The Call of Prophecy

And the Struggle over the Fate of Caliyon

Troy C. Reeves

Edited by
Natalie Forman

iUniverse, Inc.
New York   Bloomington

iUniverse books may be ordered through booksellers or by contacting:

iUniverse
1663 Liberty Drive
Bloomington, IN 47403
www.iuniverse.com
1-800-Authors (1-800-288-4677)

ISBN: 978-1-4401-9184-8 (sc)
ISBN: 978-1-4401-9183-1 (ebook)
ISBN: 978-1-4401-9182-4 (hc)

Front cover art illustrated by Paul Brookes:
Tattooist and Owner of Ink Dreams Tattoo Parlour in Westbank, BC, Canada

Printed in the United States of America

iUniverse rev. date: 12/30/2009

The Saga of Caliyon

The Call of Prophecy

*The Shadow Unleashed**

*Twinning of Fate**

* Forthcoming

This book is dedicated to:

my God for the ability to

bring my dreams to life,

my wife for her support

and belief in me,

and all my friends and guild mates

across the land for encouraging

me to pursue this path.

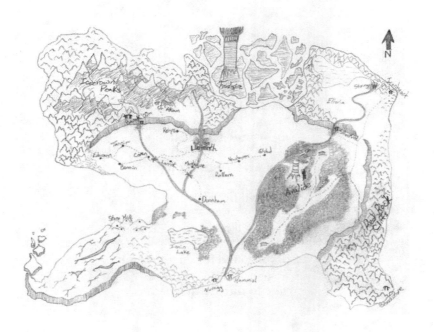

I

Twin glowing orbs of bronze scanned the occupants of the cavern. Valkyyrak, the oldest among his kind, seethed with malice as he moved the intense beacon of his gaze from his kin to the cowering interloper trembling unconvincingly before him. Patient and long-suffering by nature, Valkyyrak was not accustomed to being forced into action, especially by something as puny and insignificant as a human being. With the silence pact of the elves broken, Valkyyrak knew in all his wisdom that he and his kind would soon become objects of curiosity and wonder, just as the other fae creatures would be. But Valkyyrak feared not these curious and fragile humans. No... Valkyyrak feared something greater. He feared their potential for destruction and their ever-growing ignorance of the order of life. These broken vessels would bring about the darkness that the fae had feared for countless generations. Now, as if sent to mock Valkyyrak, a self-proclaimed scout had wandered into his domain and found far more than he anticipated. Held motionless beneath the mighty foreleg of his oldest ally, Sargeron, this ill-fated human stood wide-eyed with a sense of wonder coupled with a defiance that betrayed his true intentions. Valkyyrak could read the emotions from this pathetic whelp with great ease, and what disturbed him was the human's resolve to retaliate lying just below his feigned fear.

"Release him, Sargeron, I wish to speak a moment to this curiosity first." The low rumbling speech from Valkyyrak, much like a remarkably clear growl, resounded with power and authority. The captive scout began to stir toward the direction of the voice.

"You can talk common? I never would have thou—" The human's words were cut short as Sargeron applied a touch more pressure on his already bruised body and elicited a yelp that made both Valkyyrak and Sargeron nod with satisfaction.

"Valkyyrak, we both know what his intent is. I would suggest disposing of him immediately."

"Your objection is noted and considered. Trust me my friend... release him."

With a resigned sigh, Sargeron removed his foreleg and took a step back. The human stood proud and looked backed at Valkyyrak as he dusted himself off nonchalantly. Whether or not it was conscious to the human or merely instinctual, his left hand began to finger one of the hidden twin blades strapped to his waist. The following chorus of growls from behind him brought his hand away from the blade as he stepped forward cockily and approached the ancient one before him.

"Dispose of me? Should I fall today there will be others to take my place. The wrath of Lorenth will descend upon you beasts as it has descended upon all the beasts of the western plains, for Seneschal Dean himself will welcome the chance to bask in the glory of your death and submission—fear will descend upon this place."

At the mention of this other human, Valkyyrak and several others paused in contemplation. Finally, the great one spoke. "I find it a hallmark of your deceitful nature that you would not mention Arimas, the bearer of truth and forerunner of the Lightbringer. I believe in your words we may have uncovered some sign of the seed of corruption and as his faithful, you are no longer of use to us."

With dawning realization, the human scout swiftly unsheathed his twin blades and leapt toward the exposed throat of Valkyyrak, intent on shedding the blood of at least one of the beasts that surrounded him. Valkyyrak did not even hesitate. With the speed of a viper he recoiled on his hind legs, his magnificent golden wings unfurling from his scaled body to stabilize himself as he reared back, and enveloped the human in a blaze of dragon fire that reduced the interloper to ash in an instant.

"It is time. Tonight we hunt and feed for mid-winter night is fast approaching and the hour of darkness grows nigh. Leave the human beasts this time lest we draw too much attention to ourselves. Hunt far to the southwest." In audible agreement, the many dragons occupying the northern Icecrown Peaks bellowed together as each dispersed to their own lair, leaving Valkyyrak and his mate Dalaria alone in the great lair to await the coming of dusk.

*   *   *

It was just a dream... it had to be just a dream!

It was just a dream... wasn't it? Reyald thought desperately to himself as he fled, panicked, from the thick copse of trees behind him. A wild-eyed glance behind him showed only a few of his fellows following, running for all their worth from the unspeakable terrors they had just witnessed. No words passed between the frantic men as they moved their heavy, stolid bodies gracelessly through the tall grasses covering the expanse of land between forest and river. Once hard and fearless, the foresters had been reduced to shaking shadows of their former selves as they continued their flight, abandoning tools and provisions alike as they made their way back to their camp in the west. The expressions of honest fear painted on the faces of the other running men told Reyald that they had seen what he had seen: trees that uprooted themselves and wrenched axe handles from the fists of foresters who had only just begun swinging, only to turn the tools on the men themselves; and sensual young females clad in little more than atmosphere that appeared from the heart of the woods and using some supernatural enchantment, coaxed many of the men deep into the core of the forest.

Dead. They were all dead, except for Reyald and the handful of men who followed his scrabbling footsteps toward freedom... As for the unfortunate others, the starry-eyed men led blindly into the depths of the forest by the laughing coven of bewitching nymphs the likes of which the men had never seen before, well, there was no time to consider their fate.

What Reyald and the rest of his people were soon to learn was that the time had finally come for those living in the lands of Lorenth to discover that they, and the native beasts that had already been cowed by human progress, were not entirely alone.

When brought before Covenal Farin Guilian, who despite his relative youth as compared to the other two covenals of Lorenth was well-respected by the seasoned men who accompanied him, Reyald and the few other survivors recounted what they had seen in vivid yet unbelievable detail. The guardsmen thought them all mad, but the covenal gave the men his full attention, and concluded that the glaring absence of four out of every five of the foresters that had departed only hours ago had to be taken seriously. It did not take Farin long to give the orders to pack up camp and retreat to Lorenth with all haste.

A missive to Lord Arimas, High Inquisitor and Priest-King of Lorenth was dispatched within the hour of the foresters giving their report, in an effort to ensure that news reached Lorenth should tragedy befall the rest of the lumber camp. Camp activity was furious as supplies were gathered and stowed, carts were loaded and tied down, and horses were saddled and harnessed to prepare for the steady retreat. Luckily for the covenal and the remaining men, there was no pursuit from the forest. Nothing seemed to want to venture beyond the river, shallow though it was, and it was thought by the solemnly departing contingent that the body of water must serve as a border into the dark forest and the fantastical creatures that existed within.

The mood was somber as the remaining foresters, laborers and covenal escorts made the slow, encumbered four-day journey back to the capital, and the heavy curtain of silence that had fallen upon the men did not rise until they eventually completed the final stretch toward home.

Upon entering the massive stonework outer wall gate of Lorenth, a senior gate guard on duty gave the familiar show of respect to the covenal and handed a message to him containing instructions to make haste to the king once the carts had been unloaded and the men dismissed. After a quick debriefing with his guards, the covenal slipped a few extra coppers to his stable boy to ensure his mount would be well watered and fed, gathered his thoughts, and made his way to the inner gates of the fortress.

Nearly as impressive as its outer façade, the inner wall of Lorenth was both a work of defensive genius and aesthetic wonder. Several guard towers dotted the top of the inner wall. Each tower was built with the same stonework and they appeared as just another part of the wall itself. The width of the 'smaller' inner wall was still large enough to march six soldiers abreast with room on either side to spare. But it was the careful etchings and embossing of the inner wall that set it apart as a functional work of art. The crest of Lorenth was carefully detailed on either side of the iron portcullis, and raised tendrils that resembled vines entwined the crest and snaked around the inner wall all along its length until terminating at another matching set of Lorenth crests that marked the smaller eastern and western entrances. Being built around a majestic waterfall, the engineering that harnessed the forces of water also siphoned some water from the collection pool behind the fortress and allowed it to flow through carefully built channels throughout the center of the city where it bifurcated around the main entrance of the inner wall and flowed beneath the crests of Lorenth exiting the city beside the twin main gates on either side where it was reunited with the mighty Ardun River.

Seneschal Dean was the first to greet the covenal as he made his way toward the king's inner sanctum, much to the younger man's lament. The seneschal, second in command of Lorenth, and executor and judicator of all disciplinary matters and fortress security, was, as always, garbed in the impressive royal battle dress that ensured his status was never forgotten. His meticulously groomed sideburns and goatee, in shades of gray matching his longer, shoulder-length hair, gave him a regal and wizened appearance, yet, as always, he wore the same supercilious expression on his face that he wore whenever he had dealings with anyone other than the king himself.

Farin was more than well aware that there were those who whispered among themselves that it was Seneschal Dean who really ran Lorenth, while Lord Arimas was but a puppet or a figurehead. Since the foundations of Lorenth and the advent of political positioning, Arimas, the once inspiring warrior-priest, had seemingly laid down his maul, an iconic symbol of power, in favor of his scepter, the symbol of leadership. Though few proclaimed this theory publicly after the seneschal had two citizens publicly punished and made to make reparations to the city and to the king by toiling for six months of sewer detail, the rumor continued to persist among Lorenth's lower classes. But, Farin maintained faith in his king, along with the majority of Arimas' people, who knew in their heart of hearts that Arimas was a true and good leader. For, as many tales of strength and prowess as there were that surrounded Dean from the years of his youth and his entanglements with the wild beasts of the western hills, there was not one battle that did not have Lord Arimas at its forefront, and it was always his own trusted stone battle maul that claimed the lion's share of victories.

"Trouble in the east I hear?" inquired the seneschal arching his eyebrows, subtly insulting the younger man by foregoing the traditional handclasp that one man of power accorded another.

Farin nodded slowly, making every effort not to allow his long standing animosity to betray the false respect he paid to the seneschal. Even still, he chose to speak a few carefully selected words to the seneschal to cut this conversation off as short as possible and follow through with his orders to meet with the king.

"Yes, Seneschal, there were several unexpected... developments that must be brought before the king. Good day, Seneschal." Farin made an attempt to circumvent the man who now allowed a look of twisted amusement to cross his face even as the seneschal moved into the gap to prevent his hasty retreat.

"Farin, Farin, Farin." Dean shook his head in disgust. "This conversation is not over until I deem it to be over. Remember your place... Covenal. You were sent with the king's authority to claim and conquer that land, and yet all you return with is hands that are empty save for fairy tales. Walking trees and naked girls killing seasoned woodsmen in a matter of minutes? Pah! While I did not expect anything more from you, Covenal, our king does. Perhaps he was misguided in his acceptance of your selection for the eastern border detail."

"With all respects Seneschal, I would not be so—"

"Enough, Covenal... *now* our conversation is over. His Excellency has been waiting for you and it would be most unwise for you to keep him waiting this late in the day."

"Seneschal." With a perfunctory nod, the covenal excused himself from the seneschal's antechamber. He waited until he had turned and begun walking away before letting his hatred show on his face. There was so much latent rage swimming freely through his blood... so much history between the seneschal and the covenal of the eastern border detail... so much pain buried just beneath the surface of Farin's composed exterior.

Love has often been the cause of disputes among Lorenthians, and uncivilized as it may be, these feuds have spread even among the nobles of Lorenth. It remained no secret that Covenal Farin Guilian, then a battlemaster, was due to wed his love interest of youth, the apothecary and herbalist Jesslyn Rinidark. Even though they had courted for nearly three years, there was one man who sought to impede this union and take her for himself. It was none other than his immediate superior, Commander Dean, the second-in-command of the main expansion effort prior to the laying of the foundation of Lorenth many years ago. Though Dean was never obvious about his intentions, his methods were calculated and precise. Farin was often tasked with the advance party and this of course would keep him in the field for weeks at a time while Dean could batter the emotional resolve of Jesslyn day after day. Fear kept her silent in the face of this onslaught while love kept her faithful to Farin and as if made of iron herself, she remained steadfast—much to the great inner frustration of Dean.

If only the university had been established by this point—answers to the many questions surrounding Jesslyn's unexplained sickness and death may have been found. Hidden beneath a veiled threat, Dean had once warned Farin never to deter him from any goal or ambition. Dean fully intended on becoming seneschal one day, maybe even king, and his intent was clear. Dean was a natural leader. All deferred to him and to this day he is known for quick and decisive action coupled with wisdom that befits one of his rank and stature. Yet few saw the calculating and almost vile nature of Dean. When thwarted from something, he became like a threatened viper, full of malice and venom capable of overthrowing his opposition without a sound or a trace.

Farin had never forgotten that mid-winter's day when he returned from yet another uneventful advance mission to find his Jesslyn sleeping restlessly, feverish and sweating profusely. She never did awake to say her goodbyes or to tell Farin what ill befell her, yet Farin surmised that Dean was the orchestrator of this. When Dean was informed of her death, he donned a façade of surprise and concern and even had the nerve of extending that concern to Farin with his condolences and two days rest to grieve. While all others left the room in shock, Dean allowed the faintest of smirks to cross his lips while his eyes boiled with vengeance and satisfaction in having truly achieved his mission. If Dean was never to gain Jesslyn's heart and affections then he would ensure that no one else could either. Farin was dumbfounded. Truly alone now, and suspecting that his commander was now his enemy, Farin made the choice those many years ago to shield his pain and transform his countenance into one of strength and to find a way to allow Dean enough time and opportunity to reap the sorrow which he has sown so freely into the heart of Farin. That day still had not come.

Now the seneschal and second only to Arimas, Dean made sure to keep his contempt for Farin hidden, only striking at Farin in subtle ways, such as lashing out at Farin for some ineptitude that more than likely was not Farin's fault but could be contrived as Farin's responsibility. In service to the priest-king, whose mandate was justice and equity for all, Dean was hailed as a bastion of strength and champion to the ideals as set forth by Arimas. Farin alone knew better. Where there may have been others who could testify to the darker side of Dean, they had all been conveniently reassigned to distant settlements due to sudden failures in service, or worse, had met death during redeployment into unconquered terrain. Thus Dean remained unchallenged while Farin, long-since promoted to the respected rank of covenal, was forced to battle with the subtleties and hidden attacks of Dean while maintaining his own personal strength in leadership.

Not a day went by when he failed to reflect on the pain of losing his beloved. The sight of Dean only made matters worse as he continued on his way to see the priest-king. Fortunately, he had his emotions well under control by the time he reached the grand entrance to the hall of kings. He stopped only to run a nervous hand through his short, roughly shorn brown hair now showing some streaks of gray, before proceeding to where Arimas stood waiting. Before announcing his presence, and breaking Arimas' reverie, Farin studied his king and their surroundings for a moment. The great man, only a little more than a decade older than Farin, stood patiently at the dais, gazing out a broad window toward the east, from where so much trouble was soon to come. His balding head was still framed by short, white hair that ran into a well-groomed beard, although his preference was to shave his chin, creating a unique look for the priest-king. Although his age had started to show earlier than the seneschal, the fine lines that were now visible on his tanned skin added more to his presence, coupled with a resolve and depth of thought still evident behind his deep blue eyes.

The splendor of the hall of kings was something to marvel at. The gold embroidery and the crimson silks that adorned the dais and the throne room proper held the impression of importance as if it were embedded into the very stone. The royal armory, sealed behind the twin iron and stone wrought doors, housed the various battle honors and regalia for the priest-king to meet the needs of whatever audience or enemy he would be facing. The left wall was reserved for the king, while the right wall housed the full complement of the royal guard battle dress. Chainmail under armor complete with polished gold-stained steel plate adorned with the crest of Lorenth and shoulder guards capturing the roaring maw of the lion stood neatly ordered, row upon row, twenty-four sets in all. Impressive as the armor collection was, the rear wall was adorned with all the weaponry for the royal guards and the king himself. The longbows, tower shields, and triple-forged blades of the royal guards shone in savage beauty. And in the center of the wall, hanging upon the iron brackets rested the legendary weapon of Arimas himself, *Retribution.*

Arimas, skilled in both blade and bow, preferred the strength and weight of the battle maul. A massive work of steel framing and stonework adorned with only two perfect sapphires along the iron shaft and gripped with braided leather molded to the hands of the king. Wielded in battle time and time again, *Retribution* was a weapon that commanded respect and awe, especially when wielded by the priest-king. The covenal couldn't help but still be captivated by the magnificence of the hall of kings, though he had seen the inner court several times now. These were surroundings grand enough to humble even the greatest of men. Tapestries of the southern conquests that immortalized Arimas in the fury of battle against the great bears, the large gilded crest of the House of Lorenth, and even the ample windows crafted with such grace and precision to spill the late sunset light across the floor as if the halls were set afire—if others thought the inner wall to the fortress was a work of art, they had obviously never been in the inner court of the king. Finally moving to approach the great dais, the covenal bowed at the waist, and announced his arrival. "Covenal Farin Guilian, your Excellency, recently returned from the eastern border with grave and unusual tidings."

Arimas, reluctant to stir from his inner thoughts just yet, remained standing motionless before finally acknowledging Farin. "Welcome home, Covenal Guilian." The large, broad-shouldered man who was now starting to show signs of his age turned the intensity of his gaze toward Farin after another long pause, and then crossed the dais to where Farin stood respectfully at attention. "It sounds as if you and your men have had quite the adventure," he said, grasping Farin's shoulder warmly. "I am glad you made it back to Lorenth safely."

"Thank you, my lord." Farin bowed his head. The king's unexpected sense of concern over Farin's personal safety caught him off guard for a moment. Even during a time of marked failure, his monarch still chose to extend grace to his officers. The king dropped his hand and gestured for Farin to follow him to two carefully positioned seats.

"Now, we have much to discuss. Your missive has been considered at length during the past few days. I confess that I am inclined to believe you and your men, but there are many others in the court who deem this missive to be nothing more than a poor excuse for the failure of the covenal of the eastern border detail to complete his duties for his king. Lorenth has prospered greatly, and it will continue to prosper, but as you are well aware, this city consumes a great deal of resources. For my people to survive, and thrive, I am dependent on the careful and continuous expansion of our northern and southern borders." Arimas now turned toward the covenal. His countenance was that of a patient and kindly man, yet behind his deep blue eyes was a zealous resolve that demanded unquestioned obedience.

"We now control all the best land that the north and south has to offer and that is why your task was paramount. To the east lie unknown lands and a forest of such magnificence that with careful thinning it should be able to sustain the city for generations to come. Yet, all you have brought for me to present to the court is a very bizarre tale of living trees and wild children. I sense no deception about you though, and I do not think of you as a man creative enough or foolish enough to concoct a tale like this merely to have an excuse to return to Lorenth in failure." Arimas smoothed down his beard and wiped his brow before continuing. "However, I am pleased that the lowlands up to the new river have been secured, and your previous reports have been weighed in the light of this incident. The lowlands are to be cultivated in short order and some are to be turned to pasture to expand our livestock supplies—for that I am thankful."

Arimas rose and began to pace around the room, his long legs making short work of the space. Farin took the cue and also stood, placing himself at the position of attention while Arimas continued his pacing. The priest-king sighed audibly before speaking, "I am greatly troubled with this latest turn of events, Covenal, and not solely because the seneschal reacted to your missive with such vehemence when I shared it with him. In my times of solitude and reflection, I have often felt that a great tension was building in the heart of Lorenth and I have not been able to shake this unsettled feeling. Your report rings with truth and further confirms my concerns. Perhaps in our pride we have finally come to understand our limitations. Perhaps we need to reflect and handle this new land with tact and a hesitation born from respect of what we do not yet know or understand."

Behaving as any senior ranking soldier should, the covenal remained at the position of attention—stalwart, observant, and silent. He absorbed all the information that Arimas shared, and made inferences on the information that was not spoken. The sudden lull in the conversation prompted the covenal to engage Arimas once again.

"My lord, never before have I come across anything that shook me like this. I have held my pride and led my men countless times before and neither terrain nor beast has ever unhinged my men like this. For once in my life I witnessed true and unbridled horror in the faces of men I have served my liege alongside. If you will grant me the leave to express myself plainly, it is my professional opinion that we investigate this dark wood, and that we do so with the extreme caution that you too have just mentioned. Though many have often surmised that there are other sentient races among us, perhaps now the myth will become truth and perhaps we can learn from these creatures. Perhaps we also might be able to open trade negotiations with them if this incident is handled properly."

"Wisdom hangs in your words, Covenal, and you impress me with your forthrightness. Rest assured that I will relate this matter to the court and that the merit of your words will be presented at a time when change will be instituted to bring forth the most good for our nation. I will confer further with the seneschal and perhaps with some enlightenment his negative position will be replaced with tolerance and, dare I say, acceptance." The king paused in his pacing and faced Farin again. "That will be all for now, Covenal. I must ponder the events of the day without interruption, for many burdens of the past are once again troubling me and I know not the reason as of yet. Return to your quarters and on the morrow I would ask that you continue with your regular duties and ensure that your men are properly tended to before the court sits again. It is likely that you will be tasked again shortly once we determine our next course of action."

"Thank you, your Excellency."

"Go with the light, Covenal."

Following his dismissal from the king's court, the covenal left in the manner that he came; however, this time he did not stop to parry words with the curious seneschal. Farin made his way back down the long corridor, stepping into the evening. He walked through the courtyard and past the inner wall, venturing into the lower city with a purpose in his step and a fire in his eyes. Even in a city so well cared for as Lorenth, street dwellers and hawkers pawning whatever wares they could produce still managed to creep into the lower city, casting a pall upon the radiance of Lorenth.

"Buy some bread m'lord? Fresh still, it is."

"You said that last week Aggie. My bread was baked right this mornin' m'lord a-and I even gots some cheese for ya too if you be needin any."

"Good luck charms and talismans of protection 'ere m'lord. Blessed by the priest-king himself dey are!"

The covenal came to a halt, faced the charm dealer, and stepped out the shadowy streets and into the street light. The dealer quickly took a step back when realization crossed her face as recognition flashed through her eyes. "You dare hawk goods under false pretense such as this? Am I to believe that Arimas himself has sanctioned these goods and indeed would advocate that they bring luck and ward evil? Speak woman!"

"B-beg pardon m'lord, I meant no trouble an' certainly no disrespect. Tis been a hard summer for me and I just wanted some coins to feed me family sir. Me husband was killed in the southern expansion and the court will not hear my pleas for help."

Unsure whether this too was another fabrication to glean sympathy, the covenal scoffed and waved her off as he continued his walk down the street. One of these days, he thought to himself, he would have to submit a plan to the courts to rout out the filth in their city while also working to legitimize the claims of any truly impoverished families that should be the responsibility of the court. But, that would have to wait. As Farin turned the last corner of his route and approached the barracks, he addressed the gate guard—Falorn was his name if he remembered correctly—and inquired after his second in command.

"The commander isn't here, Covenal, he... uh, was enjoying the attentions of young Miss Ven—"

"That's quite all right sergeant, his affairs in this matter are his own; however, I want a message given to him when he returns that I must confer with him on the morrow after sunrise."

"Yes, Covenal."

After a brief walkthrough of the barracks and several minor corrections issued to his men regarding hygiene and deportment, the covenal left the barracks and made his way back into the upper city and the officer's grounds. Change was in the air and though uncertain about what was to come, he found his uncertainty oddly refreshing for once. His service to Lorenth over the years had been fairly predictable, even routine to this point. The expansion efforts remained unchallenged and with their training and development of better protective wear and weaponry, the native beasts were no match for the ever-growing and ever-reaching empire of Lorenth.

Yet now there was uncertainty. Fear as well had begun to take root in the city. Rumor began to move throughout the denizens of Lorenth as if on wings of shadow. For once there was an obstacle that hinted at an intelligence and sentience that could thwart the efforts of the Lorenthian expansion and force the question of the human ideals of supremacy in the west. Failure had never been an option for Arimas, or for the people of Lorenth. It seemed likely that the battle-hungry seneschal would advise the king that a full military detail was needed to curb any mystical threat that he refused to believe in. And, should the seneschal be successful in this, the ramifications to the covenal could be severe. Farin wondered if Dean would have him deemed 'unfit' for honored service to Lorenth, and ensure that he was sent back to one of the lesser colonies in the west to administrate over some menial cultivation or livestock operation.

But there would be time enough to worry about that tomorrow. Farin let out a heavy breath of relief as he approached his estate, one of three specifically reserved for the covenals of Lorenth. Before calling for his housekeeper to open the doors for him, Farin stopped on the front doorstep and stared up into the newly moonlit sky. In the stars he saw the ephemeral shape of his lost beloved's face, and felt a sudden rise of emotion. If Jesslyn was here, he thought, she would know just what to say to ease his heart and put the world right again. Whispering a silent prayer to her while kissing his fingers in remembrance, Farin shook off the surge of melancholy and entered his lonely white stone mansion. He alerted his staff to his presence and then took a quick supper of slightly stale bread, red wine, and fresh, sharp, orange cheese. After seeing to a few random matters of importance, Farin settled himself into bed and willed himself to sleep.

II

"*Eth aloni tul`venarii*, mistress. The glades have awoken."

"*Ashanda eth reiis*, cousin. The time of prophecy is upon us. Woe to the humans for their darkest hour approaches. It is time to alert the mistrunners and glade wardens and dispatch a summons to the Æthian and the council of the nine. Time will be critical to bridge the unbalance before the darkness can fully gain strength. The human remnant must be isolated and preserved in hopes that the Lightbringer may be found before the Spawn of Chaos has established himself completely."

"Are we to break the silence with the humans then?"

"They have already broken the silence of their own accord, yet we will not engage them for a time. Their curiosity will not be satisfied until their greed for power and dominion is shattered against the mighty glades that ring and shield us. The winds tell me that the dryads have begun to mate. With the birth of a new generation of dryads will come the birth of a stronger, more sentient glade and the guardians too shall awaken in more trees as we brace for the darkness that is fated to come. Courage cousin! Hope shall endure, and in time even these impetuous humans will gain wisdom for some are destined to call us friend. *Nishana tel`anorii*, cousin."

"*Nishana tel`anorii*, mistress." With a deep inclination of her head, the glade ambassador departed from the Matriarch's chamber and quickened her pace as she approached the calling circle. Raising a simple wooden flute to her lips, she blew a discordant pattern of notes toward the mistrunner guild to the north, another pattern of notes which varied in pitch more so than the first toward the glade wardens of the south, and finally another pattern that sounded like birdsong to the Æthian and the council far to the east. The music of the flute became almost visible in the calling circle as each dispatch dissipated within the deep green boughs of the mighty trees that encircled the majestic Elvin capital of Avalide. Serenity and strength shrouded everything beneath the trees and even the dwellings of the elves, each carefully grown over time by skilled elves that were gifted with a mastery of the treesong. The Matriarchal Commune was grown from the very heart of sixteen mighty oak trees, their branches still embracing the structure as if it were but a sapling. The vines that covered the walls gave birth to a myriad of white and lavender flowers which spread their scent throughout the entire glade. Each elven structure was similarly grown in this manner; however, only the guild halls were grown with beauty that rivaled the Matriarchal Commune.

Although all elves possessed some affinity with the treesong, none could truly compete with the members of the guild of the *Essen`dril*. Within each new generation of offspring, one or two younglings would be found that had exceptional talent with the treesong. Those chosen to become *Essen`dril* were often removed from regular teachings well before their first age cycle and sent to apprentice with the guild masters who would aid the younglings in refining their craft. The *Essen`dril* were harmonists by nature. These were the druids of life and harmony and were truly creatures of the balance. With each song and each gift, Avalide prospered and flourished with the magic that permeated the air of *Illu`Dar*. As with all creatures of balance, where the *Essen`dril* were capable of creating great beauty and structures to house the Elders and Council, they were also noted for being able to command the treesong to weave destruction, a talent that was not easily replicated by the majority of elves.

It was their Æthian brethren who were the known masters of destruction. Also harmonists at heart, their powers came from the ambient magic that dwelled in all things, and from the elements themselves. Where the *Essen`dril* typically channeled changes that gradually occurred over time, with what others might interpret as love and care, the Æthian could wield their power for good or ill within a moment. Theirs was the power of the *Trinactria*—the magic of the ether—which was long thought to exist in three planes: the plane of elements, the plane of the corporeal or physical, and the plane of the spiritual.

Within the Æthian enclave there were two distinct disciplines. The Ætheron were arcanists who specialized in the plane of elements. They could harness the wind and the rain, conjure mage-fire, and summon great lightning storms, casting their deadly bolts with care and precision. They could cultivate the land and improve upon the natural order of life by summoning and weaving the elements and infusing strength into the life around them.

Their spiritualist counterparts were the Æthanon, delving into the spiritual plane and capable of healing and mending the broken, even restoring the spirit to a fallen creature before their natural life cycle had finished. Although known for being master healers, the Æthanon were also elves to be feared for they were also skilled illusionists, able to bend the minds of weaker foes to see and feel things which did not exist, command all forms of light to shield and confuse or render the arcanist invisible. Even under dire circumstances, some of the Æthanon believed that they could summon the spirit host to aid them.

Though all the Æthian could control some aspects of the corporeal plane, none could achieve the level of skill needed to truly become a master of the corporeal. Indeed, this was an area where the *Essen`dril* and the destructive power of the treesong gained respect from the Æthian, for the treesong was a corporeal magic that, when used aggressively, could shake the very earth, shift rocks or sand, and even cause roots to sprout from the ground, entwining or crushing in accordance with the *Essen`dril's* will.

The time had now come for the elves to move into the darkness where prophecy no longer spoke. For generations, the elves grew in power, mastering themselves and their environment yet remaining secluded from the human nation. Some thought the humans were too primitive to be of any use. The scholars and sages would often dispute the scrolls of prophecy, thinking that the humans could not possibly be the race mentioned in the prophecies. Still others sat

17

and watched with curious interest. What came so easily for elves took humans much more effort to master, yet master they did, and though a short-lived race, the humans were careful to develop a written language to store their learning to better equip the next generations to follow. Elves in general cast little thought to the human advancement after watching them for several generations in their infancy.

Despite the hopes that following the completion of Lorenth the humans would slow their resource-stripping expansion toward *Illu`Dar*, such hopes were not to be realized. Steadily and predictably the human encroachment continued while the sprites, who had spent much time spying upon the humans, gradually withdrew back into *Illu`Dar* when at last, the silence pact would be broken with the first assault on the guardians.

After years of waiting, events began to unfold at a pace that Evianna was finding somewhat distressing. The ambassador still had much to accomplish this day before the council was to converge. The magister had requested an audience with her, and Ethoni only knew what he could want from her now, besides his customary allusions to those deep-set affections he felt toward her that remained unreciprocated. The magister was noble and powerful, pleasing to look upon, and would make an ideal mate for her; however, Evianna knew that the responsibilities set before her and him were great and confounding their professional obligations by introducing an element of courtship simply would not be prudent in her eyes. Nevertheless, the magister was able to remain professional whenever he found a legitimate reason to summon her again.

Today he would likely want a first-hand report on the human's assault of the glade and would also have some valuable insights on the impact that the dryad mating would have on the western border. And with treant guardians soon awakening, perhaps the ancient Oakenroot might be willing to convey his insights. The new spring would bring about the births of a new dryad generation and indirectly bolster the borders of *Illu`Dar*. That was still many moons from now, but if the prophecies were to be trusted then these next few months would bring about the darkest time in the history of human kind. The long-held fear was that this time of darkness would inadvertently plunge the fae creatures into the plight of the humans as the corruption begins its spread.

With the sudden retreat of the humans back to their city of stone, the glades grew quiet in reflection. The call had been sent forth from Avalide. The wardens and mistrunners were to be mobilized in preparation for what was to come and the council of the nine would be meeting shortly to decide what role the elves and the other fae would have in this approaching darkness. Time would not be friendly now.

When the glade ambassador finished her dispatches in the calling circle, she paused, canting her head to the left and listened— listened to the treesong deep within her and the magic coursing through the life all around the enchanted glades. The clear musical song of the *aethia'lyys*, or shadow lark in the common tongue, could be heard above the treetops, its harmonic lament calming the ears of all who would take the time to listen. Only during the transitions from dusk to dawn and then in the evening from sunset to dusk could the shadow lark be seen with the unaided eye—the ethereal wings and plumages that shone a pale incandescent blue as the bird floated amid the tree branches and into the skies above. Still being too early in the day to behold the shadow lark, Evianna Windrunner simply listened. Within several short minutes, the answers to her summons began coming in from the elven guilds confirming their preparations and their anticipated attendance at the council meeting. Gathering her essence, Evianna summoned the owl spirit to encase her as she took her new form. Gliding up on silent wings, she vanished into the shadows of the tree branches and flew east to the magister's enclave.

*   *   *

Xe`Talis walked through the southern glades toward her old and gnarled Lifetree—one of the few treants who maintained a lifebond with a dryad. Long had she been happily joined with Sereven Windsong, one of the elder elves who once bore the honor of being a warden of the glades, but a large part of her heart would forever be united with her tree in a way that Sereven was only now beginning to fully appreciate after all these years.

"I've missed you, my old friend," the dryad elder whispered as her hand gently caressed the knobby bark of the old elemental guardian of the glades.

"I felt your presence draw closer nearly an hour ago, Xe`Talis. What brings you out here to visit an old gnarled cedar like me?" Even though his slow and rumbling speech was accompanied by the sounds of wood creaking under stress, Xe`Talis could discern the great pleasure within him at her arrival.

"Life stirs within the heart wood once more, Grimleaf, and this time, not from any efforts of the elders."

"I thought as much. There was a loud pulse within the glades as well. The forest is growing stronger."

"Only six of my daughters managed to mate... jealousy burns within my other young, each having been ready to mate for longer than any of us care to remember."

"Patience never was something you were skilled at, Xe`Talis. They are still young by the forest's standard and their turn will come. Walk with me down to the river." The weathered treant, at least five times the size of the dryad elder, walked slowly beside the dryad who had to step nimbly through the trees at a quick pace to keep up with her guardian. They made their way through the southern glades toward the forest edge, both of them caught up in their memories and their hopes for the uncertain future of *Illu`Dar.*

While few understood the intricacies of the age-old forest elementals, fewer still understood the nature of dryads. While under most circumstances they appeared as gentle creatures, the dryads were by nature a savage race. Their lives were entwined into the life of their tree and should one perish, the other would perish as well. Whenever a dryad reached her age of maturity, she would often become restless and agitated and would begin to actively seek out a sentient male to mate with. Unlike most unions that resulted in offspring, when dryads mated, the traits of the male species were never expressed in the child. All dryad children were born female, and remained short in stature, appearing to others as children though in reality they would grow as old as their tree, often hundreds of years in age.

Very few dryads had borne children to date. Until recently, when the humans invaded their glade, the elves had been the only ones to mate with the dryads. However, they were wise to the dryad ways and many only formed an alliance with them. Occasionally, an elven male, typically a glade warden or a mistrunner, and a dryad female would couple together and produce offspring. With the birth of a new dryad, the magic of *Illu'Dar* would awaken a new guardian in the elder glade and produce a new sapling in the heart of the forest. The sapling was bound in life and death to the young dryad as she was bound to the sapling. As dryads grew and matured, they would come to develop a close kinship with the awakened guardian, but would often retreat into the heart wood to rest in the boughs of their Lifetree, communicating in ways only dryads could understand, singing songs of hope, of lament, and of vengeance.

Several dryads, some tied to the ancient guardians from the time of creation, represented the rest of the dryads in the alliance with the elves. Of the original twelve dryads, ten still thrived and each of these dryads had taken elven mates and continued to share their lives with them. Throughout time, these dryads and the elves grew to admire and value the diversity that set each race apart and made them unique, and together helped foster the alliance that enabled both races to live independently yet together within the magic of *Illu'Dar.*

However, the new generation of dryads were centuries younger than the elders, and fewer of the next generation dryads came to mate with the elves. Few people could ever understand the sacrifice made when an elf willfully chose to mate with a dryad. Elves were immortal by nature and one of the first couplings between a dryad and an elf resulted in the reduction of the male into nothing but a fragile and mindless shell of the elf he was before. Doomed to a life of mindless devotion to the dryad, the forest groaned in protest at the injustice brought onto this elven child of the forest. Release from this bondage was eventually granted when the male's seed was no longer needed. The dryad severed the tie that kept the male alive and he finally perished, his body accepted into the forest and drawn into its depths to provide nourishment to the glade. Such was also the fate of the humans who succumbed to dryad charms.

Although there were several other unions with elven males that produced close bonds of love between the elf and the dryad, the elves could not accept the tragic possibility of the past and, out of fear, few did not even consider the frequent advances of the hundreds of new dryads that had reached maturity. With the case of the elder dryads, the mating ritual did not harm any of the elven males but instead fostered a deep, almost spiritual union with them. Some even thought that after being united with the same dryad for generations, these few elves came to hear the whisperings of the glade and could even share in some communion with his mate's Lifetree. What eventually started to produce hope for successful unions between elf and dryad quickly degenerated when two of the elder dryads perished with the sudden death of their Lifetrees, unexpectedly causing the subsequent death of their elven mates, as well.

The invasion of the humans was a momentous time for the younger dryads. While each of the dryads was at least a hundred years old, most had never mated before. The dryads were driven into frenzy when several men were lured into the forest and taken by these female predators. Predator was a fitting term, for once the first dryads had seduced the men into mating with them, not being a magical race like the elves who displayed incredible resistance to the dryad effects, the men were all reduced to nothing more than mindless slaves, consumed completely by the other dryads. Unfortunately, the human males could only be successfully mated with for several weeks before they began to spontaneously die, taking their seed into the forest floor with them. All in all, close to one hundred dryads were able to successfully mate with these few captives before they died, leaving at least as many to wait in frustration for the next opportunity to mate.

Eager anticipation now flowed through the heart wood as many of the impregnated dryads sang to their Lifetrees, rejoicing in the gift of life that was now blossoming inside them. Even the *Essen`dril* who tended to the forests made several visits to the heart wood to comfort and share in the joy of the many expectant dryads that were moving into a new phase of their life.

Bethalyyn Leafwhisperer and Rallegan Timberwood were two of the druids who frequented the heart woods, moving through the Lifetrees and singing their multi-vocal discordant treesongs that warded each tree in range of their voice against all manners of evil and decay. But, while their presence within the heart wood was always welcomed, it was the younger druid Tavendia Amberdawn whom the newest generation of dryads were drawn to. There was a noticeable gentleness in her treesong and a power that ran incredibly deep. She would often meander in the forest singing her songs of hope and imbuing all life around her with the desire to thrive and reach new heights.

"What was it like, Xe`Fiera?" asked Xe`Janis as the two dryads accompanied Tavendia on her afternoon walk.

"It was like a fire burning within that could not be quenched and did not consume. I hope that more men stray into our glade again! But, this feeling is completely different. I can feel the beating of my daughter's heart deep within me. My reality is shifting and my mind is sharpening."

"That is your *nuna`aelia*, Xe`Fiera," explained Tavendia. "Even within elven circles, new mothers find themselves developing an awareness that helps shape them in preparation for the caring of another. Embrace the changes as you would embrace the young one within you."

Xe`Fiera nodded and smiled while Xe`Janis allowed the forming question within her mind to show upon her face. "Tavendia," Xe`Janis began, "why have you not taken a mate yet?"

Tavendia smiled as she debated side-stepping the question entirely, but then felt that the dryad deserved at least some sort of answer. "I... simply have not found one to my liking, Xe`Janis. Like your elders who still remain with their mates in a bond of love, I too am searching for one to complete the song in my heart."

The two dryads smiled at the metaphor, knowing all too well the power of the druid's song already. To think that her song was somehow incomplete would imply an untapped greatness locked away inside Tavendia.

"I long for you to share our joy, Tavendia. You have always been like a sister to the dryads and your joy is our joy, even as your sorrow will be our sorrow."

Tavendia smiled warmly at Xe`Fiera and then reclined upon the ground, the gentle wind caressing her face and playfully carrying some fallen leaves around her body and over her earthen-toned robes. She gazed for a time into the dark green canopy of branches that sheltered the *Illu`Dar* and lost herself in thought as the two dryads took up places beside her, listening to the heart beat within the ground, the laughter dancing in the branches, and the song playing through the hearts and minds of elf and dryad alike.

* * *

Sleep would not come for Arimas this night. As his wife slept peacefully in their large bed, the priest-king continued in his incessant pacing and pondering. Could twenty-five years have passed already since Lorenth was but a thought nestled within the deep recesses of Arimas' mind? Long days and even longer nights had passed since that time when the council had appointed the zealous, young leader to carry them through the unsteady paces of raising the nation that is now known as Lorenth. The vigor that once characterized the priest-king seemed but a dream to the aging monarch as he continued to walk his unchanging path back and forth, moving from the window, to the entrance of their chambers, to his side of the bed, and then repeating the cycle over and over again. The events of the day weighed heavily on his mind. There was something that continued to bother him about the unrest of his seneschal, something he could not place his finger on. He sighed and slowly shook his head as he extending his thoughts and prayers once again to his unknown god, praying for wisdom to penetrate the cloud of uncertainty. Finding a spot to sit near the window, he reached for his old journals and let his mind wander back to those familiar events all those years ago...

"You fought bravely today, my friend," Arimas commended the man standing silently at his side. "Your expert tactical positioning on the left flank in particular saved many lives when that unexpected attack from the mountain cats came. I find it refreshing that I can learn from my seneschal just as you mention often that you learn from me." The handsome, clean-shaven young ruler, scanned his surroundings with his deep blue eyes and then clasped Galan Vilarin, his seneschal and most trusted friend, on the shoulder as they looked back over the fields of battle. The council had entrusted the priest and king Arimas with a task of seemingly impossible proportions: expand the human empire east and select a suitable site for their crown jewel, the city of Lorenth, the capital that would forever etch the name of Lorenthians into history.

"I must confess Arimas, I relied heavily on Commander Dean's tactical appraisal of the situation once the beasts attacked. Once again he shows incredible potential in the ways of battle. The men are loyal to him already... he is a champion of sorts."

"Dean. Again it is his name that I hear. I, too, have seen first hand evidence of his skills. I do not believe in chance, Galan. Even though you and Melsa have been mentors to me throughout my early years, I believe that there is something to the notion of fate that the scholars are so intrigued with. There is something intriguing about this young Dean; he is destined for greatness."

"No more than you are, Arimas. The men also have seen the way you wield your new maul. I knew you were skilled in the blade but even I am tempted to stop fighting and watch you swing your weapon around as if it were little more than a twig."

"This weapon just feels... different. It is more like an extension of my body than any blade has ever been. I cannot explain the sensation; the masons certainly outdid themselves on this masterpiece."

Arimas and Galan looked over the land that would become the seventh settlement for Lorenth. Although many had been pressuring Arimas to choose a site for the capital city, Arimas took their opinions and carefully stowed them away knowing that when he found the right spot he would know beyond a shadow of a doubt. Already, tradesmen were carting off carcasses of the recently slaughtered beasts for meat and hides, while the elder apothecary, Tannis Chissam, and her talented daughter Rebekah, applied their healing arts to the injured soldiers.

"Have you thought of a name for this one as well, Arimas?"

"Reiys. The soil is adequate but the climate is a bit cooler, which may limit what will grow here. However, stone and ore are in abundance, and the lands available for pasture are excellent, making this an enviable spot for raising livestock."

"I am impressed, my friend. First Larriot, then Montague, and now Reiys, and all within a moon cycle! While some may criticize the speed at which you are expanding our lands, no one can ignore that your efforts are for the benefit of our people. We could double the settlements we have now and we would still have people itching to settle down in a place of their own. You are a wonder, Arimas. How you were able to rally this... rabble into an organized force has amazed the council. I think one or two members may have even been stunned into silence, which is a feat in and of itself!"

They both broke into hearty laughter. "How can you say that Galan? You are married to one of the council! I imagine your lady wife would not be so pleased to hear you speak such things!"

"Ah, Arimas. I love Melsa dearly, but you will not fully understand my jest until you find yourself finally married off." The older man nudged his liege knowingly, and the two broke into a fresh bout of chuckles. Something about the end of a successful battle lightened the men's spirits, especially those spirits of the ones in charge.

The laughter continued for a short time as the two leaders of the human expansion effort continued walking through the crowds of citizens and soldiers, nodding their approval of the work underway and stopping to give gentle guidance when things were not moving as planned. Marriage. True, Arimas was in his late twenties, but people had been hounding him for several years already to get married and sire an heir to a throne that had not yet been built. Humans were certainly committed to their vision once a vision had been laid before them. Arimas helped cultivate that early vision and he alone would be held accountable should that vision fail to come to pass. Yet that pressure did not sway him in the least. Patience was a virtue that few possessed in such a broad measure as Arimas.

After the discovery of yet another river, and the establishment of Montague along its edge, Arimas had sent scouts up and down the river. The river met with the Ardun River that ran past Coren so Arimas hesitated in giving this river a new name. He decided that these rivers were one and the same and therefore this river would also be labeled as the Ardun River. What really interested him though were the scouting reports from the northern part of the river that told of a waterfall more impressive than anything that had been witnessed before—even far more splendid than the waterfall in the river valley near Tannir. If this were true, perhaps Arimas would be able to test the engineers' new ideas of harnessing the power of water to be part of the foundation for his capital.

A fast moving river was also the key to the building of the various aqueducts and cisterns that would provide clean water to the city while also providing an opportunity to push human waste through a proposed sewer system with incineration facilities that would be located below the foundations of the city. Arimas was careful to contain his excitement until they had Reiys established with basic supports before pressing on back down through the hills shadowed by the impressive mountains to the north.

"Arimas, I did have one other matter of state to bring to your attention."

"Oh?"

"Earlier this morning I received another update regarding the status of the Guard. Dean has been weeding out his division yet again, and three more soldiers have been relocated to Edarann, Bonnin, and Tannir. They were deemed unfit for duty and have all been tasked with the management of more 'acceptable' tasks suited to their skills, which Dean claims are mediocre at best. Also, two others that were to be similarly demoted met unfortunate ends today in battle. Dean apparently thinks that their deaths today have restored some of the honor they were set to lose and wants honorable mentions to be made during their memorials."

"What is it about Dean's division that sparks this sudden demotion of all these fine soldiers? There have been no complaints as of yet about his procedure, has there?" Galan shook his head in response to Arimas' query. "Then as much as I find his methods somewhat less than ideal in this matter, perhaps it is those same methods that have caught all of our attention on the field of battle. Perhaps his 'pruning' is making his division more superior in battle and creating more cohesion among his men."

"That thought does indeed hold merit, Arimas, but it still concerns me that he is so quick to make these choices without consulting myself, you, or even the council. Is that not a bit presumptuous of him?"

Arimas considered the words of his mentor who, for years, had been like a father to him. Galan had never steered him wrong in the past, yet Dean was becoming an undeniable icon of victory. Arimas was only a few years older than Dean, but that did not stop him from recognizing the same fire of ambition burning behind Dean's eyes. If only Arimas could harness that enthusiasm to an even greater purpose... more topics to ponder at a later time.

"It is presumptuous, I suppose. Perhaps we should appoint someone to administer justice for Lorenth. Someone dedicated to enforcing the wishes of the council and regulating disputes between soldier and citizen alike."

Galan smiled that proud smile once more. "That is an excellent idea Arimas. Appointing a judicator, or administrator, or a—"

"A magistrate." Arimas paused while letting the word flow off his tongue. "Yes, I think that title would encompass all the areas of responsibility attributed to that station."

"A magistrate... yes, I do believe you have seen to the heart of the matter once again, Arimas. Will you be submitting this motion to the council at the next meeting then?"

"Yes, I think that would be appropriate. Were there any other matters, Galan?"

"None. Shall we move on to the tents?"

"You are free to go, Galan. I would like to spend some time in meditation before returning. There is something deeply spiritual in these hills, in these mountains. I feel almost overwhelmed with the power of creation in this place. Life is all around us here in a very real way, though my eyes betray what I know my heart can sense."

The seneschal bowed his head in acknowledgement, not understanding his lord's deep connection with the earth but moved by it just the same. Before taking his leave, Galan handed Arimas the stack of parchments he had been holding, which contained various other reports about the mundane details involved in ruling a nation. It was no wonder that humans were a disorganized lot prior to rallying behind the vision of their young leader with a dream bigger than everyone else's put together—who else in full presence of mind would consent to managing this effort?

Arimas, wanting to ensure a clear mind for his meditations, flipped through several of the reports now in his hands and looked for anything that needed immediate taking care of. He paused after a moment, noticing a trend in the actions of Dean's advance party. One soldier was constantly tasked away from the camps... Dean's own battlemaster, and a young man barely old enough to enter the Guard: Farin Guilian. This young soldier had thoroughly impressed all of his commanding officers during his short two year service and, as such, had become the youngest member of the Guard ever promoted to the position of battlemaster. With that promotion, Guilian was attached to Dean's unit and within only a few short months, Dean had tasked him no less than six times. While his first impressions of this pattern of events raised some concern, Arimas quickly discounted it, chalking the occurrences up to Farin's excellence in service and the subsequent respect of Dean in his abilities.

Arimas' memories leapt ahead several weeks from that point. The expansion efforts had continued and not even the beasts could slow their advance. Everything was being completed as planned and without incident... until that day...

With Reiys adequately established, the priest-king had begun the movement east yet again, this time venturing back down to Larriot to see its progress for himself before heading slightly northeast, toward the thundering waterfall mentioned in the scouting reports. He could not have predicted that such random evil would befall the camp as its occupants rested just beyond Larriot's borders. The advance party had returned to the settlement to find it rife with what they had taken to calling the sleeping sickness—a strange illness that the apothecaries had never encountered before. The apothecaries had determined that it was something present in the water based on the patterns of water consumption, yet that was still not enough information to link the events that transpired.

The first stage brought the fever, then the long and restless sleep, and finally, death, though thankfully, while many individuals had fallen sick—those who drank water from the wells—few actually lost their lives to the illness. But, with those who did perish, no connection or pattern could be found between the men and women who died or survived. First to fall were several soldiers throughout the camp, followed by two tradesmen, and two apothecaries, including the elder apothecary and their newest herbalist, the young Jesslyn Rinidark. What pained Arimas even more than these other losses was the sudden and tragic passing of his seneschal, who also fell quickly to the incurable disease.

The priest-king sought answers, but the few surviving apothecaries were at a complete loss as to why these few had died while the rest of camp remained ill. Arimas instinctively sought out the wisdom of his mentor and seneschal, but he was gone. Melsa Vilarin, now a widow, had elected to remain on the council, stating that the work would help occupy her distressed mind. Meanwhile, Battlemaster Guilian, who apparently had been courting the young Rinidark for several years, had undergone a transformation of his own. The gentle-spirited military achiever adopted a countenance of a battle-hardened warrior to wall off his inner turmoil as he set his mind on his task of service that had been set before him.

"There will be a reckoning for this day of evil," began Arimas that night. The intensity burning in his eyes left no doubts in the minds of his followers that he intended to find answers to the questions that many were silently whispering among each other. "Those that have been taken from us prematurely will be remembered for their deeds, for the joy they inspired and the meaning they brought into our lives. If I find that this illness was brought upon us by the devices of wicked men in our midst, then they should rue the day they sought to break our spirits in such a manner."

Arimas spoke with authority mingled with compassion as he addressed the gathering throng of Lorenthians that stood somberly just outside of his tent. He lifted up his favored weapon, now heavier with the burden of the lost souls that fell while serving under his command. "I hereby name this weapon *Retribution*, and swift will be the punishment it deals should I cross those responsible for this plague. I can only hope that it was fate that has treated us so mercilessly these past days and not the wrath of a wicked soul lurking among us.

We will remain here in Larriot for one day to mourn and bury our dead and then we must continue on eastward. Stay your hearts against fear! So long as I draw breath into my body, I will not stand for any injustice, especially when committed upon another citizen be they of status or not. Mourn this evening and attempt to get some rest in preparation for the recommencement of our journey."

True to his word, the morning of the second day saw the continuation of the eastern advance. The dead were buried and the soldiers, tradesmen, and citizens all made their way north of Montague to pursue Arimas' great hope from what he had read in the scouting reports. While the mourning had ended publicly, Arimas was no fool. He knew that the mourning would continue silently for the many people who depended on the priest-king for words of comfort and the vision of encouragement to bolster their resolves. The slow march east brought a reward to everyone as all beheld the culmination of Arimas' vision.

Arimas stood at the foot of the great waterfall and knew beyond any uncertainty that he had discovered the future site of Lorenth. The council stood behind him, jaws dropped and eyes large as they openly displayed their awe at the sheer beauty and power of this work of nature that would be channeled into the heart of their crown jewel.

"This is perfect, Arimas," commended Counselor Melsa Vilarin. "Know that Galan would have been proud of you. You have become the leader that he envisioned and you honor his memory by your excellence and perseverance. Though the time of his passing is still fresh at hand, I do think it is time you appoint a new seneschal, Arimas. Galan would not expect you to shoulder the burdens of Lorenth alone."

"Indeed, Arimas," began Counselor Renlar Fin. "Cirra and Nolan, as well as Jarl and I, believe that a new seneschal might give the people something else to celebrate over. We also have been thoroughly impressed with your endeavors. You have superseded our expectations and now we all follow you not by result of appointing you, but through choice alone. You have done what no one else attempted before... your Excellency."

Arimas was taken back by the sudden show of respect from the older counselors as they all inclined their heads toward him. The mention of replacing Galan so suddenly did not sit well with him, yet he could not argue their reasoning. The building of Lorenth would be a tremendous undertaking and he needed a capable person that both a king and his people could depend on. There was only one strong candidate that Arimas could think of to take Galan's place. Perhaps Dean would make a fine seneschal. If he excelled at this final promotion like he excelled in everything else he set his mind to, then Lorenth would benefit greatly with him as its deputy commander.

The council had unknowingly set him on a path doomed for failure but Arimas had somehow navigated the storms of life, defeated the attacks of the beasts, and survived the onslaught of the sleeping sickness to lead his people to a place they would build together. A place where every citizen would give of their time and expertise to build Lorenth into a city that could weather even tougher storms and provide a place of refuge for all.

"I give you the foundations of Lorenth!" shouted Arimas as he pointed toward the thundering waterfall, while *Retribution* hung freely at his side. "Together we will move boldly into our future as, together, we build a place of commerce and education, command and respite... a place where all Lorenthians will be welcome. Together we will build a home for our nation that will stand the test of time and will feature all the talents of our skilled tradesmen. Rejoice and celebrate the dawn of a new era... Lorenth is born!"

Arimas sat in his chair and smiled as fatigue finally began to impress itself upon his weary mind and body. He vividly remembered the cheers and applause of the humans coupled with the awe and devotion of the council, but what he never saw that day were the watchful eyes of Commander Dean and his hidden supporters. Blind to all who stood before the waterfall, there were many other eyes silently observing the rapid advancement of the fledgling nation as well. Some were curious, some were speculative, and some were even fearful of what the rise of this nation would mean to rest of the sentient races hidden throughout the lands of Caliyon.

From the earliest of days, humankind prospered. A curious and innovative race, these creatures, the youngest of Caliyon's kinds, made quick use of their surroundings. They added to their knowledge base constantly, adapting and learning at a fast pace as they successfully took new knowledge gleaned both from their environment and the species that they encountered, synthesizing that knowledge into the development of their own unique civilization. Also the shortest-lived species of Caliyon, humans soon realized that they were to be survived by their plans and ideas, and the notion of needing 'more time' was a constant complaint throughout every generation.

During the ascent of human civilization, all of man was united. Largely exploratory in nature, humans devoted much energy and will to the task of expanding their hold on the world. Inspired by the fine craftsmanship of several abandoned structures discovered by an early party of explorers, human masons finally began to achieve—after a long process of trial and error—some level of success with stonecutting. Eventually, a form of mortar was created that would eventually allow the creation of the human's first stone buildings.

With this new means of erecting hardy shelters came the desire to form permanent settlements, where men and women could couple and birth families in safety and security. And as the meager population of humans started to grow, so did their need for space.

Soon, once abundant forests and flourishing streams were being destroyed in the wake of human expansion. Pride so often precedes failure, and in honor of their numerous accomplishments, humans continued to build bigger and taller edifices to leave as legacy to those who would follow. Their crowning achievement was the city of Lorenth, the pearl of the Western hills. Human architects and tradesmen worked for nearly ten years on the city that was to be their capital, boldly erecting the King's fortress around a natural waterfall. Using the mechanical technology that had been so far created, engineers developed machinery that was built within the fortress walls to harness the force of the water and provide some rudimentary form of power to the burgeoning city. The citadel and the temple grounds made up the eastern and western sides of the city, while the lower city, though not as elaborate as the fortress but as equally well crafted, was primarily built with the concerns of industry, commerce, residential needs, sewage management, and water delivery in mind.

The university, originally planned to be housed on the fortress grounds, was later decided to be built as the focal point of the lower city. Within those halls, the minds of man advanced in leaps and bounds, with both male and female students delving into the arts of alchemy, chemistry, metallurgy, and weaponry. As great feats were achieved, never once did a human question the superiority of their race. The humans were scientists and scholars above all else, now, and though their domination of the known lands of Caliyon had been largely uncontested, the human race was to soon find themselves humbled by something they did not know existed. Magic.

Magic was something foreign to humans. In their expansion to this point, not once did the humans encounter any creatures of fae or mystic origins. Though human masonry was attributed to the discovery of small buildings built for child-sized men, no evidence of such a creature had been found to actually exist. And, while mothers told stories of faeries and sprites to ease their children into sleep, no such creature had actually been seen by any reliable source. However, the time was now upon the humans for their expansion to be brought to an abrupt halt—the day when man, in all his ignorance and pride, crossed the Ellorian River and entered the elven forests of *Illu'Dar.*

While life of all types bustled throughout Caliyon, the priest-king of Lorenth slumbered at long last, ignorant of what was happening around him and his nation. While silent eyes watched and unknown prophecies came to fulfillment, the human monarch left the concerns of the day behind as a new day would quickly be upon him and those concerns would be ready and waiting for him to bear yet again.

III

"*Please don't leave so soon, love! You've barely just arrived!*"

"*I know, Jesslyn, my heart. This is equally as hard for me to bear, but you must realize that I have no choice in the matter. Commander Dean had a new tasking for me the very hour I returned from the previous one.*"

"*Farin, please, listen to me.*" *Jesslyn paused, doing her best to fight back the tears welling in her gray eyes. She swallowed thickly. "He visits me constantly while you are gone, Farin. I believe he won't ever do anything in public that may be considered indecent, but I fear for what he may do in private, especially now that he is sending you away almost all of the time. Can you not just stay home, become an apprentice to father? Why must it be the Guard that is your calling? Father could train you to be a journeyman carpenter well before our first children are born and then we could—*"

"*Children? Love, we have a marriage to finish planning first before we even start thinking about children. Sometimes I still wonder if we are just big children ourselves some days.*" *Farin's teasing wink earned him a small smile from his beloved, and he held out his arms to her. Jesslyn moved into his embrace, wrapping her arms around him tightly and tilting her head back for a kiss. Farin pressed his lips to hers, letting himself get lost in the sweetness of her for a moment. Jesslyn broke the kiss to look into Farin's eyes. She stroked his smooth face affectionately.*

"How can I bear to be apart from you again? You, my soon-to-be husband, who looks at me in a way that a cold-hearted man like Dean never could."

Commander Dean was becoming an issue that Farin was not skilled at handling. The enemy without was one thing—a quick thrust of a sword and it was over; an enemy within was another matter altogether and Dean's cryptic warnings about thwarting his pursuits contained enough veiled threats that Farin had begun to doubt the integrity of the war hero that many believed Commander Dean to be. Others had warned Farin not to dig too deeply into matters concerning Dean, for the man had eyes and ears everywhere and little occurred around the camp that Dean was not privy to. The latest news was that Terrance and Esan had been killed today, and Ullan, Kefler, and Wade, had all been reassigned to be manifest administrators or supply assistants back in Edarann and Bonnin. All five of them had at one time or another warned Farin about Dean. This was hardly a coincidence, but nor was it concrete proof of anything, either.

As he stood with his betrothed, all Farin desired was to leave the Guard and remain at Jesslyn's side. Yet, something deep inside him told him to maintain the path he was on, to pursue truth at all costs. Someone would eventually need to stand against Dean without fear, and all Farin believed he needed was a role model to help coax him into becoming more than just another soldier... a man like Arimas. Arimas was someone to emulate. Integrity was at the core of every word spoken and every action taken by the priest-king. Arimas was a catalyst for change and those willing to support his vision would partake in the coming era which would lead Lorenthians into the dawn of a new and prosperous age. Lorenthians... it was still a term that Farin found awkward to use, considering there was not even a site selected for the city. Yet, the vision of the city and all it was to stand for birthed hope in those who used the name, inspiring many to speak of Lorenth as something that already was instead of something yet to be.

But what future would exist for Farin if he tread upon the love of his Jesslyn and chose the life of service that he had already embarked upon, instead of life as a tradesman like his soon-to-be father and master crafter Caleth Rinidark? Jesslyn had hinted that *father was making something special for them as a gift, something that would be his finest work yet. Farin had no doubt. Everything Caleth laid his hands on turned out beautifully.*

Tired of thinking of the future, and of Dean, and wanting to focus solely on the lovely vision before him, Farin took Jesslyn's hands in his. "Are you going to stay with me tonight, Jess?"

Her response, a slyly playful smile, instantly aroused him. The young woman innocently began chewing on her lower lip while twirling a lock of her golden hair around her fingers. "I will try, love. Father suspects us already, but I will be sure to go to bed early tonight to eliminate his concerns... for now, at least. Father is actually working at his shop for at least another hour or so..." Her words trailed off as Farin began to blush ever so slightly before ending her passionate torture by kissing her again.

"I have stayed too long already Jess, as much as I want to stay longer. I need to check with the men and ready our supplies for the morrow. I too will be in bed early but I hope to be awakened by you later. I love you."

"And I you Farin... I will see you tonight."

The disturbing dreams of his past faded once again as his nightmare shattered the fragments of peace and contentment he found re-living his final, long dead conversation with the woman he would love until the end of time itself. Unlike the warmth that flooded his unconscious mind when he remembered Jesslyn's smile, this nightmare brought with it a sense of unspeakable terror and dread that would often continue into his waking mind. Without invitation and without warning, his nightmare began yet again...

Standing upon the altar with the maelstrom of dark magic swirling around him, Dean raised his hands in submission. His coal-black eyes flashed with a green nebulous glow as shadowy vapor began to slowly seep from the corners of his eyes. The sky steadily darkened as an unnatural storm formation grew directly above and a thick cover of greasy clouds spread, smothering the sky. Tendrils of ebony and violet light reached down like boneless fingers and began to twine around Dean as he maintained his position. Slowly, Dean began to change in appearance. First his hands and his head, then his torso and legs, until what stood on the altar was physically nothing more than a remnant of the man, a grotesque caricature who maintained a mere shadow of Dean's features and the ever-condescending eyes whose gaze now pulsed with a sickly green color. Peals of thunder rolled across the sky, the implied lightning not witnessed until Dean dropped his arms and took a deep breath, drawing all the shadow and the darkness into him. A single column of lightning blasted into Dean at which point the sky cleared and the sun reappeared.

"What have you done Dean?"

"I am Dean no longer... I am Kaaldean. I am your doom!" Anger and fury boiled behind those green eyes as the newly birthed Kaaldean thrust out his arms and unleashed two entwining tendrils of violet and black shadow with lightning speed, enfolding Farin in a vice-like grip and sending him to his knees in agony.

"No!" Farin exclaimed as he sprung, panting, out of bed. Sweat beaded his forehead and into the nocturnal makings of his beard, and had seeped from his body into his now-soaked clothes. Visibly shaking, Farin waited a moment for his breath and his heartbeat to return to their regular rhythms before walking shakily to the window. Dawn was still several hours away, he thought idly to himself, before allowing his mind to revisit the dream that had just awoken him. Once again, Farin found himself wondering what the significance of this particular recurring dream was. Never had he obtained any answers to this dilemma, and this morning would be no different. Jesslyn, as always, remained in the forefront of his thoughts and throughout times like this he often found himself wishing for her comforting presence more than usual.

Calmed by the thought of Jesslyn, Farin turned from the view out his window and crossed the room to his desk. He ran a strong hand along the smooth surface of the piece, which had been crafted from wondrously strong black oak and etched carefully with the seal of Lorenth and the crests of the Guilian and Rinidark families. Jesslyn's father had spent several months carefully crafting this work of art as a wedding present for his soon-to-be son and had also thoughtfully added, in clear detail, the crossed blades depicting Farin's rank at the time, that of battlemaster. Farin's fingers glided along its varnished surface. Caleth Rinidark was indeed a master crafter and had even created some of the famous pieces in the hall of kings. This desk, though, was one of his best works, and remained one of his last. Some say it was heartache that led Caleth to drown himself following the death of his only daughter and the last of his family, while others, such as Farin, believed there was more to the story than that. One more thing Dean would have to answer for... eventually.

Farin trimmed the wick on his lantern, but before he lit it decided instead that all he would need was some candlelight, and lit a rosy wax pillar and set it in its stand on the far side of the desk before sitting down. No longer lost in the darkness, he reigned in his wandering mind and focused on the events in his nightmare, trying to remember each detail.

These nightmares were occurring more and more frequently now. Years ago, he could have counted on one hand how many times he had been disturbed by this dream. Now the nightmares were plaguing him every night, or every other night, and each time the nightmare was the same. Dean, becoming a creature of evil right before Farin's eyes, drawing into himself a power of such vile intensity that, once directed at Farin, left him crushed and dying. And then, he would awake.

Farin could remember certain details now that were always present. There was a dais of some sort, or an altar, he wasn't sure, and the place was dark... no it was daytime but it grew dark and then later became day once again. Farin quickly pulled out his parchments and began to journal this fragment of memory. He still had no idea where this altar was located and if it even existed, but one thing was sure—Farin would do whatever it took never to be alone with Dean during the day where it involved the investigation of some religious artifacts or places of power.

Knowing that this had to be more than a simple nightmare, Farin tossed the idea back and forth about reporting these occurrences to Arimas, beseeching his council as High Priest and not as King. Yet, as his sanity still remained somewhat in question already due to the ordeal at the Dark Wood, Farin wasn't confident that would be a good decision. Bringing a repetitive bad dream to the priest-king would be a sure way to prove his failing competence as a leader, getting him relocated back to a small western hamlet conducting livestock and harvesting audits until death finally embraced him.

His thoughts wandered once again to the dream that preceded his nightmare. Even now, Jesslyn's smile still brought a small reprieve from the shadow that loomed over his soul every time this nightmare tore him from slumber. While he may have been a simple man to some and a soldier to others, there were many who knew Farin to be a man of sound mind and commendable spirit. A man, like the priest-king, that pursued the truth of matters. Modeling his behavior after his priest-king proved to be one of his wisest choices to date, yet even after all these years, he still had only suspicions about the final days of his beloved. Try as he might, he could not keep his mind from wandering back to the pain and the deeply held emotions of loss that occupied a large part of Farin's wounded heart...

No goodbyes were exchanged between Farin and Jesslyn as he sat, miserable, at her beside. Her feverish body kept her silent and asleep while she suffered through the advanced stages of the cruel illness. Farin prayed fervently that whatever she had he would contract as well, so that he could die with her, for life without his lover seemed meaningless. But death did not call for Farin. Instead, it tore away the last threads of life holding his beloved in the plane of the living. Vowing that one day he would see her again, he kissed her pale face one last time before putting to death a large part of himself.

Arimas' recent recommendation for those in mourning to attempt getting some rest was the hardest recommendation for Farin to act upon. Twice, he tried to close his eyes and lose himself to slumber, and twice he woke from visions of Dean clothed in shadow with an intent to kill. Perhaps this nightmare was only his internal processing of all the grief his body and soul harbored and that he refused to give in to. Perhaps, with time and healing, the nightmares would pass. But for now, the horror of the earlier events continued to gnaw at the heart and mind of the restless Farin.

As Farin lay in his bed, tossing and turning, various images from the past several days played across his mind. The young man had noticed Dean's occasional exchanges of wrapped packages with several people who were not uniformed men. Farin had even followed one of these tradesmen back to his tents but did not enter, as the sign that displayed the services of an alchemist gave him the information he needed to know. What could Dean be using an alchemist for? Could Dean have descended so low... could he be responsible for such heinous evil? Had he the power to do such a thing? Farin was now sitting upright in his bed.

And to what end? The sinister smile on Dean's face as he left Farin alone with his dying lover that one final time sent his thoughts spinning further in deep and dark directions. If Farin's suspicions were true, and not just a feeble attempt to lay blame at the feet of a man he hated, what could a lowly battlemaster do against the commander himself? It certainly appeared that Dean was weaving together a web of followers from both the military and the trading sectors, which could make him an even bigger problem later on if the man was not handled soon. But, no matter what Dean did or did not do, accusations were worthless without any proof, so the path of inaction was the only path open to Farin, a fact that caused him no end of frustration. Perhaps the lack of pursuit would encourage Dean to slack in his attention to detail enough that proof of his treachery would be plain to everyone... or perhaps Farin would need to bide his time even longer and wait for his day of justice.

Expecting a reassignment back to the west that never came, Farin continued to harden himself through duty. If Dean could attract support from within the ranks, then perhaps a man standing for honor and justice—as their king did—would also be able to attract a following of his own for that eventual day when Farin would seek to expose Dean for the fraud that he was. Farin later realized that it was his respect from the ranks that prevented his reassignment. He now volunteered for the tasks that carried him away from camp and away from the plotting eyes of Dean. He had found a way to increase the distance between himself and his commander, which inadvertently prevented any coordinated attacks upon him personally for many years to come. To Dean, Farin was likely just a loose end now—a broken shell of pain and remorse that would ultimately remain unproductive and unassuming. Farin would do little to alter that perception. Farin just needed time. Time to plan, time to deepen his relationships, and time to heal.

Farin returned from his nostalgic grief of times past. Knowing that he should sleep, yet still troubled in mind and spirit, the covenal of the eastern border detail capped his quill and stowed his inkwell, slowly standing to stretch out a minor kink in his back. He blew out his candle and checked his bed. The linens were mostly dry as he laid down once again, trying to capture at least another hour or more of sleep before the events of the day were upon him in full and unrelenting force. Though sleep was long in coming, Farin did eventually drift off once more.

*   *   *

Alone in the dark, Dean stood looking out his window and watched as the candlelight of Covenal Guilian was snuffed out. For years he had been having the same dream: someone, or some*thing*, calling him by name, although his name in the dream was changed to Kaaldean. At first, Dean paid little attention to the dream, as odd as it was. But, when it began to reoccur with stunning clarity over the years, and with ever-increasing frequency, the dream had become something of a private fascination for Dean. Unanswered questions filled his head. Although the feelings and emotions persisted into his waking mind, most of the finer details of the dream remained unclear. There was tremendous power in it, and in him, Dean knew. And Farin! That whelp was one part of his dream Dean couldn't forget, and didn't want to forget. For, the feeling of finally crushing Farin with that inexplicable flood of power was the greatest sensation the seneschal could ever imagine truly experiencing. Could such power be real? And what role did Farin play in unlocking this mystery?

Several weeks earlier, Dean had first noticed candlelight coming to life across the courtyard in the covenal's estate after Dean himself had just woken from his dream. At the time he had thought it odd that Farin was awake at this early hour, but did not consider it further until he saw it again tonight, the first night since his return from the eastern border. Was it possible that Farin was having dreams as well? While the shadows of his chamber concealed the vile smirk that ran across his face, Dean pondered the chances and the significance of these matters. The covenal's report spoke of unnatural entities in the Dark Wood. Perhaps it was with these creatures that Dean could trigger this dream to become reality—to unleash this mystical force... this magic into being.

Dean looked back toward his bed chamber where Kasee, one of his favorite playmates, slumbered. Her body only partially covered by the linens that Dean had disturbed when he had awoken, Kasee's bare chest and thigh lay fully exposed. Dean smiled again. Wherever there slept a man of power, you could find one woman, or three, who wanted position and power of their own, even if their role was nothing more than chambermaid of the powerful seneschal. Dean's wants were not as simple, notwithstanding the curbing of his insatiable carnal lusts. In the morning, he might enjoy Kasee's affections once or twice more before sending her on her merry way as little more than a servant, while he would dress alone, donning his mantle of seneschal and masquerading as the most loyal servant to the priest-king Arimas while conducting his own personal agendas on the side.

Dean wanted Arimas' position, though he never overtly let his private feelings supersede his unwavering diplomacy and carefully fabricated loyalty. His personal envoys had been gathering intelligence that never made it to the King's ears for years now, and his network was becoming something rather remarkable. His favorite were the small guild of assassins he labeled the Drucharii—serving as spy, thief, and assassin when needed, and granted immunity from the laws of the land so long as they were careful to avoid capture. Only once was one of his Drucharii apprehended by authorities. The seneschal made the risks clear. In the public eye of Lorenth, the young assassin, barely in his second year of service to Dean and just recently appointed as full Drucarii, was executed for murder and theft. At least he was well trained enough to conceal his associations with the guild and with Dean, and take those secrets with him to the grave.

Dean's dispatches to the south reported nothing the border covenal hadn't already stated in his reports, and the latest fishing colony and lumbering facilities were already well underway. When the initial warning from Farin arrived by messenger nearly two days ago, Dean immediately sent out a new envoy to confirm the tales of these wondrous beings inhabiting the eastern forest now labeled as the Dark Wood. News on that front would be arriving over the next day or two, and Dean eagerly awaited it.

What troubled him most, however, was the envoy he had sent to the northern peaks. The town of Reiys was a well-functioning colony nestled into the foothills that preceded the mighty mountainous range called the Icecrown Peaks. Reiys was prospering in its mining and stone working capabilities and was even achieving some measure of success in farming the land and raising livestock. These measures were enabling the town to grow more independent and self-sufficient of Lorenth, though the townspeople were careful to maintain faithfulness to the king and remitted all resource tributes as decreed from Arimas for the continual expansion and development of Lorenth. But, reports of some thirty head of livestock suddenly vanishing one night last month led the seneschal to investigate the area more closely. Some residents were claiming that massive carnivorous birds were to blame but in all the expansion to date, Dean had never encountered an animal able to wreak so much havoc in such a short time.

Dean's envoy, also a skilled Drucharii in his own right, had been sent to the area to investigate nearly three weeks ago now, and still neither Dean, nor any other members of his intelligence network, had received word.

But, this too would have to wait until morning. Dawn was fast approaching and the notion of sleep and the attentions of his bed mate later were more a priority right now. Dean walked away from the window, slid back into his bed without so much as a noise, and rested once again.

* * *

"Sir, Commander Barros reporting for assignment."
"Come."

With the arrival of a new morning, Farin checked his rampant thoughts from last night and turned his full attention upon his subordinate officer. The commander walked with pride in his step and confidence in his demeanor as he came to the position of attention before the covenal. Farin took a quick glance over his second-in-command, nodding in approval of Barros' polished silver armor gleaming with the crest of Lorenth; the scarlet cape signifying his position of command, trimmed with the gold embroidery of his station; and the winged helm held professionally to the commander's left side. Hadrin Barros would make a fine covenal already with his exemplary record of duty. His licentiousness with the younger women was perhaps his only weakness, but he could not help that women were all attracted to power, and he had enough power to spread around. Despite this particular peccadillo, Farin counted on his second-in-command, and knew that Barros' council could be trusted and his friendship, although strictly professional with the covenal, was honest.

"Please Commander, have a seat and talk with me for a while." Farin extended his hand to the leather chair at his right and waited for Hadrin to sit before moving to close the office door. Once he was confident their conversation would not be overheard by passers-by, Farin reclaimed his own seat. "I want you to speak plainly Hadrin, and leave formalities outside of my office for now. I need to speak openly and truthfully with a man that I trust and respect as both a leader in my command and a friend." Hadrin nodded and did not hesitate for a moment.

"What is going on Farin? The men are restless, rumors are spreading around the city that our border detail is to be decommissioned and reassigned to other units. Are you to be stripped of rank as well? I may not have seen what the foresters saw, but like you, I know the men and they would simply not fabricate that entire ordeal. Not only are they good, honest men, they are also not clever enough to come up with such creative tales."

"I agree with you, and I have already conveyed my professional opinion to the priest-king himself, but there is an enemy within that I fear I will have no victory against. I am constantly being berated and ridiculed in my leadership and it is only a matter of time until he sways the mood on the council and they see me as he sees me."

"You speak of the seneschal." Farin nodded slowly before the commander continued. "I have been quietly observing the few exchanges between the two of you over the years and it troubles me to see such a dichotomy between Dean's public countenance and his private one when dealing with you."

"Again, your astuteness in discerning the truth of the matter speaks greatly of your character, my friend. Yes, Dean and I have long been opposed to each other and he would have had me stripped of all rank long ago if it were not for my successes in both training and expansion—at least until now. Arimas believes the reports and has assured me that he will convey his support to the council, but nonetheless, we are to be ready to mobilize at any moment. Today they hold council, and I expect to be summoned shortly after to answer for the disaster at the Dark Wood and the deaths of our foresters. Ultimately, as covenal, I am responsible for this failure regardless of reason, and I will accept their judgment such as it may be. I may not agree with the results of the council but, like you, I am a soldier and I will follow the order that is given."

"What of the men, Farin? The eastern detail has been together for nearly ten years now. Our training is superior, our death toll is non-existent until now, and our results have been consistent for years. Several of the Guard have already expressed their displeasure at the possibility of being reassigned to a new covenal, or a new detail altogether. Surely Arimas will pursue the truth of this matter despite the seneschal's plotting against you."

"Would that you were right my friend, would that you were right. The men will follow you, Hadrin. Should I be stripped of title and position, I have no doubts that you will be the next covenal of the eastern border detail. You have proved your capabilities time and time again and you have long been ready for a command position of your own. I have told Arimas the same. I do not fear for the men, as your time is near at hand."

"I thank you for the confidence in me, Farin, but there still is the matter of the Dark Wood. If there are sentient races that live among the trees then should we not attempt diplomacy first? Have you any direction from the council about this?"

"Very little." Farin leaned back in his seat and steepled his fingers together thoughtfully. "If I know Dean like I think I know him, he will call for immediate seizure of the forest through conflict, to vindicate the deaths that we have sustained. He deems the unknown to be hostile, and will show whomever he encounters no mercy. He will flaunt the words 'honor' and 'justice' while he attempts to press his own agenda for reasons that I cannot fathom as of yet. I fear that something is drawing Dean into the forests and I am unsure if we will be able to deter him from altering the destiny of Lorenth."

"You are sounding more like a researcher than a covenal, Farin. Your thoughts are becoming less rational the more that you talk about Dean and his..." Hadrin stopped in mid-thought as his eyes narrowed. "You really believe what you just said don't you?"

Farin paused a moment before finally nodding slowly in agreement. He knew that his words would sound odd. Not once had he dared speak of his dreams to anyone. But, times were changing, and Farin knew that now was not the time for self-censure. Knowing that Hadrin was loyal to him, and therefore could be trusted, Farin began to relate the broad details of his dreams. Then, as Hadrin became more comfortable in his role of confidante, he probed further until Farin found himself sharing even the finest of the details of his recurring dreams. For a long time after the covenal had finished speaking the two men simply looked at each other, unsure as to who should be the first to break the silence.

"This changes things, Farin. I agree that this should not become public information to the council or even Arimas for you are likely to be thought of in an ill light and your ability to command will certainly be in question. Continue to journal what you can remember as it comes to you but show no one until something can be substantiated from your dreams. This does not bode well, Farin. Even now I grow uncertain as to what truly lies in the Dark Wood. I can only hope that the council will see reason and will elect for diplomacy over open hostilities as we wrestle with the defeat we have suffered."

"I, too, hope for reason to win over rage. Thank you for your candor, my friend. I need to walk for a time to clear my head. I will return by midday and until then I would ask that you debrief the men as you see fit and have them ready to mobilize at short notice. Keep the mood light and let the men enjoy some simple comforts as they rest, for I know not how long it will be before we are able to rest again."

"Permission to take my leave, Covenal?" Hadrin stood once again before his superior and squared his broad as he made the official request to end their conference.

"Permission granted. Dismissed, Commander." With an exchange of salutes and the faintest hint of a smile on Hadrin's face, the commander turned sharply and made his exit from Farin's quarters. Alone again with his thoughts, Farin opened his journal and reread some of the scrawled fragments of his dreams. More and more he felt unsettled about approaching the Dark Wood and he could not shake the feeling that his dream was somehow related to events that would transpire in his near future.

* * *

Dean smiled to himself as his disheveled servant, Tiana, dressed hurriedly and left the great chamber without a word. After a vigorous finish with Kasee hours earlier, he had then summoned Tiana into his chambers as dawn crested and grew into a bright new morning. He mused idly to himself as he slid into a waiting robe. He had likely been a bit more aggressive with Tiana this morning than she would have liked, but to her credit, she had wisdom enough to keep her mouth shut and her legs open. Something inside of him had thrilled at the expression of fear on her face as he forced himself upon her form moments after she entered his chambers. Dean had to admit to himself that he thoroughly delighted in her tears and her terror. He would eventually woo her back, offering sweetly worded promises that he would never abuse her like that again. He had made those same vows before though not to this degree, and naturally, the young servant girl would once more surrender her body to him in an effort to affirm her place in his favor. Pathetic, Dean thought, with a mixture of lust and disgust. But it was these women and their desire to achieve some semblance of social status as the concubine of the

48

mighty seneschal of Lorenth who fed his desires and entertained his carnal demands.

Was it pride that led him to bend his own rules of decorum with his bedmates? Was it simply that his lusts were not being satiated anymore and violence was the spice needed to enhance his pleasures now? Or was it a manifestation of these new sensations rousing within? Something was beginning to change deep inside Dean and he liked it. Like a burning cauldron of liquid metal deep within, he felt a growing sense of malice and disdain catch flame in his soul, churning slowly, with purpose and gradual amplification. When this building of desires would culminate or end was not certain, but he felt more powerful and in control every day. He knew that his time for glory had to be coming soon. Soon, Dean thought to himself, his hands balled into tight, white-knuckled fists, he would finally come to power, and supplant Arimas once and for all. Soon, Dean thought, Lorenth would be his.

The seneschal slid back out of his robe, letting it slide to the floor into a puddle of rich silk as he stood naked in the center of his bedchamber. Viewing himself in the large gilt mirror that graced the eastern wall of his chamber, he admired his flawless body, studying the well-honed perfection of his physique. Eventually he grew tired of admiring himself and he began to dress, carefully choosing the ceremonial seneschal garments that he would wear when addressing the council today. This forest to the east was a key component to his vision—that much Dean knew. After so many years of living a second life of concealed deceit, not knowing when he would receive his due, he had unknowingly been given this insight that resonated deep within him as absolute truth.

This knowledge had to be connected to another new development within Dean—a subtle awareness that seemed just out of reach of his mind. The more he tried to reach it, the more his senses sharpened and his awareness increased. More and more he could feel his environment, more than simply seeing it or perceiving it. It was something he could not fully explain or describe but the entire process enthralled him. With each passing day he found himself reaching out to this awareness and allowing it to sharpen him, replacing his weaknesses with unexplainable strengths. A loud, single knock upon his chamber door stirred him from his thoughts.

"Come."

One of his servants opened the heavy door with careful precision and shut it behind him without a sound, bowing low to the seneschal. "Pardon the intrusion, my lord. The council will be convening within the hour and my lord's presence is requested." Dean nodded his approval, and the servant dismissed himself once again, leaving Dean to speculate on the events of the impending council. Feeling the slightest draft against his cheek, Dean turned toward the southern-facing wall that overlooked the lower city. Standing silently in front of the silver and green drapes stood one of his Drucharii, sealed missive in hand and poisoned blades stowed neatly to both sides of his crimson and black studded leather jerkin.

Dean walked toward the Drucharii, careful to stay out of view of both the main door and the window. Vlaros, one of the more experienced of the assassin's order, inclined his head and extended the hand with the missive held carefully in it toward the seneschal. Dean took the letter, broke its seal and began to read the latest city intelligence that had been gathered and compiled from the network of spies he had spread throughout the city. More reports on petty crime in the poorer districts, coupled with hygiene problems and illnesses. One record regarding Counselor Orden Feld, whose wife was occupied with attending to her ill sister, detailed an evening he had spent enjoying the company of Llise which proved to be rather informative. Llise, one of Dean's best female Drucharii, had seduced the aging counselor for far more than he had reckoned he would pay for her attentions.

Other reports of lesser interest were included but Dean merely skimmed these, pausing only when he came upon Alic's report on Covenal Guilian. Alic was another Drucharii tasked with watching Farin's actions from the moment the covenal returned to the city and this meeting between the covenal and his commander was most interesting. Unfortunately, their discussion, whatever it was regarding, had been held behind closed doors and far from any window. Even worse were the quiet tones they spoke in. Nothing of use was gleaned from the conversation but Alic mentioned that they spoke at length and a very troubled looking Farin eventually emerged from the command quarters to take some air and a walk. Interesting indeed. What was Farin planning? What had he discussed with Commander Barros? Alic was good and he had no doubts that Farin would slip something meaningful when he least intended too and then Dean would have more insight.

"Have you any word on Larkin?" The intensity that was even now burning behind the eyes of the seneschal gave Vlaros some paused but he asserted himself with proper respect as he answered.

"No, my lord, he has not contacted the guild in sometime. Garrin and Warric were sent to Reiys to find Larkin and they sent word yesterday that his horse was found in the hills below the Icecrown Peaks. Unfortunately, no sign of the man himself was anywhere nearby. Orders my lord?"

Dean considered the implications of this news before answering. "Larkin is dead. We must assume that he found the beasts responsible for the disappearance of all the cattle near Reiys. He would not fail otherwise. He was a master woodsman before becoming Drucharii and I have strong doubts that he simply fell ill in the mountains." Vlaros nodded in agreement with Dean's logic.

"And what of the others, my lord?"

"Have Garrin and Warric return until we can better decide on a course of action to investigate this growing concern near Reiys. I'd rather not lose two more of the guild at this point. Until then, you have your orders."

Taking his dismissal in stride, Vlaros inclined his head once again and moved back toward the green and silver drapes. With well practiced moves, Vlaros displaced the right drape and pressed his fingers against the series of small nodules in the brick wall behind. A small panel made of nothing more than plaster, but carefully painted to resemble the same textured brick that made up the rest of the wall, slid open. Once again Dean felt the gentle draft of cool air that escaped from the narrow passageway that descended along the Seneschal's outer wall and terminated in the stables of the courtyard below as Vlaros disappeared into the darkness, quickly and quietly. The panel closed behind the departing assassin as silently as it had opened.

It was now time to make his appearance at the council. The information from Llise would be most useful today as the general feeling among the counselors was one of keen interest in the Dark Wood, and not one of retribution. He would play off of this feeling and recommend a course of action that would both satisfy the council and accomplish Dean's own agenda. This he had no fear of. In time, even the counselors would be his puppets and then his dreams would be nearly realized.

* * *

Farin was no one's fool. His uneventful walk gradually led him toward one of the nearby lakes just outside the city walls. The place was serene, and allowed him the opportunity to think through the matters of the morning. But, also, it gave Farin the chance to confirm a suspicion. The covenal ventured farther around the placid lake, watching the sun reflect off the clear and still surface. Also reflecting off of the calm surface of the water was an image of a dark, slender figure disappearing into the shadows of a nearby thicket of trees. Farin only caught a glimpse of the man's reflection once, but once was all that was needed. Never directly looking back to give away his newly acquired knowledge, Farin simply nodded to himself and turned, continuing on his way back around the lake and toward the command quarters to await further instructions from either the council or the priest-king himself.

* * *

"Seneschal Dean, what is your opinion on the matter concerning this most unusual report from Covenal Guilian?" Lead Counselor Cirra Bethanin, aging in years but still with the presence of mind befitting one of her station, gazed intently toward Dean as he made his approach toward the council. In the earlier moments of the council meeting, several lesser matters were discussed that Dean had already learned of, thanks to his own information network. The council discussed the need to improve sanitation in the lower city, as well as the popular demand for an increase in the town watch for the better regulation of the increasing levels of petty crimes throughout Lorenth. Arimas made an appearance as well, discussing at length his meeting with Farin and stating that he found no incompetence in his report or conduct when he spoke with him but also diplomatically refraining from advocating that all that was said was, in fact, truth. That he would leave to the council, and was yet another reason why Dean longed to supplant Arimas. He was an effective leader, true, but Dean could be better... Dean *would* be better.

"Although I concur with the decision regarding Covenal Guilian's competence in this matter, I still remain disturbed at the sheer loss of life sustained during this mission. I question the covenal's ability to continue to lead effectively in his current role. His men are shaken, and no retaliation attempt, or even rescue attempt, was considered before he terminated his task and relocated his entire camp and supplies back to Lorenth. Perhaps the covenal has lost some of his nerve and would be better suited with a less stressful assignment elsewhere. I leave that for your consideration.

In reference to my proposed course of action, I have given the matter some considerable thought and I feel it would be best to send emissaries of peace toward the river and the wood beyond, and seek to understand what life exists in this wood and whether they intend peace or harm. It is also my suggestion that we not approach the wood in secret but in full honors and colors, complete with dignitaries and trumpeters to announce our arrival at the river border. Should diplomacy fail, and no response forthcoming, then we could consider sending unarmed scouts into the wood to determine what presence, if any, the enemy has in these lands. Should ill befall our scouts then perhaps a volley of flame arrows into the trees would flush out the assailants so that we could detain them and give our propositions to them for their consideration."

"Well thought out, Seneschal," commented Counselor Melsa Vilarin. "Any issues with this plan, counselors?" All around the room the majority of the counselors shook their heads while others simply sat quietly, listening and watching. "Well then, those in favor of the seneschal's recommendation, please stand." Without any voiced objections, the counselors stood one by one, accepting the suggested plan with unanimous support before taking their seats again.

Lead Counselor Bethanin stood once again and addressed the seneschal. "Such is the decision of the council. Seneschal Dean, you are dismissed. We shall await your preparations and expectations of the council and the city at your earliest convenience. We would hope that your plans will be timely and set to commence within the next two weeks."

"You shall have activity before the week is out, Lead Counselor. My planning also took into consideration military and supply requirements and I will have everything brought before you in a more finalized state before the evening meal."

"Thank you for your thoroughness, Seneschal." Dean nodded to the Lead Counselor, turned on his heels, and proceeded out of the council chambers and straight to his personal chambers.

IV

*L*ittle is known of the dragons of Caliyon and even less has been recorded save in the librams of the elves housed in the glades of Avalide and in the frozen wastes of Frostspire. The nomadic dwarves of the Gray clan, who also occupied the cold northern regions, kept to themselves and though they knew of and respected the dragons, they chose to limit any interaction with them, preferring to tend to their continual delving beneath the earth.

The dragons were creatures birthed completely of magic. Unlike the elves and the dwarves who were born humans but then were radically altered through the touch of Ethoni, the dragons were the spontaneous result of the imbalance. Long before the humans organized themselves into a functioning society and long before the elves and the dwarves were as scholastically and intellectually advanced as they are now, the dragons came to be.

Corruption seeped into the world and infected all creation little by little, although its conduit had not yet revealed itself and thus its influence would remain minimal. With the purposeful and insidious infusion of even these small traces of the corruption, creation itself groaned in agony and responded in a violent shearing of the planar fabric. In the far reaches of the north where life struggled to thrive and where the corruption would find little, if anything, to influence, the power of the *Trinactria* flared and swelled creating an Ætherstorm that tore the northern skies into shifting shades of blue and green. There, in the eye of the Ætherstorm, grew a calm which became a planar rift allowing the magic of the three planes to ebb and flow and finally coalesce. The Ætherstorm lasted exactly one full moon cycle. During that cycle an unnatural darkness was cast upon the north as deep within the planar tear the first spontaneous creatures of magic were born.

Unlike the creations of nature which are born helpless and weak and grow to maturity, the first dragons to soar the skies of Caliyon at the conclusion of the moon cycle were mighty, powerful, and were the perfect culmination of the three spheres of magic. They were fully corporeal, being creatures capable of great physical feats. They were fully elemental, possessing knowledge and skills of the arcane. They were also fully spiritual, able to detect truth and lies, able to speak with their minds across great distances, and most notably, were able to pass on to the next generations all the memories and learned traits of their life through the dragonblood. Physically they were creatures resembling both a great four-legged lizard and a bat. Like the lizard, dragons grew in size every year of their life. Like the bat, the dragons could glide almost silently through the skies on featherless wings made of the toughest bone and sinew.

Where the dragons differed was another thing completely. Being creatures of magic like the elemental guardians, they were incorruptible. Being creatures of life and of fae like the elves, they also inherited the same ageless immortality. Dragons had no equal among the beasts of Caliyon. They were a sentient race and one of the most ferocious, equipped with talons on their fore and hind legs, tails as stout as a tree, and rows of glistening teeth making them formidable just from their physical assets alone. Coupled with their intellect, mastery of elemental fire and their divination capabilities, the dragons were truly a force to balance the corruption that seeped into all of creation at a measured, almost patient rate. The single most defining attribute of the dragons was yet to be discovered by them or others. As the only living creature composed of all three spheres of magic, dragons were completely immune to outside magical influence.

Socially, dragons functioned as a society of equals. They never exhibited a pack-mentality or instituted a single alpha leader among them. Granted, as a society, each dragon paid additional respect to the ones with greater experience and held those particular expressed ideas in a somewhat higher regard then others, often allowing their own ideas to be dismissed as they deferred to the elders and their wisdom. Although dragons chose to live in caves, lairs, or as some even preferred, in high mountain peaks and plateaus, only a fool would think of them as primitive. It was rumored that some dragon lairs were created with such planning and thought that they could rival even some of the elven guild halls. To underestimate a dragon was the first step toward one's death.

When the planar rift was sealed, only four dragons emerged in full winged glory. Valkyyrak, clad in perfect layers of golden scales, his head crowned with two long spire horns. Sargeron, the flying shadow and master of the night skies, was clad in black scales and savage tail barbs. Upon his face were several smaller horns that were dwarfed by five straight long horns that shielded the upper portion of his neck. Dalaria, though noticeably smaller than both Valkyyrak and Sargeron, soared with an eagle's grace as her trim, scaled body coursed through the night sky. She was the first to light up the skies with a mighty jet of dragon flame. Clad in her deep blue scales and bearing two pairs of twisting horns of differing lengths also projecting behind her head, she would prove to be one of the most magically adept of the four, able to see with truesight and farsight. She would also be the one responsible for the self-learned *Skarlagnos*, the telepathic thought capabilities between dragonkind. Fyysara was the huntress of the four. Emerging from the rift last, she soared low and purposeful, scanning the mountainous region and taking a visual inventory of the terrain and the wildlife. Her crimson scales were but a pale reflection of the fury that burned within her. It was Fyysara who felt the weight of the prophecies and it was her heart that was most guided by the spirit realm. Also very adept in the arcane, she quickly became known as the Guide and historian for dragonkind.

As the four dragons visually claimed their new territory, they settled on the plateau of the region now referred to as the Icecrown Peaks. Should a human attempt to cross the expanse of mountains between the rift and the peaks it would take days or even weeks, yet these dragons were able to cover this distance in mere hours. The Icecrown Peaks were so named for the distinct plateau that was ringed in by a complete circle of jagged and broken mountains giving it the appearance of a crown from far off. Strategically, this plateau was far enough south from the rift to be much more temperate of a climate as it bordered some of the lowlands and hills that made excellent hunting grounds for the dragons and yet afforded them the privacy of the peaks to remain isolated from the humans who would eventually cross their threshold many years later.

Initially, the dragons tested their new abilities and took dominion of their new terrain, forging bonds between each other that would continue for generations to come. In time, Dalaria and Valkyyrak felt so strongly about their connection that they took each other as mates and began working on a new lair together. Sargeron and Fyysara were another matter. Fyysara, who carried prophecy within her, bore much trouble in her heart for years, and neither she nor the others ever fully grasped the true weight of these burdens until many years later. While she felt a pull toward Sargeron in response to his own strong attraction to her, she insisted on refusing him for several years out of fear of what their union would mean for the prophecies. Instead she hunted, and brooded, and even began working on an oversized lair that she maintained was just for her, while Sargeron remained the ever-vigilant guardian of the peaks, flying high on silent wings and remaining unseen to any would-be predators foolish enough to enter the plateau or the snow-topped forests leading to it.

It wasn't until the births of their friends' younglings, Zharra and Maelyyk, that Fyysara finally accepted Sargeron as her mate. When she saw how those two eggs were flame-licked for years, awaiting some unknown time to hatch, and when she saw how fragile the infant dragons were when they broke through the heavily hardened outer shell, she knew that if the dragons were to stand a chance at survival, mating and guiding of the generations to come would be part of the solution, not part of the problem. The four were nearing their three hundred and seventieth year of age. Valkyyrak and Dalaria had mated some eighty-seven years ago and their two eggs had remained unhatched for at least fourteen years. Time was not on their side. Fyysara embraced her destiny, and Sargeron joined her in the well-crafted lair that had been a single dwelling for far too long. Their joy and passion would rival that of Valkyyrak and Dalaria and it was not long until three more eggs were submitted to the long process of flame-licking that would eventually bring about Nostrimus, Vaanadu, and Sycaris. It appeared as if all were finally right with Fyysara as she opened her heart to Sargeron and welcomed the joy that she had denied herself for so many years. Inwardly, though, she still found herself holding fast to those same fears, constantly distracted as she attempted to puzzle out the meaning of the dark prophecies that clouded her fate. She had a job to do, and a race of dragonkin to guide and so, daily, she buried her troubling thoughts and willed herself to focus on accomplishing what was required of her.

Fortunately, dragons grew fast. Though often taking years to hatch, waiting for some predestined moment that none but the hatchling knew, once they broke through the almost impenetrable confines of their eggs, they grew at unprecedented rates. Within months an infant dragon could hover and glide; within the first year they were strong enough to fly. Nostrimus was particularly keen when it came to hunting and by his fifth year was already able to take down smaller animals unaided, learning from the now much older Zharra and Maelyyk who both had completed their mastery over dragon flame. Sycaris was a dragon much like her mother and Dalaria. Though her hunting skills were never as developed as Nostrimus or Vaanadu's, she was the first of the three new hatchlings to spark a flame and later, only a year after Zharra and Maelyyk, was the next able to sustain her flame and master it. And, like her mother, Sycaris too felt the weight of the prophecies. Much to her constant disappointment and confusion, instead of commiserating with her youngling on the burdens they were both to bear, Fyysara refused to open any discussion with Sycaris regarding the meaning of the clouded prophecy that they each carried in their hearts.

So it was that the dragon race prospered. Valkyrrak and the other three ancients had surpassed their millennial age and watched as their descendants thrived and learned. The gift of the dragonblood continuously imparted all of the dragon's combined previous experiences to the next generation, and then to the next, allowing the younger dragons to keep stride with the elders in conceptual knowledge, thought not in practical knowledge. With each new generation, scale colors differed and eventually others could draw connections between a dragon's colors and their individual strengths. It appeared that gender had a significant role to play, as well.

The azure-scaled dragons typically were the most magically adept, followed closely by the crimson-scaled dragons. As if the elemental plane were reflected in their scales, the azure dragons often held great power over the forces of ice and water, being most at home in the cool of the Icecrowns; the reds on the other hand, were masters of fire and typically found greater comfort within elaborate lairs deep in the earth where the fires of the deep could radiate upward to the surface. Of the reds, only Fyysara and Sycaris were female, and as well, were the only ones to feel the weight of the prophecies. The male reds like Vaanadu were not concerned with the prophecies and thus devoted more of their time to the mastery of the element of fire. Vaanadu was obviously red in skill, yet was proud and patient like his father, Sargeron the black. Though not as savage in appearance or horned for battle, Vaanadu was a guardian at heart, and noble, using his arcane prowess to turn the tides of battle.

The greens, like Nostrimus, were a blend of arcane prowess and martial skills. Like the color of their scales, they were most at home among the trees and rivers of the lowlands, building simple lairs in the rock or ground and feeding off the wildlife and provisions found nearby. The black dragons were a mystery. Often savage in appearance like Sargeron, of all the dragons, the blacks were thought to be the most deadly. Their insights into the mind of their prey made them the most lethal and efficient of hunters. Their spiritual mastery gave them exceptional skill in truth-telling and with often quick-tempers, those who thought to fool a black dragon were often disposed of without hesitation. The blacks were also the best advisors and diplomats so long as their passions and tempers were held at bay.

Far rarer than the black dragons, the gold dragons were noted as the most benevolent and typically possessed the best leadership qualities. Where most dragons excelled in one sphere of magic more than the other, the gold were almost a perfect balance of the corporeal, the spiritual, and the elemental. Though not as adept in the arcane as the reds or blues, the gold dragons could command magic respectably, though often for shorter durations. Though not as savage as the blacks or greens in martial skill, the gold dragons used cunning and agility to overpower and outwit their foes while using their claws and teeth most effectively. Though not as gifted in the spiritual areas like the female reds and the blacks, the gold dragons were almost as strong in truesight, farsight, and truth-telling, and were not easily beguiled by anyone.

Although Valkyyrak was never appointed as the leader of the dragons—and truthfully, neither he nor the others would even attribute that title to him—when others would observe the dragons in council, it was evident that many would defer to Valkyyrak's wisdom and often would align themselves with his notions and plans for the betterment of all dragons.

Zharra was something altogether different, as were several others who would follow. Occasionally, a dragon was hatched with a metallic hue. The gold certainly would be included in this category; however, as their skills were obvious, they were often thought of as being in their own category. Various shades of gold, such and bronze and copper, began to surface throughout the generations. Those bearing the more earthen metallic tones often were more martially adept and equipped than the gold, yet possessing lesser elements of the balanced magic that characterized the gold. Maelyyk, was the earliest of the copper colored dragons, and was a natural leader like his father. He spent much time channeling his limited mastery of fire into the betterment of lairs and other flame-borne crafts while asserting his place among the other martial forces to be reckoned with.

Zharra was considered a platinum dragon. Her scales were of the palest blue—almost white—yet were incredibly hard, like those of the gold. The platinum dragons, as well as the more rare silver ones, were almost purely spiritual dragons, yet surprisingly, they did not feel the weight of the prophecies like the two female reds. They could sail on soundless wings, vanish in plain sight through the bending of light, or completely dominate the mind of a lesser foe. Zharra eventually learned how to create copies of herself and project those copies along with her farsight to be able to appear in illusion form and interact with others as she saw fit. As the dragons continued to thrive, the elves and even the dwarves began to suspect that if the weight of the balance were true, then the corruption must be growing as markedly as the skills and wonders of the dragons.

It was as a result of the elves that the first emissaries were sent out to the dragons and likewise to the dwarves in order to build relationships and alliances among the three prime fae races. Until then, the dwarves had remained silent, delving into the earth and forging masterful works of martial skill and craftsmanship. Aerinyyr the truth-sage, one of the elders of the Æthian and an adept in the arts of divination, was the one responsible for locating the dragons and the ten distinct clans of dwarves and subsequently, for opening the way for extended communication. Although only two of all the dragons felt the pull of the prophecies, nearly all of the Æthian and the *Dsa`carii* spent season after season studying and divining the truth behind the prophecies and recording their insights to magically bound parchment before housing them in the twin libraries of Avalide and Frostspire. The elves were equally as troubled about the silence found in the prophecies that Fyysara and Sycaris referred to as the shrouded prophecy, yet neither race could gain insight into this matter. The hope of Aerinyyr was that if the dragons, elves, and dwarves could unite and gather all the collective wisdom and experience of the fae races together, perhaps the guiding light of prophecy would be easier to follow and a method to abate the rising corruption could be uncovered.

Locating the dragons was easy. The elves of Frostspire were but a few short days east of the Icecrowns and through the creation of the reflecting pools, Evianna would relate the plans to Nyssia Dv`arek, one of the *Dsa`carii* frost magi and ambassador to the Frostspire council of three: Valeris Sy`yn, Tinovis Fyr`eth, and Yserth Tel`andris. The Ice Elves, more commonly referred to as the *Dsa`carii* or storm weavers, were a unique blend of elf that awakened far to the north of *Illu`Dar* and settled into the frozen wastes. Linked in spirit and mind to each other, the *Dsa`carii* were all arcanists and diviners. Even more pale in complexion than their forest dwelling counterparts to the south, the *Dsa`carii* were consumed with expanding their knowledge and effectively secluded themselves in their monumental keep, a magnificent structure that defined the north-eastern horizon. Frostspire was a synthesis of stone and ice that was held together with tight bindings of magic.

To many, Frostspire appeared from far away as little more than an observation tower. Yet, if a creature chose to undertake the journey into the frozen wastes to see for themselves, what they would find was entirely different. Encasing the entire structure of Frostspire was a pale blue nimbus that served as both an anti-magic shell as well as a buffer to reinforce the structural integrity of the spire. Each level was systematically built upon the next with care, precision, and purpose. The base was as wide as the council chambers on the topmost level and each of the ninety-nine levels was large enough to provide thirty to forty complete circular accommodations for the magi, including space for the common area with portal gates at the center of each floor.

The spire was separated into three major sections: the living communes which were comprised of fifty levels, the training facilities which occupied thirty levels, and the next ten levels were reserved for the libraries where all the research would take place. The top-most nine levels were the council chambers and the battlekeep, often called the Eye of the North, where the council of three, along with the elder magi, would observe and study through plain sight and farsight. The eye was shaped slightly differently than the circular form of the rest of the spire. The walls were arranged in a twelve-sided shape with apertures that allowed those within unrestricted views of the frozen wastes. From each corner of the wall grew an inverted talon-shaped spire that arched menacingly into the sky, giving the appearance of a twelve-fingered hand reaching to the heavens above. Though the base material used to construct the spire was a black and gray stone composite, the ice of the northern wastes was given free reign to consume most of the tower giving it the appearance of jagged, blackened glass.

The *Dsa`carii* were the first to divine the secret of portals as their spire had no stairs but a central energy gate that flowed from the base of the spire to the council chamber at the top. They were also the ones to create the reflecting pools to facilitate communication between Avalide and Frostspire. Few of the *Dsa`carii* could handle the warmer regions of the south without obvious difficulty. Of these few, Nyssia was one of the more talented of the frost mages and was quickly elevated to the position of ambassador. To be an elven ambassador of Avalide or Frostspire required three things: mastery level accomplishment in one of the three planes of magic, proven trustworthiness and efficiency as a leader in their own right, and the ability to expedite communications through the mastery of shape-shifting.

Nyssia had early on mastered the shape-shifting technique, becoming a swift blue-ringed swallow. Once Aerinyyr had uncovered the dragons and tasked Frostspire with their observations and study, Nyssia quickly began working on molding herself into a similar form, for the dragon was by far the most enchanting creature she had ever seen. Thus, her chosen form was now a blue drake. Though infinitely smaller than the dragons she had spent years watching in silence, Nyssia's drake form was much larger than her original elven form, and was nearly the same in features to the dragon, though unscaled and more sleek in shape. The six appendages did pose a problem, however, as Nyssia had only four limbs to make use of. Thus, her drake form could only replicate the wings and the hind legs. The blue drake was beautiful in its own right, and the differences mattered little as in her chosen form she could cover the two week journey to Avalide in little more than a day.

Though different in form and skill than the elves of *Illu`Dar,* the *Dsa`carii* felt the bond between them early on after their awakening, and within four moon cycles had made contact with their elven kin, building ties with them while developing their own unique culture far to the north. Nyssia, the ambassador to the *Illu`darii,* and Thaelvin, ambassador to the dwarves, made the flight to Avalide following the final completion of Frostspire many generations before to begin the process of creating the first reflecting pool in the warm capital in the south; Draevor, ambassador to the dragon nation, and Larros, ambassador to the humans, remained in Frostspire to begin the work on the second pool in the council chamber of the *Dsa`carii* and to oversee the linking of ether energy to facilitate the communication process.

In total, from the forging of the arcanite castings and binders, the arcing and fusing of the crystalline power matrix, to the final setting, regulating, and testing of the working pools, the process took roughly eight and a half moon cycles. The final pools resembled a small swirling dais of ether energy that stood three spans off the ground and measured a full six spans in diameter. Each were set off to the right of the council seating chamber, close enough to be seen by all the council members when communications were initiated, but placed so as not to obstruct court functions. The Æthian of Avalide watched with keen interest as the final ether links were forged and immediately thought of ways to replicate the process with different applications.

When Nyssia and Thaelvin stood on the pool to announce the completion of the *Illu`Dar* matrix, their vision blurred as they witnessed an overlay of the Frostspire council chamber that sat upon their natural vision of the council chamber in Avalide. The Frostspire council stood in awe as perfectly clear projections of both Nyssia and Thaelvin stood on their own pool giving their reports and bowing before stepping off the pool to await confirmation of the test results. Likewise, when Draevor and Larros stepped on the Frostspire pool, they too experienced the same slightly distracting but fascinating sight distortion. The clarity of the projections and the respective greetings of both Draevor and Larros followed by the council of three to the *Illu`darii* cemented the bond between the two elven races and resulted in a weeks-long celebration in both capital cities that would later become an annual tradition. This celebration was aptly named Frostfire in honor of the specializations of each race in the differing elements of water and flame.

With the pact of silence issued from Avalide, Larros, ambassador to the humans, had yet to make first contact with the humans and merely stood in the Eye of the North using his farsight to observe their development and expansion farther east. A time would come when these humans would need to be enlightened to the fae existence but until the pact was broken, which those magi who spent their time lost in their visions as guided by prophecy warned would be broken by the humans in time, contact with this race was prohibited.

Thaelvin, ambassador to the dwarves, made contact following Nyssia's connections forged in Avalide. The dwarves were divided into ten clans spread out over much of the known land. The dwarves were a very communal race, with strong ties to both clan and kin. Thus, when Thaelvin first approached the gates of Ur'Akam to meet with clan chief Korigan Goern of the Gray clan, more commonly referred to as the grays, news of the meeting quickly spread throughout the other clans until meetings began to occur in all of the dwarven strongholds across Caliyon. The grays were the most acclimatized to the cold of all the dwarven clans. Inhabiting the lower mountainous regions of the Icecrowns, the grays knew of and respected the dragons that soared the skies above. While the dragons claimed dominion of all the land and skies of the Icecrowns, the dwarves were content to delve farther into the earth, unlocking a world of rare beauty, including forges that captured and harnessed the power of the deep, magnificent subterranean chambers and greathalls, and indeed, even a world not so unlike what others might see on the surface. The grays made such a life of exploring the world below the surface that they spent little time above the ground, giving their skin a pale ashen appearance and giving them remarkable night vision. Yet with their keen night vision came a great sensitivity to the light of the sun and as such, many grays simply did not find reason to venture to the surface unless absolutely necessary.

With this fragile balance of order between all creatures of fae came a growing fear that eventually the corruption would shatter this order and send dwarf and dragon, elf and elemental, and all other fae alike into a spiraling decay that would consume what magic remained in Caliyon. The dwarves continued their master crafting deep in the bowels of the earth, revealing residual magic found in precious gems and ores that once united with the stone and fire resulted in weapons of such elegance and brutality that few could withstand them. Even the great Ssaraki that burrowed far beneath the dwarven strongholds fell and knew fear for the first time when these power-imbued weapons were held in the hands of a skilled warmaster. The elves, in an attempt to hold this fragile order together, grew restless and began to make preparations for the unlikely event of a war among the fae, while the dragons made their distrust abundantly known and never did entertain emissaries to approach the Icecrown Summit until much later. The elementals, ever watchful and incorruptible, grew quieter as if the breath of destiny could be lost among the words of the races. And throughout all this uncertainty, the humans, ignorant and full of pride, continued to expand and dominate over the west, content in the false assurances that they had no equal or adversary greater than the beasts of the wild. Change was coming and it was Aerinyyr who once again forced destiny to reveal its plan before the time was upon them.

V

*L*ike a heavy heartbeat echoing its rhythmic sound over and over again, the dreamers, locked in their state of induced sleep, began to pulsate with each beat, moving in time to the melody that only they could hear and feel. The dream had become more intense, more real than ever before. Each beat built upon the last, creating a crescendo that drove the dreamers into a state of restlessness that none had ever before witnessed.

"Eth hador bet ysaris!"

"Tali venit usir nyyven!"

"Eth hador bet asarii!"

When the third dreamer shouted out her own four words there was a pause, a moment of complete silence, and then, rending the very atmosphere of the world came a shrill piercing sound that resonated like a song in a piece of crystal, immediately followed by a ripple of force that burst through Avalide bearing a deep heartbeat that, until that moment, had been silent to all but the dreamers. The winds of the world grew still and even the leaves dared not rustle as each elf picked him or herself up from the ground and wiped away the solitary tear that graced the left cheek of all who felt the dream that was not a dream.

* * *

"*Eth aloni tul`venarii* mistress. I bring word from the dreamers."

"*Ashanda eth reiis* Sylande, tell me the words as they were delivered."

"*Eth hador bet ysaris, tali venit usir nyyven, eth hador bet asarii.*"

The Matriarch's unlined face paled as she instantly recalled the prophecy and she whispered softly, "The tear is falling, hope is born alive, the tear is calling…"

"The dreamers have been awakened and have been unable to re-enter the dream since they spoke. They sit together in awe, as one drunk with love or lost in the deepest of thoughts. They have not opened their mouths to speak again."

"Nor will they again, Sylande. The dream is over and the tear has been awakened in the light of the corruption. Quickly, find Aerinyyr and tell him that—"

"I know, Matriarch," Aerinyyr interjected as he made his way unbidden into the Matriarch's chamber. Elegantly attired in crimson and gold embroidered robes, and bearing the scepter of the truth-sage, an ornately woven rod of unbroken wood that twisted upon itself in almost impossible ways and housed several small lavender and cyan blooms that never withered, he stood as one with authority and offered a small smile to the Matriarch before continuing.

"The balance demands much and has now cast a shadow upon the hope that for years we have been waiting for. The essence of Deimar is alive and searching for the Lightbringer while even now the corruption has found a seed within which it can cultivate itself and manifest in corporeal form. The time for fear and doubt is passed. If there is to be hope against the shadows, then all the creatures of fae must come together and present a united front that may insulate us all from the corruption that is soon to be unleashed. I am certain that dragon and dwarf alike felt the call of the tear and if we convene together for a council of the races, new truths will be discovered."

"I believe, as I always have, Aerinyyr, that of all of the elves you alone have discerned the truth of this grave matter. How we are to bring all the fae together suddenly is a matter that escapes me yet I will leave the arrangement of this council to you. May hope guide us as we enter the dream that is no longer a dream."

"The council is already at hand, Matriarch. Missives were sent out several days ago detailing the location of the council that would need to be held following the tear's call. Forgive me... I did not intend to supersede your authority. I simply reached out to the dream some time ago, and, though I am not called or gifted as a dreamer, the dream reached back to me and gave me a glimpse of what was to come. Laid upon my being was a caution to breathe not a word of the tear until the dream became no more, lest the balance be shaken before the hope was ready to surface. We convene in three days atop the Ellorian waterfall, in the vast fields and highlands yet unscouted by humans and where even the dwarves and dragons can rest in comfort in a cooler climate. Though uncertainty remains in the hearts of the fae races, the call of the tear is greater, and I was assured that equal representation of the races would be in attendance. I would ask that you and I and the magister make haste to the Ellorian falls while you leave the tending of Avalide to a steward for the next few days. Frostspire will also be sending ambassadors as you should be noticing any moment."

Within the council chambers the reflecting pool ebbed and fluctuated until images of Valeris, Tinovis, and Nyssia stood on the dais as each inclined their head touching their fingers to their lips.

"*Eth aloni tul`venarii* sister, we have felt the call of the tear. It is time to stand against the shadows," Valeris spoke directly to the Matriarch.

"*Ashanda eth reiis* sister, the time is close, yet there is much to do before the seed of corruption has fully matured. Are you to meet us in the Ellorian highlands?"

"Yes, it shall be as you have said. I cannot speak as to whether the grays or their kinsmen will be there, but it appears as if there is activity upon the Icecrown summit. Perhaps we all may finally behold the wonder and terror of the dragons at this meeting."

The Matriarch nodded in agreement. "Then I look forward to seeing you again, sister. It has been far too long." With a parting smile, the image of Valeris and her fellow *Dsa`carii* faded as they stepped from their reflecting pool in far off Frostspire and left the Matriarch, Aerinyyr, and Sylande alone in the Matriarch's chamber once again. "Evianna shall remain in Avalide while we are in attendance at this gathering. Sylande, return to the dreamers and speak only this to each of them… 'rest in peace for the dream has ended.' Then send word to Evianna that I wish to speak with her." With a low inclination of her head, Sylande took her leave and began her return to the dreamers.

"The magister is ready to leave at your order, Matriarch. I spoke with him before coming to see you. All is set and the events are in motion such that we cannot control their outcome. Should you not have anything to ask of me then I too shall take my leave to finish my preparations."

The Matriarch shook her head as Aerinyyr took his leave. The truth-sage was a mystery to her. Though he paid respects to the Matriarch and her station, it was evident that she held very little power over him, and in some ways she felt that his influence on events far outweighed her own. His words were always carefully chosen and measured in pitch and tone. The calm and sureness of all that he said and did emanated from him, evoking trust and peace in all who had dealings with him. Mystery indeed… a master elementalist and diviner was certainly a formidable ally to have with shadows fast approaching. Shaking her head at her wandering thoughts she glanced once more at Aerinyyr as he turned around the corner of the chambers and left her vision. Nodding to herself, she turned from the court chamber and headed toward the library to search out the scroll that held the prophecy which had been fulfilled today. Perhaps there was more to it than she remembered.

*   *   *

The other keepers looked to Sylande as she entered the dreaming chamber, shaking their heads in sadness at her silent question. There in the center of the room, in the same position they had been in when she left them, sat the three dreamers—that same empty, wondering stare still etched on their faces. Kneeling down beside the first dreamer, Sylande touched her face gently and whispered the matriarch's words.

"Rest in peace for the dream has ended." Without waiting to see the reaction those words inspired, Sylande moved to the second dreamer, and then the third, repeating the same message each time. It was not until Sylande had finished speaking the third and final time that there was any result. When the last dreamer had heard the words, the three smiled as one and in one voice they made their final call.

"No more dreams, for now we rest."

The triumvirate embraced one another, holding each other tightly as their bodies began to shimmer. Their legs began to take on the look and texture of the wooden chamber floor as inch by inch the dreamers grew into each other and into the space beneath them. In mere seconds, where the elven dreamers had once laid, stood a tall Rowan tree, rooted into the dreaming room itself. Vines began to spread out from the base of the dreamers' new form until the entire chamber was covered in thick, green, healthy foliage. The keepers, Sylande, Llaine, Illisa, and Ashandi, stood in wonder at what they had witnessed. As they approached the base of this new tree they could almost hear it breathing as if asleep, the new foliage moving in rhythm with each breath.

"Rest well sisters... it comes well deserved." Sylande laid her hand upon the oddly warm trunk of the tree, and in the knotted bark, vines, and leaves saw what remained of the three dreamers. Turning to the other keepers and gesturing for them to take their leave, the four keepers made their way out of the dreaming chamber and headed for the river glades where they could reflect on what they had just seen and to discuss a new direction for their service to Avalide.

*   *   *

Approaching the vast holds of the Avalide librams, the Matriarch paused as she reached the impressive structure. Unlike the rest of Avalide, which was grown with the help of the mighty trees that held each building in its tender embraces, the Illuallarii was nearly incorporeal in substance and appearance, as if resting between the natural world and that of the unnatural—which was not far from the truth. In the early years of the elven awakenings, elves, dryads, sprites, elementals, and all manners of plant and animal, sentient or not, communed together in perfect harmony. Being primarily fae creatures of the forest, both the forest elementals, more commonly referred to as the silent watchers or treants, and the air elementals were the most sentient races in the glade and were quick to develop bonds among each other. While the treants took up permanent residence in the glades, some living in symbiotic unity with the dryads, the air elementals came and went as they pleased, bearing an allegiance to no one. One of the air elementals in particular found the elves fascinating and after watching their progress for years, she finally made her presence known to the Matriarch and offered an exchange of mutual benefit.

The air elementals grew increasingly restless as time passed and few even knew of their existence save the elves. Being creatures of both the corporeal and elemental planes, they normally assumed a defensive posture, remaining insubstantial until provoked, at which point they could render themselves corporeal for the briefest of moments and strike with deadly speed. Being aligned to no one was the pinnacle of their freedom yet it left them without cause or purpose and their ever-wandering and observing became tiresome. On the other hand, the elves were enthralled with all manners of life and magic. Researchers and arcanists alike, they were careful to record all their findings, including prophecy and history.

When the air elemental who called herself Shandari came to meet the Matriarch to offer her friendship in search of meaning and direction, the Matriarch gave Shandari both. The gift would be volumes of histories collected and scribed over generations as well as the prophecies stored in the first library—the collection of the dreamers when the shroud was not yet upon them detailing the makings of the world of Caliyon, the birth of magic, the triad known as the Sar`Eth`Deim, and the arise of the incorruptible races, namely, the dragons and the elementals.

The Matriarch saw in Shandari an opportunity to harness the strength of wind and provide answers to a race that knew little of themselves. The Matriarch offered Shandari knowledge of what was and all that would be as well as all new tomes yet unwritten and not yet dreamed, if Shandari would become the Lorekeeper and defend the histories and prophecies from destruction and decay. Shandari was pleased with this offer and the alliance between the air elementals and the elves began with a simple exchange between two individuals.

The Matriarch had no idea what would eventually transpire in Avalide as the elemental took her task quite literally. Air elementals from all four winds arrived in Avalide as Shandari began the construction of the new library in the location specified by the Matriarch. Construction was a poor word for the process, which involved creating shears in the fabric of the corporeal realm much like the planar rift from which the dragons had emerged from many generations before. What grew out of this shearing was remarkable. As if inspired from the surrounding elven architecture, the elementals created a building that was, in appearance, much like the grand guild halls that decorated Avalide. But, in the case of the library, there were no trees suspending the weight of the structures or caressing each wall both inside and out. The library simply... was.

Suspended in both air and time, the walls would shimmer and twist all natural light as it entered the building, giving the inner space a dream-like appearance. Yet, there was some strong element of permanency in existence, for the library was more than simply air or the substance of dreams. The bridge that crossed the gap was grown from the nearby trees and was certainly real, the walls were hard and elaborate in design, and the doors—which only opened upon the arrival of anyone with elven blood—felt sure and resilient as if crafted to endure even the end of days. Inside, row upon row of shelving was created as several more elementals came to be a part of the new beginning with the elves as they too sought meaning and direction.

When this masterpiece of elemental and elven architecture was finished, all of Avalide came to marvel at the new edifice standing in a place of prominence among the guild halls of the capital. The Matriarch, robed in her ceremonial best—a long silken robe cut of the deepest purple that accentuated her pleasing frame and ample bosom, with golden thread embroidery all along the sleeves, back and chest—stood at the entrance to the library as several elementals began shifting into their corporeal state to allow the masses to see them.

"What has been done has never before been done and for this, elves and all fae creatures will honor the air elementals as you have taken upon yourselves the noble duty of safeguarding the knowledge of the ages, of dreams, and of things that have not yet come to be. Our gift to you will be knowledge and purpose. Let all the collections of lore, history, and dreams be brought to the elementals and entrusted to them for keeping and preserving, while they in turn have full access to the knowledge of things that have been and are yet to be. Learn what you will from the tomes and scrolls, our new friends, and I charge you with only one task. Let not dust or decay, sword, or enemy deface or destroy the collection of works that will lie within, and aid us as we tread on your new domain in search of the wisdom of the past and the future as we see fit. Will you accept this charge?"

"We accept your charge..."

"Matriarch Cheyandra Silversong, beloved..."

"of the wood,"

"leader of the elves,"

"and friend of the elementals."

In perfect unity, the five different responses of several of the nearby elementals echoed with sincerity and truth as a deep contentment washed over their ephemeral features. Shandari stepped forward once again to speak with the Matriarch and address the elves nearby.

"We are not solely of this world, children of the wood. We reside in both the corporeal plane, as you call it, and the elemental plane, where death cannot touch us and where time has no effect. Before the founding of nations... we were, before the great trees walked and watched... we were, and even before the balance brought into existence others like ourselves, born of water, fire, and of stone... we were, yet we wandered and listened without aim or reason for... we simply were. Let it now be known that in the elven woods called *Illu`Dar* where the sun rises in the eastern lands, the elementals of air have found their aim and reason. We accept your charge with honor and vow that neither destruction nor decay will corrupt the knowledge housed within the Illuallarii, a name chosen among us elementals to honor the *Illu'Dar* lands and the elemental breath of life that chose us before all others. Come as you will and we will guide you to the tomes that you wish to see. We shall be the Lorekeepers, and woe to any who would seek to threaten us or violate our charge and the vow that we have made this day."

That was the beginning, which now seemed so long ago. The Matriarch once again shook of her reflections as she stood in the entrance of the Illuallarii, and moved forward, watching in unceasing wonder as the massive doors of the library swung wide on silent hinges without aid of anyone, elf or elemental alike. As always, she witnessed the hosts of elementals gliding through space and time, sorting and searching and shelving the histories collected over centuries. When the elementals were not organizing or assisting others they were most often found sifting through the pages of each and every record, committing to memory text and verse and chapter in mere seconds, building their own body of knowledge so as to be a better resource to others than the physical histories themselves.

"How can we serve you, Cheyandra?" Jerarin, one of the male elementals and the gatekeeper of the Illuallarii, spoke softly and pleasantly, never condescending even though the elementals paid no attention to title or station and often referred to others by their birth name only.

"I am in search of two of the older prophecies, Jerarin... the ones that talked about the end of the dream that was not a dream, and the silence of prophecy."

"I find those records most unusual, Cheyandra. We have debated their meaning often within these walls and still there is no unity as to the exact meaning; however, we have often tried to read into the passages too much and perhaps the simple answer is the correct one."

"That, too, is what I was wondering. Today perhaps will change your interpretation for the dream has now ended in our midst and the dreamers are asleep for all time now."

With that statement came a sudden hush throughout the library as several other elementals stopped what they were doing in order to hear the whispers of the softly spoken words being exchanged between the Matriarch and their fellow elemental. At least two dozen of the library workers were brazen enough to approach the couple. Jerarin, who was trying rather unsuccessfully to hide his excitement, prompted the Matriarch to continue.

"Aerinyyr reached into the dream some time ago and was warned that the Tear of Deimar would awake and call for the Lightbringer. Today, the tear made its call and the dreamers were enthralled in their visions until I passed along the words to set them free and give them their final rest. The keepers are without direction as the dreamers have now passed into the eternal sleep and need no one to tend to them any longer. All of Avalide felt the call and the wave of emotion was breathtaking. Even now, Aerinyyr has set in motion events that will bring about the first council of the fae races atop the Ellorian waterfall three days from now. I would ask that Shandari send one of your race to be present, for the balance has shifted yet again and I believe the time of shadow is so upon us that prophecy shall speak no more for a time."

"The simplest answer"

"was indeed the correct one it seems"

"Cheyandra. Then did we see darkly but now"

"we see clearly. The dream"

"that is not a dream has ended and the"

"shadowed one draws nigh"

"and still there is no Lightbringer."

The wave of unified voices of the elementals was always difficult to focus upon and even though this was their way of communicating in larger groups, as she had witnessed countless times before, each similar exchange still fascinated her.

"As always, the balance has shifted again and now the darkness will run free with terrible haste until the balance shifts to favor those not of the darkness. Long have we trusted in the hope that the Lightbringer will come, and even though we fear he has not yet been born, still we shall trust in the prophecies and prepare ourselves for the time of shadow."

"You are wise beyond words, Cheyandra. Did you still wish to view the records of which you spoke of moments ago?"

The Matriarch probed her thoughts in an attempt to weigh what other details could be hidden in the scrolls that were not discussed already through the recent casual dialog. "No, Jerarin. I am satisfied with our discussion, and now must return to my chambers as I prepare for the great council meeting. I thank you for your time, Jerarin. You have been a comfort."

Before the Matriarch could make her way out of the Illuallarii, Jerarin hesitated for a moment, his hand frozen in an outstretched position as if listening to words that only an elemental could hear. "Shandari has received your message, Cheyandra, and will accompany you herself on the third day. I am pleased to have spoken with you again."

With that, the nearby elementals vanished into insubstantiality as they all returned to their tasks. The Matriarch left the Illuallarii, not sparing a moment to watch again as the silent gates swung closed behind her. Even now, the charge issued to the elementals to protect the librams and tomes within from all, including eventual decay, was something that she didn't fully appreciate until after the tomes were housed in this wondrous place.

It was thought by many broad-thinking members of each species that should an entity, or creature, dwell in more than one plane at the same time, then they are neither in either plane fully and thus are immune from the impact of either plane. Such was the case with the air elementals, and now the Illuallarii. Air elementals did not age, but their agelessness was different from the immortality of the elves. Nothing seemed to change for them. They existed, but remained apart from the world, creating an unnatural disconnect between reality and time. They were the first extra-planar creatures that the elves had encountered, and thus, several of the Æthian dedicated much study toward these creatures that now dwelled in their midst. Some hoped to discover a way to walk through planes at will, folding space and time to cover large distances instantly; others thought to reach a state of dual planar existence through the mastery of their elemental disciplines and thus eventually become elves of similar structure and capability as the air elementals. Yet, neither of these had become a reality, and so the study continued.

Once safely within her chambers, the Matriarch paused briefly to contemplate the list of tasks that still stood before her. She wanted to have an audience with both Evianna and the magister before the third day. The council meeting with the nine would also need to be amended in light of the quickly approaching gathering of the fae races. Decorum would demand at least a brief appearance by the Matriarch to present this new information to all of the assembled dignitaries, and she would be required to establish a time to present both the results and decisions made at the council of fae races and discuss the impact upon Avalide. For now, that would have to wait. With the shadow of corruption looming, and the sudden revelation of prophecy being fulfilled in her very presence, the Matriarch knew that the united council meeting of the races required careful preparation. Calling her maidservant to her chambers, the Matriarch sent a dispatch to the magister to meet with her at his earliest convenience. Sylande would undoubtedly be returning with Evianna shortly and so she would use this short time to gather her thoughts and check her emotions.

VI

*D*iscussions around the summit grew more intense each day. Draevor Tel`yys had come again last month making mention to Valkyyrak about an alliance of the fae races in hopes that the elven nations in Frostspire and in Avalide might share knowledge and learn from one another. On the surface many liked the idea of having allies, yet deeply rooted in the heart of every dragon was a natural independence and an inherent understanding that theirs was a race that had no equal. Though not prideful in their dealings with the elves, who admittedly were far more advanced than the humans, few dragons could reconcile the need to include others in their private world, which for generations had seen no need to allow the inclusion of others.

The dwarves were another matter altogether. The dragons knew from their elven ambassador that twelve distinct dwarven clans were now thriving in various parts of Caliyon. Of these twelve, the dragons had only seen the Gray clan, who also made their home deep inside the Icecrowns and who, for that same reason, fascinated many of the dragons. The stone lords were rumored to have crafted lairs as elaborate as those crafted by the dragons, as well as tools for hunting. Solitary creatures much like the dragons, the dwarves presented a certain appeal to their neighbors, yet both races remained content to know of each other while refraining from making contact.

As usual, Fyysara continued to struggle with the meaning of the shrouded prophecy and the subsequent turmoil it caused within her. Sargeron had noticed that through the passing months his mate had become more and more aloof, often staying out late at night, soaring the midnight skies with Sargeron, or, more often than not, alone. Tonight she flew solo, feeling strongly the need for seclusion. Something was about to become clear tonight, and Fyysara wanted no distractions around her. Sycaris tried once to speak with her mother before she began her ascension, a tinge of something akin to fear in her voice. The younger dragon tried to explain to her mother that she may have divined some sort of truth about the shrouded prophecy, but even though Fyysara accepted the fact that Sycaris was no longer a hatchling—in fact, that she was now thought of as an elder second only to Fyysara, Sargeron, Dalaria, and of course Valkyyrak—still Fyysara's pride refused to accept that Sycaris could possibly glean truth out of a prophecy that had troubled Fyysara for well over a millennia. So, she dismissed her daughter once again and took flight to clear her head. Scouting out the lowlands to the west for hunting grounds to report on she flew fast and low, speeding through trees and over cliffs, banking sharply and letting the thrill of the flight consume her. It was then that fate and destiny flew like an arrow straight into the heart of Fyysara.

Like a ripple in time, a piercing song that resonated as if harnessed in crystal tore through her mind causing her left eye to water as a sudden rush of emotion and understanding flooded into her mind. The shroud was lifted and finally she understood her fate as exuberant joy and hope quickly became replaced by sheer terror and violent anger. Preoccupied as she was with this sudden revelation, her last thoughts were of Sargeron and her daughter as she flew headlong into the side of the mountain, snapping several bones in her armored neck before falling at great speed down into the lowland river area below. The sound of her death echoed throughout the entire river valley, creating such a stir in the land that the heavens echoed with it.

*   *   *

Sargeron felt a deep unease as he patrolled the night skies. Something was wrong and for once he felt powerless to stop it. There was something unusual about the exchange he had witnessed between his mate and his daughter earlier. Sycaris had never before appeared so afraid or so adamant about deterring Fyysara from any other flight. With Fyysara likely leagues away soaring and scouting, he figured the best option before him was to return to the summit and speak with his daughter about their earlier conflict. For hundreds of years the two females of his heart had debated the prophecies and honestly, he wanted nothing to do with this source of continual contention between the two most important females in his life.

Arriving back at the summit, Sargeron found that circumstances did not bring about the conversation he had hoped for. Several dragons rested idly while others either roamed atop the summit or flew softly above the vicinity. The large black found Sycaris where he always did when she was upset with Fyysara. But unlike every other time, he did not find her pacing about. Instead, the younger red stood frozen, transfixed, her gaze one of sheer wonder. Sargeron felt a most unusual feeling pass through him. Something deep within his breast stirred and he felt a single tear form in his left eye as a ripple of emotion passed through him coupled with a strange crystalline musical sound. Sycaris too had a tear forming in her left eye and for a short time all was silent.

Then, suddenly, the supernatural peace on top of the summit was shattered as Sycaris roared in desperation and anger. Never had she broken a silence with such power. Her cries shook the very peaks of the Icecrowns, causing several dragons to stir and fly down to where Sycaris still remained in a stupor of rage, disbelief, and sorrow.

"Sycaris! What is it?" shouted Ysiel, one of the much younger blacks, as he shoved through the throng of gathering dragons.

"Something is amiss brothers and sisters..." offered Azaryyk, a middle aged bronze dragon.

"Daughter, speak! What troubles you, Sycaris? What have you seen?" questioned Sargeron forcefully as Valkyyrak, Dalaria, Vaanadu, and Maelyyk also appeared among the others. For a short time no one else spoke. Slowly, breath crept back into Sycaris.

Again she roared in anger, tears now openly running down her crimson scales, as she turned toward her father and shifted her gaze toward Dalaria and Valkyyrak.

"Did you feel it?" Sycaris asked, her voice trembling with emotion.

"Yes Sycaris, we all felt it. What was it?" Dalaria replied in little more than a whisper.

"The Tear of Deimar has awakened and the Lightbringer has been called." With that statement several dragons reeled. Both Valkyyrak and Sargeron made attempts to approach Sycaris but a warning growl and a raised talon from Dalaria stilled both of the ancients.

"What of the shrouded prophecy Sycaris? Have you received new insight?" Dalaria prompted. Sycaris began to tremble once again and focused all her attentions upon Dalaria. Unsure at her ability to voice what she saw, she spoke to Dalaria using the *Skarlagnos.*

"I saw mother die Dalaria... I felt her pain and love and regret all at once before it ended suddenly."

"Are you sure that is what you saw?" Even though she asked the question, Dalaria knew Sycaris' words to be true and pain began to gnaw at her own heart. *"What of the prophecies?"*

"Damn the prophecies! Mother is dead. She saw what she was to become and flew blindly into her death. The shroud was lifted only to reveal to her the fate that awaited and that the time of prophecy has ended. The corruption has begun to grow beyond limits. The seed of corruption is alive and soon will bring the shadow and I stand here powerless to do anything! My dreaming eyes are blind Dalaria!" Eyes burning with fury stared at Dalaria as if challenging her to doubt her visions while the others watched the silent exchange between the two great females.

Dalaria bellowed in anger and frustration as she turned toward the gathering of dragons. She gazed intently at Valkyyrak, drawing strength from the love that she found burning behind those twin golden orbs, and then she turned toward her dearest friend Sargeron, never breaking her gaze as tears began to cloud her eyes. She too chose to extend her thoughts to everyone nearby.

"Fyysara is dead." The skies awoke with fury as all of the dragons roared in disbelief and sorrow, save the three that could not utter more than a single breath: Sycaris, Dalaria, and Sargeron, trapped in his devastated shock. *"Our guide has passed from this plane and has left the mantle to her daughter Sycaris. But prophecy has been silenced now and we know not how long this will last. Even Sycaris, with all her talents and skills, has been blinded to the prophecy... but she did uncover two things... the Tear of Deimar is awake and calling, and the seed of corruption is being positioned to bring the shadow into the world."*

Sycaris hung her head as wave after wave of emotion washed over her. The other dragons backed away as the ancients all approached the new guide in an attempt to offer some measure of strength and comfort. But comfort was not to be found here this night. That would come later. For now, grief was all that held the remaining three ancients and Sycaris together as the lament of the dragons continued throughout the remainder of the night.

*   *   *

With the rising of the sun came the discovery of the race of dragons. The thunderous sound that shattered the silence of the night hours earlier was heard all through the river valley and in the human townships of Coren, Edarann, and Tannir. The local town guard dispatched several scouts to investigate the river valley and what they found was beyond description. Nestled beside the base of the mountains was a great winged beast partially buried beneath the earth and stone that had tumbled down from the mountain above. Never before had anyone seen a beast so impressive or beautiful. Easily measuring at least ten times larger than the largest beasts they had ever witnessed, the sight and smell of the fallen creature made the horses nicker with unease as the scouts pressed them close. Deep crimson scales as hard as the stone that buried it clad the beast from head to tail with the exception of a softer underbelly that was almost a pale yellow in color. The beast appeared to have died on impact for there were no signs that it had struggled trying to remove the earth and stone that had crumbled on top of it.

What really disturbed the scouts was that they had never before seen such a creature. Had it been flying the skies for years? Or had it just materialized? Recent news from Lorenth spoke of a mysterious disappearance of cattle from the thriving township of Reiys and perhaps now these scouts had partially solved this mystery. One thing was sure... news had to be sent to Lorenth and orders needed to be received regarding what was to be done with the remains of this beast once they figured out a way to remove the great amount of debris that effectively entombed the entire torso, most of the wings and three of the four legs.

Two scouts, one from Tannir and the other from Coren, elected to stand watch around their discovery while the rest of the scouts returned to their townships to report the discovery to their local Captain of the Guard and await further instructions. There was no hesitation on behalf of the three Captains of the Guard. Swift riders were dispatched to Lorenth immediately to bear the news of the beast in the river valley, while regular messengers were dispatched to several other local townships to bear news of the findings. By nightfall, the town guard had to task several other soldiers to enforce security around the beast as peasantry, nobles, and even off-duty soldiers alike all journeyed to the remains in the valley to see for themselves the truth of the stories that were quickly spreading throughout the towns.

A sense of reverence and awe overcame all those who beheld the great beast, and to the frustration of the soldiers and scouts attempting to secure the area, several citizens made attempts to press through the barricades in order to touch the fallen creature. Once, as the sun began to set, everyone held their breath as a massive shadow blotted out the sun. As they searched the skies some reported seeing a blur of green soar with great speed in the western sky but no one could say for sure what they saw. Finally, by the second watch after nightfall, Covenal Erikk Masaad of the northern border detail and his troops arrived on the scene and quickly reinstituted order. The locals were instructed to return to their homes and the soldiers and scouts of the township were affirmed for their duties and dismissed to their Captains.

As Covenal Masaad stood in the shadow of such a great beast, he felt truly insignificant. He removed his left gauntlet and placed his bare hand on an exposed portion of the beast's scaled neck, surprised at the heat that still radiated from the beast that, if reports were accurate, had now been dead for nearly a full day. Replacing the gauntlet, his thoughts quickly strayed to the investigation of his long time friend and peer, Covenal Farin Guilian. He admitted to himself that he feared his friend was losing his competence, for the ridicule that ran wild through the barracks in Lorenth and among the other border detail encampments was extreme. The creature before Erikk easily fit into the same category of 'unbelievable', and his peers may have ridiculed him if there were not so many witnesses here today to confirm the findings. When next he encountered Farin, Erikk resolved to apologize to his friend and buy a round of ale at the tavern for him. For now though, Arimas himself would likely be enroute to examine this beast and would provide more instruction to the covenal at that time.

The troops were busy establishing a perimeter and resuming camp discipline. Torches were lit and sentries were posted as the covenal prepared for a long and uneventful night. The priest-king wasn't likely to arrive for at least a day or two, and there was nothing more to be done. But, no sooner had the covenal entered his command tent to unpack his gear, when several deep roars thundered in the skies above. He ran out of his tent in time to see three more of these terrifying beasts begin to encircle the encampment. Individuals of lesser discipline would have broken rank and scattered, but the covenal's men held their positions.

"Hold your positions and ready your lances, men! Do not provoke the beasts, but engage if attacked. Our priority is to preserve the discovery for the priest-king." In response to their leader's words, the men dug in their heels and watched the skies with trepidation, uncertain as to what was about to transpire.

* * *

Their grief still not abated, Sargeron, Sycaris, and Nostrimus circled the broken body of their mate and mother. The dragons had realized too late that the lesser races, in their curiosity, would likely take an interest in the discovery of a dragon and thus the search started much later than they had intended. Sycaris, using remembered fragments of the emotions and visions that Fyysara had experienced just before her death, narrowed down the search. In her heart she knew that her mother's body was somewhere to the southwest and the three of them searched the land in detail, flying at slower speeds to ensure they effectively covered the terrain. Nostrimus was the first one to discover the location of Fyysara's broken body. Even from his height, he could clearly see her broken form and could also discern the rabble that closed in around her. Anger swelled in his throat. He immediately accelerated past the site as he began to track down Sycaris and Sargeron to lead them back to Fyysara. Locating both of them was time consuming but the three made their way back to the site at great speed, Nostrimus leading the vanguard.

By now night was well upon them, but the lack of natural light did not hamper their vision. In the few hours that had elapsed from when Nostrimus first scouted the site, a large contingent of human soldiers had begun establishing a camp around Fyysara's body. When Sargeron saw with his own eyes his mate, broken and partially entombed, he unleashed a great bellow which Sycaris and Nostrimus echoed in sympathy.

"How dare these humans claim my mate for some spoil of war!"

"Father, perhaps these humans are just curious," projected Sycaris. *"Let us be reasonable about handling this situation. Valkyyrak warned us about this possibility, and also said that not all humans were like that spawn of chaos we encountered before."*

"I know Valkyyrak. I will not dishonor him or our kind... but I do not have to be pleased with what I see before me."

"Father," began Nostrimus, *"let us simply assert ourselves and speak plainly with them. They have broken the silence pact, the Tear is calling, and eventually we will need to get to know these creatures below us. Mother cannot stay there as she is. Perhaps it is time to instill the fear and respect of dragonkind into the hearts of these humans as we remove mother and give her a dignified place of rest in the Icecrowns."*

"Very well... I suppose this could get interesting. Let us speak openly with these humans and remove Fyysara from this undignified place."

The three dragons descended toward the river valley floor, each approaching the encampment from a different side. As each one landed, not bothering to do so with grace, the humans were forced to brace themselves as the very earth beneath them shook. They shifted their vision between the three incarnations of death that stood before them, tension building within as each man struggled with the decision of whether they should flee, or fight. The covenal, who had moved to stand with his men, stared openly at the three dragons, taking in the other red scaled beast noticeably smaller than the dead one, the green one which was much more savage looking and equal in size to the dead one, and the menacing black scaled one, easily much larger than the dead one, covered with horns and spikes from head to tail.

"Hold your ground men. Hold!" shouted the covenal in an attempt to bolster the resolve of the soldiers.

"Lower your weapons human. If we desired your destruction then you would already be dead." Sargeron growled in a clear and deep voice, much to the shock of the humans. "I assume you have authority of voice. We would speak openly with you."

Standing in utter confusion that these beasts could talk inspired a new sense of dread in the heart of even the covenal. Taking a few breaths to ensure his voice did not quiver, he ordered his men to stay their weapons and fallout behind him to the right of the command tent, while he took several paces forward to meet with the biggest of the three.

"Pardon great ones, but what manner of beast are you?"

Nostrimus extended his neck to full length and stopped inches from the now trembling human leader as he too growled, "We are not beasts, we are dragons!"

"Patience Nostrimus, they were merely asking an ignorant question. Let father handle this." Nostrimus stepped back and reluctantly gave the human some space.

Sargeron glanced back and forth from Sycaris and Nostrimus and then focused his attention toward the human before him. "What do you call yourself, human? Or would you prefer I continue calling you human?"

"No, my lord. I am Erikk Masaad, covenal of the northern border detail, and officer of Lorenth, our capital city here in the west." The covenal offered a bow as he regained his full composure, knowing now that these 'dragons' were not interested in making war this day.

"I am Sargeron the black, guardian of the night skies and ancient of the Icecrown Peaks. These are two of my offspring: Nostrimus the green and Sycaris the red, Guide and historian as was her mother whom you have set this encampment around. I am not here to trade tales or make friendships, nor am I here to ask that you surrender my mate's body to me—that I most seriously demand and expect your compliance with."

"We meant no harm to your mate, Lord Sargeron, we found her like—"

"Enough, Covenal Erikk Masaad. I do not think your race capable of bringing down one of the four ancient dragons so do not try to appease my grief or my anger. Rest content in the knowledge that I do not direct my anger toward you as of yet." Sargeron looked again to his two offspring. "Uncover her, both of you, so that we can leave this place."

Nostrimus and Sycaris began to dig out their mother's body from beneath the rubble, tossing boulders the size of a small horse with ease. A strange strained sound escaped Sycaris as she continued her work and the covenal was uncertain what to say. Was the dragon crying? His mind now became preoccupied with what Arimas would think of this great failure when he arrived in the morning.

"Arimas we know of, and your report to him will be sufficient. Fear not the wrath of Arimas for he is marked in the line of the Lightbringer."

The covenal stood dumbfounded that Sargeron simply read his thoughts as if they were spoken words. What was the line of the Lightbringer supposed to mean? How can dragons read the thoughts of men? There were so many questions, so many things he wanted to understand.

"Now is not that time, Erikk Masaad. Hold your questions, for understanding will come later. I, however, have one question to ask of you. Who is the human called Seneschal Dean?"

"He is second in command of Lorenth, second only to Arimas the Just, wielder of *Retribution* and Priest-King of Lorenth."

"I thank you Erikk Masaad. I would like to meet this Arimas. However, that too will have to wait. We are leaving now and I am taking my mate with me. Seek us not in the Icecrowns for our kind is not open to uninvited guests and I cannot guarantee your safety should you stray into our lands. One warning I would leave with you. Beware of this Seneschal Dean."

"Thank you for speaking with me, Lord Sargeron. Will we see you again?" By this point Sargeron had already turned his massive body around and was approaching the uncovered form of his beloved. "Lord Sargeron?"

No more words were given to the humans and none were exchanged between the dragons as Sargeron nuzzled the face of his mate one last time before unleashing a loud roar into the sky followed by a jet of flame that lit up the darkness and made all the troops, including the covenal, take an extra step back. Then Sargeron and the other dragons unfolded their great sinewy wings and lifted off the ground. Sargeron gently encircled the base of the neck and tail of his mate as he struggled to lift Fyysara's limp body into the air. Nostrimus flew beneath his mother once Sargeron was high enough and together they distributed her weight so that they could manage the long, slow flight back to the Icecrowns. Sycaris watched the two fly off as she took another look at the humans below, who had now fixed all their attentions upon her. She inclined her head toward the covenal in a show of respect, and then she too took off after her brother and father, leaving the awestruck humans behind in the darkness of their encampment.

VII

$\mathcal{D}$eep within the heart of the Lesser Icecrown Mountains resided a collection of dwarven clans that had united together to form the hold known as Barak`Dûm, Barak`Dûm was a true dwarven hold, comprised of three of the largest clans: Dûm`Ald, Dûm`Keld, and Dûm`Eth. Torgrim Varr, originally of the Dûm`Keld clan, had no equal in strength or canny intelligence, and was appointed King of the hold. Under his guidance, the dwarves of Barak`Dûm prospered.

Nearly a generation earlier, their clansmen to the northeast, led by Korigan Goern, had suggested connecting Barak`Dûm with Ur`Akam to increase trade between the clans and provide quicker access to each other if ever the other clans were in need of aid. Thus, the Great Stoneway was agreed upon and completed in little under fourteen years. Reaching for leagues beneath both the Lesser Icecrowns and the great peaks themselves, the passage was a feat of dwarven genius.

The Great Stoneway was decorated with stonework pillars spaced every twenty spans that had been elaborately chiseled to reflect the skill of the dwarven stonecutters. Each section of the passage was girded and braced in case the under rock layers ever shifted or gave way. The ceiling was excavated to reach over twenty-five spans tall, and the width of the passage was nearly thirty-two spans wide, including the several spans of empty space on either side that were left vacant in case repairs were ever needed. The Gray clan provided the strange colspar crystals that, when embedded into the stone pillars, emitted an incandescent blue glow that acted as a source of constant light. Such were the lights in Ur'Akam.

The dwarves of Barak`Dûm, however, did not delve as deep as the Gray clan. They preferred living among the mountains, close to the surface where carefully crafted sun wells could be cut into the stone, illuminating much of the greathalls with a natural, though dim, light source by day. By night, all of Barak`Dûm was illuminated by torch light. Travel to Ur'Akam was infrequent at best, because those of Barak`Dûm often found it unsettling to travel into the depths of Ur`Akam for trade, simply because the darkness felt somehow more absolute and impenetrable in the deepest parts of the earth. Business was usually conducted quickly and preparations were made in short order to return to Barak`Dûm after enjoying the usual pint or two of mead near the greathall of Ur`Akam.

The bronze furnaces that thundered below the greathall of Ur`Akam, however, were something worth seeing. The grays were masters at fuelling their furnaces with the heat of the depths, and the assortment of rare gems that could only be excavated in places of great heat and pressure were coveted items for trade. Four times as large as the forges in Barak`Dûm, these bronze furnaces billowed day and night with white hot flame, searing the impurities of the ore and tempering the ore and rare metals that the grays were famous for.

One could almost lose themselves in the rhythmic *thrum-thrum* of the furnaces as hundreds of smelters, miners, temperers, and crafters hovered around the twelve mighty furnaces that were fuelled by liquid rock. Each furnace was carefully constructed to regulate the intake of this molten rock into the lower chambers allowing it to churn by propellers crafted of tempered truesilver, the only metal that once tempered and cooled could not be forged again. The heat was then siphoned from the lower chambers by a series of bronze tubes that created a manageable and even heated surface on the middle and upper levels of the furnace. As the heat would slowly dissipate from the molten rock, the cooler rock would sink to the bottom of the propellers to then be guided back out of the furnace on to the exhaust ramp which would deposit the cooler rock back into the fires of the deep, where the process would repeat itself.

Efficiency and stability coupled with the rare gems and ores of the deep produced warehouses of untempered truesilver ore, silver, gold and bronze bars, and iron, copper and occasionally mithril bars to be set with either infused gems or stonework settings made of black basalt, limestone, occasionally some crystallized quartz but more commonly, granite. Apparently Korigan was preparing for a war, yet there was no enemy to fight. Those of Barak`Dûm privately questioned the actions of the clan chief, yet, out of respect, they kept their opinions silent and simply marveled at the armories and the vast assorted stocks of warhammers, mauls, and bladed-edge weapons.

Such was life with the dwarves. Master craftsmen and honor-bound in fealty to their clan chief and family, a dwarf would spend their typical day delving or shaping, forging or crafting, while others—namely those of the Gray clan, the Stormgarde, the Ironheart, the Silverfist and the Hammul—would train with the weapons of the armory. The women were usually found tending to the children and the home, teaching the young, or studying the roots, gems, fungi, lichens, and even the dusts of the rock to explore their uses in healing or infusing.

Dwarven women were often times the scholars and scribes of the clans as well; however, when a male dwarf would prove himself exceptionally adept with literacy and scholarly practice, he could choose to join the women in the runehalls. Those who studied infusion worked with dusts that could imbue certain gems with a radiant aura that could help speed up natural healing rates. Some lichens, when applied to chainmail armor, would stain the silver color to a deep green, while both hardening the surface until it was stronger than iron plates and making it resistant even to the hottest temperatures of the fiercest furnace. Through experimentation and careful recording of their successful formularies, the runehalls became a source of pride among each clan.

Differing formularies created a variety of knowledge that could be shared with their dwarven kin, though often before any sharing of knowledge was done, competitions to judge the best were often held each year, alongside traditional sporting events, sparring with practice weaponry, and a full three days of heavy drinking for both male and female alike. The celebrations of Runeveld were highly anticipated by all ten clans and each year they alternated the location of Runeveld between the great hold of Barak`Dûm and the distant north-eastern battlekeep where the Stormgarde and Ironheart clans made their home above the Ellorian waterfalls, in the highland plains north of the *Illu`Dar* and far to the southeast of Frostspire.

Runeveld was still several months away, but already several clans were sorting through their formularies and practicing their skills with the blade and hammer. While most were sleeping there were still many throughout the clans that would continue at their craft or their practice well into the late of night. It was during this time when the most unusual sound resounded throughout hold, clan hall, and battlekeep. It was the purest song any dwarf had ever heard and it was only one solitary note that resonated as if it were encased in crystal. Wave upon wave of emotions tore through the dwarves all around Caliyon as a sudden blast sent most to their feet. The great white furnace fires of Ur`Akam were cooled to a pale blue, the music of the waterfalls hiding the entrances to the Silverfist and the Stormgarde clans were stilled, and within moments of this strange music, even the walls of Barak`Dûm shook with a force so great that the southeast tunnels completely collapsed.

As each dwarf stood and contemplated the significance of what had just happened, all noticed the wet stain of a solitary tear on their left cheek. The effects lasted but a moment. The waterfalls sang again and the furnace fires returned to their white hot state but, in Barak`Dûm, the collapse of the south-eastern tunnel was irreversible. The terrible crash was enough to awaken most of the dwarves in the hold and several headed toward the south-eastern tunnel alternate routes, including their hidden entrance into the river valley, to investigate.

No one was prepared for what they found. There, trapped beneath an unmanageable mass of rock and dirt rested the easily recognizable, horribly broken body of Fyysara, the greatest of the red dragons according to the tales of the Gray clan. This would not bode well for either the dwarves or the dragons as attention at last had been drawn to Barak`Dûm, which had remained hidden for generations. There were no answers to be had or comfort to be given. The dwarves reported back to Torgrim, who made plans to dispatch word to the elves known to be in contact with the dragons. However, before the king had finalized his plan with those gathered before him, Thaelvin, the Frostspire ambassador, arrived and was escorted to the King bearing news from Aerinyyr of Avalide that would further unsettle the dwarves of Barak`Dûm.

* * *

The dream wasn't the same this evening. For the first time, it ended abruptly, just before Dean completed his transformation into Kaaldean and unleashed his wrath upon Farin. The seneschal awoke, his blood pounding and the despicable taste of fear on his tongue. Even his body ached with an imagined pain that burned all over his body. Lianne, yet another of his bedmates, was startled awake by the seneschal's violent stirrings and promptly tried to offer Dean some comfort. He would have none of that, however, and roughly pushed her away, throwing his legs over the side of the bed and standing to pace across the length of his chamber. He eventually stopped at the same window through which he had previously espied Farin. True to his suspicions, within several minutes the candlelight began to burn once again in the covenal's chambers.

Dean shuddered. He distinctly remembered that sound… a piercing shrill note that sounded like it resonated through crystal. That certainly was never a part of the dream before. That one note ripped him from sleep and brought a sensation of fear and pain that he had never before encountered.

Despite Lianne's pleadings for Dean to return to bed, he continued to stand there in the dark, a brooding and ominous pillar of ego and strength, and watched Farin's candlelit chamber from across the officer grounds. Half afraid to return to sleep and half too agitated to even attempt it, he remained fixated on the events that were unfolding before him.

*   *   *

The dream was different for Farin this night and he wasn't sure why. He awoke suddenly, well before the dawn, and for a few moments simply sat in his bed and pondered what had just happened. Raising a hand to push back a lock of hair that had fallen across his face, he felt a wet touch on his skin and wiped from his cheek a single tear. He stared in disbelief at the touch of moisture. Had he been crying in his dream? He didn't remember doing so... but then again, he often didn't remember everything from his slumberous adventures. Today he felt like he remembered everything. He quickly lit his candle and pulled out his journal as he began to frantically copy several of the missing pieces of his dream.

It was the same dream that he had been having for years, until the moment when death was to overtake him. Somehow his dream counterpart knew he wasn't completely dead, that he was something different. Not alive though, for he could still feel the pain of seeing his beloved Jesslyn once again. There was also a song; a chime of pure music that echoed through the night and the dream. It was the most beautiful sound he had ever heard and it reminded him of a note resonating in a piece of crystal, a tone that elicited an overwhelming sense of warmth and hope as the shadows around him lifted and he awoke in his bed. That was definitely new and very different from before. It was as if something had changed the course of destiny and set him free from Kaaldean's malice for all time.

Farin knew that he should sleep once more, for today or tomorrow he would be leading the soldiers in formation to present their colors and honors at the forest border once again. Dean, in his calculating wisdom, had specifically demanded that Farin head the formation. First to the front, first to die was the saying, and Farin wondered if the noose around his neck was already starting to tighten. He needed to be at his best if he was to survive the plotting of Dean over the next few days. He would not fall without a fight.

Satisfied with the new additions to his journal, he stowed the pages once again under the loosely attached bottom of his desk drawer and successfully hid them from any who would snoop into his affairs. He then blew out his candle and returned to sleep with a pervading sense of hope covering him and comforting him. Rest came easily for once.

* * *

The mood was somber all across the Icecrowns as Sargeron and Nostrimus flew without sound or emotion to the frozen lake at the lowest part of the summit. Laying Fyysara's broken body down in the middle of the ice, Sargeron and Nostrimus took their place back in the sky as dragons of all ages came to honor the memory of their guide and ancient. The sky began to darken with the sheer number of dragons flying above. Valkyyrak and Dalaria descended to Sargeron's level, silently communicating their mutual sense of loss and sorrow to Sargeron. Eventually, Valkyyrak addressed his kin.

"Brothers and sisters! Today darkness has fallen. Never before has one of our kin been lost to us. Words cannot define the sorrow that burns in our hearts. Fyysara was more than our guide, she was mother, and mate, and friend. Let us light up the skies with a fusillade of flame as we honor her memory and dedicate this hollow as her final resting place." With that final admonition, all those present arched back their strong necks and launched mighty gouts of flame into the early dawn sky. It was later heard that those below in the township of Reiys witnessed this event in wonder, seeing only a giant pillar of flame erupt amid the snow topped peaks above.

It was hours later that Draevor arrived at the dragon summit. Tensions were high and many were not prepared to entertain the Frostspire ambassador at such a dark hour but Sycaris admitted him into their presence, believing that his timely arrival was not by chance but by destiny. When Draevor was told about the tragedy that had occurred he stood in shock for a moment before speaking.

"Lady Sycaris and all of dragonkind, please forgive me for intruding upon your grief. I would never have thought to continue with my message were it not for its sudden relevance to all our situations." While Draevor continued to speak, more and more dragons let down their guard and descended to the summit to hear what the elven ambassador had to say. "Many of you know of Aerinyyr the truth-sage, who has played active rolls in bringing the fae races together. Several days ago, I was asked to begin preparations for a journey to the Icecrowns to deliver a message that had absolutely no meaning or relevance to me until late last night, which I now believe was a significant time for you all, as well as for the dwarves and the elves of Frostspire and Avalide. As I stand here before you now, there are also seven other messengers making their way to each of the independent clans, including Thaelvin, the dwarven ambassador, who has been sent to the dwarven hold of Barak`Dûm to speak with King Varr. Each carries this same message.

"Fyysara and Sycaris both have mentioned the shrouded prophecies to me. Those of Frostspire and of Avalide have also spent much time lost in the labyrinthine prophecies and we too have discovered a common darkness that we could never fully understand. The time for understanding is now upon us and Aerinyyr has requested at long last a union of the fae races in the Ellorian highlands two days from now. Elf and dryad, dragon and dwarf, and even some of the elemental races, have been asked to send representatives to discuss the meaning of the shadow that has now silenced prophecy altogether.

"The Tear of Deimar has awakened as you all have felt in your spirit. Hope is born once again in Caliyon and it is this hope that will bring about the Lightbringer—the child of prophecy that is destined to stand in the wake of corruption's advance. We now believe that the seed of corruption is also alive in the world and dwelling in the realm of men. Through ignorance, the seed of corruption will inadvertently bring the shadow over all of Caliyon and in order to support the Lightbringer, perhaps the union of fae races and the sharing of wisdom and knowledge will create a front of strength that will bolster the Lightbringer is his time of need."

For a time there was no discussion. Dragons of young and old pondered the elf's words. Draevor knew never to press the dragons and thus he waited with patience, allowing the impact of his words to sink deep into the hearts of his listeners. It was no surprise to Draevor when Valkyyrak the Ancient, the magnificent gold dragon, approached the center of the summit and fixed his ominous bronze orbs upon Draevor.

"Long have we discussed the notions of creating an alliance, Draevor. As you know, we lead lives above the petty concerns of the lesser races. Yet, fate has entwined our destinies now, and perhaps listening to your ideas may be of use. Do not press this issue, Draevor. Leave us now and let us continue in our grief. Some of our number will be present at this gathering at the appointed time. I will be there as well."

Valkyyrak ended the meeting with those few words, not spoken with anger or irritation, but with certainty and an expectation that he was to be obeyed in this matter. Draevor bowed deeply to Valkyyrak as he made his way off of the summit, waiting until he was well into the snow-topped forests before shape-shifting into his preferred flight form of a sleek white and black specked falcon. There was much to report to the council in Frostspire and he, for one, had some unanswered questions that he would be directing to Aerinyyr at the gathering.

* * *

All around Caliyon the dwarven clan chiefs and the king, together with their advisors, counselors, warmasters and runemages reflected on the elven messages that they had received, calling for a united meeting to discuss the Tear of Deimar. All those who were awake during the surreal crystal song that rang through hold and fortress alike, for reasons unknown to them, felt a sense of compulsion to attend the gathering. Clan chiefs, and the king, felt the same compulsion, and trusted that this was a decision being made of their will and choice and not as some persuasion or mind spell of the elves. Runeveld was still months away and perhaps it would do some good to see the other clans beforehand. If the reports were true, then even the mighty dragons would be in attendance. Whether this meeting would be the beginning of some great coalition between the races or simply a dreadful argument about some age-old prophecy that had apparently fallen silent, the dwarves were not certain... but at least it would provide an opportunity for each clan to brag of their newest runes and formularies while perhaps enjoying the spiced mead of Stormgarde.

Travel was another issue. The highland clans would of course be able to reach the meeting in two days, but those in the far south and those in the north or west, like the Gray clan and those of Barak`Dûm, were weeks at best from the meeting, even should they leave that very night. What worried these dwarves was that the messengers had told those out of range that they would be assisted in their travel, but were not told in what way. Several dwarves thought the entire notion was doomed to failure because even on the fastest steeds there would be no way to cross the human lands into the *Illu`Dar* and then take the northern routes up above the lower Ellorian waterfall to reach the highlands. But all doubts were set aside when on the evening before the appointed day, the dwarves of Barak`Dûm and of the Gray clan were visited by a small host of air elementals who brought with them a strangely shaped wing made of silken cloth, equipped with harnesses for twenty passengers and tethers held fast by the elementals.

"Now I 'ave seen everything!" grumbled Korigan to his brother and military commander, Durgan. "What would you 'ave us do with this contraption, masters of air? Dwarves cannot fly, and nor were we meant to. We are creatures of earth and belong on the ground."

Shifting into her corporeal state, one of the air elementals approached Korigan. "Peace, Korigan the gray. We shall carry you and your fellows to the meeting should you allow us to be of service. This instrument was simply fashioned to harness our efforts and lighten the load as we speed you with all haste to the meeting on the morrow. We shall be traveling throughout the night and should you wish, we can veil your eyes during travel to abate your fears. As you must know, there is no way to reach the highlands by the appointed time. We assure you, we would never let harm come to any entrusted to our care, as Aerinyyr the truth-sage has charged us personally to attend to all matters of your comfort and safety. Will you not allow us to serve you in this matter, Korigan the gray?" Though her form was still mostly insubstantial, her features were strikingly beautiful and Korigan found it very hard not to trust her.

Looking from side to side at the men he had selected to accompany him, which coincidentally numbered at twenty, he saw that some showed little to no displeasure at the notion, while others even appeared slightly curious at the thought of being borne through the sky with naught but a cloth wing and maidens of air bearing them. "Aye then, lady. We shall trust you in this. Let us get this over with then."

It took mere moments for the dwarves to approach the wing and secure themselves to its frame with the simple harnesses, and then even less time for the elementals to bear the wing aloft. Accelerating at an incredible rate, the air elementals bore the dwarves of Ur`Akam into the evening sky and sped toward the Icecrowns, and eventually toward the Ellorian highlands.

* * *

While the elementals of air were swiftly bearing those of Ur`Akam and Barak`Dûm aloft, Aerinyyr had sought out those of the plane of water to attend the council as well, requesting their aid in the transportation of those from the Hammul and Nuragg clans whose holds were encompassed by water. When the rivers running deep into the cisterns of their underground caves tunneled down from the surface came alive and took shape before them, clan chief Forin Hammul III and clan chief Gimmel Thaineson of the Nuragg were completely bowled over with shock and awe. After the five Hammul dwarves and the seven Nuragg dwarves each boarded their sturdy rivercraft at sunset on the day before the gathering, the water elementals propelled them at unbelievable speeds along the waterways. They sailed past the western border of *Illu`Dar* and then without altering the horizontal plane of their watercraft, the elementals supported the hulls and lifted them directly up the Ellorian waterfall against its natural flow to lead several stunned dwarves into the highlands above.

The Silverfist and Bloodstone clans needed no assistance, for while there was some travel required, the distance was easily covered through their individual conventions. Located deep in the north-eastern part of the plains, on the northern borders of the *Illu`Dar*, the Silverfist clan was known for their engineering capabilities and more than likely would be happy for the opportunity to show off one of their latest inventions that undoubtedly would be bearing the few to the meeting.

The Bloodstone clan, located far to the southeast in the midland mountains called the Red Rock Cliffs, had a different way of travel. Over the generations of delving and forging, building keeps and greathalls as their kinsmen did, the Bloodstone clan became one of the first to encounter and forge relationships with the remarkably large and powerful stone elementals. Generations past, in a cooperative effort to show respect for the land around them and the habitat of the stone elementals, Shaemir Gorund, first clan chief of the Bloodstone clan, requested direction from the elementals so that their subterranean expansion would not displace the land held in high importance to the elementals.

From this exchange grew a mutual respect and understanding between the dwarves and the elementals... a respect which later grew into a close friendship during the leadership of Chorim Shaemirson. While their strength was formidable, stone elementals were vulnerable to blunt weaponry akin to what the dwarves made and an idea was fostered among both the Bloodstone dwarves and the stone elementals. Dwarves were slow on their feet, though possessing great strength in arms, while the elementals were able to cover great distances with ease. The elementals would be the ideal counterparts to the dwarves who wielded the weapons that represented the greatest weakness of the elementals.

Thus were born the Stoneriders, a small division of fifty of the bloodstone elite. These dwarven combatants were equipped with crimson-stained chainmail and black iron pauldrons, helms, and breastplates. Their weapons of choice were their dual bronze warhammers with long sharpened spikes on the opposing side, and a small supply of polished-silver throwing axes attached at the bases with leather thongs that hung from their girdle. To further add to their menacing demeanor, leather slings reinforced with thin, molded rods of iron were draped around the front of the neck of the earth elementals which allowed for two bloodstone elites to mount on the back of a single elemental. These elites would then wander into battle with stone arms flailing and crashing, bronze warhammers crushing, and when distance was required, the polished silver throwing axes could be hurled at great distances with remarkable cleaving accuracy in the hands of the trained elite.

Now was the time when Orin Chorimson led the Bloodstone clan. Being given the honor to ride with the bloodstone elite, Orin and his honor guard of nine elites mounted their five lumbering elementals, setting out on the three-day journey across the midland mountains and up into the Ellorian highlands.

*   *   *

Dawn was beginning to rise over Avalide and Frostspire on the morning of the meeting that would supersede all other meetings. Although the dreamers slept and prophecy was silent, Aerinyyr was able to answer the Matriarch with a level of certainty that indeed all races were en route to the meeting place. While tempted to doubt that such representation could be arranged and mobilized in only three days, the Matriarch maintained faith in her truth-sage and nodded to Evianna that it was time for the four to depart. Touching fingers to lips, Evianna bowed and took the place of steward in the Matriarchal Commune while Matriarch Cheyandra Silversong, Truth-Sage Aerinyyr Riftseeker, Magister Edarath Lightweaver, and Lorekeeper Shandari of the race of elementals took to the air in their flight forms and made the short journey north.

*   *   *

"Yserth, it is time. We leave for the gathering now and will return with haste at its conclusion. *Syl anoth hamen anarii,*" admonished Valeris Sy`yn.

"*Tel anarii beth ari`thesala, Valeris.* My eyes shall be fixed upon Lorenth and upon the advancing shadow. Larros will remain here until your return, at which time he shall open communications with the humans at Lorenth. Speed be with you all," replied Yserth Tel`andris. "We have slightly shifted the north winds to the east to clear the skies to aid you."

Valeris nodded her approval to Yserth and then fixed her attention upon Nyssia and Tinovis. In the council chamber, Nyssia took the form of her blue drake, while Valeris and Tinovis shifted into a pair of white-feathered great eagles, and together the three left the council chambers of Frostspire, heading south toward the soon to be historic gathering of Caliyon's mystic races.

VIII

The council had received the complete summary of Dean's plans for the Dark Wood expedition two days previous, as promised. Already things were mobilizing and would be ready by late that day, or early the next. With a good-paced ride they would be approaching the forest edge within three to four days from now. It was then, Dean was confident, that his reality would collide with the dream at last.

Would the inhabitants be open to diplomacy or would they descend into brutality once again? Either way, under the guise of peace or the pressure of war, Dean had to make his way into the forest. Among the soldiers of Lorenth and the royal guard of Arimas, curiosity was peaking and a subtle sense of fear was looming. Many discounted the stories and half-truths that were openly circulating about Farin's ill-fated expedition the week before, but there were some that were influenced. Dean did nothing to stem off the fear that was mounting. Anything that eroded the credibility of Farin would inevitably make Dean's job easier. Leading the diplomatic advance would be Farin and his ever-loyal eastern border detail. This time, hopefully, if peace could not be achieved, Farin and his men would be the first to meet the power of the Dark Wood and fall beneath their strength. And, if the tides were to turn in such a way, the noble and victorious seneschal would lead the counter-attack to bring honor to Lorenth and further increase his support among the nobles and peasantry alike.

Dean lost track of time standing in the dark. He wasn't sure how long it had been since Farin's candlelight was extinguished, but it didn't matter. Fatigue had long left him and now in the early morning hours he would attend to the *other* part of his plan. Change of shift would soon be happening as the fourth watch of the night took their post before the dawn approached. Lianne had fallen back asleep in his bed, and should she awake to find him gone, she would never inquire of the matter. Besides, he would return before dawn broke.

Quickly donning a pair of simple brown leggings and a shirt, unadorned gray leather boots and gloves, his black leather jerkin, and his dark gray hooded cloak, Dean approached the hidden wall in his chamber, and quickly descended into the courts below. He skulked in and out of the numerous shadows cast from the city lamp lights upon the buildings and alleyways as he navigated the upper city. His destination was close. Dean detested the location of the guild this year. Part of why the Drucharii were so successful at remaining hidden was that they kept moving their semi-permanent base of operations every year, before anyone could act or organize any action if they caught wind of any localized activity. Usually, the members of the guild chose areas within the vast sewer networks of Lorenth; however, there had been times when they would leave the city and occupy the forests in various locations. This year they were once again in the sewers.

Sewer entrance number seventeen was tucked at the rear of the temple area, among the short trees along the inner wall of Lorenth. As usual, there was no one about. The guards approaching the end of the third watch were often tired and inattentive to things happening *behind* the gates or walls that they were watching. Few people had keys to unlock the sewer covers. The seneschal of course had the keys, as did several counselors, for accountability reasons only. The other key holders were the captains of the night watch and two undisclosed members of the royal guard.

Within the assassin's guild, only the Drucharii held keys which were unlawfully and unknowingly copied and these had been provided to the guild from Dean himself. New thieves and would-be Drucharii were assigned to apprentice full members often responsible for guild management, relocation, security and training, as well as secondary duties involving intelligence or assassination activities within Lorenth only.

Motivation and compensation were built into the guild's foundations. Simply stated, all the spoils of a target went to the assassin. Thus, if a Drucharii assassinated a target outdoors where fear of observance was high, then the spoils would be limited to what the mark was carrying or wearing. However, should a Drucharii plan out an assassination, tracking the mark over time, and learning their movement patterns in order to expose their weaknesses and ultimately gain access to their place of residence, then the compensation would be substantially greater.

No dues were paid to the guild and there was no fear of authority so long as their actions were not made public. Recruiting from outside the guild was not a common practice, as each new member further increased the risks of exposure or corruption from within. Thus, the final test for any new thief to be granted assassin status and access to the Drucharii training phase was two parts. The first step of a would-be Drucharii was to assassinate a member of their family while being watched by a full Drucharii, who would evaluate both commitment and completion. The second and final step was to then successfully assassinate a mark of the guild's choosing, in order to evaluate skill and planning. Should a thief fail or refuse to complete their task, they would forfeit their life to the guild and would be immediately executed without opportunity to contest or reverse their decision. Such was the code of blood among the Drucharii, and there were no exceptions. Among these few thieves and assassins was a mandated honor and respect... everyone else was fair game.

The wretched stench of human waste and stagnant water rushed into Dean's nostrils as he began climbing down the access ladder of entrance number seventeen. Carefully replacing the sewer access cover and locking it from within, he made his way down onto the stone ledges that ran down the length of the sewers. Debris and traces of garbage floated along the filth that gently flowed along the stone channels even though garbage was stipulated to be collected and burned outside the city and not dropped into the sewers. Moving by instinct, Dean circumvented the various obstacles in the sewers, being careful not to step into the raw sewage beside him until he approached the service tunnel for the southeast section sewers and stopped once to rap against the metal grate.

Rap rap-rap-rap rap.

His men were well trained. Reaching out to that increasing awareness and drawing into him the scents of filth all around, Dean could somehow *feel* more than see the two who had their crossbows trained on his back as he clattered the pass code into the grate. Again he sensed the two who waited at the end of the service tunnel to confirm his identity.

"Welcome my lord. The Drucharii await your orders inside," whispered one of the assassins on watch. Dean nodded slightly, pleased that the assassin soon to be made Drucharii had kept his voice low and his tone respectful. Approaching the guild entrance, a hidden access from off the service tunnel through a breach in the stone channel, he stepped into the excavated and well-lit hollow just outside of the sewers and into the cool and dank underground hall which was big enough to accommodate even the council of Lorenth when in session.

"Impressive, Dhax. This room is considerably bigger than the last time I was here. I've come with something fun for you to do for a change," Dean stated with a gleam in his eye.

"Fun? Now you definitely have our attention. As for the hall, we just recently found more supports to expand this room, my lord. Next will be the planning room which will connect over there." Dhax pointed to the wall across from him and behind where Dean was standing.

"Not bad for only six weeks. I want everyone out of this room save for you and your best six for this briefing. Time is critical. I have places to be seen before the fourth watch is over."

"Understood, my lord. Vlaros, Llise, Otto, Jaerik, Sorren, and Naethan on me, the rest of you are dismissed. Return by dawn." The shuffle happened within moments as thief, assassin, and Drucharii alike hastened to heed the Druuarc's command. "This would have been a great opportunity for both Warric and Garrin, or even Deidre, but Diedre only arrived in Reiys this evening, and I estimate that it will be another two and a half days before the three return. Nevertheless, these six have proved their skill and commitment more times than I care to remember, my lord, and we are yours to command." Dhax, his one eye pale and scarred, the other a sharp piercing blue, bowed low as the six other Drucharii present followed the lead of their Druuarc.

"My friends, I trust your spoils have been rewarding, for your work has been impeccable. Never in the last year have I even heard wind of any assassination attempts but oddly, this new disease that is passing through the lower city is quite 'catching' and has hidden many answers from those with half a brain. You all have done well. When I take the throne and disband the royal guard, I will install the blood order as my personal bodyguard and extension of my intelligence arm, instilled with the power to mediate and judicate throughout the city as they see fit.

But I have come tonight with a purpose. You seven are to leave immediately for the Dark Woods and hide where you can around its borders on our side of the river. I suspect that our sickeningly loyal Covenal Guilian has uncovered some truth in the forest and I would not have you wander into these woods alone or without orders and provisions. You will be the unofficial vanguard to ensure that peaceful negotiations do not take place. Bring spare horses, the strongest nets you can find, and any concoctions that may aid you in capturing any of the natives." Dean took a moment to gather more thoughts before continuing.

I want you to spread out around the border of the forest and observe what you can from our side of the river. Bring spyglasses, bring crossbows with noxious barbs, and most importantly, bring fire! I want flaming sacs lashed onto several bolts and shot into the trees or whatever you think will catch fire. I want any compounds that you have created that burn easily and spread quickly to be thrown into the flames to bolster them and encourage the spread, and I want this to be the last day that Arimas draws breath. If any of you get the chance amid the chaos to fire a bolt into Arimas, then take it... but make it appear as if the shot came from the forest and not from the men. Pandemonium will reign when the armies of Lorenth gather in front of the Dark Wood and then we can see what these trees are hiding among them."

Secretly, the Drucharii present grew increasingly unnerved as the seneschal talked about the forest. Dean was not the patient and calculating puppet master that he once was. The few gathered could see that the orchestrator of their careers had begun cultivating an even deeper lust for power. Dhax, who had worked with Dean more than any of the others, privately wondered what the results would be as Dean released flurry after flurry of orders. The Drucharii were not trained to be reckless, but it was obvious that Dean was asking them to commit to actions that he had not thought through entirely. Disobedience was not an option, though, and questioning the seneschal was also out of the question, so perhaps this rash, bloodthirsty Dean would carry them into a new chapter of the guild's existence. Perhaps he did know what was going on after all. Dhax kept his ruminations to himself. He nodded appropriately when Dean turned to him for acknowledgement, and his one good eye gleamed with the promise of chaos and mayhem that the week's end would undoubtedly provide.

When Dean was sure that his trusted few fully grasped his intent and more importantly, his timings, he nodded to them all. "Gather what you need to make this operation quick and efficient. Our time is at hand and the hour is ripe. Failure is not an option for the blood order." With that, Dean turned back to the service tunnel and vanished into the night once more.

Retracing his steps back through the sewers, he continued to test the limits of his awareness, noticing that if he concentrated all of his effort on submitting to the awareness within that even the small specs of filthy sewer life became noticeable to him. There was something about the nature of the being that amplified his ability to sense it, yet he still did not completely understand.

Exiting the sewer entrance brought the unwelcomed light of an early dawn sky, and Dean realized he must have been underground longer than expected. The fourth watch would be nearly ended and the gates would soon open to allow commerce and politics to resume all through Lorenth. He quickly locked down the sewer entrance again and began his return to the courtyard and the hidden ladder leading to his chamber. Carefully, the seneschal crossed the temple grounds using what little natural shadows remained to cloak his trespass until he could almost make out the last alley that would lead him to the stable courtyard.

Just before entering the alley, he paused. Again he felt that extra-sensory warning that he was being watched, but the sensation was vastly different and much clearer than those he had experienced earlier. Careful to keep his face hidden beneath the hood of his cloak, the seneschal took a quick glance over his left shoulder and started at the sight of Arimas on the top stair of the temple. The priest-king seemed to stare directly at Dean and through him, as if peering into his soul to discover his true identity. Dean cursed under his breath as he turned and vanished into the alley. How could he be so careless! Arimas always went to the temple early in the morning to pray and meditate. Dean hastened into the courtyard and deftly climbed his hidden stairwell, cautiously stopping for a moment to ensure that he was not being followed by Arimas, or anyone else who might be in pursuit.

Thankfully Lianne was still asleep when he entered his chambers. He removed his garments, stowing them all beneath his large four post bed until he had an opportunity to burn everything. He would need to acquire another set of common clothes. Still angry with his own carelessness, he slipped into his bed again, and willed his pulse to slow. Gradually, Dean's confidence erased his earlier alarm, and his ego soothed away any lingering fears. Arimas knew nothing, and it was the priest-king's ignorance of his swiftly approaching fate that re-awakened the burning hunger for power in Dean. He turned his attentions to the woman in his bed, and watched Lianne as she continued to sleep. Of his three favorites, she was the most beautiful and sensual of them, easily matching him in carnal appetites.

Dean felt himself burn with lust and arousal, and unconcerned with her reaction, jerked the sheets from atop her body, revealing to him her nakedness. His eyes wandered ravenously from her breasts down the entire length of her, taking in the soft puckering of her skin as she started to respond to the chill in the air. Then she began to stir. Feeling the predatory gaze of Dean upon her, she smiled and stretched like cat, her chest heaving, her limbs loose, and her eyes inviting. Dean reached for her roughly, his hands straying from her breasts down along her stomach and thigh as she turned and encouraged him to dominate her wholly.

*　*　*

Arimas left the temple area with a troubled spirit. He had just caught sight of someone wandering the grounds well before the night watch was over, someone who, his instincts told him, was up to no good. And that someone, who had to be from the upper city, was less than everyone thought. Equally troubling was that Arimas felt this uneasy presence before he actually saw him. This odd sensation was what led him out of the temple earlier than normal, at exactly the right moment to find himself only partly surprised to see the back of this stranger walking away from the temple area and approaching the shadows of the alley leading toward the citadel and the fortress, the magistrate's compound, the gardens, the stables and the courtyard. When the stranger suddenly stopped and looked right over his shoulder into Arimas' eyes, a chill had washed over the leader. Part of him wanted to pursue this man to obtain some answers, while inside, a part of him like a scared boy cried out for shelter and held his pursuit at bay.

Since awaking last night to some surreal musical note piercing his sleeping mind, nothing has been the same. He had felt truly alive since that event, as if something long dead had been resurrected. Arimas was getting along in years and his queen, the ever-loving and beautiful Verona, was also awakened when Arimas sat up in bed. She had smiled her private smile as she reached up and caressed his face, wiping away a solitary tear that she found on his left cheek before sharing her love with the man who had cherished her and protected her over the years. Verona was eleven years younger than Arimas. Although the marriage was arranged by the council at the time of Lorenth's completion ceremony nearly twenty-five years ago, it didn't take long for the priest-king and queen to cultivate a sincere appreciation for each other... an appreciation that grew into a powerful friendship, and then a deeply committed and passionate love.

For reasons unknown to anyone, Verona had failed to quicken with child. Despite having tried for years, even resorting to a series of various tinctures and remedies from the apothecary for aid, the king and his queen had not been blessed. As a result, Verona felt she was only half of a woman and half of a queen, unable to produce an heir to the throne and continue the legacy of her husband. Verona internalized much of this turmoil, which acted as a barrier between her and the members of court, and thus she chose to spend her days in the various wings of the citadel and the fortress, training alone in the armories where she became adept with the blade and bow or occasionally spending her time lost in the libraries of Lorenth.

Arimas and Verona led a private life of passion and devotion that the public would never see and likely couldn't fathom. They were the best of friends, the most honest of critics, and the most passionate of lovers. They found joy nearly every day during the quiet times of ruling a nation as great as Lorenth. Counselors and magistrates, soldiers and citizens, each with cares and concerns that could weigh down many lesser men, came before Arimas for council, prayer, advice, or ruling, and each he met with patience, understanding, and fairness. But it was those few quiet times in his day when he would dismiss the council for a time, when the citadel would be shut to the public in order for the citadel members to have times of prayer and feasting, when Arimas would search out his beloved bride and lose himself in her love.

That morning, Verona, her bare legs and arms still wrapped around him after a night of deep lovemaking, had drawn him close and pleaded for him to stay with her a little while longer. "You *are* indeed a wonder my dear. Must you head to the temple so early?"

"I need some time to dwell on the meaning of this song, love. I will return by dawn to join you for breakfast."

Smiling to himself at the memory of their earlier exchange, Arimas continued walking along the upper city streets, unaware of how the sun cresting over the horizon set him alight with its gold and red hues. Like a living symbol, he basked in the glory of the light that reached back into the sky as the heavy shadow of night began to lift more completely. The watch bells tolled twice and the iron portcullis separating the upper and lower city swung wide, allowing all to come and go through the city at will. In his time of meditation upon this odd crystalline song that stirred him in the night, one thing became clear: something in the world was about to change and Arimas would either adjust to this change or likely die beneath it. Those thoughts would continue to occupy his mind as he entered the fortress and made his way to his private quarters to share his breakfast with the queen on what was looking to be the start of an interesting day.

*   *   *

It was nearing noon when, led by their Druuarc, the six Drucharii made their way out of the sewers, choosing to exit far down in the lower city near entrance number five. The only watchers at this particular entrance were the large bilge rats and the occasional disease-infested peasant wandering aimlessly as he or she drifted in and out of consciousness.

"H-hey youz! Whacha doin' there with all dem fanc—" One unfortunate peasant was stopped mid-sentence as Otto launched one of his throwing knives straight into the man's throat.

"Well placed Otto. Now, we all know our stories should we be asked. Llise and Jaerik can head through the gates now, then you three, and Otto and I will follow at the end." Dhax spoke in hushed tones as Otto retrieved his knife, careful to wipe the blade clean on the peasant's tattered clothes before stowing it among his other concealed weapons. As usual, when exiting the city they all chose non-descript clothing and groomed themselves reasonably well to mitigate any curious questions as they blended in with the general populace. Their horses were already laden with their supplies and tied up near the Silver Ram tavern, where two assassins were idly watching the horses from across the street. Once Llise and Jaerik approached the tavern, the assassins left their observation areas, casually wandering away as they too disappeared among the general citizenry. It took less than fifteen minutes for the seven to acquire their horses and leave the main gate. No one was detained or questioned. No one even passed them a second look.

Approaching the designated gathering area, Dhax and Otto reigned in their horses as the other five were watching their approach. Naethan and Vlaros were stowing their canteens while Llise concentrated on fixing the straps of the black and crimson studded leathers she wore now that the non-descript clothing was no longer needed. With little more than a nod from Dhax, the seven headed out toward the east, Dhax and Vlaros riding two by two at the head of the column, each leading an extra mount, with Otto alone providing the rear guard, and also leading an extra mount.

Their ride was largely uneventful. They rode for several hours the first day, trying to recoup some of the lost time from their late start. They were still several hours from Newhaven and the turn to Rallorn was near and rather tempting but it would have set them back more than it would have aided them, should they have ridden toward Rallorn that evening. With nothing to shelter them this evening, they all ventured off the main road until it could barely be seen and made their camp for the night.

The morning brought with it a slight chill and the seven were mounted and riding well before the sun was high in the sky. Several traders and merchants were on the road from the nearby townships. The occasional farmer with his horse team and cart, heading into the capital to sell his wares, passed by the seven riders, and most did not even bother to study the swift riders in crimson and black. The weather remained clear throughout their travels toward the Dark Woods, the gentle north breeze whistling through the sparse collection of trees providing relief from the direct heat of the sun. The group only stopped twice to water the horses and partake of some of their travel rations. They did, however, stop to buy some fresh bread from a baker in Newhaven as they rode through the township around midday. They kept moving until well into the second watch of the night at which point they found a grove of trees off the main road and set up a small camp where each assassin took their turns at stealing a couple of hours of sleep.

Before dawn fully broke into the eastern sky, they were riding once again. The main road ended once they cleared the newly established settlement of Falstad, which was shaping up to be a grain and livestock operation. The small band of assassins kept to the northern outskirts of the newly forming settlement to minimize the chance that any early morning workers would be around to witness their passing into the unworked lands farther east. With only one crude, beaten-down dirt path to follow through the eastern border, the Drucharii traveled in single file until the borders of the Dark Wood finally became visible. Accounting for another two water and rest breaks, Dhax estimated that they would near the river and the Dark Wood by early evening at the latest.

By now, the seneschal, King Arimas, and Covenal Guilian would be well on their way to the Dark Wood, which left a window of approximately two days to setup, observe and prepare for the arrival of the official party from Lorenth. Silence disciplines were maintained throughout the long day of travel as the seven continued to race across the ground. Their horses had run longer and faster in the past and were well bred for endurance in the open fields, so little concern was given to them now. They were watered frequently and to be fair, they were not driven at their maximal speed yet, as the Drucharii chose to drive the horses for much longer hours instead of at much faster speeds.

As the sun began to set, they could hear the sounds of a large waterfall off in the distance and they could finally see the river flowing near the forest's edge. There was an unnatural silence emanating from the forest as if it were simply lying in wait for some unsuspecting traveler to violate its borders. The horses began to nicker nervously the closer they got to the river. Otto, Vlaros and Naethan began to exchange glances, wondering when Dhax would order them to dismount and begin their preparations.

"This is close enough for my liking. Dismount and survey the surroundings on our side of the river," Dhax ordered. He and the other six jumped from their saddles and began to unload their stores and supplies. Dhax paused for a moment, pointing to a cluster of three larger trees. "Secure the horses there and carry the supplies well off this trail. We will make camp farther north toward the waterfall and that ridgeline where the smaller hills are."

With precise actions and expert discipline, the seven carried out their individual tasks, relocating their supplies to the preliminary camp, and then beginning their initial survey of the forest border after dividing into three groups of two. Meanwhile, Dhax scouted out for a better place to tie the horses, somewhere far enough from the road to never be seen or heard. Llise and Vlaros followed the river to the north, while Naethan and Otto headed south, leaving

Jaerik and Sorren to set up where they were already digging out their spyglasses.

The silence grew heavier. Nothing in the forest moved; no sounds were heard. Not even the leaves were rustling. Vlaros jokingly commented that it should be called the Dead Wood instead of the Dark Wood which earned him a sly grin from Llise followed by a sharp jab of her elbow into his ribs. Their watch that night revealed nothing. Dhax had found a suitable site much farther north and by the time he had relocated all the horses to the new site, the others had gathered at the campsite to debrief the Druuarc about their findings.

"Nothing moved, Dhax. Nothing even stirred," stated Llise.

"Same on the south side," began Naethan. "The place feels dead."

"I felt the same thing," added Vlaros. "It feels almost like the forest knows we are here."

"While this sounds all fine and good for a child's story, unfortunately I felt nearly the same thing too, Dhax," Sorren stated. "The spyglasses showed us nothing. Not a bird or even a leaf twitched. It is as if the wind itself is afraid to cross into the Wood."

Dhax took each piece of information in as it was presented, knowing that his best would not contrive such matters. After several moments he replied, "Whether or not the forest is alive and watching I do not know, but perhaps the morning light will reveal things that the setting sun and darkness would choose to hide. We sleep in shifts again tonight. At first light we start over. I want those vantage points set up to both observe the forest and prepare for the strike upon Arimas as the rest of them approach. Tomorrow we toss the fire kegs into the forest edge to spark our little welcome. Dean said to stay out of the forest but he said nothing about weaving our destruction along its border."

Several of the Drucharii began to chuckle softly at the last comment while the seven began to prepare their bed rolls. As usual, Llise and Jaerik prepared their bed rolls together. While she used her body as a tool to glean valuable information from the nobles of Lorenth who were not accustomed to the forward advances of a sensual, well curved, and long-legged blonde beauty, privately, she used her body and heart for pleasure with Jaerik, her original mentor and the one who watched and comforted her when she had to kill her father as a young assassin. Though she succeeded in passing her critical trials, Jaerik knew her well enough to know that the bond between her and her father was very strong, and a part of Llise died that day as she tearfully approached him in his sleep, slit his throat clean and true to minimize his pain, and then threw herself upon his lifeless body, openly crying until Jaerik entered the window to help her withdraw. She had kissed her father goodbye one last time, turned over some furniture and stole a couple items of value to make it appear as if a robbery had gone wrong, and then vanished into the night with her mentor and eventual lover.

That had been well over six years ago now. Llise had transformed from the reckless, troublemaking flirt to a cold and calculating vixen with no regard for human life. Even now, little joy ever showed on her face. Jaerik was the only one to ever see her smile. While he was able to see the little girl that dwelled beneath the hardened and callous exterior, no one else even attempted to get close to Llise. Attractive as she was, any unwelcomed advances upon her were often met with a dagger positioned at the juncture of the offender's groin. Needless to say, her reputation preceded her among the assassin's guild and while many considered her a trusted ally, all except those with a death wish gave her a wide berth.

The morning brought further frustration. The members of the group spent the day alternating their efforts between watching the silent forest, checking their firebrands, and preparing the fire kegs, tossing them along the forest borders as they waded in the shallow parts of the river. The heavily reinforced nets that Otto had worked on earlier were also concealed on their side of the river and positioned at the two most strategic locations. Each of them reported the same sense of unease, as if being watched, but try as they might, there remained nothing in sight that could account for this feeling. So, the Drucharii shrugged off these feelings, believing it to be little more than their nerves set on edge. The army of Lorenth would be nearing the forest by tomorrow, likely, and still they had little information to pass on to the seneschal; however, at least the second phase of their mission was in place, and should the meeting parties be inclined toward making peace, the Drucharii would see to it that the "forest" would act unfavorably to the hosts of Lorenth standing at its border.

The day ended much the same as it had the night before, with a general feeling of unease and frustration at the sheer lack of activity within the forest. Something was happening within the shadows, of that the observers were sure, but damned if they could get anyone or anything to even hint at what was awaiting the assassins' next move.

IX

The departure from Lorenth did not go smoothly. Dean rallied the men as usual, cheering their determination to serve Lorenth and hailing their envoy as the bastion of hope that would lead Lorenth into a new era of discovery. Arimas, however, was not his normal self. The moment Dean walked into the room, Farin noticed Arimas' eyes widen as he immediately picked out Dean among the crowd, as if he had almost felt his presence enter the courtyard. What was more unnerving was that Dean did the exact same thing. Once their eyes met, Dean immediately dropped his eyes and shouted out, greeting the soldiers and the royal guard and beginning his rally. From that point on, Arimas had a disconcerting sense of caution in his eyes.

Then, just as they were about to begin the march out, two messengers from the towns of Coren and Tannir, both located a fair distance west of Lorenth, sped into the courtyard to deliver messages to the priest-king. Farin wished that he could have heard the exchanges as again he watched his king's eyes take on a new expression. It was obvious that the matters being spoken of were of grave importance for Arimas immediately approached several of his counselors. After another exchange of words, there was some nodding of heads and looks of excitement that crossed the faces of the counselors. By now, Dean had finished addressing the men and was blatantly watching the disturbance over the heads of those gathered.

Arimas returned to the waiting messengers, passed on his reply, and dismissed the riders while counselor Nolan Weiss approached four of the royal guard who immediately stepped out of formation to attend to the priest-king. Arimas and the four guards made their way out of the courtyard while Nolan took the position among the army as the advocate for the council of Lorenth, prepared to diplomatically represent the capital and the priest-king in the discussions with those of the Dark Wood himself.

Farin, still standing in curiosity, swiveled to face Dean's direction in time to take in the ferocious frustration that clouded the seneschal's face as Arimas strode from the courtyard. Something was terribly amiss, yet Farin, leading the vanguard with his eastern border detail in their best dress, and with Commander Barros at his side, was powerless to do anything but carry on with the orders that he had received from Dean and the rest of the council.

Within the hour, Dean issued the marching order and the long line of soldiers eased off the reigns of their mounts and the procession began its exodus of the upper city along the main street leading to the broad gates atop the Ardun river. Numbering well over two hundred strong, the procession began with the eastern border detail dressed in their finest. Polished silver armor decorated the men, and the armor plating covering their warhorses was draped with the colors of Lorenth. The few scarlet capes belonging to Farin, Hadrin, and several of the battlemasters in charge of smaller divisions flew in the gentle breeze as the leadership rode near the front with Farin at the head.

Behind the border detail followed several of the Lorenthian honor guard: volunteers mostly, trained and armed with lances and long swords, wearing simple coats of chainmail and riding atop unadorned mounts. Several men bore pennants from Lorenth while others carried the trumpets and other horns to announce the arrival of Lorenth to those of the Dark Wood.

Following the honor guard rode Counselor Nolan and the seneschal, the official representatives of Lorenth, with twenty of the impressively clad royal guard atop their equally impressive warmounts and bearing their savage triple-forged blades which hung idly across their shoulders. The royal guard made up the rear party; the gold lions on their shoulder armor elicited awe from any who witnessed their passing, making the impressive image of the eastern border detail pale in comparison.

Once they left the city, the ride went reasonably smooth. Farin knew these roads well as these lands were under the mantle of his responsibility. Breaks were well used and the horses given time to water and graze as the war party passed several settlements. Even with the breaks, they made fairly good time. They took a small detour south to reach the township of Rallorn where they made camp on the first night, careful to keep the animals on the outskirts of town where they pitched their tents and set up camp.

After a restful and uneventful night, scouts were sent into town to acquire some additional supplies, which was another of Farin's responsibilities. When one of the scouts brought local tavern talk of a small scouting party that passed through Newhaven not two days past, Farin began to piece together some of the frustrations of Dean. He was plotting something, and he would bet that his sights were fixed on more than just the forests of the east. Farin thanked the gods that somehow Arimas was taken out of the war party, but couldn't help but wonder about what Dean was ultimately planning.

The ride continued east, past Newhaven, until finally the group stopped to set up camp outside of the new settlement of Falstad, which Farin had established about two months ago now. He waved to the few workers who were ending their day. Already the fields were being turned over and prepared for the next spring plant even though this harvesting season was long over. The town itself was also in various stages of construction. The town hall was complete, as were several farmhouses and livestock pens. It appeared as if many of the workers had also found time to build their own houses in anticipation for their families to arrive before the winter was upon them. The beginnings of what appeared to be a granary and some stables with an attached blacksmith for tending to the horses were underway as well.

Farin struggled to find sleep that night. Since that odd change in his recurrent dreams two nights before, he had not had another. For the last two nights he had been sleeping peacefully and uninterrupted. He mused at the significance of this but nothing became clear. Sometimes he almost missed the interruptions and the nightly pondering about the meanings and hidden stories that must lurk beneath the surface of his understanding, where perhaps his fantasy mind collided with his cognitive mind. Tension kept building inside him as an uninvited sense of trepidation began to surround him. Why was this all happening? Would there ever be answers to these mysteries? Farin wrestled with the notion that somehow he had caught a glimpse of some future event, for how else could he describe what had been happening to him over and over for years? He had felt the stirrings of change deep in his spirit for some time now, but never had it felt so close. Something was about to happen and that anticipation made what little sleep he did get fitful and sparse.

Morning came too early for Farin. The camps were struck and the tents loaded. Once again, the armies of Lorenth marched with pride, flying their honors and colors, and made their way from Falstad to the bare path that would eventually lead them to the river and what lay beyond. Approaching the forest from afar brought back the fear and the memories of his men, scared for their lives, and the unbelievable sights that they had claimed to witness... the same sights that Farin had accepted as truth on their behalf and in front of Lorenth.

Creatures of intelligence usually do not simply want to destroy everything around them simply because they could, do they? A nerve was struck deep inside of Farin. Was this potentially how other sentient races viewed the people of Lorenth? Were they nothing more than barbarians of the land that killed every beast that opposed them? Were they savages that cut down every tree and excavated every stone in their path solely to mark their place? If this were the case then perhaps it would take more than honors, flags, and trumpets mingled with fine words to appease these beings of nature who may have witnessed the humans destroy everything in their path for generations.

Only an hour later, Farin looked to his left and saw what remained of the campsite where he and his men had thought to begin cutting the giant trees within the Dark Wood. The forest's edge kept drawing closer and closer and within the next few hours they would finally arrive, likely in mid or late afternoon. The last few hours for Farin felt like a lifetime. His men, those who made up the eastern border vanguard, were resolute and professional, yet Farin wondered what, if any, fears were lurking beneath their polished steel, threatening to cause them to break and run like ordinary, undisciplined men.

Three hours later, the inevitable order was given. The honor guard lifted trumpet and horn to mouth and began sounding their cries into the borders of the forest, announcing their presence for all to hear. The last hour of travel toward the Dark Wood brought no challenge, no emissaries of the forest, no stirring within its borders. There were no walking trees or half-clothed young female girls flaunting bodies that belonged to much more mature women. This was to be a day of ridicule for Farin. Should Dean have his way, Farin would be a curse word from this day forth and no one would ever mourn the loss of the inept covenal of the eastern border detail.

*   *   *

"Talonyyr! Eth athariel nina telu vadii?" questioned Evianna in the elven tongue.

"I did not leave the glades without reason, ambassador. The sprites brought us word of seven riders in black who now lie in hiding around the borders of our glades. They have nets and devices to cast fire into our trees and among the guardians. I cannot be completely sure, but several sprites heard mention of another group of humans coming and that this other group comes in peace. These seven riders were not sent to represent them. They show no light at all around them and I fear that they are messengers of the seed of corruption."

Evianna pondered carefully the words that Talonyyr brought to her ears. The Matriarch and the others would likely just be starting the meeting above the Ellorian waterfall and there was no time to seek her council. As steward of Avalide, the burden was hers alone to bear and she must think and act quickly.

"Have you seen the other party with farsight?" Evianna inquired. Talonyyr shook his head as Evianna nodded and let her eyes glaze over in an attempt to extend her vision into the spiritual realm. She searched far to the west, following the broken ground until her vision began to blur at a small human town that was beginning to be built. She tried pushing her farsight farther but everything went gray.

"I cannot see them, either. We must protect the glades above all else. If they attempt to enter our forest with ill intent then strike them down to the last man. However, should they bring peace then we will gather to meet and discuss openly with them for the time of silence is past. I leave now to request the presence of the Æthian and the *Essen`drill* and to see whether their superior giftings can discover the nature of the party that follows. Do not show yourself to the dark riders. If they mean to capture us then woe to them for it will be the last thing they ever try to do. Return to the glades, Talonyyr. Gather the other mistrunners and have some wardens join you and keep the wood still until the other party arrives. I will join you on the western border by tomorrow and I hope to have some arcanists, a spiritualist, and a druid or two among us."

Talonyyr touched fingers to lips and forehead before hastening from the Matriarchal Commune back to his section of the glades on the western border. The elven *Ryl`idohan* blurred his image as the mistrunner accelerated through the forest toward the nearby guild halls and smaller watch posts to call his brothers to silently bear arms along the border of the western glade.

Evianna also departed, gathering her essence and taking the form of the owl once again as she flew with purpose toward the eastern conclave wherein the careful studies conducted by the Æthian and the *Essen`drill* took place. Resuming her natural form once she entered the enclave, Evianna quickly scanned the area for those she had built great respect with. Valeck Silversong and Bethalyyn Leafwhisperer were already deep in conversation when the ambassador came within earshot.

"The forest is alive with restlessness, Evianna. Valeck and I were just discussing this matter. Is this why you have come?"

"Yes, Elder Druid. Talonyyr is assembling the mistrunners and wardens along the water's edge even as we speak. A large arm—"

"Has the Matriarch condoned this course of action, ambassador?" inquired the arch mage. "While I recognize your role as steward, it behooves you to initiate hostilities of any kind without consent of the Matriarch, or at the very least, those of us in the council of the nine."

"My intent is not to engage these humans but to prepare ourselves should their intentions toward us be less than peaceable. Seven dark riders have brought nets and fire with them and even now they lie in wait. Yet, behind them rides a large army of humans. I have come to hear your wisdom in the matter and perhaps seek use of your divination skills in order to ascertain the nature of this larger force that marches beyond my range of farsight."

Valeck considered the words of the elven ambassador carefully. The mention of nets and fire was certainly something to prepare against so arguably her hasty actions were in the best interests of Avalide. Bethalyyn nodded toward the arch mage as Evianna watched on. Valeck's eyes began to mist over as he entered into his farsight, reaching considerably farther and quicker than most with any level of mastery with this talent. It was not long before the lost look in his eyes departed and seriousness crossed his face.

"It is as you say, Evianna. It may well prove that your hastiness was the best course of action. You have done well in this matter. As to the nature of the army that approaches, it is hard to tell... I see several sources of light surrounding a focal point of darkness. There is much uncertainty and much that we must wait to understand fully. I would join the *Ryl'idohan* in preparation if you ask it of me."

"As would I, Evianna."

"This was my intent all along. Let us make haste to the forest's edge," proposed Evianna as she looked back toward the arch mage. "Would you speak with Narissa as well?"

"I will take care of that, Valeck. You gather Phaelen and Shae. Evianna, thank you for your quick action. We will make our way to the border shortly. *Eth aloni tul`venarii*, ambassador."

"*Ashanda eth reiis*, Elder Druid... Arch Mage."

Nodding to both of them as they inclined their heads in return of the acknowledgement, Evianna shifted once again into her owl form, and on silent, feathered wings she made her way out of the enclave and down to the river where the tenuous situation was already building.

* * *

Arimas was lost for words. The messengers of Coren and Tannir brought unbelievable news about a winged beast larger than twenty horses that had collided with the mountains and fallen dead into the river valley where Erikk Masaad, covenal of the northern border detail, now stood guard. Arimas had battled nearly every sort of beast known to man but this was truly something for anyone who respected life in all forms to behold. Taking only a small personal guard from the main diplomatic party toward the east, Arimas made all haste to send word to Verona about his sudden change in plans as well as to reflect on the sickened feeling he had when he felt Dean come into the courtyard this morning.

Why had he experienced that same feeling once again? Surely his most trusted military advisor and the seneschal himself could not be same vile presence he felt while in meditation yesterday morning. But, when Dean had turned to face him, deep in those dark eyes had shone a gleaming hatred and an evil that was never there before. Arimas took pause and wondered just what sort of web he was being led into. Was it fate that brought those two messengers to him only minutes before he would have departed with the army for the east? Was it something more powerful than fate? His choice was clear. He needed time to contemplate what these new feelings about Dean meant and this was the perfect opportunity to visit Covenal Masaad again, to obtain his most current updates personally and see this tremendous finding for himself.

After kissing Verona another time, allowing her intoxicating smile to burn itself upon his memory, he set aside his scepter and gripped *Retribution* once more, allowing its weight and power to wash over him and bring forward memories of the countless battles fought with the deadly yet primal weapon. Too long had he held the scepter and too long had he been lost within the political entrapments of managing Lorenth... too long indeed since he purposefully held this devastating icon of his youthful reign. When he closed the armory doors and turned to face his four royal guards with *Retribution* in hand, each of them raised their eyebrows while three of them began to crack large smiles.

"That is the *real* Arimas we remember, my liege," quipped Anton. Long in service to Arimas, and one of his best friends, Anton was chosen as captain of the royal guard when it first was founded. He had remained one of Arimas' closest advisors and was the most honest of his friends. It was only when he was alone with these four that Arimas would allow his complete disregard for position to shine forth.

"Yes, I know. Only now that I have taken up *Retribution* after all this time do I realize how much lighter it can be compared to the holy scepter. We travel west, my friends. There are things happening that I do not understand and there are people I have trusted that I fear I no longer can. We ride for the river valley near Coren, where Covenal Masaad awaits our arrival to show us a beast that rivals anything we have ever seen or heard of before. If we ride light and fast we should arrive by nightfall, and I would leave this instant."

"You know our pledge to you, Arimas. Where you go, we go. Always. Let's see this beast of yours," smiled Rorrick. The priest-king and his guards left the hall of kings, stripped their warhorses of their heavy plate adornments and chose for themselves their lighter suit of silver chainmail and hardened leathers. Several attendants quickly came to remove the armor from the courtyard and left to house them properly in the armory while the five adjusted their saddles and sped out the front gate of the upper city. The royal party led their horses down into the lower city and out the main gates, taking the road west toward Tannir and then onto Coren, while, to the east, the golden heavy armor of the royal guards sent to escort counselor Nolan and Seneschal Dean were seen gleaming in the distant sunlight.

Seeing the priest-king was always an event for the local peasantry to remember and embellish upon, but this day, many simply stared in open shock as Lord Arimas and four of his royal guards tore through the various settlements, stopping only to water the horses and take water for themselves. Most people new better than to interfere with the king's business—especially when anyone could decipher that his Excellency was in a hurry and setting a fast pace for the horses; however, occasionally one of the royal guards would have to shout, "Make way for the priest-king of Lorenth!" to get someone to clear the roads and let the party ride past.

They reached the township of Coren by nightfall, as Arimas had predicted. Celebrating the horses for their tremendous ride today, the five dismounted and requested fresh feed and new straw for their mounts and a careful grooming for each of them when they arrived at the barracks of the town watch. The stable hands complied with honor, never before seeing such magnificent steeds. The Captain of the Guard came moments later and bowed low to the priest-king.

"Your Excellency, Covenal Erikk Masaad awaits you in the officer quarters. If you and your guards would follow me then I shall bring you there now."

"Lead on Captain." Arimas and the four royal guards made their way past the barracks and the stables to a small but well-built single-roomed dwelling. From the outside, it was plain brick with a thatched roof and a decent size chimney, but once they entered, they found it to be a two level building with the reception area up top and a staircase descending below the ground level to a rather nice gathering area below. A great hearth opened off of a roaring fire that led to the chimney they had noticed from outside. Covenal Erikk Masaad stood from his comfortable seat to welcome Arimas, and held himself at the position of attention until he was addressed.

"Relax, Erikk. We have ridden long and hard to see you and get your latest report and I would prefer not to bother with the formalities of command and titles this late in the evening, when it is just us present. Please sit and speak plainly with us." Erikk nodded and smiled, calling for the serving boy and requesting stew and bread be brought for the visitors as well as a cold stein of ale for all, including himself and his own Captain of the Guard.

Arimas and the royal guards sat, ate, and drank, never letting a word of Erikk's report fall on deaf ears. Winged beasts that shook the very ground when they landed, speaking common with ordinary men, spouting mighty gouts of fire into the night sky, reading the mind of the covenal and speaking of Arimas himself as being marked in the line of the Lightbringer, not to mention uncovering the half-buried dragon with little effort and then flying off into the darkness above… this simply was beyond reason and defied explanation. The tale was as unbelievable as Farin's report on the Dark Wood, but when Erikk expressed nearly the same sentiments and assured the others that his entire division of well trained soldiers could attest to the validity of this report, Arimas and the four royal guards exchanged glances and nodded, believing that their tiny reality of manageable beasts and the sheer lack of other sentient races was shattered. For once, the humans of Lorenth felt small and insignificant in the light of the unknown.

"And you say that this Sargeron… he was bigger than the dead dragon you found?" inquired Arimas.

"Much bigger my lord. He referred to her as his mate and one of four ancient dragons. I did not have time to inquire about the meaning of that but I would expect that there are at least two other dragons as large as him. His son, the green one, was Nosta—, no… it was something like Nostrima, and he was easily as large as the dead female ancient while his sister, Sycaris I believe, was noticeably smaller than the dead ancient. I have never seen anything so amazing, my lord. He read my fears, saw my thoughts as if they were plain words and answered my questions before I had even uttered them."

"This changes things you realize. Did the dragons give you any information about their intentions? Did they give you any warning or council?"

"Oh! How could I forget… forgive me, my lord, but before they flew off, Lord Sargeron told me three things of tremendous import. The first was a warning not to pursue them into the Icecrowns. The second, a mentioning of you. Lord Sargeron said that he wanted to eventually meet you, though he claimed it was not yet time. I still do not understand how he even knew of you. He was familiar with your name well before he plucked it from my mind."

"You digress, Erikk. What was the final thing he said?"

"Beg pardon my lord. I do not know an easy way to say this, but Lord Sargeron inquired about the seneschal and asked who he was." At this revelation, Arimas felt that same sickened feeling arise in the pit of his stomach. "I told him his station and function in Lorenth and then the dragon quite clearly warned me to beware of Seneschal Dean."

No one spoke for quite some time. The serving boy came to refill the ale steins but was waved away by the covenal. Anton leaned toward Arimas and whispered something to him that no one else heard. Arimas nodded and sighed.

"Covenal... Captain... I have not spoken of this with anyone outside of these four men whom I have loved as brothers and trusted with my life. Why I am choosing to share this with you I am not sure, but now is the time for truth and trust to lead us into the next era of Lorenth. There are things happening around us that we do not wish to accept and cannot understand, yet it must be so. We are not alone in this world as we once thought. Our pride and achievements could be gnashed to pieces in a heartbeat should we bring war upon ourselves with the rest of the world. I will die before I let that happen.

"Unfortunately, I believe this warning from Sargeron to be more than relevant and timely. Two days ago now, I was awakened from sleep with the most beautiful sound I have ever heard. Your report seems to place this disastrous event with the dead ancient around almost the same time; it may in fact have been the same time and the same event. Why this has happened I am not sure, but like Sargeron told you, the time for answers has not yet come so I will stop asking 'why?' and start asking 'what?' What do we need to do now? Since that night, I have been changed in some way. I cannot say how, but what I can say is since that night, I have begun to sense evil. I feel its presence when it is close. And I have felt it twice now when I crossed paths with Seneschal Dean. I would have tried to ignore this extreme unease, but coupled with the warning of Sargeron, I dare not treat these feelings lightly any longer.

"If Seneschal Dean is in fact an enemy working from within, then it will be hard to determine whom he has corrupted and how deep his influence runs. He must not be given any further opportunity to gain ground. Even now, I have sent Dean and Counselor Nolan with Covenal Farin Guilian and his eastern border detail toward the Dark Wood on a mission of peace, or so I believed. Now I fear for the fate of the good men I entrusted to Dean, as well as for the fate of any future relations that may be had with those of the Dark Wood.

As it stands now, we are a full two days behind Dean and the men of Lorenth. We have ridden our horses hard today and we simply cannot catch up with Dean now, even if we could expect more from the horses in their fatigued state. We ride for Dunnham tomorrow morning so that I can speak with Chase before moving on to Lorenth from there. I need you both to begin spreading the word throughout our settlements that all soldiers loyal to me and to the good of Lorenth guard themselves against the division that would seek to undermine the foundational truths of Lorenth. I will deal with Dean when he returns. I cannot allow him to poison good natured men into becoming corrupt ambassadors of wickedness.

I will need you both for this task. Rout out evil from your ranks. Give men the choice to leave in peace if they are not loyal lest they be discovered as enemies and killed as would befit any enemy of Lorenth. All those who leave are to head south beyond the river and never return to Lorenth. They may take their families and all their belongings in order to start anew but they will no longer be granted shelter under the protection of Lorenth."

The mood was somber when Arimas finished speaking. Words that bore such heaviness and responsibility were laid on the shoulders of two men who in turn were to draw unto themselves men they could trust and duplicate the process to ensure that all enemies of Lorenth be given the chance to leave in peace or die by the sword. Nothing further was discussed this evening. Sleep was hard in coming to all seven men as each pondered the weight of Arimas' words and the impact that those words would have on all of Lorenth.

X

The marching order changed once they arrived at the forest. The sun was late in the sky and within the next hour or two at most, it would begin to set and would cast its shadows upon the Lorenth encampment. The eastern border detail spread out in two ranks of thirty men wide, followed by three ranks of the honor guard behind them, while the remaining honor guard began setting up camp well behind the wall of soldiers. Counselor Nolan and the seneschal made their way to the front of the formation while ten royal guards flanked them on each side. Farin received a nod from Dean indicating that he was to join the leadership near the front of the procession. With an inward hesitation that not for one minute showed on his face, Farin spurred his horse forward stopping to the left of Nolan, while Dean remained on his right. With a one-handed motion, Dean silenced the trumpets and horns. Then, all was quiet. Dean looked around at the forest, drew in a deep breath and stood in his saddle to shout in a loud and commanding voice.

"Peoples of the wood! We come with noble intent and to offer sincere apologies for the grief we have caused you in recent days. Our ignorance led us into your lands and we wish to make amends and speak plainly of friendship and trade. Would there be any among you willing to speak with us?"

The silence that long lived in the heart of the forest broke as the very trees seemed to stand taller. Then, out from the shadows emerged a crowd of tall, thin, fair skinned people with elongated ears and long flowing hair in shades of silver and white, gold and yellow, and a hundred hues of brown. Some kept low profiles, barely rising above the low lying shrubs and trees near the river's edge. These were dressed in various types of armor that were made of materials that did not resemble anything crafted in Lorenth. Others were clothed in long flowing robes; many bore scarlet and orange patterned robes while some were dressed in a pale blue.

One simply stood watching the men of Lorenth from across the water, dressed in a robe of earthen tones of green and brown with a mantle and cloak that appeared as if it had been made entirely of leaves. Clutching a gnarled longstaff with a pulsating crystalline headpiece atop it she simply watched. No facial expression was recognizable in her perfectly featured face... a face of striking beauty to the men of Lorenth.

"So we meet the Seed of Corruption at last," began Valeck Silversong, brother to the Matriarch and Arch Magus of the Ætheron. "Long have we studied the prophecies and long have we watched the growth of your race. Do not think to stand there and cloud the minds of those who have long stood here, before you were but a thought, with your lies of good intent and false pretences of making amends. We have watched the dark riders that were sent before you. Nothing is veiled from the eyes of the elves of *Illu'Dar*. Were it not for the hosts of innocents that you lead to our borders we would dispose of you once and for all."

"You are a fool if you think we would entreat with one such as you," added Narissa Amberdawn, another of the Æthanon gifted in the ways of healing and divination. "There is only one whom we will entreat with. The Lightbringer will descend through his line, and the world lies in wait for the child of prophecy to be born through the man you follow, the man by the name of Arimas!"

Mass confusion broke out among the ranks of men as Counselor Nolan suddenly, with an animal moan, pitched forward in his saddle, blood running freely around the bolt that had just been lodged deep in his neck. Dean was furious. Not only did these elves refuse to speak with him, but they also revealed that Arimas and his descendents would bring about some Lightbringer. But what descendants were these? He had no children and his queen was barren, so how could this be? Before they could state Arimas' name, though, his fool Drucharii had fired upon Nolan. Nolan! It should have been Arimas slouched there, bleeding and dying. How could everything go so wrong so quickly? Dean realized he had to act fast before the men began to turn on him as well.

"Foul trickery! Men of Lorenth! They have killed the Counselor Nolan and mean to destroy us all! Stand firm and hold your ground, men!" Dean's words left the men in a state of conflict. The words spoken from the elves did not imply that they were in danger but that Dean was in danger, yet the counselor was dead and now the seneschal of Lorenth was issuing battle orders that were expected to be obeyed. The men of Lorenth were about to form up when Covenal Farin Guilian addressed them all, including the twenty royal guards.

"This is not the time for blind obedience, men. Dean is trying to lead us into a war with these elves, a war that will spark chaos in all of Lorenth. I now believe that Counselor Nolan was meant to be the priest-king himself, bleeding and dying so that the seneschal, a man whose blood runs with an evil and malice darker than any of you can comprehend, could ascend the throne in his place. Open your eyes men and see what—" Farin's words were cut short as yet another bolt flew from what appeared to be the forest, and pierced through the back part of his left shoulder. Farin collapsed beneath the force and fell from his saddle, blacking out when the ground rushed up to meet him.

"Enough discord! Enough corruption! Those who value their lives will leave now and return only with Arimas. We know your face now, Seed of Corruption, and I vow that you will never enter our lands alive. Begone!" shouted Talonyyr as several of his mistrunners appeared from the shadows pointing their ornately strung longbows, already knocked with arrows, toward the men.

The Drucharii, who had been watching the chaos unfold, were waiting for an opportunity such as this to present itself. With the presence of arms from the elves, Otto, Vlaros, Sorren, Jaerik, and Naethan unleashed their firebrands toward the hidden kegs along the forest's edge. The first bolt met its target and sent a mighty blast of flame into the trees behind them. Several of the guardians thrashed about as their leaves and bark became engulfed in flames while a fair number of mistrunners yelled in agony at the searing of fire across their fair skin. The Æthian were not quick enough to stop the first flaming bolt but those that followed simply stopped in mid-flight as the arcanists focused a minute channeling of their essence on putting out the fires. The druid began to close her eyes as the sky darkened. Then, in a sudden rush of wind, the four remaining bolts spun on their axis and traveled straight back to their targets. The druid then focused her energies on the water in the river, causing a wall of water to rise straight up and collapse into the forest, dousing the flames that were threatening the guardians and nearby elves.

Llise, Otto and Dhax stood with mixture of fear and rage as four of their comrades buckled beneath their own bolts. Llise rushed to Jaerik's side, only to find him already dead. In a blind rage she grabbed two heavy nets and leapt into the river, casting them toward several of the elves on the shore. Talonyyr could feel both her pain and her rage but still he issued the silent order and several of his mistrunners launched their arrows into her body, stopping her in her tracks and staining the Ellorian River red with her blood. The nets caught flame before they reached the elves on the shore as the Æthian channeled their essence of fire into them. Suddenly aware that they were facing a far superior foe, Otto and Dhax made their retreat back to where the horses remained.

It was then that the men of Lorenth broke rank by order of Commander Barros and began their unlawfully ordered retreat back to Falstad. Farin regained consciousness in time to see his men riding out, but could not find his voice to call for aid. He knew he was losing a lot of blood, and had barely enough strength left to feel fear as his worst nightmare approached.

"You!" Dean scowled as he drew his blades and approached the fallen covenal. "I should have killed you myself years ago. Arimas is not here to hide behind and now your men are fleeing! The circle is now complete. First I killed your Jesslyn and her doting father and now I finally get to drive the knife deeper and kill you!" Dean paused in front of the broken body of Farin, watching the fury flood into Farin's eyes at the mention of his long-dead love.

"You have already lost Dean," Farin croaked weakly. "Lorenth will not welcome you back and your plans to kill the priest-king have failed. Jesslyn is at peace and now I can be at peace alongside her."

Dean roared, and raised his blades, but before he could plant them firmly in Farin's already weakened body, something strange began to happen. Dean could almost feel the druid looking at him and before he could fully brace himself, a great blast of wind took him off his feet and sent him flying back into the long grass behind.

"Leave him!" The druid thundered, her hands still hovering in mid-air and her eyes a fierce shade of emerald.

"This is not over Farin!" Dean screamed as he scrabbled to his feet. "I know you have seen the dreams. I will be your doom!" Dean hurriedly stowed his blades, whistled for his mount and then rode off north toward the waterfall and away from the men who had begun their retreat back to Lorenth.

Farin again faded into darkness. Knowing that his time was short, he formed the image of Jesslyn in his mind and began to allow the memory of her to warm his heart. During his last moments lost in the darkness from which he did not expect to awake from, his eyes opened to see a female elf dressed in blue staring into his face and into his soul. For once in his life he felt completely vulnerable and drifted again into darkness as she smiled at him.

* * *

Farin had no concept of time when he finally awoke and found himself in the strangest of places. He was lying in one of the most comfortable beds he had ever slept in, within a room that appeared to have been made inside the hearts of several great trees. Natural sunlight poured in through many smaller windows also grown into the walls. The room was large yet simple. No pictures adorned the walls and the only decorative elements were the furniture, each a piece superiorly woven together without the use of nails or joints, and vines that bore beautiful flowers he had never seen before.

"Those are the *ost`anellia*, or Winter's Kiss, in your tongue. We elves celebrate life and harmony in all things and at all times. We are children of the balance and this flower blooms as the chill of winter approaches and withers as the summer heat falls upon the glades. As you will have the opportunity to learn, your bitter winters cannot trouble us within the *Illu'Dar*. We are the magi of the elements and the chroniclers of history. You may call me Narissa."

Farin was too overwhelmed to respond. The elven woman dressed in her long ornately tailored blue robes stood before him smiling at the infatuation that spread a pink blush over his features. Elven women were perfect in face and feature and her words rolled off her tongue like music. He felt like a pre-pubescent boy looking at a woman for the first time, and had to gather all his composure to speak in a complete sentence.

"I thought I was dead. Then I awoke and saw you and now I am here. How long have I been resting in this place?"

She chuckled, though not in a condescending manner but as a light-hearted laugh, "You have been sleeping for the last two days while I have been tending to your wound. I brought you here to shelter you from the hatred of the Seed of Corruption who even now has begun to walk the path of shadow. Your time to face him has not come, for face him you shall, but there is much for you to learn before that day."

Dean... the last thing Farin remembered about the seneschal was the hatred burning in his eyes as he raised his blades in preparation of delivering the death blow. Some unknown force had saved him and had sent Dean flying away from him. Then Dean referenced the dream... had someone stolen his dream journal? Had Dean also been dreaming the same thing, knowing the fate that was in store for Farin and the immense power destined to flow in and through Dean? Melancholy spread over his face as he looked into the eyes of the healer.

"I know the fate that awaits me, my lady. Long have I had the same dream over and over again, until a couple nights ago, when it suddenly stopped recurring." Narissa's intense look of interest compelled him to continue. "In my dream, Dean stands on a dais and becomes filled with shadows. His features change and then he takes on a new name, Kaaldean. Then he unleashes these tendrils of black and violet shadows that entwine and crush me. It is then that I would normally awake."

The elf hung on to every word that Farin spoke, nodding at several places as if none of this information was a surprise for her. She came around to his side and gently laid her hand upon his shoulder, infusing a sense of comfort and warmth into him.

"You will suffer greatly Farin Guilian, the redeemed and the guardian of the light. You must keep hope, even when all hope seems lost, for it will be at your weakest and darkest hour that you will find your greatest joy and strength."

"But how can you know these things? How can my dreams not shock you? How can you touch me and I somehow feel stronger and more at peace? These are things that I cannot fathom."

"Calm yourself, Farin. In time, you shall learn. Though you may not understand the magic that dwells at the heart of Caliyon, you can see its effects all around you. Your fate, and that of the Lightbringer, is partially entwined, and it was that fact alone that drew us to you."

"Is this why you only saved me? Why didn't you help the counselor? He was innocent and did not deserve such an early death."

A tear formed on the healer's face. "Once the spirit has left the body there is nothing that can be done without violating the balance. It was too late for the counselor, but I found you before you had passed fully into shadow. I know you have many questions, and perhaps I can help answer some this way." She knelt beside Farin while he was sitting upright in his bed and placed both her hands on either side of his face forcing him to look into her eyes. "Open your mind to me Farin. Open your mind and see."

Thousands of images began to flow into Farin's open mind, stripped of all sense of normal parameters. He saw the elves in their awakening and development, their mastery of the spheres of magic, the young child-like race known as the dryads, creatures made of air and trees, and then the discovery of the dwarves and the mighty dragons, creatures beyond reason and of tremendous magical and physical strength. More and more knowledge kept flooding into Farin's mind: prophecies, the Illuallarii, the council of the nine, the Frostspire elves in a desolate place called the frozen wastes. It was becoming too much for him to handle. He was about to cry out when the elf finally cut off the exchange. Farin lifted his hand and touched the small trickle of blood that had begun to run from his nose.

"You are stronger than I thought, Farin, but I am sorry for pushing you as far as I did. Do you now understand a little of our world and our ways?"

"Yes," Farin replied. He paid no further notice to the blood on his face as he braced his head in his hands in a feeble attempt to massage the newly forming headache pounding at his temples. "That was the most amazing thing I have ever experienced. I had no idea that there was so much hidden life in these lands." Farin paused for a moment. "Forgive me for my ignorance, but you are the most beautiful woman I have ever seen. I find it hard to believe that you are centuries old. How is this possible?"

The healer smiled once again, touching his face and infusing yet another ounce of strength into him while clearing the blood from his nose. "We elves are not like humans. We were infused with the magic of Ethoni a long time ago and thus we do not age as you, nor do we die as you. I know this is hard for you to understand but I will bring you to the libraries if you like, when you are well, and I can show you the true history of the lands, and of Caliyon."

"What is Caliyon? You have mentioned it a couple times now. Is that what you call this place that we are in now?"

"Yes, but Caliyon is also the realms of the dragons, the dwarves, and even your lands wherein dwells your capital of Lorenth. Caliyon is all the lands from west to east, north and south, and encompasses all life in all three planes of magic. Even now as we speak, all the magical races of Caliyon have gathered above the waterfall to openly talk of this Dean who will eventually become Kaaldean. Do you know the significance of this name change?"

"No m'lady. I thought it odd but I did not realize that there was any meaning behind it. Why is everyone afraid of Dean? He is just a man."

"Oh that he were just a man, Farin. The prefix *Kay-El* in the ancient tongue, transcribed to 'Kaal' in the common tongue, means 'soul stealer.' He has been touched by the shadow and has begun to walk a path that will ultimately end in his complete submission to the same corruption that has been slumbering beneath Caliyon for as long as we have existed. The corruption is the incarnate negative balance, created by accident through the pride of Sarik, one of the three deities that originally governed the creation of Caliyon. It is this corruption that has been seeking a vulnerable soul to consume in an effort to unleash the shadow upon all of Caliyon.

The fae creatures, those who were birthed of magic through the influence of Ethoni, have been able to resist the corruption in its advance into our world, and while there have been cases where the corruption has attempted to strike at our world, it has been unable to fully corrupt any who were created by Ethoni.

It was Deimar, the third of the deities, the creator of the positive balance and the creator of your race and of all life, both animal and plant, who was left vulnerable in the attempt to restrain Sarik from breaking the balance of Caliyon. Thus we have been watching your growth and advancement for many years, knowing that of all the races, it would be the humans who would be most susceptible to the corruption of soul and who would eventually give rise to the seed that would bring the shadow upon the world."

Farin had no idea what to say. His entire concept of reality was being shattered in the presence of this elven healer. He should have died from his wounds, yet he lived. He could have lived out the rest of his life in ignorance, yet now with the revelation of all that his reality was lacking, he could not go back to live in ignorance any longer. His life was now a gift, granted by this elven beauty, and he would learn all that he could in an effort to bring unity and reconciliation between their races. In some ways, Farin felt like a child, lacking in knowledge and turning to the wisdom of those who had come before.

"What would you have me do now m'lady? In my heart, I would choose to stay among you and learn, and then take what I know back to those who would stand against the coming darkness that you speak of. I know Arimas to be a man of indomitable spirit. Though I know that he, among others, would make an excellent ally, I find myself wondering how we could even be of use to those as fair and powerful as the fae creatures. We are a broken race when compared to you and to be honest, I detest this feeling of ineptitude that I feel while sitting here."

"You have strength that you do not realize, Farin. Humans are an impetuous race. Yet, with your relatively short time awake among the living, you have been able to develop proportionately faster than any other race in existence. Even now, change is happening among the humans. In time you will fully understand the nature of your dreams and the effects that those dreams have been having upon you. You are not alone in this, Farin. A time is coming when your wisdom will expand into the realms of magic. This we fear most of all, for your learning will come not by instinct as it has happened with us, but through experimentation and research, which are two traits that will forever set humans apart from the fae races.

"Come Farin. It is time I show you the histories of the Illuallarii and the Lorekeepers that guard the mysteries for all time. When we are done, I would like to introduce you to our Matriarch. She has guided us for generations and she will have much to ask of you and much to tell that will both aid and inspire, I am sure."

Slowly, Farin rose from the soft comfort of the bed beneath him and stood tall once more. He was dressed in a pale linen robe that was rather comfortable, to be honest, but was certainly not masculine enough in his opinion. He stretched his left arm and rotated his shoulder, testing the limits of his would-be-fatal wound. Were it not for the tenderness and some slight pain with movement, he would scarcely believe that he had nearly died. Farin extended the fingers of his good arm to the back of his shoulder and found the skin where he had been struck neatly closed. The young covenal could not even make out the lines of a scar.

"How did you—"

"Hush Farin... I know you do not understand our ways fully, but you will. Walk with me to the Illuallarii."

Farin and Narissa made their way from the Æthian healing ward into the general enclave. The structure was breathtaking. Orbs of some incandescent energy were suspended in the air by nothing visible to the man's gaze, and gave off a clear light to illuminate the halls in the day and in the evening. Like the room he had woken in, the entire structure seemed to be grown from within the trees, which to his natural mind was impossible. The same flowers and vines continued to grow all over the roof of the building, creating an atmosphere of solace.

"How are these buildings formed m'lady? I saw some images but I cannot fully understand how this came to be."

"I will show you once we have departed, Farin." The two left the Æthian enclave and made their way toward the Illuallarii, Farin taking in deep breaths of the crisp air and drinking in the scents of the vast diversity of flora that surrounded him. Several elves that saw Farin stopped and nodded politely, while others raised their eyebrows and continued on their way. None, however, showed anything more than mild curiosity.

Narissa touched Farin's hand and pointed toward a young tree growing nearby. The mismatched pair stepped from the main pathway and approached the tree. Narissa smiled at Farin, and then knelt beside the tree, lowering her face toward the trunk and beginning to sing in a language that clearly was not even elven. Farin blinked as he saw the tree grow before his eyes. The thin trunk began to thicken, the limbs appeared to strengthen, and the leaves grew slightly larger and began to fill more of the branches as this young tree seemed to take breath for the first time. Then the song changed slightly. From within the trunk itself, a small object began to form and grow from the tree until the small wooden shape fell into Narissa's open hand. Then the 'wound', if one could call it that, simply healed over as the young tree stood strengthened. Narissa took the beautiful thin object and handed it to Farin.

"What is it? It is beautiful."

"It is but a small flute that will mimic the calling of the *aethia`lyys*. That was the treesong. I am not nearly as strong in its use as the *Essen`drill* are, but all elves command some level of proficiency in the treesong. This is how Avalide was grown. We strengthen the trees and they in turn allow us to be embraced in their strong branches as we shape our structures with care and careful timing so that we never harm the trees who have agreed to let us live among them. Do you understand now?"

Farin nodded hesitantly as they returned to the path and continued on toward the Illuallarii. Farin placed the small flute to his lips and blew lightly. His heart clenched at the sheer beauty of the resulting song. Again, a little more confidently, he blew the whistle, and above him he could hear several other similar calls respond to him. Try as he might, he could not see anything and thus he wondered if this were just another part of the magic within the flute.

"The *aethia`lyys* cannot be seen in the light of the day or in the darkness of the night. Only when the sun is setting or rising in that transitional period between both night and day can the splendor of the shadow lark be seen. We are here now, Farin. What you are about to see has never been witnessed by anyone other than creatures of the fae. You may not understand what will be before you, but simply watch with your eyes to see and try to watch with your senses to understand."

The two crossed a wondrous bridge that appeared to connect to nothing. It was just empty space. Yet, Farin did as Narissa suggested, and tried to quiet his natural mind, letting his emotions and feelings stretch out curiously. There, on the fringes of his vision, shimmered something like a building but Farin could not make out any details other than the fact that there was in reality something at the end of the bridge that could not be easily seen.

Approaching what looked to be the main entrance, Farin paused as the massive doors began to swing open without assistance. He followed Narissa into the odd structure, still not sure of his footing as much of the place appeared insubstantial and part of his linear mind refused to believe he would do anything other than fall through the floor. Suddenly, there stood before him a creature seemingly made of nothing more than air, yet who was still able to maintain a certain level of permanence, apparently at will.

"How can we serve you, Narissa," Jerarin asked the elegant druid.

"I have come to show young Farin the histories of Caliyon, beginning with the dream records of the Sar`Eth`Deim. It is time the humans began to understand what they have long misunderstood."

The air elemental looked toward Farin and seemed to study him for a moment. A brief moment of realization dawned in his eyes as he turned toward Narissa again. "This one is marked as well as linked with the Lightbringer."

"Yes I know, and I have told him much the same, yet we mustn't inundate him with too much information. His road is long and the key to his success will be preparedness through knowledge. Please take us to the histories, Jararin."

"Of course, Narissa. If you and the Redeemed Guardian would please follow me I will take you there now." Farin took pause as this unusual title was given to him yet again. Narissa had worded it slightly differently if he recalled, but essentially the two mentioned the same thing about him. Marked... linked... redeemed... guardian... the very thought that his life was not in his control but suspended by some sort of invisible set of scales disturbed him greatly. How could anyone know for certain what the future would bring? This was not rational or even plausible... was it? He stopped suddenly and placed his left hand around his temples trying to massage away the still-lingering headache.

"How can all this be? You mean to tell me that my life is predestined? How can anyone know for certain what the future will bring? I have choices. I am Farin Guilian of Lorenth, not some redeemed and marked man twisted around the fate of this Lightbringer you speak of. What if I choose to ignore all that you both are saying and wander out into the forest, stumbling on my own way back to Lorenth? I cannot simply believe that my life hangs in some sort of balance that will determine my every step!"

Narissa looked back toward Farin with a deep compassion in her eyes while Jerarin glided back to him and answered. "It is not completely how you think, Farin. Prophecy never lies, yet those who are under its guidance do indeed have the power of choice. But it is in the choices that you make that the prophecy will be fulfilled. You may attempt to change the prophecy through your choices. Sometimes the thread of prophecy will shift to reflect your choices, but then you must also understand that a true prophecy will often account for your attempts to deviate from what was established and thus again you would have fulfilled prophecy. Think of it not as a leash that pulls you forward, but a mirror that is simply reflecting what you choose to do. You humans normally remember what was passed, while we elementals simply study and observe what is yet to be done, nothing more."

Farin stood wrestling with what Jerarin was saying, trying to find the breach in logic. Yet, for some reason he found himself accepting these words as truth. He figured that his ignorance was simply an obstacle that would need to be overcome, and perhaps here, in this library of sorts, he would find more answers to all his questions.

Two other creatures of air similar to Jerarin appeared holding various volumes and two slim rolls of something that resembled parchment. Jerarin nodded and thanked them, took up the materials then laid them out on what appeared to be a table made of the same insubstantial matter as the walls around him. Farin kept trying to see with his senses, but it was simply too difficult for him and at best he could only discern vague shapes.

"Why are these all written in common? I would have thought they would be in a script I could not understand."

Narissa answered, "We fae chose to learn your tongue because it is a simple language. It is easy to transcribe and it provided a means to facilitate communication with all races. Please sit Farin, I will show you words of the past. Words that will help you understand the importance of your race, the Lightbringer, and the shadow of corruption that is threatening to consume Caliyon. Open your eyes and see plainly. Open your mind and believe."

XI

The men of Lorenth were camped outside of Falstad once again when Dean finally caught up with the main body of troops that had retreated by Commander Barros' decree. Farin and his meddling border guards would answer for this breach in the chain of command. Farin likely would not have lasted the night with that wound he sustained—that thought made Dean smile slightly, until his dream recollections refuted that faint hope.

These elves were indeed powerful and possessed a knowledge that he must learn. How could they do those wondrous things? The trees, the air, even the water was under their command, and for all their planning and efforts they might as well have not even been there. He must keep reaching out to that awareness deep within. When he felt that elf with the staff summon the wind against him, he was party afraid, yet partly fascinated because he was able to brace himself as a result of his heightened awareness. With practice and experimentation he wondered what even he could be capable of.

What he was not counting on, however, was the perimeter defense established by the honor guard and the border detail. As Dean approached the sentries, they did not raise their lances or swords to admit the seneschal into the camp.

"What is the meaning of this!" exclaimed Dean.

"We have been instructed not to grant you admittance into the camp, Seneschal—Commander Barros' orders. It would be best for all of us if you simply returned to Lorenth and took this issue up with the priest-king and the council." There was no hesitation or fear in the soldier's voice as he delivered his message clearly and with conviction. Dean raged inside, but instead of exchanging futile words with the soldiers, which would do no good, he decided to make haste to the city and perhaps sway the council first before Arimas caught wind of this ordeal. Just as he prepared to leave, he felt eyes on him again. Obviously there were people watching him being turned away by the sentries, but this was somehow different. It was not the same feeling he had when Arimas walked into the same room, but it was similar and it gave him pause. He immediately locked on to the eyes of Commander Barros who likewise was staring intently at him with a defiant challenge in his gaze. Farin trained his pets well.

Dean returned the glare as he turned his steed around from the sentries and circumvented the camp on his way along the main road back to Lorenth. If there wasn't to be a war with the Dark Wood, or the Illu-something-or-other that the elf mentioned, then perhaps it was time to pull his alliances within Lorenth and force a new order upon the city. Time was his issue now. Before he arrived at the camp, he had crossed paths with Otto and Dhax, the only Drucharii to survive the complete disaster at the river. They were now well on their way back to the guild. He would need to speak with Dhax and the other Drucharii again soon to determine the best way to infiltrate the city while at the same time, drawing those loyal to him from within to support the initiative. Change was coming, whether or not Arimas was ready for it.

* * *

News of the dragons, and of Arimas' visit with the Captain of the Guard and the covenal, began to spread like plainsfire across the townships. Many listened with keen interest as the rumors of civil instability within the leadership of Lorenth met their ears. Some could not accept that the seneschal could be implicated in this ordeal, yet, when the official word came to them from their local town watch, there was little room to doubt. Trouble had begun to fall upon Lorenth and the priest-king was demanding loyalty from all who called Lorenth home. In the distant townships, loyalty was not in question. Arimas had ensured the safety and provision of all the townships over the years, never increasing the quarterly tributes of goods back to Lorenth, and giving all those who helped build their towns a chance to prosper and live in peace under the protection that Lorenth provided.

It wasn't until the town watch approached the townships closer to Lorenth that some began to choose exile over death. For several hours after the initial news was broken, no one would openly admit to being disloyal, but after the town watch had departed and ensured that everyone knew that no harm would come to those who chose exile willfully, several families began to pack up their belongings, loading up their carts with as much as they could carry including tools, provisions, and even salvaging some parts of their existing homes with the hope of making the process of rebuilding easier.

As one family openly declared their choice for exile, eventually others became bold enough to follow until several families from townships all over Lorenth, including Reiys, Newhaven, Larriot, Bonnin, and even Montague—previously thought to be completely loyal to Arimas—began their preparations to head south.

Arimas was shocked that Dean's insidious poison had spread so far, and he began to fear what he would encounter upon his arrival back in Lorenth. He had made the choice not to return directly to Lorenth in favor of helping to spread his new decree personally to some of the southern townships while Erikk and Breden, the Captain of Coren who had attended the officer's meeting the day earlier, began passing the decree to the north and the west. Arimas was no fool. He began to recognize the pattern that was presenting itself to him the closer he got to Lorenth. Dean's influence would likely be the greatest inside Lorenth itself and if he were not careful, he could very likely be walking into his own exile, and perhaps death.

As he left the southern township of Montague, the closest of the townships to the city, he knew that he could not simply wander back into Lorenth with only his four royal guards and thus, his decision to seek out Covenal Chase Harman of the southern border detail, who made his home in the southernmost township of Dunnham, could produce some much needed aid. Although he considered moving east toward Rallorn and Newhaven, time was becoming critical so he decided to adhere to his original plan of making Dunnham his final stop before returning to Lorenth. Covenal Masaad or Captain Breden would likely make their way into the eastern townships on their own initiative, regardless of his own actions. Arimas' priority now was to speak with Covenal Harman, first to appraise him of the current developments and then to request his men as an escort to display strength of arms upon his return to Lorenth the following morning.

Nothing could have prepared Arimas for what was to be found in Dunnham. The morning of his arrival there, the king walked into the middle of what looked like a civil war, with the covenal and nearly half of his entire border detail fending off those who would choose exile with their families behind them.

"Arimas, we must be careful. This doesn't feel right," commented Garron, one of the royal guards, as he began to unsheathe his dual blades from his position atop his steed. Arimas nodded to his friend and to the others as Anton, Rorrick, and Dayle drew their blades as well. Arimas lightly touched *Retribution*, which was now secured loosely beside his saddle near his left hand.

When the covenal saw Arimas approaching unarmed, he turned toward his men and raised his arms in salute, crying out in a loud voice, "For the glory of Lorenth and the glory of the seneschal!"

Arimas reeled. Those who he had thought were loyal to him, the covenal and the covenal's men, were loyal to the traitor Dean. The other half of the border detail, those who did not follow their faithless commander, quickly began to rally to the side of their priest-king. Arimas nodded to his royal guards and the five dismounted and stood their ground as Arimas unlashed the restraints around *Retribution*. He hefted the handle in the grip of his strong hand and allowed the weight and power of his legendary battle maul to infuse him with the otherworldly zeal that drove fear and respect into the heart of his foes. He waved back the border detail and told his royal guards to stand down for a moment as he focused on the covenal moving to lead the charge against him.

When those loyal to Dean saw Arimas with *Retribution* in hand, several stopped in their tracks unsure as to whether they truly wanted to test their skill of arms against the legend himself. Arimas did not hesitate. With *Retribution* hanging low to his left side, almost dragging in the dirt, he closed the gap between him and Chase, leaving the lesser players in the current battle to stop and watch. Chase, blind with a rage as wild as Arimas' was controlled, lunged quickly with his blades toward the priest-king, only to find himself slicing through thin air as Arimas deftly sidestepped the traitor's blades. With the momentum that he generated with his sidestep, Arimas circled, swinging *Retribution* in an arc as he swiveled his body and smashed the weapon full into the center of Chase's chest. The sound of stone hammering through bone echoed throughout the township as the dead covenal crumpled to the ground, blood oozing freely from his slackened mouth.

"ENOUGH!" shouted Arimas with all the rage and authority he could muster. Even his royal guards were struck at the sheer amount of anger and authority that flowed through that one word. The divided border detail simply stood in shock and awe that the fight had lasted little more than five seconds... that the aging priest-king was still able to wield *Retribution* with all the skill and grace that had made him a legend. Some took in the dead body of Chase near his feet. The former covenal's entire chest was concave, sunken and depressed from the force of the killing blow, and muddled with the fluids seeping from the fatal wound. Blood continued to flow from the dead man's mouth, pooling like an unholy halo around his head. Some spectators lost their fortitude and turned away to vomit while others simply stood waiting in fear of what would happen to them now that Arimas' wrath had been incurred.

Arimas stared down all those who had stood against him mere moments before. Righteous zeal burned in his eyes as his gaze traveled from man to man.

"I see before me men of wavering integrity and loyalty. Such is NOT what Lorenth was founded upon. However," Arimas took a deep cleansing breath before continuing, "Lorenth was also not built upon the blood of our own. Do not think to deceive me, men. While I may appear to be the same Arimas you once thought you knew, I feel more alive now than I ever have, and I see things more clearly than you can imagine. I can sense your loyalty and your vile intentions now in a way that I cannot fully understand or explain.

"If you are loyal to Dean and to his cause, I give you one chance to leave my sight with your lives. I have given freedom of travel to all who leave Lorenth in peace, but after my decree is issued, any disloyalty that is routed out will be treated as treason and those so judged will suffer the same fate as Covenal Harman. If you are loyal, form up on my right, in a single rank facing me. If you choose exile, then you must leave now. You have forfeited the right to gather your belongings; however, your families will be sent out after you when you depart. They will not suffer harm and neither will you if you begin heading south now. You are never to return to these lands, for Lorenth will not offer you shelter or quarter again."

Arimas extended his senses and noticed a darkness that dwelled within several of the men before him. Many appeared to weigh their options and began to break out of their ranks and walk away from Arimas. Those that were loyal to the king did as he had asked, and formed up in a single rank. Some of the individuals from the opposing side that were either weak-minded or simply just followers chose loyalty to the crown once again, dropping their weapons and making their way to the right side to join those in the single rank facing Arimas. Trying desperately not to let the mass betrayal here in Dunnham bring emotion to his eyes as so many once-loyal soldiers made their way south, Arimas adopted a stance of indifference and waited until all the men had either begun their walk south or laid down their arms and joined those on the right. Arimas then turned to his four trusted royal guards and whispered simple directives to each of them.

"You who remain have chosen loyalty and will be remembered for doing so. For those who stood against the revolt I extend to you honor and dignity befitting your character, and to those who have laid down arms in search of forgiveness, I ask that you each take three paces forward and present yourself before me. You will be forgiven and your disloyalty will be forgotten but you must once again earn your place among the border detail that stands behind you. Thus, you will all be stripped of command and rank as you prove your loyalty from now on through your actions and not simply your words."

Several men took three paces forward as instructed. Arimas approached the nine soldiers who originally stood with Chase against their king while the royal guards formed up behind the nine and walked between the two ranks, measuring their pace with that of Arimas. Of the nine men that stood before him, his new awareness detected that familiar, vile darkness, still lurking heavily in the hearts of six of them. Knowing their hearts were still plotting against him and that they would seek to sow more discord among the border detail if he allowed them to stay, as he passed each one that was harboring darkness within, he gave of the members of his royal guard a quick look. At this signal, the indicated royal guard remained behind the individual in question, saying nothing nor alerting them to their presence. When his four guards were in position and when he was at the very end of the line in front of the sixth member in question he spoke again.

"Nine stand before me seeking forgiveness and searching for redemption under the wings of Lorenth. Only three are sincere and shall be granted forgiveness." Eyes began to widen in horror as Arimas struck down the guard in front him, *Retribution* crunching into the neck and shoulder of the soldier before him and contorting the traitor's head into an unnatural position. Arimas reclaimed *Retribution,* and allowed the body to crumple to the ground. At the same time, his four royal guards ran their triple-forged blades through the backs of the other four unsuspecting guards. Amid the strained cries of the dying four, each of whom was looking down in disbelief at the blades protruding through their chest, the last guard, who had not been executed yet, broke rank and ran toward the south with all the speed he could muster.

"Anton!" Arimas shouted. The captain of the royal guard quickly calculated the soldier's path of flight as he launched his second savage, balanced blade toward the fleeing soldier. The blade spun end-over-end four times before embedding itself in the right shoulder of the fleeing soldier, just shy of where Anton had intended to strike. The soldier yelped in pain as he fell to the ground. He tore the blade from his back, blood flowing freely from the deep wound in his shoulder, and began to crawl on hands and knees away from the golden priest-king, who stalked with a measured pace toward him, closing the gap with each long stride. Passing Anton's bloody blade, Arimas raised *Retribution* again and crushed the ankle of the fleeing soldier, stopping the frantic man in his tracks. The traitor flailed in agony, turning over on his back in the process until he finally faced Arimas, tears of fear in his eyes, and hands extended in silent pleading for mercy. Arimas knew he could not break his own decree now. He had to follow through with the sentence that this soldier had earned with his actions. Arimas swallowed his regret as the weight of his decision began settling upon him. No words were exchanged as Arimas raised *Retribution* one last time and silenced the soldier's final screams with a single blow to his chest that savagely broke several ribs, ruptured the beating heart, and collapsed the lungs before another breath escaped.

"It is done." Arimas walked back to his men, and to those final three who stood mute after witnessing the savage yet just punishment that was administered on their comrades. He picked up the second blade of Anton as he allowed the remorse to finally affect him, his righteous wrath and zeal being replaced now with compassion for those who betrayed their friends, their land, and their king.

The four royal guards cleaned their blades and sheathed them once again. Anton grabbed his second blade from Arimas, who held it with the hilt extended toward him. Placing his free hand on Arimas' shoulder as he took the blade, Anton sensed the sorrow that tore at the heart of his king and friend. He tightened his grip in a subtle gesture of empathy, which Arimas acknowledged with a nod before pulling away, leaving Anton to the task of cleaning off his second blade before sheathing it. Arimas turned away from Anton and approached the waiting men.

"Soldiers of the southern border detail, re-form in three ranks!" The remaining soldiers, including the three demoted soldiers that were still present, quickly arranged themselves into three ranks as Arimas looked them over once again. His royal guards took their places beside him, while Arimas, his left hand balancing the weight of *Retribution* gently upon his shoulder, allowed a small smile to cross his face once more.

"What is done is done. Let no one speak ill of the three among you who genuinely repented of their treachery. They will be restored and forgiven as they return to duty among you. Their commitment will be demonstrated through their actions and service to Lorenth and in time their rank will reflect the extent of their dedication and loyalty. I regret that I must now call upon each of you here to march with me back to Lorenth to secure the capital against the plots of Seneschal Dean. Whether or not your presence of arms will be required remains uncertain, but I refuse to let Lorenth fall under the calculating ways of Dean and his puppets. Let the purge of all Lorenth continue and together we shall purify our land as we transition into a new era for humanity!"

After his address was complete, the remaining border guards were tasked with the burial of the dead and the eviction of the families of those who chose exile, allowing the women and children to gather what they could manage and leave the town heading toward the south after their men. Some of the women and wives, however, were appalled that their men would choose exile over service to Arimas and pleaded with the priest-king not to be punished for the choices made by selfish men.

For the women who chose to leave their men and remain to work their fields, tend to their livestock, buy and trade with their neighbors, and provide for their sons and daughters, Arimas granted independence from their foolish mates, and allowed them their request to remain in Dunnham. A studied scan revealed no malice or treachery among those women who chose to remain and thus was his decision made. Evening came and fell upon the township of Dunnham. The innkeeper and the stable master provided rooms, food, and provisions for the horses, and the priest-king and his four royal guards enjoyed a brief evening meal together before they retired. The dawn of the day when they would return to Lorenth to deal with the conspiracies of the seneschal was fast approaching.

Arimas tossed in his sleep. The weight of command bore down upon him as misplaced feelings of guilt refused him a full night of sleep. He awoke twice, and spent hours wrestling with the events of the day. Beasts fell beneath *Retribution*, not men... not *his* men. When Arimas awoke again from his third attempt at snatching sleep, he decided it was time to rise. He moved from his bed, took a kneeling position on the cleanly swept wood floor, and, as was typical for him, he began praying and seeking guidance beneath the first rays of sunlight filtering through the open window of his room. He had no definitive answers about what he would encounter today, but he felt reasonably sure that Dean would not be back in the city as of yet. This was the third morning since the departure of the armies of Lorenth. With the number of soldiers traveling with Dean, it was likely that he would only be arriving at the forest today. Should they immediately begin returning to Lorenth, he would not expect to see anyone from the war party for at least another three days from now, giving Arimas approximately a one or two day window within which he could prepare for the return of Dean.

The innkeeper again provided food, serving up a wonderful breakfast of sharp orange cheese, fresh milk, eggs, and a subtly herbed bread that filled the tavern area below with a pleasantly distracting aroma. The five finished their meals, thanked the innkeeper for his service, and headed out to the stables where their mounts were groomed and prepared for the day long ride back to Lorenth.

The leaderless southern border detail had also presented themselves in full sets of armor for themselves and their mounts, their lances cupped in their saddles with pennants flying from the tips in the early morning breeze. Arranged in two ranks, both man and horse stood proud and faced the priest-king as they awaited their marching orders. Arimas would need to discuss with the council a suitable replacement for the covenal of the southern border detail, but until that time, he would make do with what was available. The priest-king scanned the ranks of the men looking for the dual crossed swords that would indicate a battlemaster, or the crossed blades with the crest of Lorenth above them that would indicate a commander. Although he found no commander, whom he presumed was one of the ones to head south with the other exiles, he did spot two battlemasters among the ranks and he called the men forth.

Troy C. Reeves

"Battlemaster Kalian Turron at your service, your Excellency."

"Battlemaster Ulric Morgan at your service, your Excellency."

"Good morning, men. It would be unfit for me to simply appoint a new covenal without the council's direction, especially since neither one of you have demonstrated your capabilities in the requisite commander rank for any length of time. That being said, the men need leadership and you two shall be the ones to administer it. Leaving all pride aside, which one of you is the more senior battlemaster?"

Kalian immediately looked to Ulric and nodded, "Battlemaster Morgan has served longer than I, your Excellency."

"Very well." Arimas then addressed the soldiers before him. "Battlemaster Morgan shall be acting commander of the southern border detail until such time as a suitable covenal has been found or trained. You are to respect his authority and command as you would anyone bearing the crossed swords and crest of Lorenth. Battlemaster Turron will serve as his adjutant and will also be given the respect of rank as the second-in-command. Today we march for Lorenth. We shall stop once in Montague to water the horses and replenish our supplies and then we will finish the remaining ride to the capital."

Then turning to Ulric, Arimas added, "The detail is yours to command. We leave as soon as you have your men ready."

"Yes, your Excellency." Ulric saluted the priest-king as Kalian took up his place in front of the men. With a quick command, the southern border detail shifted formation into a dual-column with the battlemaster and the acting-commander leading the procession. Arimas and the four royal guards took up the position of the vanguard and together they left the township of Dunnham, heading north toward Montague, and ultimately, Lorenth.

*   *   *

Dean rode his horse to complete exhaustion on his panicked quest to reach the gates of Lorenth. In less than two days he completed nearly the entire return trip back to the city where he would place the final wheels in motion to salvage what he could from the disastrous developments he had suffered. He didn't eat. He didn't rest. He didn't even take the time to water his mount. As he neared the final few leagues toward Lorenth, its outer wall gates clearly visible, his horse finally collapsed, sending Dean slamming into the ground with such force that his cloak tore and the skin on his legs, face, and hands was scratched deep enough to draw blood. He cursed and spat upon the horse, giving it two kicks in an effort to get it back on its feet. But, the horse was dead and would suffer his abuse no longer.

Nearing the end of the first watch of the night, Dean finally made his approach to the front gate and was greeted by a full contingent of guards, some of which he swore were men of the southern border detail led by Covenal Chase Harman, one of the few military allies he had deep within Lorenth.

"Open the gates for the seneschal! I bring urgent news for the priest-king!"

"And what would you tell me, Dean?" Arimas stepped out into the open upon the ramparts above the main gate. Dean felt sick to his stomach. This was never a part of his dreams! How could everything fall apart so completely? His men, his assassins, the plans to dispose of Arimas and his puppet council... all ruined. "Would you tell me of the treachery that you have planned, the traitorous words you have planted in my people from Reiys to Dunnham and Newhaven to Edarann? And what of Chase Harman? Would you tell me of his revolt in the south? No wait... how about the ilk you have planted all through Lorenth itself?"

This was not the same inept and aging Arimas that he had been plotting against all these years. The patriarch had that long-forgotten fire back in his eyes again—even *Retribution* was being carried where the priest's scepter had been days before.

"Do not waste your breath with an answer, Dean. There is nothing you could say now that I would be interested in hearing. Choose exile along with your followers and head south beyond the river's banks or stand where you are and bleed your lies and filth upon the stones that have long stood for truth and justice. Should your face be shown in Lorenth or in its townships you will be struck down without question. I will purge the streets of Lorenth of all that hold sway with your lies. There will be no hiding. Every building, every alley, every sewer, and every patch of tree or shrubbery will be flushed of your filth until only those loyal to Lorenth remain. Leave now and may the gods have mercy on your accursed soul!"

Torn and bruised, Dean unleashed the full power of his hate as he glared back at Arimas. Working up enough moisture in his mouth, he spat on the pavement at his feet before turning from the crossbowmen stationed upon the ramparts above and beginning his cold and lonely walk south. He knew with thanks to his ever-growing awareness that revenge would be his in time. For now, he would lay low, cultivating a position of strength once more. Vengeance will come, thought Dean as he strode forward, and one day Lorenth will fall beneath the wrath of Kaaldean.

The night went on longer than any battle Dean could remember fighting. Stumbling along the road in the dark, battling fatigue and frustration, Dean felt like giving in to the voices inside his mind and fading into the shadow of death. Following the south road toward Dunnham, he finally arrived in Montague by late in the afternoon on the following day. Though business was being conducted as usual, the sight of the bruised and bloody Dean caused those who were out among the streets to give the man a wide berth. Others tucked within their homes began to shut their doors and close their windows, wanting nothing to do with the one who had incurred the righteous anger of Arimas. Hungry and furious, Dean broke through the doors of the first set of stables he came to, which happened to belong to the town's barracks, and stole a chestnut mare. The two guards didn't even get a chance to sound an alarm before Dean ran both of them through with his gleaming blades.

Mounted once more, Dean pressed through his fatigue and rode throughout the afternoon and evening, passing by the outskirts of Dunnham and noticing several freshly dug graves near the edge of town. It wasn't until he reached the river that he started passing fellow exiles, and finally noticed just how many of them there were. Several had abandoned carts and supplies, as they couldn't manage the efforts of crossing the river. Some took the longer route around and traveled west toward the Ardun Ford were many were then able to bring their carts and horses through the shallow point in the river and into the less fertile southern plains that would eventually lead into the Stone Hills and the heated wastelands below.

It was no surprise to Dean when he at last reached Innin Lake, the last large southern body of water besides the Ardun River, and found the hosts of exiles whose same path he had been following. Arriving late in the evening to the welcoming sight of torchlight he noticed that some were camped in tents around the lake, while others blocked their carts and either slept on top of them or beneath them in the natural shade offered. Urgent whispers broke through the camp as Dean approached. Those that were still awake could scarcely believe that Dean was as injured and broken as he appeared in the firelight. Some watched wide-eyed as he passed their camps, while others nodded in welcome and greeted him with his title, showing him the honor he felt was due.

"Seneschal, come and drink m'lord, you have traveled a long ways," commented the middle-aged commander, Erran Zorn, who was now the most senior ranking officer besides Dean himself. Dean nodded his acceptance of the welcome warily, taking in the surrounding men and women as he edged his horse closer to the gathered circle. He was pleased to notice in the throng several of his younger, untrained thieves and even some of his assassins dressing their wounds, though he did not sight one Drucharii among them. Dean dismounted carefully, stiff and sore from his travels, and was about to address those around him. But, before he could speak, his knees buckled beneath him and he collapsed, losing consciousness completely.

Dean woke a couple of hours later when the clatter of the exiles bustling about with the breaking of dawn stole what little rest he may have been able to muster. Someone had dragged him into the command tent and laid him on a somewhat comfortable bed roll to rest. He felt bruised all over. Still dressed in his armor and his torn and bloodied finery, Dean massaged his temples and stretched out several of the kinks in his back before standing and exiting the command tent. The need for sleep pressed at him from all sides but proper rest would come soon enough. For now, there were things that had to be initiated first. Fatigued as he was, if there was ever to be a second stand against Arimas, it would begin with some semblance of unity and order.

"Exiles of Lorenth rally to me!" shouted Dean above all the clamor of conversation and small talk throughout the camp. Those who witnessed Dean's arrival late last night were already standing near and awaiting his greetings while those that had been sleeping began to chatter among themselves at the condition that their seneschal was in. Many stood to listen while others stopped what they were doing and moved closer to hear.

"Lorenth has scorned us for desiring a better capital, one that would embrace change and care for the needs of all. We will not be defeated like this! Our story will be heard and we will receive proper recompense for the sorrows that we have been made to endure these past few days. Where Arimas has judged you, I will not judge you. We are free people, and we shall unite as free people and build for us a place of our own with the skills and talents that we each possess. Come, my friends, and let us work together on building a new city worthy to house the visionaries that stand before me now, as united we establish a new way of life for all those who follow us."

The men and women around Dean stood and in one voice echoed their support. And thus, the work began. Many were familiar with the establishment of new settlements from their work with various border details, and the basics of industry and housing would not take them terribly long. In fact, Dean estimated that this particular settlement would develop rather quickly because there was at least ten times the number of workers here than were usually sent to establish a new settlement. These exiles also had motivation, and a wounded pride that drove them harder and faster than force ever could.

With the small pockets of trees in the area, Dean knew that forestry would not be a viable industry for the exiles. But there was stone... an abundance of whitewashed limestone and a pale green flecked granite that could be used to build residences stronger and better then the wooden housing typical of Lorenthian townships. All the prized stone went to the crown capital, the jewel of the west and the namesake of Lorenth. Dean would gather even more support as he used this additional rationale to further add to his benevolent status among the easily misled peasantry that had proved themselves as his devoted followers.

While there were many hands to make quick work, there was no initial vision for the layout of this new settlement. Dean had the soldiers limit the workers to foraging, fishing, salvaging, scavenging and hunting. Dean ordered three teams of soldiers and citizens to return to the ford in all haste to retrieve the numerous carts and supplies that were simply abandoned along the river's northern edge both to the east and to the west. Those supplies could support the people for several weeks and logistically, that amount of provisional waste this early in any new development was unacceptable.

Once the salvaging detail had been sent out, Dean also gathered several soldiers to begin an inventory and a census of all those who were present. The gathered exiles were to be organized by family and name, and were to be identified by their trade and whether or not they brought the essentials to work with, or whether they were in need of space and tools to craft once more. Dean arranged the various work assignments, dispatched his troops for the census, and left the remainder of the soldiers in charge of establishing and maintaining an acceptable level of camp discipline, at which point Dean, aware that he was nearing another collapse due to sleep deprivation, left the command to Erran and sought the comfort of his donated bedroll once more. Before retiring, though, Dean made sure that Erran had received instruction to enforce some level of camp discipline and silence while Dean then slept.

XII

$\mathcal{A}$ cool northern breeze mingled among the mid-morning rays of sunlight that splashed upon the highland fields of Elloria. The great waterfall, which began beneath the ice-crusted lake above, flowed with such magnificence as it crashed into the basin below. Most that stood before the sight of it were momentarily struck dumb with awe. Continuing to meander through the highlands, the widened river flowed gently until accelerating into the lower waterfall that lead into the Ellorian river which itself flowed around the western borders of *Illu'Dar*.

This day would be a day for all fae races to look back on with wonder. The three elves and the air elemental from Avalide were to first to arrive in the highlands, followed shortly after by the nearby Ellorian dwarves of the Ironheart and Stormgarde clans. The elves inclined their heads to the numerous dwarves of the two clans that arrived. The dwarves were captivated by the beauty of the elves and stood in awe when the air elemental materialized and introduced herself to them. The three races knew of and respected the others, but this first meeting with the various racial leaders filled each group with a sense of dignity and pride. The pathways for diplomacy and eventual alliance talks were finally open.

Throughout the afternoon, a dryad elder of the *Illu'Dar* as well as many more dwarves continued to arrive, some through mechanical engineering and others being borne on a silken wing. The Frostspire elves from the north flew into the center of the gathering, two great white eagles and a smaller blue drake that, once they had landed, shape-shifted back to their original forms, much to the awe of the dwarves who had gathered. The Hammul and Nuragg clans arrived in their rivercrafts, followed by the Bloodstone clan, who came on the backs of five massive stone elementals. The bloodstone elites and Clan Chief Orin Chorimson smiled their bearded smiles when they beheld the fascination by even the elves at their entrance as they dismounted and greeted the elves and their kinsmen.

Valeris and Cheyandra exchanged glances. Nearly all the races had appeared to attend the gathering to discuss the Tear of Deimar. All, except the dragons. The elves continued to greet and introduce themselves to the various clans of dwarves, also stopping to show their respects to the dryad elder here to represent the guardians of the forest and the dryadic coven. The elementals communicated with everyone, but maintained a very unemotional tone which initially was thought to be a lack of interest or respect until the elves explained about the nature of the elementals, and the incorruptible essence of each that made them almost perfectly neutral.

The greetings and informal introductions led them well into the early evening, until Valeris nodded to Cheyandra to begin the formalities. Choosing a large flat rock near the river's edge so that elf, dwarf, dryad and elemental alike could hear, Cheyandra channeled her essence of spirit to amplify her voice as she began to address the large gathering around her.

"History is being created in our midst today! Never before have we all gathered to discuss the veiled threat that looms before us all. May today be the start of a long-standing alliance between all fae races as together we stand in unity to repel the corruption that has long threatened to consume the lands in shadow. Tonight shall be a night of harmony and fellowship. Let us begin the evening with music and song, dance and feasting, as we all share in the uniqueness of our races. My kin from Frostspire have assured me that their stormweavers have already tasked themselves with guiding the winds to keep the following days and nights clear for us to speak without concern for the variable weather. Our official discussions shall begin at dawn."

The elves would have preferred to start the talks much earlier in the day, but Valeris had previously warned Cheyandra that dwarves demanded feasting and celebration at any gathering in order for it to be deemed worthy of their time. Bringing all these races together and immediately launching into deep discussions could be considered impolite at best, and offensive at worst. Thus, the elves came prepared to reacquaint with each other, sharing in pleasant conversation while getting to know their hopeful allies.

The evening was pleasant overall. There were several cook fires set up around the dwarven sites where the offensive smell of searing meat or fish began to nauseate some of the elves. Those who were especially bothered had to restrain their tongues and be mindful that to their knowledge, the race of elves was the only race whose peoples chose not to eat anything that was a part of the balance. To no surprise of the elves, some of the dwarves of the closer clans had also brought casks of their meads and ales, along with steins, to share their famed drink with those around them.

While the elves shared in their typical diet of simple fruits and nuts foraged from the land, the dwarves continued in their merrymaking until at long last, the fires grew dim and the conversation had lulled to several small and occasional exchanges. Aerinyyr, Tinovis, and Edarath were deeply engaged in conversation about the foundations of magic, gently debating prophecies that presented differing views about the *Trinactria* and the various implications that each belief system could potentiate.

Meanwhile, Cheyandra, Valeris, and Nyssia spoke of the dragons, each speculating at the reasoning for their absence. Nyssia was most troubled. It was no secret that she had a certain fascination for the dragons, and the fact that they had refused to send even one emissary to represent them was greatly disturbing, especially since Draevor, the dragon ambassador, had related that Valkyyrak, one of the four ancient dragons, had given his word that he, at the very least, would be present.

The elementals, not requiring food like the other races present, wandered through the small gatherings, amusing themselves by interacting with their world as they were known to often do. In many ways, the elementals were not just a part of nature and creation... they were nature. They felt the water and stone and air, each ripple, tremor and breeze, like others would feel those effects upon their skin. But, for the elementals, these sensations were internalized and brought a certain amount of peace and contentment to them. It was harmonious. It was balance.

Slowly, conversations tapered off into silence, until all was quiet and at peace. Sleep came upon the Ellorian highlands for all, and the first day of the gathering was concluded. Dawn brought eager anticipation from everyone present. With the dwarven traditions suitably upheld, all who gathered were in an open frame of mind, waiting to hear the topics for discussion. The elementals surfaced once again, ready to listen as the various dwarves, clustered together in their clans, approached the riverbank and the flat slab of rock that the elves were choosing to speak from.

"Peace upon you all and good morning friends. It is time that we begin for time is something that we may find we are running out of as the days darken." Cheyandra paused, and smiled when she heard the sound she had been hoping to hear. The dragons had sent an emissary after all. As the elves began to look to the sky, all the other races followed their lead. It wasn't just one dragon that was soaring toward the gathering, his majestic golden scales glittering in the sunlight above, but a vast host that filled the sky. One by one, the dragons of the Icecrowns began to descend softly upon the highland plains as the other fae races subconsciously began clustering closer together near the river to make room for the vast amount of scale and muscle that was approaching them. Dragons of all colors and sizes came to attend the gathering as their numbers encircled all the other races, some even landing on the opposite shore of the river to hear and be heard.

When the last of the dragons had landed, the two largest ones, followed by a third blue dragon easily as big as several of the others, began to walk toward the elves, their mighty wings folded across their backs as they moved forward. It was the large golden dragon who spoke first.

"We are the dragons of the Icecrown Summit. I am Valkyyrak. I do not lead my kin behind me nor do I make choices for any dragon. We were invited to the gathering and many had a peaked interest in this notion of a gathering of fae races. Thus, many have come of their own volition to hear what you all would have to say.

We too have information about the subject of today's discussion and will share our knowledge with you at the appointed time."

The large black dragon then began to speak. "I am Sargeron the black, guardian of the night skies and one of the three remaining ancient dragons that now stand before you. Whether you have understanding of this or not, a recent tragedy has befallen us and we ask that you not pry into the grief that is still near to our hearts. We may choose to speak of this, but it will be of our choice and not as a result of your promptings."

Finally, the blue dragon began to speak. Where the voices of Valkyyrak and Sargeron were deep, booming voices that resounded with authority and strength, the voice of the blue dragon was surprisingly feminine, although much deeper of a voice than that of the elves or the dwarves.

"I am Dalaria, mate to Valkyyrak and one of the adept dragons who have learned to master the powers of fire and ice. We have long been a solitary race, amassing our knowledge not in tomes like the elves but in the very essence of our bloodlines, passing that knowledge to every generation as we thrive and grow apart from the struggles of other races. I confess that for a time we dragonkind once thought of everyone else as a lesser race. With the impossible death of the fourth ancient dragon, we have come to learn that even we dragons are vulnerable. Ignorance is a weapon that can be used against us and thus we submit to the learning of the other fae races in search of answers that can unite us all and create a world free of the shadow that my sister Fyysara grew weary of for over a millennia."

"We are honored to have you all among us. Welcome Valkyyrak, Sargeron, and Dalaria, along with all your kin who are present and those who are not. May this be the beginning of wisdom for all the races and of a friendship built on respect and understanding," announced Cheyandra.

With the pleasantries completed, Cheyandra invited Aerinyyr the truth-sage, whose intervention and planning had made the gathering possible, to moderate the council meeting of the fae races. Aerinyyr began by extending his sincere thanks for the active participation that was shown by all the races in helping to make the gathering a success. He then invited each representative of the races present to open with introductions and any initial comments that they wanted to offer to the council.

The dragons deferred their opening remarks as they had already done as much with their magnanimous entrance. Each of the dwarven clan chiefs took longer then a considerate amount of time to embellish on their holds and fortresses, runehalls and greathalls and, of course, the quality of their crafts and their mead. The dryad representative spoke eloquently and enlightened the others about the symbiotic life bond between the dryads and their Lifetrees and the awakening of the guardians of *Illu`Dar*. Xe`Deiona also briefly touched on the other elder dryads, their elven mates, and their life bond with some of the ancient guardians that had stood since the magic of Ethoni awakened the first trees of *Illu`Dar*.

The water elementals spoke much like the air elementals did, though without the often distracting multiple-voice sentence completion that the air elementals were known for. They knew that their destinies were entwined with the other fae races but many drifted aimlessly throughout Caliyon. Few had allegiances to anyone and many lacked a sense of purpose. This meeting helped to define a sense of responsibility for the water elementals as the task of guarding the waterways and the great seas beyond against the advance of the corruption was now laid upon them.

The stone elementals had chosen to align their fate with those of the Bloodstone Clan. The lumbering giants of stone spoke little but conveyed much in the few words they chose to utter, knowing the fate of all life, both fae and human, was under the threat of the shadow. The stone elementals would walk where others dare not tread and would aid the Bloodstone dwarves and through the alliance, all others as needed.

The elves of Frostspire revealed some of their history to the gathering. They spoke with pride of the Frostspire itself, its construction, the gateways, the Eye of the North, and their libraries, housed with their own records and visions, postulates and theories, and of course all their vast research into the elemental plane of magic.

The introductions concluded with Cheyandra speaking as Matriarch about Avalide, the guilds grown from the very heart of the trees through their use and mastery of the treesong, their two magi guilds delving deeper into the knowledge of both the elemental and spiritual planes in the one, and the druidic order and the pursuits of the corporeal sphere mastery of the treesong in the other. Cheyandra concluded by introducing her friend Shandari, the Lorekeeper of Avalide, who spoke of the other air elementals who had chosen alliance with the elves in Avalide where they could learn and master the histories and prophecies of the lands and forever protect them from destruction and decay within their dual-planar Illuallarii—the pinnacle creation in Avalide, incorporating elemental and elven architecture in perfect harmony.

The rest of the gathering was driven by Aerinyyr. As he revealed his outreach to the dream that was not a dream, many were convinced that the rise of the Seed of Corruption was near, which then would implicate that the balance would bring about the Lightbringer as well. Aerinyyr shared of the call of the Tear, the silence of the dream and the dreamers of Avalide, as well as the prophecies that were required to be fulfilled to prevent the balance from shifting yet again. Many could not reconcile this last point. When the dragons told of the assassin that had wandered into the Icecrowns and spoke of Seneschal Dean instead of Arimas, and then when Sargeron added the back story on who Dean was and his function within human society, the popular thought was to simply attack the humans now to rid the lands of Dean before he could cast the world in shadow.

Aerinyyr then detailed the obligations of prophecy and its weight on the balance. Many believed in the prophecies but thought that they could be changed if key events were also changed. What Aerinyyr taught conflicted with that rationale. If a viable thread of prophecy were critically altered, then not only the balance would be shifted but potentially a ripple through creation would occur in order to re-establish the thread of prophecy within the current reality. Sometimes, the simplest changes involved only a delay in the timeline of the prophecy. Those delays would then result in a greater force upon the new thread of prophecy to ensure its fulfillment. This could potentially sway the balance even more as a result of the initial compensation effect and was the main reason why they could not kill Dean now, before his part in the prophecy was completed.

Many started to accept this thinking, but there were still doubts. Aerinyyr then questioned those present about the knowledge that the fae now possessed as a result of the dragons sharing Dean's name. All agreed that knowing one's enemy would be better than not knowing. When Aerinyyr again stressed that altering Dean's part in the prophecy would not eliminate the Seed of Corruption, but merely force the prophecy to reassign a new focal point who would grow to become the harbinger of the shadow, the others finally understood. Dean was a known variable and could be better watched and tracked by those who sought to stop him.

Evening brought about the abrupt end to discussions once again. Although the merrymaking and feasting was not nearly as elaborate or boisterous as the night before, possibly because dragons surrounded every camp and open patch of ground around the highlands, the dwarves still found ways to celebrate, eat and drink until late in the evening when sleep finally brought calm over the gathering once more.

For the last two days, Aerinyyr had been troubled but could not venture into his truesight to determine if there was any reason for his inner caution. He has passed on his concerns to Cheyandra and even she confirmed that something felt amiss. Though time never held sway over the elves, the elves felt pressured to conclude this meeting and return to the forests. Now that the camp was quiet, Aerinyyr closed his eyes, venturing into his truesight and extending his vision south toward the *Illu'Dar* and west toward the human lands. He saw heightened activity in Avalide and felt strong residual effects along the river telling him that the druids had been active today. The pang of death hit him deep in the chest as he noticed several dead human bodies on the western banks of the river. There was one other body farther away from the rest, regally dressed. Extending his vision farther west, he discovered a new human settlement being founded. On the outskirts, a much larger group of armed soldiers were camping for the evening. Whether they were regrouping for an attack or retreating from the forest wasn't clear but there were answers that had to be obtained. This gathering couldn't conclude fast enough for Aerinyyr. He opened his eyes and turned toward Cheyandra again.

"There is trouble in the west. A large force of humans rest less than a day from the western border and six humans lay dead near the river's edge. Avalide also bustles with activity. This gathering must draw to a close."

"Patience Aerinyyr. Much was accomplished today and I fully anticipate our talks to be concluded early tomorrow. Rest my friend. There is nothing we can accomplish from here right now. Tomorrow we will return to Avalide."

The morning held more discussions about lesser matters of importance. Many new ideas were raised, opportunities to share knowledge and open trade were mentioned, and in regards to the prophecies, there was a sense of agreement and unity at long last. The one major decision of the gathering was that Dean would not be eliminated by force but would be left to navigate through the prophecies while the fae began to seek out and protect the line of the Lightbringer who also would need to be preserved to prevent altering from the opposing side of prophecy. For, once Dean became the hand of the shadow, if he could eliminate the Lightbringer chosen to stand to represent the other side of the balance, Dean could force the threads of prophecy to reassign a new Lightbringer and prolong his unquestioned reign with the shadows. If Dean could perpetually extinguish the line of the Lightbringer then prophecy would hold Dean in a pseudo-state of immortality as each new thread that was cut would search for a new child of prophecy in its effort to fulfill destiny.

Realization dawned upon several faces in the crowd as Aerinyyr made clear the impact of prophecy. The line of the Lightbringer must be preserved and prepared if he was to face Dean at the peak of his corruption. The ominous task set before them all was to isolate and nurture the Lightbringer before the Seed of Corruption could cut the thread of prophecy binding itself to his life. The humans under the leadership of Arimas would need to be brought into contact and potential alliance with the fae creature before the rise in power of Dean was complete... so many tasks, so much uncertainty, and so little time according to the timeline of men. Where the dwarves, the shortest living fae race, lived on average three hundred to four hundred years compared to men, if Dean was truly the Seed of Corruption, then his ascension would be swift and his wrath would be fierce. Time rarely served the line of fae races and in this matter once again, time would be pitted against them.

As the sun began to reach midday, the first gathering of the fae races came to an end. While there were no confirmed plans to hold another meeting anytime soon, all those present saw the need and the benefit of combining thoughts and ideas. Even the dragons found some of the achievements of the dwarves and the elves fascinating. One thing of particular interest prompted discussions among many of those present. When the dwarves overheard how the two elven races were able to instantly communicate and coordinate activities through their reflecting pools, the idea was suggested that more of these instruments be created to better serve the alliance of fae races and expedite communications across the land.

While the elves saw wisdom in the plan, they ended the conversation with cryptic responses that indicated the matter would be discussed at a later date and would be given serious consideration. Satisfied with the response, the dwarves, as was predicted, were invited back to the greathall of clan chief Edon Thunderhammer of the Stormgarde clan to resume the real feasting that many looked forward to every other year during Runeveld. The elves graciously declined the invitation, but did make mention that experiencing a true dwarven feast would be a matter of some great interest.

Thus parted the dwarves, starting on their way toward the northeast parts of Elloria, where the fertile highland plains and the rocky peaks housed two of the clans. The Frostspire elves said their farewells to their southern elven kin, the dragons and the others, taking their flight forms once again and preparing to head to the skies above. When Dalaria saw Nyssia begin to change into her form of the blue drake she gasped. Nyssia failed to ponder the implication of her shape change in front of the dragons. She immediately began to shift back when Dalaria stopped her.

"Peace, our sister! How is it that you can change into a being so near to us that you could be considered kin?"

Nyssia continued with her shift back into elven form and replied, "Forgive me if I have offended you, Dalaria. Elven ambassadors are masters in their sphere of magic and also skilled in the ways of shape-shifting. When we first learned of your existence generations ago and sent Draevor to greet you, I used my abilities of farsight to behold your splendor. Since that day I have found yours to be the most elegant and powerful of forms that I could endeavor to model. It took me several weeks of practice before I could finally mold myself into your form, paying careful detail to tail and wing dimensions, talons and head shape and horn pattern. I could not do scales properly so I chose a simpler skin type. But if this offends you then I will not continue in this any longer.

Dalaria appeared to be communicating with the other dragons, although none of them were actually vocalizing anything. She looked from one to another, often nodding her head before she returned her gaze to Nyssia. "We find it both amusing and an honor that you have chosen our shape to replicate, and we have no quarrel with you for doing so. This shape-shifting talent of yours is quite interesting to us, Nyssia. We may indeed have some things to discuss with you at length when time is more accommodating. For now, go in peace and know that the dragons hold you in high esteem, elves of the north. We shall speak with you again soon."

With those final words, Valkyyrak let loose a mighty roar, stopping all the communication around the highlands as the dragons unfurled their strong and sinewy wings. Like a rainbow ascending into the evening sky, the dragons of the Icecrowns took to the air on their flight back toward the northwest, well past Frostspire and deep into the frozen north wherein lay their lairs and the summit that they claimed as their own. The elves of Avalide and Frostspire watched the elementals of air and water begin to dissipate. The dwarves declined their assistance in the unnatural travel arrangements, preferring to take the long way home after their merrymaking in the Thunderhammer Greathall. The dryad elder also began her way back to the forests, sprinting across the fertile plain on bare skinned feet as if moving with the wind in its gentle, rhythmic dance.

Smiling to each other once again, Valeris and Cheyandra touched fingers to lips, inclining their heads before both the three

Dsa`carii* and the three *Illu`darii shape-shifted and left the highland plains of Elloria behind them, ready to convey the successes of the gathering to all those in their cities as they prepared for the next major event in the timeline—the negotiations with the humans and the identification and protection of the Lightbringer.

XIII

*U*nder the guidance and watchful gazes of the healer and the elemental, Farin spent days in the Illuallarii reading scroll after scroll of history and prophecy. He would never have imagined that such a vast amount of knowledge could be contained in one place. The libraries of Lorenth were not half as impressive when compared to the collections of the Illuallarii. Even though much of what he read today competed with his own perceptions of truth and reality, he came to an eventual acceptance when presented with the diverse amount of information that all appeared to interconnect. But still, prophecy felt unnatural to him. Farin continued to struggle with the feeling that his steps were being led by some invisible puppeteer, fate, destiny or whatever those around him chose to call it.

Farin feared that his reading was troubling his hosts or at the very least, wasting their time, but they simply smiled and encouraged him to continue. Farin idly thought that if he were immortal like the elves, a few hours compared to forever was not much time at all. In any event, he knew he was privileged to be the first human ever to see the elven city and share in the knowledge of the ages before him. He finished the last of the scrolls that had been placed before him, which, if he understood the words correctly, was not a true dream record. Rather, it was a compilation of several individual pieces of prophecy from dreamers, and women of other areas, that all referred to the same, or very similar, event. The prophecy of the tear was something that stirred him in the very center of his being. The thought of what this corruption would be capable of and what terrible responsibility would inevitably fall on the Lightbringer was a weight upon Farin and he knew not why.

He then recalled the air elemental's greeting to him earlier as well as the titles that Narissa addressed him by. Probing the two about these titles, he began to inquire about the prophecies that mentioned the redeemed one, or the marked one, or the guardian of the light. Jerarin went to fetch the applicable scrolls, but Narissa stopped him.

"Farin, there are some things that you must accept in faith. Seek not these prophecies. I would have you learn and grow, not stand in fear under the shadow of our arcane wordings. Even as we elves have spent much time in study of the prophecies, there are many that are vague and may hold different meanings in the light of the truth once fulfilled. Rest your mind Farin."

Farin was an officer, a leader of men, and a man who needed to know what lay in his path before committing himself to a certain course of action. Yet, when standing before the wisdom and beauty of this elven healer, he could only nod in acquiescence and let the matter drop.

Hunger had begun to affect Farin now and his eyes felt dry and sore from all the time he had spent pouring over all of the scrolls. He indicated the same to his hosts, thanking Jerarin for the pleasure of making his acquaintance and for the assistance while in the Illuallarii. Jerarin offered what appeared to be a smile of sorts, nodded to Narissa and then began to restock the prophecies that he had been reading back into their assigned place in the shifting walls of the Illuallarii.

Narissa and Farin left the dual-planed structure the same way they entered, Farin stopping this time to watch the massive gates close independently on their silent hinges before following the elf maiden. Taking in the long ribbon of golden hair that hung down Narissa's back in long gentle curls, and the delicate shape of her very desirable figure, Farin felt himself moved to bravery.

"M'lady, might I ask how old you are? I understand that you showed me memories in my mind that were centuries old and, that you are a part of those memories. I mean no disrespect by asking you this, I am simply curious."

"Elves do not concern themselves with age as time does not hold sway over us, Farin. We live in longer groups of time that we refer to as age cycles. I myself have recently entered my fourth age cycle. I know this means little to you but think of it as you would think of your children. The first age cycle is a time of learning and growing. For you this may be your 'childhood' I believe you call it. For us, our first age is often a lengthy one for it is in this time that we grow considerably, both physically and mentally, experimenting with our newly discovered skills in the treesong and in the planar masteries before choosing a particular focus.

The second age cycle is typically one of mastery and maturation, much like your time of adolescence. We practice and refine our disciplines, we assume roles of responsibility, and often times, we spend much time in research of both the prophecies and the wisdom of the ages, as well as researching our field of study." Turning from the bridge in front of the Illuallarii, Narissa extended her hand in front of Farin, motioning for them to continue walking toward the celebration hall where they would partake of the midday meal. They continued on together while Narissa added more to her explanation.

"The third age cycle is when many elves begin considering the choice of a mate and the raising of younglings. As you can appreciate, this age can be rather time consuming. Elves, as you are starting to understand, strive for harmony in all life, and the sanctity and development of our young is a matter of honor and pride among us. Time is not a factor for us as we impart wisdom upon the next generation, leading and guiding, channeling and shaping their young minds and ambitions."

"Do you have a mate and younglings?" Farin interjected somewhat nervously, realizing too late that his words may convey more than he was intending to.

Narissa smiled yet again, "Yes, my mate is one of the Æthian diviners and together we have three younglings who even now are about to enter their third age cycle. Aaira has chosen the way of the Æthanon like her father and I, and Tavendia was honored to be accepted among the *Essen`dril.* Gildar followed his closest friend Talonyyr into the glades to serve as a mistrunner. Our line has been blessed and has brought much honor to our name. Have you a mate and younglings of your own?"

The unexpected question caught Farin off guard. He immediately thought of Jesslyn and their frequent whisperings in the late of night about how many children they had planned on having together: two boys to carry on Farin's line, and a daughter who would have Jesslyn's gray eyes. The memory hit so fast that Farin was forced again to smother the emotion threatening to rise. Narissa read Farin's face as if it were no more than a scroll in the Illuallarii and could see how her question pained him. Before she could offer comfort to Farin he looked back at her as they were nearing the celebration hall and with strength in his voice he answered her.

"There was a time when I had found love in the arms of a woman. We had talked of children and marriage, her father had given his blessing and welcomed me into his family as a son, but fate was cruel and robbed me of her. I believe that it was Dean, who had worked to possess the woman I loved, that extended his cruelty to her innocent spirit and poisoned her with some foul herb that sent her into a fitful sleep from which she never woke from." Farin swallowed, scrubbing the palm of his left hand against the days-old beard that shadowed the lower half of his face. "She was gone so quickly... a part of me died alongside her that day."

Compassion showed strongly on Narissa's face, and she gently shook her head in sympathy when Farin paused. Narissa looked into Farin's eyes as she responded to his grief. "Death is a weapon sharper than anything forged in the flame. I cannot remember how you feel, for death has not plagued elven kind for a long time, not since two of the guardians died, and with them, their elder dryad and the dryad's elven mate. Such sorrow has long passed from thought but not memory... yet the pain has become distant and now is but a shadow of what we once felt in its presence. I wish you happiness again, Farin." Narissa paused all of a sudden, her eyes beginning to widen slightly. "Have you seen your love since she passed into shadow?"

Thinking this to be a rather odd question he simply answered no, until she prodded further. Farin grew anxious at her intensity and then stopped himself as he thought about his answer.

"Seen her? In my waking hours... no, but long have I remembered her face, her kiss, even the scent of lilac and roses that perfumed her hair. My last visit of the dream that I spoke with you about... I remember, I saw her then, when I was struck down by Dean during his transformation into Kaaldean. I can only imagine that if I fall beneath Dean like my dream has told me, in the afterlife I will be reunited with Jesslyn. This gives me some measure of peace."

Narissa pondered his words carefully, knowing in her soul some of the threads of relevant prophecies that Farin was now alluding to without his awareness. Those she would keep secret, for their interpretation, whether true or false, could so drastically alter this fine thread of prophecy that sharing her knowledge of them would do more harm than good.

"Then take comfort in that Farin. I do not believe that you will meet your end like you fear. There is much that is uncertain about your destiny, and much will depend on you and your choices. You are not being led blindly, remember. The mirror of prophecy shows us a glimpse of what will be but it does not interpret that glimpse for us, thus for many, its meaning is relative and subject to individual interpretation."

Farin offered her a weak smile as they continued into the celebration hall where Farin was invited to partake in the midday meal. When Farin unsuccessfully searched the table for the main course, Narissa told him quietly that the elven role as creatures of the balance and protectors of all life prevented them from killing animals for meat. They were foragers of the land and never found difficulty being able to meet their nutritional needs simply and plainly. For Farin, this indeed was different, but a pleasant change nonetheless. He ate until he was full.

*   *   *

It was still early in the afternoon when Cheyandra, Aerinyyr, Edarath, and Shandari descended beneath the rich, deep foliage of *Illu`Dar*. Eager to report on the council activities to the Æthanon and Ætheron enclaves, the Magister took his leave after shifting back into elven form. Shandari also took her leave, heading to the Illuallarii to relax among the various tomes and scrolls. Of all the topics housed in the Illuallarii, she preferred the dream records. There was a fascination about the sleeping mind of the elves that compelled her to study the minds and memories, finding truths buried within the dream records and understanding, perhaps even more completely than the elves sometimes, the finer implications of various threads of prophecy.

The Matriarch and the ever wise truth-sage returned to the Matriarchal Commune where Evianna was awaiting her arrival.

"*Eth aloni tul`venarii* Matriarch."

"*Ashanda eth reiis* Evianna. Tell me of the humans that approached the western border."

Evianna looked up in surprise before shifting her gaze to the truth-sage beside her. "I have much to report, Matriarch. While you were away the humans marched out to our western border with propositions of peace, yet within their midst the Seed of Corruption sought to start a war with us." The Matriarch raised her eyebrows at this last comment while Aerinyyr began to close his eyes, shifting his vision and entering his truesight as he began to search for something unknown to Evianna or to Cheyandra.

"He calls himself Seneschal Dean and he had sent dark riders several days in advance to prepare to interrupt the peace talks. Talonyyr Silverleaf brought word of their presence and I told him to still the forest and watch from the shadows while I sought out the arch mage in the Ætheron enclave to scout the west with his farsight to confirm reports from some sprites about the larger group of approaching humans.

"I rallied the defenses, had the wardens and mistrunners watching the riverbanks while I summoned the aid of several Ætheron and Æthanon, as well as Bethalyyn Leafwhisperer and Narissa Amberdawn. The darkness of this Dean was so plain to see as he mixed words with us, promising peace and offering insincere apologies while standing in front of a host of men deceived and not evil themselves. The seven dark riders then tried to implicate us by opening hostilities on one of their own, a nobleman with authority to represent their capital city."

Aerinyyr snapped out of his truesight with great haste and interrupted her. "Did he exude a clear mark of light, Evianna? Was that Arimas that died on the western bank of the Ellorian?"

"I cannot say for certain, Truth-Sage, but there is one who can answer that question for you. There is a human among us even now. One also linked with the Lightbringer, but whose fate is shrouded. Narissa has been tending to him as he was injured when attempting to stop the chaos that Dean was creating. He nearly passed into the shadow himself."

The Matriarch now addressed Evianna with authority. "We must speak with him Evianna. This was not expected. I am not disappointed with your choices; I am just... surprised that you would bring him among us without counseling me. In any event, your quick response to this uncertainty is well appreciated Evianna. I know my trust in you as steward was well placed. Please lead us to this human."

Turning toward the entrance of the Matriarchal Commune, Evianna began to lead Cheyandra and Aerinyyr toward the Æthanon healing circles but stopped abruptly as the healer in question walked in, accompanied by a rather fair looking human male dressed in naught but a white linen robe laced at the back to aid the Æthanon in attending to his wound.

"That will not be necessary Evianna. *Eth aloni tul`venarii* Matriarch. I would have come sooner but I have been aiding our guest in his healing process as well as sharing with him some of the histories. May I present to you Farin, the redeemed and guardian of the light."

Cheyandra gave a questioning look back to Narissa when she heard the title addressed to Farin. Narissa nodded in affirmation. Cheyandra looked at Farin then returned her gaze to the healer. "*Ashanda eth reiis,* Narissa. And blessings of life upon you as well, Farin. It is an unexpected honor to have you among us. I am Cheyandra Silversong, Matriarch of the *Illu`darii,* and this is Aerinyyr Riftseeker, my truth-sage and guide and one of our most powerful diviners and arcanists. I would be honored to have both of you come in, sit and speak openly with us."

Farin had no desire to do anything other then speak with the elven nobility. Nobility may not have been the best word but the titles they called themselves by must be akin to that of king and queen and he would afford them no lesser amount of dignity and respect than were they indeed nobles of that station.

"I am honored to be among you all. Forgive me if my words or address offends any of you. I am unfamiliar with elven ways and I would not want my ignorance to ill represent me." Even Aerinyyr seemed slightly impressed with the manners of this barbarian from the west. Perhaps there was indeed hope for this race after all.

The three elves and the lone human spoke at length for several hours. Some of the conversations between Narissa and Farin were repeated for the benefit of Aerinyyr and the Matriarch. Farin also began to share what he had begun to learn from the scrolls and prophecies. He showed remarkable insight already thanks to the tremendous amount of knowledge that he had been given and was able to understand the fundamentals of the elven race as it was presented to him.

The Matriarch shared some of the key points from the gathering, as well. Farin was dumbfounded when Cheyandra spoke of the various clans of dwarves, the elementals of water and stone who made an appearance, as well as those of air, and of course the vast host of dragons that arrived late but where key participants in the discussions. Farin tried his best to absorb every word. Such knowledge was intoxicating. Although he had tried to spend some time in the libraries of Lorenth, that was nothing like the information he was learning right now. Arimas needed to know these things even more than him.

That thought immediately struck a deep chord within him. While he had been healing under the watchful care of the elves, his soldiers and the armies of Lorenth had returned to the capital and would likely be relating to Arimas the death of Counselor Nolan and of the covenal of the eastern border detail. Farin had been left for dead on the river's edge. While the retreat was well ordered, again, there was to be no recovery of the dead at the hands of the Dark Wood… well, that was what he thought the impression would be. It wasn't until all the conversation had ceased and three pairs of elven eyes were locked on his face that he stirred out of his musings.

"What troubles you Farin? I see great concern in your eyes." Aerinyyr certainly was a truth-sage if his interpretation of the title was correct. This elf seemed to have such a deep connection with all life around him that falsehoods and truths were laid bare at his feet.

"I am sorry, honored ones, I was thinking about Lorenth and about Arimas. It is likely that I will be thought dead and that news will be brought before Arimas soon. The sights that I have seen and the knowledge that I have gained over the last few days are too wondrous to keep to myself; of all men, Arimas is the one who needs to know what I now know. For the last few weeks we were afraid of the forests. Many, including myself until recently, called this place the Dark Wood. I now understand the pain that your guardians must have felt when we in our ignorance thought to harvest the great trees. These forests are not dark... they celebrate life of all kinds and the magic that permeates the very air is intoxicating to one such as me.

"I am a simple soldier. Commanding men, though requiring skills unique to my position, is still a small achievement compared to the vast knowledge you all have been able to amass in your generations upon these lands. It is overwhelming to me at times when I think that the majesty of the fae races lies in patient wait for the fall and rise of men, a race untouched by magic but apparently prophesized to turn the natural order of life around and sink the creation in shadow. How do I respond to things like this? I try to keep my mind open and not see with just my eyes. There is much to learn and little time to learn it I fear, for if Dean is the monstrosity that you all believe him to be, he will press his attack upon Lorenth soon, seeking to supplant Arimas and begin the corruption in the great city itself. I feel like I must do something to help but I know not what."

Aerinyyr looked more intently toward Farin, speaking in his calm, measured voice. "I see strength in you that I have not seen before in the other humans I have observed. Your time among us is indeed coming quickly to a close, but not for the lack of desiring your company but for the very reasons that you are speaking of. For years there has been a silence pact between the fae races and the humans. Now the time for silence has passed. It is long overdue for those of the *Illu`darii* to declare peace and open up the paths of trade and diplomacy with Lorenth. I am confident that the *Dsa`carii* ambassador will also be heading to Lorenth shortly for the same reasons."

Noticing the confused look now on Farin's face, Aerinyyr added, "Those are the northern elves of the frozen wastes that specialize in the powers of ice and storm. They are much like us in culture and appearance but they focus all their efforts on their masteries of the arcane"

Cheyandra turned to Narissa and asked, "How far along is he in his healing?"

"He is responding exceptionally well to our arts, Matriarch, and I believe he could handle the journey back to Lorenth no more than three days from now."

Cheyandra acknowledged Narissa's wisdom with a respectful nod. Turning back to Farin, she spoke in quieter tones about the significance and implication of the prophecy and the preservation of the coming Lightbringer. If Dean was to be corrected by the balance, the child of prophecy would need to stand in opposition to the corruption to allow the balance to sort itself out once and for all. What was most troubling to all present, mostly Farin but including the three elves near him, was that their fate was not yet determined.

Ultimately the only guarantee was that at some point the Lightbringer and the Seed of Corruption must meet, and that the fate of Caliyon and of the balance would not be determined until that moment. Should the Lightbringer defeat Dean, the corruption would be destroyed at long last and the Sar`Eth`Deim would be restored to power once more. But, should the corruption overpower even the child of prophecy... the thought was too horrible to contemplate and by the end of the conversation, Farin knew the tremendous weight that would be placed upon Arimas and the threat from the shadow that would lurk over him and his line.

The evening meal was eaten but not enjoyed by Farin, whose movements at the banquet table were no more than mechanical. He could not stop thinking about the dream, about Dean, and about the fate that potentially loomed over all Caliyon should Dean complete his transformation into Kaaldean and unleash the shadow upon the land. In a matter of days he would travel finally. His shoulder kept improving at a rate that he would not have expected before meeting the elves, and the long ride to Lorenth should not trouble his healing by then at this rate, just as Narissa had estimated.

Narissa left him after tending to his wound following the evening meal. She had been with him all day and he assumed that it was now time for her to return to her mate and visit with her younglings. Sleep came quickly for Farin. Lost in the absolute comfort of the bedding that was provided in the healing ward, he fell asleep to the musical sounds of the *aethia`lyys*, both from his flute and from the skies above, catching a glimpse of their incandescent blue wings during the shift from dusk to night. Perfection was the only word for what he saw. These shadow larks were much bigger than he pictured them to be. Their silent wings almost floated on top of the air beneath the forest canopy while several larks broke through the patches of setting sun to soar in the skies above the tree line. Returning to Lorenth would be bittersweet. Living within the forests of *Illu`Dar* made him feel the most at home that he had felt in years.

The rest of his stay was filled with more of the same. Occasional visits to the Illuallarii to read more of the prophecies and histories and more walks with Narissa. The conversations with his healer were always the highlight of his days, even though Narissa tended to speak more cryptically each time Farin touched on subjects that she obviously did not wish to broach.

His shoulder continued to mend under the watchful care of Narissa. Each day she would infuse a tiny thread of warmth into the tissues deep within his shoulder and every day it continually felt more sure and strong until on the night before he set out from Avalide his shoulder was healed completely.

Farin woke on the final morning of his time in the elven lands more refreshed than he had felt in years. Again there were no dreams... just peace. A fresh set of clothing was folded on the floor near his bed, and a wash basin woven from trees much like the way his flute was made stood off to the corner of the room, a gentle mist rising into the morning air indicating that warm bath water awaited him inside. He stood and tested his shoulder once again. In roughly a week he was completely healed from a near-fatal wound. He shook his head in disbelief as he walked gingerly over to the wash basin and admired the superior craftsmanship. Again, there were no joints, no nails, and no braces of metal or anything that would have injured the living wood from which this piece was grown from. Its weaves were so ornate and so complete that it surprisingly did not leak but carried the water inside as if it were a thousand fingers woven together, preventing even the smallest drop of water from seeping through its cracks.

It would be pleasing to wash and don a fresh set of clothes once more. He slipped out from under the linen robe and tested the water with his hand before submerging himself within the fragrant, warm waters of the tub. He could hardly remember the last time he enjoyed a bath so much. Cleaning was done for necessity and never for sheer enjoyment in a soldier's life, but this undeserved comfort was definitely one of the most pleasurable parts of his stay among the elves.

"Your body is quite pleasing to look upon, Farin," whispered a soft gentle voice behind him. The sudden breach of his privacy made him quite self-conscious as he instinctively sat up, splashing water upon the floor and covering his choice parts with his hands as he looked over his shoulder to see the intruder. His jaw dropped. If Narissa was thought to be beautiful, then this elven maiden was beyond description. There were distinct similarities between Narissa and this elf yet for all the generations that these elves lived, this one appeared somewhat... younger. Clad in a robe much like the one that the elder *Essen`dril* wore on the river's edge last week, she smiled a smile not unlike that of Narissa, the left side of her delicate lips curling up more than the right as her deep blue eyes glittered in the morning sun. Her mischievous chuckle told him that he most definitely was blushing all over as he broke eye contact with her and looked back down into the tub.

"I am sorry for my reaction, m'lady, I am just not... um... used to having someone as... uh... beautiful as you interrupt me while I am bathing." Farin wanted to drown himself beneath the surface of the water. He couldn't even string together a complete sentence without fumbling for words. He had to overlook the beauty of these elven maidens and simply accept the fact that they existed and that ogling and bumbling for words would not be in the best interests of Lorenth.

What made matters worse was that she apparently didn't mind interrupting him, and she appeared to have no intentions of leaving. She did however move around from the back of him to his front where he could look at her without canting his head awkwardly to look over his shoulder.

"My mother sent me in her stead this morning, Farin Guilian. I have been chosen to represent Avalide as ambassador to the humans. We are to be traveling together, and I am to provide you with protection should the Seed of Corruption seek to overpower you again."

Provide *him* protection? He quickly abandoned that line of thought when he remembered the magical prowess of the elves. In many instances here in the forests of *Illu'Dar* it was the things that were not seen that posed more of an issue than that which was seen. Remembering Narissa's response about her family and the paths chosen by her offspring he was reasonably sure he knew who stood before him now.

"You must be Tavendia then. It is a pleasure to meet you, despite my delicate position at the moment. Your mother's aid to me and her welcoming of my presence here in Avalide has been a blessing that I will not soon forget and I look forward to traveling with her daughter to my home in Lorenth. I guarantee you shall be well received by Arimas, the priest-king of Lorenth, our crowning jewel of the west."

Tavendia smiled again. "You remember small details well Farin. I have come to inform you that it is time for us to begin preparing for travel. Also, there is still one more individual who wishes to speak with you before we set out. If you are finished with your bath, then please leave the water and try on these clothes. My mother commissioned them on your behalf."

Tavendia stood there waiting for him to move, but all Farin could do was sit awkwardly in the water and blush another humiliating shade of red. The elven woman chuckled once more at his hesitation. "I see that my presence here makes you feel more vulnerable than you are comfortable with, so if it pleases you, I will turn my face until you are properly garbed."

"Thank you m'lady... it's just that... I... uh... nevermind."
Tavendia openly laughed this time as she turned long enough for
Farin to exit the tub and pat himself dry with a very soft material
that he draped over his body like a towel. No sooner had he
slipped into his undergarments then Tavendia was turning back
around and assisting him with the foreign clothing that he soon
discovered had laces in places he had no idea how to maneuver.
Farin sighed and resigned himself to her help, and the process
was completed much sooner than if he had insisted on stumbling
through it alone.

"I have never seen hair over a man's body like yours, Farin. I
find it unusual yet quite pleasing indeed. These clothes were made
from some of the artisans in the southeast part of the glades. I
hope you find them comfortable and well fitting."

Farin tried once again to shrug off the comments about how
his body was pleasing to the beautiful druid in front of him as
he began testing the garments that he now wore. They felt as
strong as leather yet were as soft as the finest cloth he had seen
in Lorenth. The black pants were well fitted and would certainly
make excellent travel clothes. The boots were a pale grayish black
color, much like ash and well measured for his feet. The tunic was
laced like a robe yet felt as tight as a leather jerkin. The various
shades of green, brown and gray were quite attractive and while
being rather functional in an outdoor setting, were finely crafted
enough to also be more than acceptable when finery was needed
to address those of higher station than himself.

He felt more like a young lord than a military covenal now but
he welcomed the change in attire. The final item at the bottom of the
pile was his cloak. The hole that the bolt passed through was gone
and he could not even distinguish where the tear in the fabric was.
He fastened his gold embroidered crimson cloak around his neck and
faced Tavendia once more.

"Everything fits remarkably well m'lady. What fabric is this?
Never have I worn anything more comfortable, yet, the material
feels durable as well."

"That is ironsilk. There are spiders near the south-eastern glades
that spin this silk for use in their webs and we have found many
beneficial applications for it, including the tailoring and weaving of

various items. I am pleased that you find the clothing to your liking. Let us now head back toward the Matriarchal Commune, for there are a few points of interest that the Matriarch wishes to pass on to both of us."

Farin nodded, looking back over the room that had been home to him for the last several days before following Tavendia down the outer hall. He made his way back through the Æthanon enclave, watching the mystical shapes and lights float above him as they rose toward the spires that were fixed atop both the Æthanon and Ætheron enclaves. Together with Tavendia, Farin walked the now familiar path from the Æthian enclaves to the center of Avalide and the Matriarchal Commune. As they walked, he found Tavendia to be more spontaneous with conversation than her mother, as she led most of the casual exchanges rather than him.

Waiting for them in the Commune was Cheyandra, and another elf that Farin had not yet met. He was taller than most, very athletically built, and garbed in an odd assortment of garments that appeared to play tricks with his eyes. The most striking feature to this elf was his long silver hair. Where some elven males would tie their hair back or arrange it with various ties to keep it orderly, this elf let his long silver locks cascade across his shoulders, around his face, and down past the middle of his back. He carried several small knives, likely for throwing, two edged blades that were very slender and of medium length, and hanging beside his dark green and brown quiver which held countless thin and deadly shafts was an elegantly fashioned longbow with carefully crafted recurves. He was a dichotomy of savage brutality and elven elegance all in one. Cheyandra waved as Farin observed the typical elven greeting exchanged between Tavendia and the Matriarch before she spoke in common.

"Farin, today you leave our glades and venture west to your lands. It has been an honor to have you among us and were it not for the importance of the message you carry in your heart and the missive to your king that Tavendia carries in her hand then I would welcome you to stay longer. Tavendia is to be your keeper and our ambassador in Lorenth and as we have shown you grace, guidance, and hospitality in Avalide, I would expect the same treatment to be accorded to Tavendia when she arrives in Lorenth. Before you leave, I would introduce you to Talonyyr Silverleaf. He is the *Ryl`idohan* of the mistrunner guild and enforces the protection around the glades, serving as our eyes, and when needed, our teeth and claws."

Talonyyr nodded toward Farin before speaking. "I watched your attempt to ward off the hostilities along the border. I saw you fall by the weapons fashioned from the human kin that lurked in the shadows. I also listened to your last words to the Seed of Corruption and saw how you were prepared to embrace a victorious death. There is honor among humans Farin Guilian, and such is what I see in you. Go with the blessing of the mistrunners. You will find friends within our borders always. I have made arrangements with Alarielle Featherbow. You are to meet her down at the river's edge where we found you, and from there she will assist you with your transportation to Lorenth. Trust her words and question not her methods for she is one of the wardens of the glade and is well attuned to the rhythm of the forest, as is Tavendia." Talonyyr offered a polite smile to the druid as she inclined her head in response to his compliment.

Cheyandra and Talonyyr led Farin and Tavendia out of the commune and onto the path that would lead them to the western border of the forest. Cheyandra extended her hand and gave Tavendia an elaborately inscribed scroll sealed with a thick opaque resin into which a symbol of a great tree had been somehow inscribed. Tavendia stowed the scroll within a compartment of her earthen toned robe and bowed before the Matriarch, receiving the blessing of speed and the protection of the glades before returning to the commune. Talonyyr inclined his head to them both and then he too left toward the northern border to return to his duties.

The walk took slightly less than an hour. Arriving at the forest's edge Farin jumped slightly when several of the large treants stirred and looked down at him with curious interest. Tavendia simply smiled and began talking in that deep treesong voice that Narissa had demonstrated the other day. Tavendia's treesong sounded more complicated than her mother's, if that was even possible. It was almost like there were two or sometimes three voices speaking out of her mouth at the same time. The treants quieted and the forest once again stood still as the elven druid and the human covenal stepped into the bright sun that, until now, was hidden above the thick, green canopy of the forest. The shallow river stopped flowing suddenly to reveal a thin patch of dry ground as Tavendia whispered beside Farin, waiting until they both had crossed to the other side before allowing the river to flow freely once more.

Tavendia led Farin along the western bank of the river heading north. The sound of the crashing waterfall was off in the distance and as he looked to the river itself, he noticed that it gradually was getting deeper and slightly broader the closer it got to the waterfall. To the left of him, slightly to the northwest he noticed another elf approaching them encircled by a fair number of horses. As the elf drew nearer, he could easily make out the curvaceous figure and soft features characteristic of the female elves, though she was dressed in garments plainer than those of Talonyyr. She also was carrying something oddly shaped that reflected the sunlight tremendously. He could not discern what it was at this distance.

The horses that ran with her nickered and tossed their heads. It had been a long time since he had seen a wild horse. The free mounts were almost playful as they trotted toward him. One was different. As the elf and the horses drew closer, Farin began to recognize the drapery and the armor plating of his mount. Everything was the same except that his bit and bridle were removed.

As the elven maiden approached Tavendia and Farin, she whistled a clear long whistle and the horses came to a halt beside her. Tucked beneath her arm was all of Farin's battle dress: plate and chainmail, polished like new and cleaned of any memory of bloodstains. She stopped before Farin, and held out the armor to him.

"You must be Farin. I am Alarielle, warden of the western border." Farin nodded, relieving her of her burden as Tavendia inclined her head to the warden. "I was bidden to aid you both in your travels to Lorenth. I will not venture far from the forest but I did take the time to find several abandoned horses whose masters were either slain or chased off. Horses are magnificent beasts are they not? So strong, so swift, and inside they long to run free like younglings—finding adventure everywhere and nowhere all at once." Farin stretched out his hand and gently patted his magnificent steed. The horse nickered softly as Farin stroke his neck and scratched behind his ear. "You are fortunate he chose to stay with you, Farin," the elf stated matter-of-factly. "You have obviously never mistreated him, for when he was offered complete freedom, he chose to wait for your return. But there will be some subtle changes in your friendship."

"You can talk to them?" Farin asked in disbelief.

"Of course. These horses were all chained to different men and women of Lorenth. Six were tied securely farther up north and abandoned by two of the dark riders who outlasted their own foul plot. And these two," she began, pointing to Farin's horse and the other fair colored steed that Counselor Nolan was riding, "were found back down by the river's edge where you and your other human, unmarked with the darkness, were struck down. I have set them free. Their eyes have seen enough hate and bloodshed and their spirits were heavy."

Farin looked into his horse's eyes and tried to extend his senses over the animal like he did in the Illuallarii, in order to see that which he could not see. For a brief instant he almost thought he felt turmoil and pride, obligation and subtle traces of fear coming from the horse. Farin looked straight into the horse's eyes and whispered softly, "I am sorry old friend. I am sorry that I have made you travel so long into such bleakness."

Tavendia and Alarielle exchanged glances as Tavendia came behind Farin and rested her right hand on the back of his neck while stroking the pale colored horse with her left. "You are learning Farin. In time you will understand even more than you do now. His name is Atarax. A strong name for a strong ally, but from now on you must learn to work together. He will not permit the use of your restraints in his mouth any longer, not since Alarielle has given him the choice for freedom and bolstered all of their resolve to choose it despite their years of training in servitude. This gentle one is Laenos. He has seen little of battle and pain, such is not his fate. He longs to run and he too has accepted freedom and will not be chained again."

Tavendia leaned in close to the pale mount and whispered into his ear eliciting a soft nicker as he shook his head up and down slightly. "Laenos will bear me to Lorenth with you, and Atarax will bear you again as before, but you must guide him with words and not reigns, with your heart and not your gloved hand."

Farin looked at Atarax again. "Very well old friend. We ride your way from now on." Farin secured his armor behind the saddle, not wishing to ruin his new clothes by adorning it then, and mounted Atarax. Tavendia inclined her head to Alarielle once more as she too mounted, though without saddle or harness, and held on to nothing except the mane along Laenos' neck.

"You will find Atarax and Laenos swifter than before. Now they run by choice, not by command, and they have been strengthened with the magic of the *Illu'Dar* as well. Take care of these creatures and they will take care of you. Ride with the wind and make haste to Lorenth!"

Farin waved goodbye as Alarielle whistled once again and the six remaining horses, stripped of saddle, bits and bridles, ran carefree across the stream and into the deep green of the forest beyond. Farin gazed after the creatures with a wistful smile. If only his own freedom could be won as easily.

"Let's get this over with," Farin stated authoritatively to Tavendia, who was affectionately stroking the side of Laenos' neck. He pressed a heel into Atarax's side. "Home is waiting, Atarax." Atarax reared on his hind legs and neighed loudly, almost sending Farin out of the saddle, before resettling his powerful body with all four hooves on the ground. Responding to Farin's gentle guidance, Atarax threw himself into a swift canter westward. Farin reeled in surprise, leaning forward to grasp Atarax's mane for balance as the horse revealed the true power that Alarielle had released. Tavendia, who had stood watching with a wry grin as Farin launched into action, urged her own mount into motion. It was a three day journey back to Lorenth, and neither elf nor human knew what would be found there when they arrived.

XIV

She could almost feel the coming darkness and it unnerved her. Of all the times for the prophecies to be silent, why did it have to be now? Mother had always hated to discuss the shrouded prophecy with her, despite her eager prying and her digging, interpreting, and comparing of one thread of the prophecy to the other until all was a meaningless and undecipherable gray. This night held no sleep for the Guide. While the others discussed the events of the council concluded not two days earlier, she stole away to think once again, as mother used to do. That thought caused Sycaris to suffer a pang of grief, as well as a tremor of worry. Tonight was not the first night that Sycaris had found herself beginning to wonder if her fate would be the same as her mother's. Would the inexplicable become more than a fascination, and evolve into an obsession that would tear her away from those in life who made her existence worth living?

Fyysara had grown more and more distant as her unforeseen death approached… almost as if she subconsciously knew that her fate was catching up to her. Why did her mother frequently choose solitude over the comfort of her loved ones? Was Fyysara trying to uncover a way to discover her eventual fate? These were just more questions that led Sycaris nowhere, save for back into the mire of frustrations that plagued the Guide of the Icecrowns. The chill of the pre-dawn sky cut at her flesh as she stood alone atop the mountain peaks she called home. From here she was able to view the magnificence of dawn in the cold barren peaks where life other than dragonkind struggled to take root.

Smiles were rare for Sycaris, and rarer still with the absence of her mother and mentor—the only other dragon to have felt the weight of the prophecies. What the elf had to say about the threads of prophecy and the impact on the balance did make a great deal of sense. Her way of viewing prophecy was slightly different, but she had to concede to the great wisdom and logic that this elf presented. While she had often thought about altering several threads of prophecy, she never once thought that those subtle changes could offset the balance to such a degree that the balance itself would reinsert those threads in unexpected ways to fulfill the prophecy, regardless.

This Dean, whom Aerinyyr had named as Kaaldean the soul stealer, made her wary—and this was a simple human! Yet they were all cautioned not to think of them as simple humans any longer. The elves inferred from several other threads of prophecy that humans would stumble into magic through their only truly remarkable trait—ingenuity. Humans, though far inferior races and unschooled in the ways of magic, were an industrious race much like the dwarves, yet with such a short lifespan in comparison, their achievements appeared to occur much faster than that of other races, where time was less of a burden. Humans were driven by purpose and necessity to better themselves and this would not lessen now that the truth of the fae existence would be soon be common knowledge.

"Sycaris, may I join you for a moment?" The perfectly clear voice of Zharra echoed in her head. Sometimes Sycaris envied her closest friend. Zharra was so incredibly skilled in the mastery of the spiritual realm. The *Skarlagnos* was difficult for many to learn, especially those of the green and to a lesser extent, those of the copper and bronze, though all did learn it eventually. Some, like Sycaris, had greater difficulty with both range projection and clarity, while others like Zharra made the concept of projection and clarity trivial. Even though Dalaria still handled much of the instruction to the younger ones, Dalaria herself had to admit that her daughter had perfected the art that the blue ancient dragon

discovered and would likely be asked to either teach the art completely or assist in the training of others very shortly.

"Of course Zharra, but I am not where you usually find me in th—" before Sycaris had finished the thought, Zharra appeared in full form beside her. This was something that Sycaris was not alone in envying. Zharra's ability to project an exact copy of herself wherever she wanted was incredible and no other dragon had yet proved able to duplicate the process. Zharra was working rather carefully with Criosys, a fairly young silver dragon nearing his first century of age, and there was talk that the young silver male was rather adept in the spiritual arts like Zharra and may be the second dragon able to perfect the art of illusion and projection.

"Once I find your mind, finding your body is easy," Zharra announced with a half proud, half teasing tone that led to her cracking a rather toothy grin toward her friend. Dawn was nearly about to break in the eastern peaks and the absolute darkness of night was not so absolute any longer. The illusion that stood before her seemed so real. It was dense and only allowed the faintest amount of light to pass through to tell you that this was not in fact the real Zharra standing in front her.

"What troubles you Sycaris?"

"I needed some time to think. More and more I understand the pain and frustration that mother must have felt for all those years. This silence in the prophecy is so distracting! When you are used to hearing something... feeling that gentle presence within your mind, and your heart, for hundreds of years... its absence is sometimes louder than even Valkyyrak's bellow."

Zharra chuckled at the comparison, but then fell silent. The truth behind the symbolism was hard to ignore. Zharra could not fully appreciate the frustration of her friend. The platinum dragon imagined that it would be much like not being able to connect with the spiritual plane, which would render nearly all of her abilities useless. Granted, Sycaris was a red, and aside from her spiritual giftings, she was equally as gifted in the elemental plane as well.

For the longest time, no words were exchanged. Zharra and Sycaris stood facing the east, embracing the glory and majesty of the sunrise that crested the peaks and illuminated the frozen basin to the south. The snow peaked mountains that spanned the horizon glistened in the wake of the sun's precious elongated morning rays. Sycaris permitted herself a smile, absorbing the beauty and tucking it away deep within her, using the warmth of the sight to stir her sense of hope, and rekindle that sense of deep appreciation for things as easy to take for granted as sunrises.

"Will you be coming home soon? Mother and father wish to speak with you. There has been much discussion about the elves, and in particular, Nyssia Dv`arek, the elf whose magic allows her to mimic our form. They wish to speak with the Guide, not for forth telling, but reflection on what is already known, in hopes that thoughts of the past may provide guidance in the days ahead."

Sycaris acknowledged her friend's words with a nod of her regal head. "Please tell Valkyyrak and Dalaria that I will return shortly."

"I will," Zharra replied. And, with that, she released her illusion, leaving Sycaris to stand alone once more in the quickly brightening morning sky. If nothing else good was to happen today, at least she was able to have hope stir in her heart once again and feel more alive this morning than she has felt in a long time.

"Thank you for sharing that beautiful sunrise with me, Sycaris..."

The internal echo drifted off before she could respond. Her ability to search others purely through the *Skarlagnos* was not nearly as refined as Zharra's was, so she just smiled and whispered aloud to the air in front of her, "No Zharra... thank you."

* * *

Zharra broke off her illusion form and stared at Vaanadu who was still slumbering beside her in their lair. So beautiful and gifted he was, she thought with adoration, unable to resist leaning down and nuzzling his neck. Not wanting to wake him, she got up and on her silent wings lifted herself up into the air, heading straight up through their entrance in the top of the mountain peak. Their lair was rare in that it utilized this type of exit. Most dragons chose to carve out entrances to their lairs in the side of the mountain that housed it, keeping a large perching area just beyond it on which to land on and ascend from. Zharra and Vaanadu had long agreed on something a little more diverse and interesting. While the entrance above the lair also served as a vent causing the temperature of their lair to be much cooler than others, Vaanadu conceded this minor inconvenience to honor the preference of his mate who preferred the cooler climates to the deeper lairs that reds were known to prefer. Their lair was a bit more southern than most, though, as Zharra also didn't want her preferences to be too inconsiderate of Vaanadu's own.

Her parents' lair was not far, though to be honest, nothing was ever truly too far for a dragon. Granted, the trip to the Ellorian highlands did take much longer than any of them had originally anticipated. None had ever ventured that far to the east before for there was never any reason to do so. Some of the younger dragons had found the sheer size of Caliyon to be staggering. It was indeed a land that kept going and going.

Zharra always loved finding a reason to come home to see Valkyyrak and Dalaria. Their lair was by far one of the more elaborate ones within the summit. Having over a millennium to develop and refine it had obviously helped, but the sheer brilliance of the designs and ornamentations carved, channeled, or burned into the walls was magnificent.

Valkyyrak was waiting for her as she arrived at the grand entrance to their lair. "Morning Zharra. Were you able to find Sycaris?"

"Yes father. She was not where she usually flies to for solitude so it took me a little longer to find her. We talked briefly this morning as we took in the sunrise over the peaks. She still hurts, father, and it is a hurt that I am beginning to understand more clearly. The silence is affecting her spirit. She described it as almost an inward presence that has been cut off after centuries of being there."

"That is indeed troubling. There is great strength in her... in some ways, more than Fyysara had. I hope that my faith in Sycaris is not ill-placed. Will she come this morning to speak with us?"

"She did say she would come shortly."

Zharra and Valkyyrak engaged in some light conversation while looking out over the frozen basin that would forever mark the final resting place of Fyysara and any other dragons that would unfortunately fall by the ill-guided hand of fate. Zharra was one of the few who visited the basin floor regularly. While it was incredibly difficult to behold, the way that the corruption of death had so swiftly begun to ravage the body of Fyysara was astounding. Her brilliant crimson scales were fast fading, turning ashen. Her soft underbelly was now in various stages of decay, as were her talons, neck, face, and tail. Many avoided the burial ground now because of the implication that this would be their fate as well, should they fall. The rapidly advancing decomposition of one of the dragon's leaders tore away at the morale of the dragons nearly as much as it tore away the brilliance of the ancient red dragon herself.

Zharra made an attempt to study the decay, to see if there was anything that could be learned from this horrific event. While death had long been a part of the chain of life with dragons—the death being exclusively doled out to their prey, of course—Zharra did notice that the speed of corruption's advance upon dragonkind was remarkably fast. She remembered studying death in the wildlife many generations ago. Many animals took several weeks to reach the same stage of decay that Fyysara was reaching in roughly one week. While she could not explain this phenomenon yet, she made mental note of its progress with every visit she made.

Valkyyrak chuckled softly as he watched several of the younglings near the large plateau nearby trying to make their first flights. Clumsy and awkward, a dragon without the skill to manage all six limbs was an amusing sight to behold. Even Zharra began to chuckle after following her father's eyes toward the plateau and taking in the sight.

"You looked just as comical at that age, Zharra." Valkyyrak nudged his daughter and let loose a more robust laugh. "Your mother had far more patience than I though. She guided you and Maelyyk almost entirely, but once Vaelis and later Karros were hatched, I tried a bit more to guide them. Thankfully Vaelis learned quickly, like you, but then your sister has always been trying to follow in your path for as long as I can remember."

"I think she has been trying to follow mother more than I, father. I've always had very little to teach a blue like Vaelis. You know that."

"I was speaking of more than simply the color of scales and their corresponding magical traits, daughter. You have a unique character and quality about you that I have seen her trying to emulate. You have made me increasingly proud in the way you have long mediated with and counseled others, and, even now, in the way you love and care for Sycaris in her great time of need. There are more to dragons that what our scale patterns determine and it is those things that I believe Vaelis has seen in you and is trying to model."

The unexpected praise from her father—one of the most respected of all the dragons in the Icecrowns—caught her off guard. She quickly attempted to shift the focus off of herself and changed the subject.

"Have you heard anything from Karros, father?" Valkyyrak paused for a moment. Mentioning her younger brother was never a terribly wise thing to do around Valkyyrak, but it had been a while since she last inquired about him.

"No... again he stays away from the Icecrowns, both in body and in spirit. I know he felt the call as all of us did, and yet, he failed to seek us out for guidance or understanding. I have long been tempted to contact him and see how he and Xarethia are doing. While I have come to expect little of Karros, I was surprised that Xarethia has been out of contact with Nostrimus and Vaelis as well."

"You know I can contact him, father. You need but ask it of me and I will seek him out. He will suffer his older sister more than the great Valkyyrak." Zharra nudged her father back with a laugh of her own. Valkyyrak looked ready to retort, but then shrugged off her last comment with an insincere gruff followed by a small chuckle of his own.

"Perhaps soon... yes, perhaps soon. I will think on it."

The two stood watching morning unveil itself upon the rest of the peaks. All around the Icecrowns dragons were starting to resume their training or practicing. Some were crafting and working on their never-done lairs, while others were flying around the early morning skies. Dalaria emerged from the lair and smiled when she saw Zharra before moving to Valkyyrak and nuzzling him gently in greeting. After bidding her family a good morning,

Dalaria made some small talk, asked about Vaanadu and what he was working on now, and also made mention of Maelyyk and his worry that was beginning to affect him much like Sargeron began to worry about Fyysara. Zharra could only nod. Deep down, she agreed with her father and knew there was a resiliency about Sycaris that Fyysara did not possess, and she shared his hope that Sycaris would find a way to channel this frustration into something useful.

It wasn't long before the three saw the familiar slender red wings deftly cutting through the crisp northern air. Sycaris made her descent upon the grand perch, smiling when she saw the real Zharra and then inclining her head to Valkyyrak and Dalaria.

"Thank you for coming so quickly, Sycaris," Dalaria began. "I hope you have gained some sense of peace through your solitude."

"I have." Sycaris again looked toward Zharra. "Sometimes it just takes a friend to help me see things in a different light. I need to find Maelyyk soon as well. I know these past few days have been hard on him."

Valkyyrak then added, "Maelyyk worries not unlike your father did for Fyysara, but he knows you need the space and his love for you is deep. But, we did not ask you here to speak of my son. As you saw for yourself, there is one among the Ice Elves who can mimic our form and has shown tremendous giftings in matters of the arcane."

Dalaria then continued on, "I want to bring her here to learn about us more. While Draevor has long been their representative and will continue to function as such, I believe that if we have Nyssia learn from us, potentially we can learn from her. If we can follow the ways that the elves use magic, perhaps we too can achieve new directions in the application of the magic that is inherent to us. As Guide, we wish to know if there has been anything in the prophecies from before the silence that spoke about a union between the elves and the dragons, or of learning from them, or perhaps new directions in the use of our essence within."

Sycaris became serious and intent as she began to reach back through the recesses of her own mind, sorting through the myriad of dreams and prophecies that were housed there. Dalaria waited, exchanging gratified looks with Zharra and to Valkyyrak. Valkyyrak had suggested several days ago that perhaps Sycaris was suffering from, among everything else, a lack of purpose. If they could cultivate her sense of need and appreciation by those around her, perhaps the silence would be less important and she could still function as Historian, guiding others from what was already revealed and not only from what was now hidden.

Sycaris began breathing very slowly, signaling the discovery of an uncovered thread of prophecy that could aid them in their decision. Eventually, her eyes opened slowly to reveal two pale swirling orbs that looked like clouds churning. This was the first time any of them had seen Sycaris or Fyysara demonstrate this phenomenon and it was unsettling to all three of the dragons watching. Then in an uncharacteristic and low, monotonous voice, Sycaris began to repeat the dream as it was imprinted upon her.

> *Mingled sorrow on crimson wing*
> *Decay, despair, the silent sing*
> *Those of wood, of ice, of earth*
> *Entreat with those of magic's birth*
> *The ice shall fall in shapes unknown*
> *The Wyrm to shift; the drake is grown*
> *The blues in hues to mark their fate*
> *The ice to strengthen the golden mate.*

The clouded orbs that masked Sycaris' eyes dissipated to reveal the deep yellow eyes that all were familiar with. Sycaris seemed rejuvenated from her experience. Beneath the surface of her deep crimson scales burned a new flame that was beginning to surge. There was intent and purpose where they had long been seeing defeat and despair. The old Sycaris was back among them once more.

"That was unexpected," said Sycaris as she looked at her companions. Valkyyrak was hard to read as usual, though he appeared to be pondering the strange behavior that he had just witnessed. Dalaria appeared somewhat troubled and intrigued. Zharra, ever the researcher, was obviously trying to puzzle out the meaning of the riddle.

"Where did this prophecy come from Sycaris? I don't recall ever hearing Fyysara share that one." inquired Zharra, some minor frustration on her face in her attempt to fully understand the words that Sycaris had just spoken.

"From me," Sycaris whispered. Valkyyrak's eyes were no longer pensive but grew intent as he trained his gaze upon Sycaris. She then added, "I was barely older than a hatchling. I was just learning to master my flame when this particular thread came upon me. I was so excited and tried to share it with mother but she refused to entertain it as prophecy and told me that I was too young to experience prophecy. This was the first of my dreams. I fear that mother was beginning to understand that her fate would bring about great sorrow and she flatly refused to ever speak with me about the shrouded prophecy. It wasn't until I had a less important dream that revealed the link between the arcane mastery and those of blue or red scales that mother deemed me to also be a dreamer who felt the prophecies. She never spoke to me again about this thread, and I forgot about it until now."

"What does it mean Sycaris?" began Dalaria. "Some things are fairly plain. Those of wood and ice are the elves, which leaves the dwarves as those of stone. I am assuming that we are those of magic's birth and the sorrow mentioned refers to the death of Fyysara. What are unclear are the final references. Are the 'blues in hues' all blue dragons or various shades? And what of our fate? Is the 'wyrm' reference pertaining to dragonkind? Does the final line speak of me? What does the birth of the drake—"

"Let me explain it to all of you, Dalaria. You have deciphered much of its meaning already. Where you all heard words in rhyme, I simply saw a picture shifting in focus. I saw mother… broken, then I saw a host of elves and dwarves speaking with a multitude of dragons with great sorrow still heavily laden on their hearts. Then I saw the northern elves shifting into various forms of animals, including the drake form that Nyssia now models. The last picture was of a gathering of blue dragons also learning how to shift their own forms into one much like the humans yet very draconic in appearance… with you, Dalaria, as the guide that would enable our kin to learn this. You indeed are the golden one's mate referred to in the last line. The only thing that isn't clear is the reference to 'the silent sing.'

"I have had other dreams as well. I believe that the term 'wyrm' will be a label used by humans. Many will come to respect and even revere us, but there will come a day when wyrm-hunters will arise. They will attempt to kill or capture us for fame, sport, or other twisted devices that only the humans can concoct. Whether this happens or not is unknown to me for therein lays the essence of the shrouded prophecies. Should the Seed of Corruption triumph over the Lightbringer, such may be our fate."

The heavy words settled among the four dragons. It was indeed prophesized that the elves and dragons would begin to learn from each other. In this, the message was clear, but again, there was the reference to fate. What would be the ultimate result of such an exchange between the races? Is this a thread that could be altered? Would it be wise to even consider it? Was this why Fyysara discarded this thread of prophecy? Aerinyyr's cautions began surfacing anew along with the echoes of strong admonitions to protect the threads of fate, whether for good or for ill. Perhaps in her fears, Fyysara was trying to protect the dragons from a fate worse than she could bear to imagine. A fate that would present itself as good and beneficial but later would spoil and taint all things that the dragons, and by virtue of the new alliance—all fae creatures, held dear.

"I would not overcomplicate matters with giving this decision excessive thought. If the prophecies are to be trusted, and deep in my heart I know the truth of this matter, then we have created worry and doubt where there should be none. Dalaria felt strongly about this elf, and now Sycaris reveals a long missing prophecy that reveals most of what we know to be true and very little that has not yet happened, but may yet happen. I believe our choice is decided. We are to speak with this elf more and perhaps bolster ourselves in a new way as we begin to learn from the elves and teach them what they need to know as well, should there be anything to teach these scholars of magic."

As usual, the wisdom of Valkyyrak made plain the issue before the other three. While logic nullified all doubt from Zharra's mind, Sycaris and Dalaria retained some doubts, though the two kept those doubts to themselves. Valkyyrak wanted to check up on Sargeron and left the remaining details up to the three females. Before flying off, he stopped and turned to face Zharra, stating that perhaps it would be a good idea to contact Karros and Xarethia when she had some time, and as well, that perhaps she could use her projection to make contact with the elves instead of waiting for Draevor to arrive whenever it suited him. Zharra nodded. Valkyyrak then vaulted off the ledge of his lair and took flight, unfurling his immensely broad golden wings that were more brilliant than the sun.

XV

"You brought up Karros again?" Sycaris asked Zharra. Dalaria revealed nothing in her expression as the red and the blue turned toward Zharra.

"It had been a while since I last inquired. I do not see why this needs to be such a point of contention. Must pride divide the dragons? Karros has made his choices and Xarethia has made her own as well. Others have also left the Icecrowns. Warmer climates, better hunting grounds perhaps, greater independence—all these things lay south of the Icecrowns. I think it is pure folly that we have not even contacted them. Karros even said this was not a decision made against father, but more for his own growth and desire to explore more of the lands."

Dalaria slowly shook her blue-scaled neck. "Zharra, your father and I were just taken back because until he left, we had all been one large functional society here. This has been our home since we came to be and we just didn't expect anyone to leave so quickly. He never spoke of these things to us."

"No he didn't. Maelyyk and I also didn't know about this until he left. Vaelis knew. He always spoke with her, and out of respect for you and father, he did not want Vaelis speaking about his dreams to head to warmer hills."

Sycaris then chimed in, "But why would Karros not speak to you and Maelyyk too? You both are brother and sister to him as well as Vaelis."

"Yes, but think of the years between us. Maelyyk and I had mastered our arts, built our lairs, and taken mates well before he was even a hatchling. As it is, Vaelis is considerably older than he is. I don't think that Karros ever looked at me or Maelyyk as a sister or brother, but more as a teacher or mentor."

"So you will attempt to contact him through your projections?"

"Yes mother. I have already located him. I never wanted to go against father so I have not contacted him, but I have traced him. He is far to the south of us... beyond the water and the human lands."

"When you speak with him, tell him that he is missed. Will you contact the elves after speaking with Karros?"

"No, I will contact them first. Then I will allow myself the time to speak with my brother at my leisure. That is, if he actually wants to speak with me. I will be sure to pass on your words too, mother, and will let you know what he says."

Sycaris began to back out of the conversation between the mother and daughter. When Dalaria and Zharra paused in their exchange to look at her, she smiled shyly. "I am going to find Maelyyk now. His patience with me has been great and I owe him some explanations for my recent actions."

"I will seek you out later, Sycaris," responded Zharra with a grin of understanding. Soon after Sycaris' departure, Zharra and Dalaria bid each other farewell, the younger dragon ascending from the ledge and making her way back to her own mate. Lifting herself into the air, she let her wings carry her up and over the peaks that hemmed in the Icecrowns. With the slightest manipulation of her essence, she began to amplify the ambient light all around her, shielding her from all other eyes as she soared and spun, enjoying the freedom of flight without fear of being seen by any who would balk to see a dragon of Zharra's age engaging in such uncharacteristic behavior.

Her thoughts began to drift south to the small human townships below, far west of the lair-city that the humans call Lorenth. She would need to resolve those differences in her mind. They did not live in lairs but towns and cities. This should be simple enough to remember. Out of curiosity she made a turn to the south to quickly observe any changes that may be happening around the human townships. Within two hours, flying high and unseen with no fears of discovery, her sharply attuned vision allowed her to glean the information that she was interested in. Since Fyysara's death, no one had been scouting the human lands as that was something Fyysara did regularly.

As Zharra passed over the first township she felt it. It was like a wave of shadow and fear, and it washed over her hungrily. Her eyes widened and her heart began to beat faster as she searched back and forth for what could have elicited this terrible feeling. There was nothing to be seen. The humans were busy with their usual duties, although their numbers seemed considerably fewer. The same things were witnessed in the other human townships in the area as well. Many of their houses, as they called them, did not have smoke rising from the surface and their animals were gone as well. This was new. Zharra then made her approach back to the north, passing over what must have been the place that Fyysara fell. Several humans were busy studying the area, measuring out the great depression in the ground in an attempt to record the vast measurements. Outside of what they pieced together from the broken ground, Zharra didn't think the humans would be able to glean much information now that Fyysara was removed from the area and given her place of dignified rest. Having enough information to make a decent report to her kin, she turned one last time to the northeast and made for her lair.

It was midday when the elder platinum at last arrived at the opening to her lair. She released the light weave that rendered her invisible and gently descended down the aperture into the lower cavern where Vaanadu was tempering the newly excavated chamber along the western hall. Zharra stood back so as not to disturb him. She loved watching him work. Vaanadu released a solid wall of flame into the cavern and adjusted it to burn evenly across the entire surface as he channeled more and more essence into his constant flame that increasingly elevated the temperature in the room and in the rock that began to melt before her eyes. He could only maintain this level of channeling for a short period of time before he had to release the flow and rest. Drawing in deep breaths and looking over his last patch of work he nodded with approval at the rock which now remarkably resembled a reddish-black tinted glass.

"You are a sight to behold, my dear," Zharra whispered affectionately, catching the studious Vaanadu off guard. He suddenly lifted his head at her words and struck his broad visage against the ceiling of the chamber. He winced in pain but then began to chuckle as he made his way over to his mate. The differences in the male reds were so evident from those of the female reds. While it was plain to see some resemblances between Sycaris and Vaanadu, the horn patterns, and especially Vaanadu's thicker, and more rugged underbelly set apart the male reds quite a bit.

"You slipped out early this morning. Was anything wrong?"

"Not really. I found Sycaris and father wanted me to bring her to the summit to speak about the elves. Mother wants us to invite the female shape-shifter here to learn from us and, potentially, us from her."

"Interesting." Vaanadu nuzzled up against Zharra, sending thrills through her body. His intent gaze upon her made Zharra feel pleasantly vulnerable as she turned her face into the heat of his neck.

"I have to reach out to the elves and then to Karros afterward, love. There is much for me to accomplish this afternoon."

"That's fine. They can have your mind while I stay here with your body." The gruff laughter that came from Vaanadu was intoxicating as Zharra began to laugh as well, giving him a gentle shove. "I need to get back to work here anyhow. I think I found a way to make some rooms radiate more heat. When I tempered the rock like this, and channeled more and more essence into it, some of the essence became trapped within the glassed wall. Already I can start to feel the temperature in this room increase a bit."

"You still find the lair too cold?"

"I always have, but I have found a way to mitigate this issue now so the lair can still be chilled for your comfort and this room will be much warmer for mine. I may continue to excavate more deeply from this room and make a room for flame-working that will also retain much heat. It's a thought."

"A very good thought at that. I will leave you, dear. I do not know how long I will be speaking with the elves or with Karros."

"I won't even bother asking about Karros. I hope you will tell me more after though. I would like to hear how he and Xarethia are faring."

"I will tell you everything later, as long as there is something to tell."

Vaanadu rubbed against Zharra once more before turning his massive frame back toward the partially tempered wall and slowly beginning to gather his essence for another pass. Zharra backed out of the chamber and went back to the main chamber beneath the vent and exit to their layer, already feeling much more comfortable in the cooler room. It was amazing to her that Vaanadu could channel his flame into the rock and create this sort of glass to warm an entire chamber—and he was not even half done in that room. She likely would find the completed chamber much too warm for her liking, but if it brought some comfort to her mate then she was overjoyed. This was their third lair already, and Vaanadu had been more than accommodating for Zharra. It was nice that finally he could create a sanctuary where even a red could rest in comfort within the chill of the Icecrowns. No doubt the others would be excited to learn about this once Vaanadu told Sargeron and Valkyyrak about this type of forging.

Zharra rested on the ground in the corner of their lair and allowed her thoughts to drift as she opened herself up to the spiritual plane and began casting forth her vision toward the east in search of the blackened tower that housed the Ice Elves. Knowing where to look cut her time down immensely and once she located the massive pillar of rock that was heavily laden with ice all along its edges she paused to channel her essence and extend it, using her farsight to force a clear projection of herself on the ground at the base of the structure. She had never been this close to the Ice Elves' tower before and the detail and precision in the craftsmanship was superb. Surrounding the tower was a shimmering blue nebulous of energy, and Zharra could feel the magic of it crackling along her scales.

She took flight in her illusion form and flew up toward the oddly shaped structure at the top of the tower. Several openings were built into the walls of this chamber and through it she could see a gathering of elves within the chamber as three well-dressed and dignified elves stood from their seats and inclined their heads toward Zharra in greeting. Two of the three approached a swirling pillar of energy in the center of the chamber and stepped within it, only to suddenly appear on the surface of their tower where a small portal of the same swirling energy sat in a small pool beneath their feet.

"How is it that we are honored to have one of the mighty dragons at our keep yet we did not sense your arrival until only now?" spoke the male elf, Tinovis, if Zharra recalled correctly.

"I have sent a projection of myself only, friend elf. Valkyyrak and Dalaria have sent me with a missive to request an audience with Nyssia Dv'arek if you would be willing to permit her to visit with us. We still will welcome Draevor as we always have, but Dalaria believes fate has brought about an opportunity for shared learning should Nyssia be interested in passing time with us."

The female elf, Valeris, nodded with keen interest. "You are truly a remarkable race, Zharra the lightweaver. Long have we seen this day approaching and we grant your request with eager anticipation at what our races can learn from each other. Nyssia will be honored to make the trip to your summit and she will arrive by this time tomorrow, if that is acceptable to you."

Zharra was amazed that the frost mage in front of her knew her name already. Equally amazing was that she knew about her abilities as well. This was indeed a powerful arcanist and one with an astute eye for insight into the realms of magic. "That would be more than acceptable, Valeris. I will tell my mother to expect her then. Thank you for meeting with me."

"The honor was ours Zharra. *Nishana tel'anorii*" Valeris and Tinovis inclined their heads, touching their fingers to their lips and foreheads as they stepped back onto the energy pool in the center of the tower and returned to their chamber within the spire. Zharra inclined her head as well as she released the magical image of herself and returned in full presence of mind back to where her body rested in her lair.

Zharra found herself growing excited at the notion of having an elf among the dragons again. There were so many things already that the elves were capable of accomplishing with their magic, practices and skills that the dragons had never even contemplated of. The dragons had remained isolated for so long that perhaps they only discovered what they needed to discover in order to survive and take complete dominion over the land around them. It was seldom that new discoveries were being made among the dragons because until now, life was fairly simple around the summit. In reflection, perhaps it was too simple here, another possible reason to explain the exodus of the few dragons that had left the Icecrowns to unite with Karros and Xarethia in the south.

Settling herself once again, she began to extend her farsight toward the direction where her brother lay... south... searching and probing for the signature of life that she previously identified as Karros. Her vision soared across the lower Icecrowns, the human township of Bonnin, and then into the western sea where she searched farther still until land suddenly became visible. These were the stone hills and it was a barren land—dry and hot, devoid of much life. In many ways, it reminded her of the Icecrowns, only that the hills here were made of a pale rock and stood much lower than the snow-topped peaks of the Icecrowns. She noticed what appeared to be several entrances within the summits of various hills indicating the lairs of the few dragons that were here. Two of the entrances were near the base of the hills where the ground looked like scorched earth, dry and cracked, with several vents that allowed steam from the intensely hotter depths below to escape into the relatively cooler air above. Taking a quick count there were at least six lair entrances in this area, which could mean approximately ten dragons or more could now be living down here.

She recoiled in her mind once again as that feeling of shadow washing over her intensified. The sensation made her want to wretch as every nerve was standing on end—her eyes wide and her pulse racing. This was definitely not a coincidence and she would need to report this to the others. This was the second instance where this feeling overtook her, and this time it was as her mind passed to the south, not her body. Perhaps Karros knew more about this; perhaps others were feeling the same emotions here in this part of Caliyon.

Worry began to set in as she continued to scout out the surrounding areas. There were no dragons about, no signs of life other than the entrances to the lairs, and there were no sounds of flame-craft or flight. She then began to guide her vision around to the lairs. She entered various dragon homes, noticing immediately that they all tunnelled quite deep into the ground. Many of these lairs were new and undeveloped. Others seemed more complete but were functional only, not decorated with the delicate ornamentation that was dragon tradition. And even more surprising was what she found deeper within the dragon homes. Here were the dragons she was seeking. But, while she was relieved to have found them alive, she was shocked to find each and every one of them in the throes of slumber. It was well past midday and dragons were never asleep this late. Some of the dragons she recognized, yet there were some younger dragons in newly formed lairs of their own that she did not recognize. Had Karros really been gone that long?

She finally located the lair where Karros and Xarethia were sleeping alongside two younger dragons, and two hatchlings. Zharra was touched at the sight, and relieved that at least this lair had some touches of home. There was some evidence of flame-craft along the halls and the main chamber was well excavated to provide a great amount of room. The ceiling was imperfect. Karros had chosen to leave many raw spikes of rock hanging from the ceiling giving it the appearance of a mouth full of jagged teeth—creative for sure, but not in her taste. This lair had two entrances—one at the summit of one of the taller hills in the area, and the other near the base of the hills, with a multi-cavernous layout that also delved fairly deep into the softer earth beneath the hard rock above.

Zharra forced her essence into the farsight and summoned an image of herself within the chamber. The reasons for all the depth and the daytime slumber became immediately apparent. The blast of sheer heat tore into her once her illusion was summoned. Even though her body was not truly there, the effect of the ambient heat told her that this place was even hotter than it looked. As she climbed the hallways from the lower part of the lair she stopped short of the slumbering Karros with his family and observed. Karros certainly was bigger now, and his massive head horns grew back initially and then protruded forward toward his eyes and mouth. He was nearly as savage looking as Sargeron, though Karros's bronze scales did not convey the same level of trepidation that the black scales of Sargeron did. Xarethia had changed even more. As a rule, female dragons were never as savage looking as the males. Having seen so few black dragons, Zharra admired the female creature sleeping before her, because Xarethia was one of the few black female dragons that existed. Her lines were sleek and her features perfect. Her head horns were almost entwined together in a spiraling fashion that fanned out to each side near the tips, creating a striking image. Xarethia appeared much leaner somehow, as if she had been streamlined for speed.

The young ones were all new to her, and two of them were so very young she could not even determine their gender yet. The older two were male and were both a lighter bronze color, almost like the pale color of the sand atop the hills above, while one of the younger ones was black and the other a very deep red, much darker than Fyysara, Vaanadu or Sycaris. Zharra paused as she then reflected on all the dragons that she had seen prior to summoning her form within the lair. All the colors were similar. She saw no blue, or green. No gold, no bronze—other than Karros—and certainly no silver or platinum. All the dragons were of the darker pigments, suggesting a much more martial and savage breed of dragons down here, with little to no connection to the arcane that the blues and reds maintained. Even red was not well represented among those here. She only remembered seeing one truly red dragon male— Skoren if she remembered, although he certainly had changed since she saw him last—and of course that young reddish-black hatchling asleep before her now.

Uncertain whether to wake Karros or not, she decided to awaken his mind first through the *Skarlagnos* to notify him of her presence.

"Brother, please wake. I have traveled long to find you." Only silence greeted her as she pressed again. *"Karros, it is Zharra. Please wake. I need to speak with you."* The soundless whisper of her words had barely faded when he moved. Zharra leapt back in fear as Karros crossed the length of the chamber in an instant, moving to grab her neck in his powerful foreleg talons. The foot-

long claws passed harmlessly through Zharra's illusion, leaving Karros to scrabble for his balance.

"Very clever sister. I forgot about that trick of yours." Karros growled, regaining his composure and eying Zharra's projected form with little affection. "Why do you seek me out here? You should not have come. It is folly to waken a slumbering dragon with his family present and defenseless. Learn from this mistake and wait until dark before you ever try this again. As you can feel, the heat is insufferable during the day, so we sleep. It is the night that brings us out to hunt, to craft and train, and to explore."

Zharra carefully studied Karros with her senses before responding. There was a taint of corruption about him that could not take hold, but was clinging to him like a parasite attempting to find a weakness it could exploit. Something was definitely foul in these lands and her fear grew as she noticed the same corruption tainting Xarethia and the younger dragons. Karros also followed his sister's eyes and trained his senses as well, attempting to see what she saw.

"You fear what you do not understand sister. You are correct in noticing the strength of the corruption in these lands. Over the years I have been studying its advancement and I believe we understand where it originated. There is an island of rock and mist far to the southwest within the southern seas. We cannot use our farsight to penetrate the mist, and none of us have been willing to fly blindly into it ourselves to determine what lies beneath the shroud. We know that it is evil, and it knows we are here and has been trying for years to break us, but for reasons we do not understand, we are all immune from its effects. While we certainly feel its mire over us, it is like a filth that can be washed away. It does not enter; it does not corrupt. We are now the guardians of the barren wastes. Our role is to preserve the line of the dragons, even those in the Icecrowns who have ignored us and disowned us for venturing south to help protect the arrogant who do not understand the threat encroaching from the south."

Karros moved back a few paces and violently shook in disgust at the taint that was on him. Xarethia opened her eyes and looked at Karros shaking. She nearly went back to sleep until her eyes landed on Zharra, at which point she arose quickly with surprise, the expression on her face one that was mingled with joy and sorrow.

"Zharra! How I have missed you!"

"Xarethia please... there will be time for reunions later. I still have not learned why she is here after all these years of silence and isolation from the north."

"Karros... Xarethia... long have I wanted to break the silence between us but you know father. He is proud. He was waiting for you to contact him and in his pride he would not extend his care to you. Mother has been broken inside—torn between her love for father and for you. She wanted me to tell you just how much you both have been missed. The silence finally broke down father's pride and he asked me to seek you out to see how you both are faring down here. He misses you too Karros—he still speaks fondly of you when he remembers your hatchling days. Mother simply did not understand the sudden departure and quest for adventure that took several of you from the Icecrowns. I did not fully understand either, until I spoke at length with Vaelis years ago. She did keep her word but I have my ways of picking up fragments of information that led me to piece together the real story behind your departure."

Much of the anger and bitterness behind the eyes of Karros began to wane as he took in all that his sister was saying. Xarethia drew close to Karros, resting her head upon his shoulder. The play of light on the northern visitor alerted Xarethia that something was odd with Zharra.

"Zharra, are my eyes playing tricks on me?"

"No Xarethia, it is just a pro—tion of myself. I am still in m— lair in the Ice—wns. I know it takes some getting used to but in ti— I hope to be able to—"

Karros growled deeply as Zharra began flinching in pain. They both extended their senses once again and noticed the taint beginning to come in contact with the illusion of Zharra. The illusion began to weaken in front of them as Zharra felt a very real pain each time another creeping globule of mire touched her projection.

"Zharra… release the image now. Tell father and mother that I regret my anger and my pride. I will visit when I can. Report to the others about what we face down here."

Before he could finish his final words, the illusion fully degraded and collapsed, sending the creeping taint falling to the floor of the lair as it began to advance once again upon Xarethia and Karros. Xarethia watched with her senses as well and did not hesitate. She unleashed a carefully aimed gout of flame across the ground, searing the advancing mire into nothingness.

"I hope your sister is all right, Karros. The taint has never affected one of us before."

"It wasn't one of us though, Xarethia. I believe Zharra is fine. The projection was corruptible but I do not feel that she was. At least we finally have some news of home. I was so wroth with her today. I wonder at times if this constant oppression by the taint is slowly weakening us in some way."

"Don't speak like that Karros. We all have been frustrated with the constant advance of the evil from the Isle. You were awakened suddenly and simply reacted as any guardian would react when his family was near."

"But I felt her presence in my mind first. I knew she was here when I lunged at her. I scared her and scared myself with the speed of my reaction."

The two dragons stood in silence not knowing what else could be said. Karros ventured to the lower entrance and observed the sun still high in the mid-afternoon sky. He returned back inside to the slightly cooler rock that provided ample shade from the sun as he motioned to Xarethia to lie down with him again in hopes that they could sleep a little longer before the evening came upon them.

XVI

Zharra reeled from the shock of being forced back into her body so violently. After a moment of gathering her bearings, she stood and found Vaanadu less than a span from her, watching with concern etched into his face.

"What happened? I heard you call out in pain and came quickly, but you weren't responding to me."

Zharra used her heightened senses to scan her body and mind and was relieved to find no trace of the taint lingering. She looked over Vaanadu and then around the lair to see if somehow she had brought an uninvited traveler with her when her projection was corrupted. Finally reassured that they were safe, she began to breathe a little easier.

"There is great evil at work in the south, Vaanadu. Karros, Xarethia, their young, and presumably all the others down there are covered with it, yet Karros maintains that it cannot and has not corrupted any of them so far. When you look with your senses it shows itself as a slowly creeping filth that attempts to alter whatever it touches. When it came into contact with my projection, I felt such pain and fear all at once that I failed to maintain my spirit self. Even now I cannot shake those feelings from me, Vaanadu. I still feel touched by it."

Vaanadu opened his own senses and examined his mate carefully before confirming to Zharra that he could not see any trace of the living taint that she spoke of. She closed the space between them and curled her body into his, letting him comfort her with the promise that he would allow no evil to come near her while she remained beside him.

When she had finally regained her composure, Zharra asked if Vaanadu would come with her to gather the ancients and some of the other elders to report on the situation in the south, as well as to share the information passed on to her from Valeris Sy`yn of Frostspire. Vaanadu agreed and within a few moments the two made their exit from their lair and headed northeast toward the summit. While in flight, Zharra initiated the *Skarlagnos* and used it to connect with several of the elders and the ancients at once, conveying to all the sense of urgency she felt. All responded that they would arrive at the summit as soon as they were able.

There was quite a bit of stirring already by the time that Vaanadu and Zharra reached the summit. A number of younger and middle-aged dragons also drew in to where the couple alighted as they too could pick up the feeling of unease that was spreading among their kin. Sargeron was there, his black mass and brooding face showing his obvious concern. Valkyyrak and Dalaria, as well as Nostrimus and Vaelis, Manaseth and Sirrusa, Vasuni and Scyllian, and even Azaryyk and Pydriss showed up. Vaanadu and Zharra landed just as Sycaris and Maelyyk were seen cresting the eastern peaks, and stayed where they were as the other pair descended. Once Maelyyk and Sycaris were firmly on ground, Sargeron looked from his daughter to Zharra, noticing the unspoken fears that showed in their eyes.

"Tell us, Zharra. What has happened?"

Zharra looked toward Sargeron, and then to Vaanadu and her parents before beginning. "I would first like to share news of my contact with the elves. Valeris Sy`yn spoke with me, and has promised to send Nyssia to us tomorrow by midday. It appears they too have seen this meeting in their own prophecies, and are as eager to exchange knowledge with us as we are with them. But, while this is good news, it is unfortunately not the matter of great importance that led me to summon you all here.

"As my father is aware, this afternoon I sent a projection of my body and spirit far to the south to find my brother Karros and his mate Xarethia. What I found there troubles me greatly. There are a collection of lairs down in the barren wastelands where several of our kin have been languishing. Great evil hangs over those lands. I saw it with my eyes, and with my senses. There is a corruption, an almost living entity, and it is spreading like a consuming taint that clings to the dragons there like a second skin. It seems to seek a weakness to exploit in its host, and caused me great pain when it advanced on my projection. It actually nullified my magic. I did not recall the projection—the corruption made it unstable and caused it to fail. Karros says they believe they have found the location of the corruption. Far into the sea, to the southwest of the stone hills where our kin now reside, is an island shrouded with a mist that farsight cannot penetrate. Fear has held our kin at bay and none have attempted to fly blind into the mist to discern what threat, if any, exists beneath the shadows of the isle."

"What of Xarethia and Karros? Has this corruption consumed them and the others?" asked Nostrimus. Everyone around the summit was silent, absorbing the new information slowly and carefully. Zharra's reference to an island of mist, a space that was impenetrable to all magical sight, was oddly familiar to those aware of the shrouded prophecies. If this was indeed the land of the shadow, then this news was the harbinger of sorrow as the time of darkness must be quickly approaching.

"Karros said they were immune to the effects, but I wonder if that is completely true. He reacted to my presence with extreme hostility and I cannot be sure whether that was just a reaction caused by his frustration and anger toward me as a part of his past, or if it was due to the effects of the corruption on his spirit."

Vaelis shifted her thoughtful gaze from Nostrimus to Zharra, "Why would he be angry with us? It was his desire to leave the Icecrowns. No one pressured him to make his home in a part of the world so far from us."

"The complete answer does not belong to everyone here sister, but to mother and father alone. Suffice it to say that pride kept him from seeking us these many months past, and he has become bitter that we would not seek him out first. I believe I mediated through this though, as Karros did say he would return to speak with everyone when he is able."

Those gathered collectively nodded their approval of Zharra's words. So many changes had befallen the dragons in such a short time. And, at the center of it all, was the Tear of Deimar, and the hope that the Lightbringer would correct the balance once and for all.

Before the impromptu meeting was concluded, Dalaria asked Sycaris to share her own news about the old prophecy that she had only that day uncovered. More questions were raised that could not be answered, yet Sycaris confidently expressed the knowledge she did have, and asserted that her interpretations were as complete as they could be for now. Time would reveal who the silent singers were and as to their fate... again, only the future held those answers. The blue dragons that had gathered all lingered behind after the others had begun to leave and turned to Dalaria with queries regarding the reference to their kind in the uncovered prophecy. Dalaria confirmed their inferences by relating her own suspicion that Nyssia Dv`arek would bring teaching to them that specifically would benefit her and those in 'hues of blue.' Dalaria wanted the word to be passed among the other blues that all, regardless of age or experience, should be present tomorrow by midday to see what Nyssia had to say, and to give their input in the matter. All would be heard and all would choose this unknown fate together in full accord.

An uneasy silence set along with the sun on the dragons all across the Icecrowns that night. Valkyyrak and Dalaria spoke together at length regarding their son Karros, and the very serious threat that was encroaching upon him and Xarethia. Valkyyrak, normally the proudest of all the dragons, felt an unnatural need to speak with his son, to admit to his own pride and failings in the matters that hung uncomfortably between them. When Zharra had relayed the rest of the discussion to them both privately, after the gathering had dispersed, Valkyyrak was overcome with guilt and a sense of responsibility for submitting his son to this evil alone and without support from the Icecrowns.

Meanwhile, Sargeron was also taking some time to think through the events of the day, reflecting on all that had transpired recently until he finally decided to visit the resting place of Fyysara in the hopes of finding solace in her memory. He knew that Zharra had been visiting her often, yet he had been unable to look upon the broken body of his mate again. Tonight, though, Sargeron decided to face her again, and perhaps complete the cycle of grief. Descending to the lowest part of the summit where the wide lake rested under a great floor of ice, Sargeron landed softly at the back of his lost beloved.

Already he could see how death was ravaging her. Her wings, her tail, the back of her head and joints, and her neck, were all being eaten away by the advancing, unmerciful decay. The great heavy-hearted black slowly walked around to see her face but quickly averted his gaze as many of the features that he had loved for a millennia had been eaten away as well. Her scales, once a brilliant red that glowed like flames from the depths of the earth, had faded into a sickly, ashen gray color. Sargeron allowed himself to openly mourn for her again, roaring into the night sky in frustration and grief. Those who heard Sargeron in the valley below recognized his anguished voice and had the insight to give him the privacy he needed. Sleep would not come for Sargeron until very late in the darkest night when at long last he laid down on the ice at Fyysara's side and fell into fitful, dream-filled slumber.

Maelyyk and Sycaris rested together in their lair, where sleep could only be found within the comfort of each other's presence. Even Vaanadu chose to sleep beside Zharra in their lair, in spite of the cold, to offer her comfort in the light of all the darkness that approached. Fear was not an emotion that was experienced by dragons... until today.

*   *   *

The breaking of dawn brought little relief to the dragons of the Icecrown Peaks. Many felt frustrated that they were not already moving to help Karros and the other southern kin. While the dragons of the north knew the name of their enemy and knew where to begin looking for the promised Lightbringer, Karros and Xarethia would have no way of knowing about the prophecies, nor about the results of the council meeting of the fae races. This information was the very weapon that those in the south were lacking and should they not become armed with this information, they might suffer loss and sorrow in vain.

Zharra, Dalaria, and the other blues had been contemplating this very idea throughout much of the morning. Zharra agreed to attempt contacting Karros once more, but this time she would not send her projection, strictly limiting the communication to her use of the *Skarlagnos*. Those present all felt that this living taint would be unable to corrupt a voice completely within another, if that other truly was immune from the effects of this taint. Zharra told those present that she would need to wait until nightfall to attempt communication with Karros, explaining that those in the south had reversed their sleeping and waking cycles and would not be awake until sunset.

"Dalaria, a rather small winged beast that resembles one of our own is approaching the summit at great speed. I cannot discern who this is but I don't think it is a dragon. Should I engage this creature?"

"No Ysiel, she is a friend. She is an elven ice mage sent from Frostspire to learn of us and to have us learn of her and the elven ways of magic. Let her pass and treat her with honor."

"Of course, Dalaria."

"Nyssia Dv'arek approaches. For those of you who were not at the gathering, she has a remarkable gift. Some of these elves have learned to change their form and Nyssia has taken to our ways and has modeled her form after us. It will be our job to enlighten her about our ways and our capabilities so that perhaps her form will be more than just a travel form but a form with greater versatility. It also is our hope that we can observe her use of magic and decipher how she is able to mold her form into other beings of varied sizes and colors."

The elegant blue drake glided past the black dragon in the skies as she focused her attention on the summit, where a small gathering of several blue dragons, a silver dragon and another one, the beautiful pale one that Valeris had mentioned, waited for her arrival. All the eyes were focused on Nyssia as she landed with expert grace near the gathering of the dragons, recognizing the immense form of Dalaria amid the others.

"Greetings, Nyssia. Welcome to our summit. There is much to speak of, including some news that you and your kin may not yet be aware of."

Nyssia released the image of the blue drake from her mind as her features shifted once again, returning to her natural elven form much to the surprise and awe of the younger dragons that were present. Nyssia felt like a spectacle. She removed her travel satchel and cloak, laying them aside for the time being, and focused her gaze on the dragons that had gathered. All eyes remained on her and while she felt honored at the attention she was receiving, a part of her felt quite distracted as well.

"The honor is mine, Dalaria. Long have I wanted to see with my own eyes the splendor of your summit and to speak with you all as friend and not simply as ally. Today is a day where opportunity and fate collide and perhaps both races will be better served by the exchanges that we share in together."

Nyssia felt suddenly awkward as she delivered the prepared speech, hating how rehearsed and inauthentic her words sounded. But, instead of drawing attention to her feelings of ineptitude, she carried on in stride and asked Dalaria to share her news. Nyssia, too, felt an unnatural chill descend upon her as Dalaria prodded Zharra, the pale, almost metallic looking dragon, to describe the events that transpired in the south. When Zharra spoke of a living and moving corruption, several cautions flooded into her mind as various threads of prophecy became abundantly clear. Those in Frostspire and indeed farther south in Avalide would find this news of great importance indeed. Before she started volunteering her interpretations to the dragons, she would need to bring this information to the council of three and allow them to verify the validity and discuss what information would need to be shared with the other races. Panic was never an ally in negotiations and careful mediation was the secret to building effective and useful alliances.

After the news was shared, Nyssia then introduced herself to those present whom she had either met and forgotten the name of, or had not met at all during the great meeting of the races. Nyssia was amazed at how the bloodlines crossed among the dragons. Before her stood nearly five different generations of dragons, and in total Nyssia was speaking with nine dragons: seven blue, one silver, and Zharra, who identified herself as a platinum dragon. Criosys, the silver dragon, was among the smallest of the seven and nearing his one-hundredth year. Vaelis and Zharra were both daughters of Dalaria, the ancient blue dragon that she had already met at the gathering. Manaseth, the son of Zharra, and Khezhet, the son of Vaelis, were also among the blue dragons present. Auroc, the son of Khezhet was present and Vasuni, with his daughter Sirtis, made up the final two blue dragons.

So began the long process of teaching and learning from one another. Nyssia was rather surprised when Dalaria offered to help her refine the drake form so that is was more than aesthetic but functional in all ways. Nyssia was taken back with the sheer complexity of the dragon anatomy. She learned that there were little glands that ran along the inside of the neck that were responsible for flame ignition. Once contact was made with something similar to a gland but was purely magical, the dragon was able to summon the essence that the glands would ignite and with their own breath they would propel the flame until the dragon needed to rest to regain their essence. The dragons were incredibly thorough in their explanations. But, there were some things that were impossible to define using words.

During the point in the teaching about these odd, internal, magical structures, Nyssia could not completely grasp the nature of what was being explained. She ask if they could try an elven ritual known as the *Aëolyys eth`Seloria* that was used to share memories between elves. Nyssia had heard a report about one of the *Illu`darii* performing the *Aëolyys eth`Seloria* with a human who was able to withstand a great amount of information before he fatigued. Dragons, being far superior to the humans, must therefore be able to tolerate this ritual to an even greater extent.

The dragons were intrigued at the idea, and the intrepid Zharra offered to enter the ritual with Nyssia. Standing face to face, the elf directed Zharra to focus her thoughts on everything she knew about being a member of dragonkind: skills, anatomy, magical abilities, and to let those thoughts remain at the forefront of her mind. Zharra nodded in assent, and lowered her head toward Nyssia so that the elf could place her slender hands on both sides of the scaled platinum head before her. Then the transfer began. Images began to flash between Nyssia and Zharra at an accelerated rate. Nyssia finally understood the magical structures that allowed the dragons to command the elemental and spiritual magic, as well as various other small, seemingly insignificant aspects of the dragon anatomy that would indeed allow her to refine her altered form even more.

The flow of information continued until Nyssia began to see some of the deeper abilities of Zharra. The way the dragon used her knowledge of the spirit to bend light, cast projections and even speak among other dragons with only mental voice was fascinating. It was then that the flow changed. It slowed suddenly—the focus shifting to Nyssia. Images began to flow into Zharra now: Nyssia's sheer amazement with the dragons, her memories, the years of studies in the Frostspire library, and then on the process of shifting herself into whatever shape she desired. Nyssia realized then that Zharra had adapted to the *Aëolyys eth`Seloria* and was somehow using it to draw knowledge from Nyssia. The elf experienced a burst of uninhibited joy, which was soon coupled with fear as she experienced the most unusual of sensations with this dragon that she had only just met. Nyssia quickly realized that she no longer had control of the ritual. She tried to cut off the flow, to catch a breath, for the mental exchange was becoming quite taxing on her now, but she could not get Zharra out of her mind.

"Zharra please... I cannot handle any more of this!" Nyssia thought to herself, attempting to send the words to the essence of Zharra now housed within her body.

Suddenly, as quickly as it had begun, the exchange stopped, leaving Nyssia to collapse weakly to the ground. Zharra's own mind reeled, and she too was forced off of her feet as she slid to her belly and closed her eyes. The spectators split, some attending to the fallen elf, and others to their sister Zharra. Dalaria, Vaelis, and Manaseth all crowded close to Zharra, studying her for signs of life before breathing in relief when the elder dragon opened her eyes. Zharra responded to their concern, shifting her large body and taking in the sight of several other dragons, some who had not been there only a few moments before—including Vaanadu— crowding around her. Then, she looked up at the sky and noticed in surprise that the sun was considerably lower than she remembered it being only a little bit earlier, indicating the passage of hours, not minutes. Relieved and confused, the platinum dragon then sought out the eyes of the elven ice mage. Their gazes met, and they both stared at each other in awe and amazement, finding in each other a new understanding and something even greater—a strangely comforting sense of kinship.

XVII

"What happened?" Nyssia asked as she pulled herself into a sitting position and began massaging her temples in the hope of relieving the sudden onset headache she found herself suffering from... something that was quite a new sensation for the elf.

"I was hoping you would have known, Nyssia," Zharra replied, clearly confused and frustrated that neither one was able to even stand after this ordeal.

Nyssia shrugged and then commented, "How could we be so fatigued after only several minutes of this ritual?"

"Minutes?" inquired Vaelis. "Both of you were engaged with each other for several hours. We couldn't speak to you; we had no idea what was happening."

Now Nyssia openly stared at Zharra in disbelief. Dalaria approached the two and fixed a careful eye on both of them, extending her senses over the two to see if there was anything to be observed or learned.

"Zharra, can you at least tell us what you saw?"

"Allow me to offer up an explanation, Dalaria," Nyssia began. "I believe that the *Aëolyys eth'Seloria* was working correctly at first. I now fully understand how to shift into a drake capable of reproducing flame as well as handling the elemental and spiritual planes while in drake-form, though I will still have to practice this later to be sure. I had no idea that there would be so much I could learn about your race. What I didn't account for was Zharra's adaptation of the ritual. I felt her awaken to what I was doing and with that awakening the ritual changed. With Zharra's adaptation I felt her take complete control of the exchange as she began to pull knowledge from me at an incredible rate."

Zharra then offered some perspective on what she experienced. "It was remarkable. I saw her memories and pains, times of study in their libraries, and then I felt more than saw how she is able to shift her form into whatever being she wants."

Zharra paused suddenly and began to concentrate with all her strength until her image began to blur. The dragons and Nyssia watched with great interest as Zharra's massive frame began to shrink, her wings folded in on each other toward her back as her tail began to retract into the body. Her platinum scales began to smooth over. Her facial features began to change completely. Her entire body was in a state of flux: ever-shrinking; ever-shifting. The entire process only took seconds but it felt much longer as the unthinkable happened there before everyone's eyes. In the center of the gathering where eight dragons and an elf stood watching in amazement, Zharra reduced herself into a near perfect copy of Nyssia, though the dragon made several purposeful changes to identify the differences. Zharra changed the darker hair of Nyssia to the platinum color that her scales were. She retained the same silken robes that barely hid her elegant frame but also patterned the color of the robes into the platinum of her original scales to match her hair. But she did not change the eyes at all. Nestled within the beautiful sculpted features of the elven frame were two very reptilian eyes, which retained their dark blue color from before her change. Only when one looked closely into the face of this near perfect copy of Nyssia could they decipher that this being was not elven.

"This is incredible!" Zharra exclaimed in a soft voice that none recognized. The shift was truly complete. Nyssia stood before Zharra in awe. Vaanadu stepped forward in shock. He canted his head to the left and brought his head low to look into the same eyes that he had been gazing into for years. Zharra extended her soft elven hand and stroked the side of Vaanadu's face. To this much weaker flesh, Vaanadu felt rugged and edged. The scales felt so hard but the warmth she felt from him at her touch, even in this form, caused her mouth to reveal a gentle smile. Zharra then turned to Nyssia once again, and saw that tears were in both their eyes. Today would be a day that would spark such change between the races.

Regrettably, Zharra released the elven image from her mind and urged her features to return to their original shapes once more. The robe began to texture and tighten to reveal hardened scales, and both wings and tail began to emerge from her back. Her hair twisted into her typical horn patterns as her soft delicate face hardened and enlarged until the platinum dragon stood before them once again.

It was young Auroc who submitted the question that many had failed to ask. "Zharra, what made you suddenly end the ritual? We were trying to reach you for so long. Even the *Skarlagnos* was silent to your ears. We were starting to fear what was happening and had begun to call the others down here to aid us when you both suddenly collapsed. Do you remember what happened at that point?"

"Yes, Nyssia asked me to stop and I did. She was growing weary of the ritual and somehow I had taken control of it like she already mentioned."

Nyssia shook her head. "No I didn't. I only wished that it would end. I couldn't breathe; I couldn't even scream. The process was becoming overwhelming and I distinctly remember pleading in my heart for you to stop." How had Zharra known what Nyssia was feeling? Dalaria looked intently at the elf and then closed her eyes. Within moments she opened her eyes in surprise.

"She has become sensitive to the *Skarlagnos*. She does not yet understand how to control it but I can sense her presence through it." The other dragons also closed their eyes and began to nod their heads in amazement. Nyssia could feel *something* but wasn't sure what it was. It was like a probing deep within her awareness. Like a gentle wind that passes through the trees bearing the chill from the frozen wastes of the north.

"In time you will learn to control this gift that we have imprinted upon you, Nyssia. In many ways, I can now look upon you as sister and friend. We have shared what no one else has ever shared so

deeply. Even the dragon bloodlines cannot convey the intimacy between the knowledge passed on from generation to generation that our exchange has given to us."

Zharra's crystal clear voice echoed in the hollows of Nyssia's mind. Such a gift was common to dragons yet, for the first time, had now crossed over into elven hands. Perhaps it was a good thing that she did not fully comprehend how this particular gift worked. Her new trust and favor in the eyes of these dragons was not something to be treated lightly and once again, now was the time for diplomacy and not selfish indulgence. While she knew that all elves would want to learn what Nyssia has been blessed with, a certain amount of decorum was required to ensure that these gifts would not become trivial. The dragons would be the final authority regarding the exchange of information that would pass between the races.

The fears now abated, Vaanadu nuzzled Zharra's neck before heading back to their lair, presumably to continue working on his new heat chamber. The rest of the blues that were gathered as well as Criosys drew closer to Zharra and Nyssia once more as the talks and the teaching continued.

Nyssia then demonstrated her ability to shift into the drake once more, paying close attention to the new details that she had gleaned from Zharra's mind. She felt somewhat different now; somehow more complete in the transformation. Vaelis encouraged her to attempt summoning dragon fire but the technique was foreign to her. The dragon mastery over the elemental plane was completely different from the elven ways of manipulating the magic. For the dragons it was more physical. The dragons *were* magic and it was an extension of their being. She had to let go of her generations of magical manipulations and simply feel the magic within this new form. She turned her awareness inside and began to study the new structures that she had mimicked. It was so complex yet so simple, but still the ability to generate flame escaped her. The dragons near echoed her own thoughts that told her with practice these things would come to pass.

For the entirety of the afternoon and well into the evening, the dragons watched and learned both from Nyssia and from Zharra, who gave her uniquely dragon perspectives on various teachings in order to facilitate the process of information becoming knowledge to the dragons. Nyssia had to stop partway into the evening to rest, opening her small travel satchel and grabbing an assortment of dried fruits, nuts, and an odd-looking wafer that the *Dsa`carii* had created from various seeds and something the elves were becoming rather fond of—a sweet substance the humans had used for years called honey.

Zharra continued to mentor the others as Nyssia observed and ate off to the side, giving her mind a quick reprieve from all the activity of the day. While she didn't mind flying in the dark, she was hoping she could find a place to sleep here for the evening and perhaps venture back to Frostspire in the morning after a decent rest.

"You are doing it again, you know..." Dalaria had somehow managed to sneak up on Nyssia, a feat quite difficult for an ancient dragon of her size. "There is little difference between your private thoughts and those directed to another dragon, especially when someone like me is observing and listening as much with my ears as I am listening with my mind." Dalaria flashed her teeth toward Nyssia, which the elf interpreted as a smile of sorts. "Of course you are welcome to stay here. You will find the lairs of the blue dragons to be fairly cool like your own tower, while those of the red, and to a lesser extent those of the green, tend to be much warmer."

"Thank you Dalaria. This has been an exhausting day already. I do not think I would be able to tolerate entering into another *Aëolyys eth`Seloria* with even one dragon let alone all those here in order to properly convey the process of shape-shifting. I am shocked at how fast Zharra was able to repeat the process."

"My daughter lacks strength in many ways common to dragons, yet is by far the most superior in matters of the mind and spirit. It is fortunate that you chose to enter your ritual with her. Of all the dragons most suited to learning that ability it would be her. I have no doubts that Zharra will become our own ambassador to the humans and to the others in time, for out of all of us, she remains the only one able to master the mental abilities needed to cross physical boundaries with ease. Where we would need to fly, she simply projects her mind in a fraction of the time and with a fraction of the effort. I do not think it was coincidence that enabled her to learn your art so fast."

"I would not feel like I accomplished my mandate if I was only able to pass on the knowledge to one and not all who were able, yet I cannot fight through my current fatigue of mind. I am sorry if I have disappointed you, Dalaria."

"Be not troubled Nyssia. Your wisdom has not fallen on deaf ears." Dalaria too began to concentrate as her image began to distort. The process was considerably slower than when Zharra changed but eventually Dalaria's massive frame began to compress in size as she arched back and began to stand on her hind legs while her forelegs elongated slightly to appear more like arms. Wings and tail, talons and head—all adjusted in size to this new upright frame, but that was where the transformation stopped.

"I don't understand. How is it that you cannot complete the transformation?"

"For me, this is complete." As with Zharra's transformation, Dalaria's voice was also modified by her great reduction in size. "Zharra has giftings the rest of us do not possess. We blues are elemental dragons with average giftings in the realm of the spirit. Her ability to control the spiritual realm affords her greater control over the change than those of us who are masters of the elemental. We compensate for our lack of spiritual mastery with the elemental. This is not failure, Nyssia. The ability to reduce our size but retain the protection of our scales and the use of our wings to some degree is a rather unique gift and I have no doubt there will come a time when this ability will be of use."

Dalaria released the image and returned back to her original size once again while Zharra nodded to Dalaria and continued to guide the other dragons in their first changes into forms very similar to what Dalaria was able to create.

Nyssia finished her small meal and continued to watch the dragons practice. Criosys was struggling a little bit and Zharra was spending some additional time with him. Nyssia wondered whether this young silver one was also spiritually gifted like Zharra and whether or not his eventual transformations would be like Zharra's were.

Nyssia took the time to dwell on what she had learned today. She was looking forward to being alone tomorrow so she could practice summoning her flame but the dragon speech gift was something that she could only really practice here among the dragons and she was at a loss as to why she could not repeat what she had already done once. Was it easier for her to do when she was linked with a dragon mind? That could explain part of the difficulty. Perhaps in her drake form she would be more aware, provided she could concentrate on feeling the magic instead of trying to manipulate it. That too would have to wait until tomorrow. Dalaria had called an end to the training finally. The sun was long gone, yet Nyssia noticed that the dragons were unaffected by the darkness. They all looked to Nyssia and either nodded or inclined their massive heads toward her, thanking her for the knowledge that was passed to them today. Vaelis was the third last to leave as Zharra and Dalaria approached Nyssia.

"I would have invited you to rest in my lair, Nyssia, but apparently Zharra insists on having your company tonight. I trust both our races have been strengthened through what has been shared this day. You will always be welcome among us Nyssia—without invitation. Rest well."

"Thank you Dalaria. I will stop by in the morning once again to say my farewells before I return to the Frostspire." Dalaria smiled in acknowledgement of the courtesy before vaulting herself into the air and climbing toward a fairly large prominence that overlooked the entire summit and the frozen lake far below.

"My lair is a small distance from here to the southwest, Nyssia. This short flight will give us some time to speak and work on your proficiency with the *Skarlagnos* as well. Try to aim your thoughts. Concentrate on me and form the words like you did before. Remember that dragons feel magic, we do not control magic. Are you ready?"

Nyssia nodded and began her change into the blue drake once more. With each shifting of her shape it was getting easier to recreate the mental image, and the finer details were starting to become more instinctual. This time she paid special attention to her eyes, attempting to enhance her ability to see in low light. It was like a new world had opened up to her. Instead of everything lying in shadows, a veil was lifted and she could see nearly as well now as she was able to during the day. With more practice, even her vision in this form would improve. Zharra looked over Nyssia, apparently satisfied with the change, and lifted herself into the air, spiraling out of the summit and beginning her flight southwest with Nyssia following close behind.

"Try to feel the words Nyssia. Relax your mind and feel."

Nyssia found it hard to relax while concentrating on her flying. While few of the elves were fully capable of shape-shifting into a flight form, many of those that did found themselves devoting much of their concentration and energy to the particular act of flying. Nyssia tried to calm her anxiousness, knowing that her wings would continue to uphold her even if she did ease her intense concentration. Flight was always enjoyable for Nyssia, but now that she was learning to relax and let the drake form do the work, she found the flight experience even more exhilarating. Zharra looked back several times but did not pressure Nyssia any longer, though a sense of expectancy hovered between them. Nyssia tried to relax even more. She focused on Zharra, studied her beautiful wings that slowly beat the air in a gentle rhythm, and began to form thoughts in her mind. It did not appear to be working.

What was so different from before? She felt threatened then. Panic had set in. Two distinct emotions that... emotions! She had to feel the words, not only think them. Again her mind was interfering with the process. She concentrated on Zharra once again.

"I understand now."

"I knew you would figure out the nature of it soon. I know I saw more than you wanted me to see Nyssia, but I hope you can forgive me for drawing so much from you. I got lost in the vast amount of knowledge your mind contained. I should not have been studying you as closely as I did. But I do not regret. I feel connected to you in a very different way than I am connected to my kin."

"There is nothing to forgive. I did the same to you at first. I was not anticipating you learning from me so fast. I was humbled today." Nyssia paused for a moment before continuing. *"There was something else I think I learned today. I have not attempted it yet, but I believe I understand how you bend light as well."*

Zharra smiled at the words Nyssia projected then looked over her shoulder. Zharra concentrated her efforts and began to pull what little ambient light existed in the darkness and vanished.

"Practice this in the daytime, first. Having an abundance of light makes this work much easier, but as you can see, there is ambient light even in the darkness." Zharra released her light weave as the two of them continued on their south-westerly route until Zharra gestured toward a large mountain with a great hollow in the center. Zharra hovered around the aperture and then descended down into the mountain with Nyssia not far behind. Inside the lair, Vaanadu stood waiting and smiled. He then chuckled and shook his head when Nyssia descended behind his mate.

"Welcome, little sister. It is an honor to have you among us."

"The honor is mine, Vaanadu," Nyssia projected respectfully before breaking into laughter at the surprise on Vaanadu's face. Zharra began explaining the findings of the day as she closed the gap between them and nuzzled against her mate. The three spoke for a time. They talked of matters of significance and they talked of matters of ease and for the pure enjoyment of the company. Nyssia received a guided tour through the lair that night as well. It was far from simple, and the room of glass that Vaanadu was working on was beautiful and noticeably warmer than the rest of the lair. Nyssia doubted Zharra when she told her that Valkyyrak and Dalaria's lair was three times as large and far more splendid to behold, but once Vaanadu conceded that fact she believed it.

Finally it was time for sleep. Zharra and Vaanadu told her she could sleep wherever she wished as they headed to one of the larger chambers. Nyssia looked up into the night that shone in through the opening to the lair. With the endless expanse of clear dark sky above her, she curled up within the faint patch of moonlight that illuminated the chamber floor and closed her scaled eyes. She chose to stay in the drake form for the evening, thinking that it would be much more comfortable sleeping on the ground in this form as compared to her elven form. She was right.

Morning came much the same as it came every morning for Nyssia, though had she remained in elven form she would have missed the usual comforts of her large furnished living quarters within the spire. She woke in her drake form, surprised that she had actually maintained the form for the entire evening. Somehow she needed to make a decision of the will to release this image to return to elven form.

Nyssia stretched out her limbs and unfurled her wings. Hunger was beginning to gnaw at her stomach, and she found herself revolted at the carnivorous thoughts beginning to swirl through her head. She was craving meat. Hopefully this was just a side effect of assuming a predatory form such as this. Vaanadu came out to greet Nyssia and told her that Zharra had left early this morning to seek out Sycaris, the red female among them that was attuned to the voice of prophecy. A conversation with this dragon would be something to look forward to in time. For now though, Nyssia thanked Vaanadu for the company and the conversation, informing him that she intended on returning to the summit to pay her respects to the others there before heading back to Frostspire.

Exiting the lair that in itself was a masterpiece to behold, she turned to the northeast and began her short flight back to the summit. Seeing that no one was around, she turned her thoughts within once again and tried to summon the dragon flame. She tried to form the image of fire in her mind, but that didn't work. She tried forcing out the fire by exhaling with tremendous force but she only succeeded in making a rather embarrassing straining noise that made her choke in midair. She was glad no one was watching her make a fool of herself like this. Nyssia tried several other techniques and variants but the skill was escaping her so she decided to halt her experiments now before frustration overtook her.

Approaching the summit area again she saw the large green dragon hovering in patrol around the peaks above. Apparently, they alternated in sharing patrolling duties for the younger black dragon from yesterday was no longer encircling the summit. Vaanadu's brother was definitely more savage in appearance than most of the dragons she had seen, but he was still nothing compared to Sargeron. Nyssia found it fascinating how much of their abilities and strengths were linked to the scale colors. That was something else for her to eventually learn about in time. Nostrimus began to probe Nyssia's mind as she flew by but said nothing as Nyssia began her decent toward the plateau below. Nyssia landed gently near to where Manaseth and Sirtis were already practicing shape-shifting into the upright mini-dragon form that Dalaria had shown them the day before.

Nyssia finally released the image of the drake and resumed her soft and curvaceous elven form, part of her already missing the sensation of being the blue drake. She wandered over to the satchel and cloak that she had completely forgot about after landing the day before and reached inside for another quick meal as she slung the satchel and cloak back around her shoulders.

"Good morning Nyssia." The distinct voice of Zharra within her head made her look around in an attempt to locate the great platinum dragon, but she was not to be seen.

"Hello Zharra. Are you hiding this morning?"

"No, I am spending some time with Sycaris. I will speak to you more about her later but it was her mother that fell during the call of the Tear several days past. While she possesses great strength, sometimes the presence of a friend is needed to help one pass through the final stages of their grief."

"Death is something I have not had to deal with personally so I cannot imagine the depths of her pain. Please offer her my condolences, for what they are worth."

"She will appreciate your concern Nyssia. You have earned a place of respect among us here. I wish I could see you off this morning but we shall stay in touch this way. Safe flight back to the east Nyssia."

With those final words, Nyssia felt the connection wane. Zharra must have been able to direct the channel that enabled her to communicate back without seeing her—another reason to respect the tremendous power of Zharra. Multi-tasking with this new communication was going to require even more practice. While Nyssia had been engaged in private conversation with Zharra, Dalaria and several of the others had now gathered to wish her well on her travels back to Frostspire. Nyssia felt a slight pang of embarrassment at having not been paying attention to the activities around her.

"Think nothing of it Nyssia. It was plain to see you were occupied and with the speed at which you are adapting to our ways I would expect you to be able to handle the *Skarlagnos* and be present in body rather soon indeed. At least you had the presence of mind to continue to eat while you were lost in conversation." Dalaria smiled that large toothy grin as Nyssia looked down to her hands noticing that the meal she remembered barely starting was finished. Her cheeks grew flushed.

"Tell Valeris that it has been our pleasure to host you here with us and should others wish to learn what we have begun to teach you, perhaps we can arrange something else at a later time. Now that you can hear our thoughts, I expect communication to flow much faster between the elves and the dragons."

"Yes, I expect the same, and I will be sure to convey the deep honor and respect that I have felt at being accepted among dragonkind. When I woke this morning, I actually missed being in the drake form. I do not think that I will ever be the same again and I owe that to you all."

The gathered dragons watched on as Nyssia once again gathered her essence and shifted into the blue drake once more. Several of the dragons wished her safety in travel and thanked her for the instruction. Nyssia let out a simple roar of her own, much to the pleasure of the dragons, before she climbed into the morning sky and began her long flight east toward Frostspire.

Leaving the magic of the summit behind she soared in gentle rhythm, riding the warmer air currents that held up her frame above the ice-topped peaks below. Her thoughts began to wander to the report that she would be expected to deliver to the council of three. How could she convey all that had happened in mere words? She decided that perhaps the *Aëolyys eth'Seloria* would be the best way to give a complete report. Although asking one of the three to enter into this ritual with her was not proper etiquette, perhaps in light of the content that she would offer they would understand this request and grant her a ritual.

Alone for the second time that morning, Nyssia again let her thoughts stray to the practicing of the dragon flame. She felt like the verge of discovery was in reach yet it escaped her once more. For about an hour she soared, frustration mounting at her inability to master something so fundamental to the dragons as dragon fire. More practice perhaps, but this thought brought no comfort.

Flying amid the bright rays of sun, the echo of Zharra's voice brought light to memory in the center of her frustration. Practice this in daytime she said. Perhaps a shift in focus was needed. While the making of fire was more of a physiological process in the dragon form, the bending of light felt much more like the manipulation of the sphere of the spirit and the elemental together. She gathered her will and her essence within and began to harness the light around her. It embraced her as a lover, swirling and caressing her drake form until at last the weave was complete. In the crisp air of the Icecrown Peaks flew a fading blue streak toward the frozen wastes and the lands of the *Dsa'carii*. Nyssia the frost mage, the blue drake of the Icecrowns and of Frostspire, vanished in plain sight and the only sound that could be heard for leagues was the sound of her triumphant laughter.

XVIII

The purging of Lorenth continued. Arimas was relentless in his complete and thorough search for those with betrayal in their hearts. The scepter at last was laid down as *Retribution* resurrected the long-forgotten image of the priest-king. Together with his royal guard, now complete and strong at twenty-four, they combed every corner of the city. The upper quarters were laid bare before Arimas' eyes and those with ill-intent in their souls were wise to flee before being discovered as traitors. Many were tempted to think that Arimas had fallen into madness, yet there was no madness to be seen behind the eyes that burned once more with the zeal of his youth.

The lower city nearly fell to chaos when Arimas turned his gaze upon the shadowed streets. No house was left unchecked. Every inn and tavern, blacksmith shop and tannery, butcher, baker and cobbler was searched and by the end of the third day, those filled with treason that were not yet discovered were fleeing the city as fast as they could before Arimas could look them in the eyes. Once again, the people of Lorenth knew righteous fear. Arimas was indeed touched by the gods, for no lie escaped him. Those of noble intent felt true safety and security under the firm and fair hand of Arimas... the same hand that wielded *Retribution* with justice and honor.

Dean was now a name spoken solely with scorn. Those on the council that were deceived by his talents were given the chance to repent, as were all citizens and soldiers alike, yet still there were some who would choose exile over contrition, and still some who thought to fool the eyes of the priest-king. Those few tried to remain hidden, laying in wait for the opportunity to aid Dean in whatever plot he would try to rekindle. But Arimas could see the darkness in their hearts like he saw the filth that clung to Dean. There were no words given, no offers of grace, and deaf ears were aplenty when the traitors offered up insincere pleas for mercy. The royal guard struck down all who were routed out. Among the traitors, two thought to strike down Arimas in desperation, but *Retribution* was faster than their swords and surer than their feeble strikes. Blood ran into the canals of the Ardun River as the streets were painted red with treachery.

With the upper and lower cities purged, Arimas returned to the fortress to rest for a time, taking council with his royal guards and summoning Commander Barros to join him as well. Since returning from the forest not two days ago now, Hadrin had been rather diligent in his plans to summon the eastern border detail for a rather special task that would be started tomorrow. Hadrin's report on the assassination of both Counselor Nolan and Covenal Guilian did nothing to improve the priest-king's mood, yet it did confirm his suspicions that Dean had managed to assemble his own elite guards to aid him in his plot to usurp the crown. Farin was to be honored for his service to Lorenth once the purge was complete, and would be noted for acts of bravery and loyal fealty to king and country. Counselor Nolan, advisor and friend since before the foundations of Lorenth itself, was also to be remembered.

Fate indeed was not fair. The past two days after Hadrin's report, Arimas was plagued with remorse as he often reflected on the thought that it should have been him who bled and died upon the river's edge that day. While he was dragon-watching in the west, Nolan Weiss was sent to suffer Arimas' fate in the east. And Farin... Arimas was aware of the poorly concealed ill will that Farin harbored toward Dean, but had, like others, believed the younger man's feelings a result of the jealousy typical between a man and his superior. It was obvious, though, that Farin knew much more about the former seneschal than even Arimas did. There were no words that could be said that could appease this guilt that rested on the king's shoulders. The only answer to such wickedness was justice and purification. At the end of the purge, Farin's name would be held in honor once more—his death would not be in vain.

Arimas looked around at his trusted few that were now gathered in the fortress. There stood twenty-four of his best, who had bled and served in honor for years, standing in their regalia as shining examples of the strength that Lorenth stood for. Also standing by their side was Commander Barros, who had proven himself at Farin's side time and time again. Now that the eastern border detail was leaderless, Hadrin temporarily assumed its command and expertly held them in check against the plot of Dean before ordering their quick retreat back to Lorenth. Also among the soldiers in arms stood Lead Counselor Cirra Bethanin, whose advice could always be trusted, even when many on the council were deceived.

"So ends the third day, Arimas," Cirra began. "Hope is spreading throughout the streets again and darkness is failing in the light of a new day for Lorenth."

"And each of you here has had a hand in creating this new day. When allies were few and loyalties were weak, each of you stood by my side." Arimas emphasized those last few words by pointing to his royal guards first and then nodding to the lead counselor and the commander. Arimas turned and faced the commander with an inquiring look in his eyes. Barros nodded and grinned.

"Tomorrow morning the final purge begins. I am satisfied with the progress made in both the upper and lower city but there is one place that has been neglected by us for years." Even some of the royal guards had to raise an eyebrow at that comment. "As some of you know, I discovered Dean wandering around behind the temple grounds before the end of the fourth watch. I later returned to the temple grounds to walk and pray for guidance, and saw that aside from the trees and the inner wall there was nothing where I had seen Dean earlier—except an entrance to the sewers. I have even more good reason to believe that something lies in wait for us beneath the surface. Commander Barros and his men have been covertly watching every sewer entrance for the past two days while we have been purging the city proper. The commander now confirms my suspicions and there has been activity through the sewer entrances."

"There has been much activity, I am afraid," Hadrin began. "Some of my men hid beneath small piles of refuse and others had to hang their armor in favor of torn and soiled rags, to secure thorough and detailed information to report. The members of this gang of thieves enter and exit in groups of two or three. There also appears to be a rank structure among them, though I have not as yet been able to piece out the details. It is clear that Dean had a hand in their establishment, for some carry keys to the sewers and are careful to lock the entrances once they are inside. They move quietly and quickly and favor the use of short blades and hardened leathers. Some of them appear rather inexperienced, but there are several that show signs of great training and skill. Purging the sewers will not be easy. I am sure they have been listening to the mayhem above over the last few days and I believe they are preparing their own fortifications below in anticipation for our eventual investigations beneath the city, where all the filth gathers—rather figurative meeting area wouldn't you say, your Excellency?"

"Rather fitting indeed. I would like to speak with one of our engineers about the sewers. It has been long time since I even gave thought to them but I would like to know their structure and other potential entrances or exits and where they lie."

Hadrin smiled again as he produced a report and what appeared to be markings that detailed the original layout of the sewers. "I figured you would need this information so I saw to this part personally while my men were monitoring the entrances into the city. There are a team of six engineers who are responsible for the maintenance of the sewer lines. Two stay above ground and four have small working areas below. Unfortunately all four of the engineers below ground are missing and have been missing for some time. Of the two above ground, one fled with the rest of the exiles, and the other remained true to Lorenth. He maintains that he had no idea the other four were missing. I do believe him.

"He was rather helpful in providing us with these schematics that show the sewer routes as well as the intake line and the exit line which connects with the Ardun River several leagues downstream.

Along the exit line are several incineration points with a series of grates that catch the larger garbage and filth and shunt it away from the river into various collection points where the refuse is burned to ash. Approaching from the south would be difficult at best. There is a chance for a small party to enter through the entrance line but it is at the base of the waterfall and a short swim under the water. The engineer assures me that there is not much of a swim before the intake line opens into the sewer area and one could surface from the water to breathe."

Arimas waved at Anton and Rorrick to come over as the three looked over the sewer map. Arimas began to trace the intake route with his finger noticing the various bifurcations along the way as well as the sewer entrances above. Anton began to point out various areas which were larger than the other areas that would be an ideal location for Dean's followers to maintain their position and launch a counter attack. Rorrick nodded his agreement while Arimas looked on. Arimas' eyes wandered back to the intake line as he began to search for the closest sewer entrance from the intake line. Sewer number twenty-four was only a short distance away. A plan began to reveal itself.

"How difficult would it be to have a few men sneak into the intake line and unlock sewer entrance number twenty-four to allow a larger force to descend into the sewers? Perhaps we could make it known we would start with entrance number one and draw their attention to the lower city while a small select group were busy slipping into the sewers in the upper city."

Hadrin nodded. "With some occasional banging around and fiddling with the sewer locks this might indeed draw the attention away from the upper city. It should not be that difficult, your Excellency."

"Then let us tentatively plan for this. Commander, you shall lead thirty of your best men and twenty of my royal guards to the upper city with torn cloaks draped over your armor. You will remain hiding until the sewer entrance is open. Anton, you will lead the honor guard toward the lower city where you will fumble with the each of the sewer gates. Have the men borrow the armor of the border detail to confuse the peasantry and hopefully those below into thinking that our main force is concentrated in the lower city. If there is a commotion, do not quell it. Let the attentions of everyone be drawn to you until those of us in the upper city are in position.

"Have your men break into smaller groups after about one hour and have those groups begin to guard each sewer entrance in the entire city, except number twenty-four which will be our exit once we have completed the purge. If anyone opens a sewer entrance from inside, have your men strike quick and true and secure the area. No one must be allowed to escape. Hadrin, you will also arrange to have the remaining border detail mounted at the front gates and conducting random patrols throughout the city as well as beyond the gates along the river."

"Who will be heading into the intake line?" Cirra asked.

"I will take Garron, Dayle and Rorrick with me down into the intake line. We shall unlock the sewer entrance and lead the rest of the men through the sewers."

No one liked this idea, especially Anton and Cirra. "Arimas, we have no way to know whether that entrance is being watched. I do not believe this is a safe or prudent course of action for the priest-king." Anton spoke with conviction in his voice as he looked at Arimas intently.

"They will find an Arimas much more attuned to their presence than before, Anton. Fear not for me. Fear for them instead. I need you to ensure the defenses are maintained and the patrols are carried out to maximal effectiveness. I appreciate your caution but this matter is not open for debate."

Cirra appeared as though she wished to question Arimas about his decision further but refrained, choosing instead to take her seat while Anton and Rorrick returned to their place among the royal guard. Arimas dismissed everyone shortly after that, knowing that what was needed now was not more talk and planning but a good night's rest to ensure all bore sharp minds along with sharp blades into the dim corridors beneath the city. When all had vacated the fortress, Arimas approached one of the windows that looked out to the east, knelt down, and began to pray for guidance, strength, and a wisdom such as he had never prayed for before. Beneath the pale light of the rising moon, Arimas could almost feel a warmth cascade down upon his head and shoulders, infusing him with life and peace. For some reason he knew his course was sure.

After securing *Retribution* behind the large gilded doors of the royal armory, Arimas walked with a measured pace back toward his chambers. While he did feel at peace there still remained many questions that ran through his mind: thoughts of the east, and of Dean; thoughts of the exiles; thoughts of how he would manage a complete purge of the townships. There was much to do now, and even more to do later.

While he afforded Dean and the other exiles a chance to leave Lorenth in peace, only a fool would believe the fight with Dean to be completely over. Measures would need to be implemented to secure the lands of Lorenth and protect them against more than just the beasts now. Lorenth had a new enemy—an enemy with intellect and skill that was superseded only by pride. Arimas could not yet wash his hands of human blood, for deep in his heart he knew that even more was yet to be spilt.

Approaching the door to his spacious chambers, Arimas put an end to all the thoughts and cares of Lorenth. Relaxation was something that seldom came to Arimas, a fact that Verona chastised him about often. Perhaps he would indulge in some easing of the spirit tonight. His two chamber servants were at their posts as usual, both bowing low to the priest-king as he approached.

"Tomas, do you know if the queen has retired for the evening?"

"Yes my liege. She awaits you within."

"Excellent. Might I request a warm bath be drawn for me tonight?"

Tomas exchanged looks with Relde before Relde offered the next answer. "The queen has already requested a bath to be drawn for you both, sire. We brought the water inside your chamber less than ten minutes ago. Please let us know if it needs to be refreshed."

"I will indeed, but I do not think that will be necessary. I suppose I shall also pretend to act surprised." Arimas flashed them both a wide smile before adding, "Good night gentlemen."

"Goodnight my liege."

"Rest well, sire."

Arimas opened the door to his chamber and headed toward the bathing room that he and his queen shared. Very few in Lorenth had such a tub as Arimas. In time, he would like to see all in the city, or at least within the fortress and citadel, outfitted with such finely crafted pieces. Beneath the tub sat the heating room where several fires would heat large containers of water for use within the fortress while also casting their heat upon several thin sheets of metal that were secured and sealed to the bottom of each tub. As these sheets of metal heated, the water also began to draw that heat into the water slightly in order to offset the natural cooling of water when taken away from a heat source. Having a slab of hot metal beneath your feet was not the most ideal arrangement though, so the tub was also crafted with thin stone columns that ran across the metal sheet, providing a surface to sit upon that would not retain the heat radiating from the metal. Overall, the idea was rather ingenious. The only draw back was the amount of trips needed to bring the pre-warmed water from the heating room to fill the large tub.

As he turned the corner of his chamber room that led into the bathing room he realized that tonight would not be a night of relaxation after all. Arimas smiled that private smile that only his wife was privy to as he moved ever closer to the vision of seductive beauty that sat naked before him, sitting vulnerable on the edge of the tub waiting for her lover and king. No, there would be no relaxation at all this night.

* * *

The following morning, the planning phase was conducted as expected. The men were moving into position as instructed. Anton was in command of the honor guard while Hadrin and his small detachment of the border detail with the royal guard were hiding. Arimas and his select three were already lowering themselves down the back of the fortress and into the water below where they would inevitably find the intake line and whatever opposition awaited them inside the sewers.

Arimas could not fully concentrate this morning. Knowing that he needed to be fully present with his men if this was to succeed, he tried repeatedly to guard his mind from the worry that was haunting him. This was the third morning that Verona had awoken from a fitful sleep retching from a horrible sickness. The apothecary had once again rushed to her aid, given her a tincture, and told her to rest, offering little encouragement to Arimas. He had seen sickness before but this was somehow different, and the differences were what had him uneasy.

He shook his head, subconsciously believing that this motion would help him forget this worry as he focused once more on the task at hand. While they were armed, the men were not protected, as they could not afford to wear their heavy armor if they were required to swim any distance. The precious metal garb remained with Hadrin above and would be given to them once they had opened the sewer and reunited with the main force that would sweep the area below. At no point did any of the four talk. Silence discipline was maintained as the small band moved with purpose and precision into the water, descending into the chill in search for the intake line. The pounding of the waterfall behind them made their silence disciplines rather unnecessary for the moment, but as in each battle these men went into, certain rules remained, and this would be no different.

Thankfully, the report from the engineer was fairly accurate and it was a very short swim under the water to reach the intake line and follow it into the sewers where they could surface for air. All four were wary as they slowly surfaced. Weapons drawn, the four inched their way along the edge of the sewer line with Arimas taking the lead. He was casting his senses forward, which was the best way for him to describe what he was trying to do. Somehow he would *know* if evil was near. He wasn't sure how he knew this but his men learned to trust this new ability rather quickly as his thorough purge of Lorenth validated this instinct over and over again.

They made their way out of the sewer line without incident. There were no guards waiting for them and Arimas could not sense anything out of the ordinary. The four walked the short span of approximately sixty paces which brought them to the ladder leading up to sewer entrance number twenty-four. Rorrick ascended the ladder and drew his keys to unlock the entrance cover, trying his best to ensure as little noise as possible was made in the process. Whether it was blind luck that no one was guarding this area, or simply the result of the diversion in the lower city no one was sure, but none of the four wanted to waste time figuring it out. With the early morning sun streaming through the sewer entrance, Rorrick surfaced only for a brief moment, searching for Hadrin's eyes to lock on his to indicate that the way was open. Rorrick found Hadrin looking in anticipation as the men in hiding began to move quickly and efficiently toward the sewer entrance, descending into the grim and dank sewers below.

The force of men—now fifty-five strong with Arimas taken into account—formed up in ranks trying to adhere to the silence disciplines that were ordered last night and reiterated again this morning. No one talked as Arimas and his three royal guards slipped out of their wet underclothes and donned their battle armor once more. Commander Barros presented the men to Arimas for his inspection and turned over command before he too stepped back into the formation for the inspection. Arimas nodded his approval to the commander then quickly looked over his men that were assembled. He extended his senses over the men once more hoping to find nothing but loyalty, and indeed, that was all he found.

With blades stowed, each of the men of the border detail drew forth crossbows and began to load bolts, proceeding to the front ranks as they did so. The royal guards, with Arimas at its head, remained poised with their blades and, of course, *Retribution* at the ready. With their pre-assigned syndicate formations, the men broke into five groups and began to disperse down various tunnels beneath the city as they began their systematic sweep of the sewers.

Commander Barros led the first division down the western main line while Rorrick followed with the second division. The second division was to digress to the southwest at the next major junction, working beside Hadrin as both moved across the western and south-western part of the sewers. Dayle and Garron leading divisions three and four headed down the southern main line where Garron would be leading division four south and into the various service lines branching off the south main line and the larger collection points toward the center. They would work together yet would maintain their own responsibilities and would function independently when needed. Arimas led the final division directly into the center of the sewers, following the south-western main line. This way had very few bifurcations, but contained all the incineration chambers, and eventually ran into the exit line with the various grates funneling larger refuse and waste into the collection rooms prior to incineration.

Torchlight was forbidden on this mission and those not in a group being led by Arimas were even more wary knowing that none of the others possessed the same skills of detection that the priest-king was becoming even more renowned for. Each group moved cautiously and quietly. Eleven men per syndicate, six border detail with crossbows, four royal guardsmen with their savage triple-forged balanced blades, and then the syndicate leader as well, armed as he desired.

The first hour passed slowly as the men were careful and thorough in their sweep, moving almost as a single unit in five segmented pieces. There was nothing out of the ordinary in the northern and western parts of the sewers although Rorrick did take note of several excavations within the sewer walls at various points that led into collapsed sections that could have been utilized as a room of some kind. None of these excavations were ever indicated on the maps and schematics, and he made a mental note of their locations. Dayle also found similar excavations along the southern mainline, and these were also abandoned.

It wasn't until the middle of the second hour that chaos burst forth beneath the ground. It didn't matter who shot first because once the first bolt struck the neck of the ruffian patrolling the paths between sewer entrances number eleven and six, the other denizens took up the alarm as those in the border detail and royal guards under Garron's command began to take cover where they could. Hadrin and Rorrick wanted to turn their sweep toward the commotion in the east yet they obeyed their orders. They continued in their western sweeps much faster, throwing caution to the wind in an effort to complete their tasks and assist their brothers-in-arms who were now engaging the enemy beneath the city.

Arimas continued his search toward the southwest. He extended his senses around him and could detect a rather large source of darkness to his left, where Dayle and Garron would likely be fighting now. He could sense nothing else in the immediate area but he still had to ensure that he followed the directives that he passed on to his men. Leadership was not delegation only. A good leader would never ask his men to do something that he himself was not prepared to do. Divisions three and four knew their job. Each group was instructed to hold their positions and lure the rogues out to them once they made contact. Under no circumstances were they to pursue the enemy without the support of the other divisions who would be conducting their sweeps and positioning themselves behind the threat in hopes to outflank the enemy within their own territory.

The royal guards that accompanied Dayle and Garron rested against the stone walls of the sewers, swords drawn and held across their chests in patient wait for these would-be assassins to throw caution to the wind and test them in skill at arms. Garron and Dayle were more than content to wait out the barrage of bolt fire that flew past them each time one or two would venture a shot down the dark tunnel. The occasional yelp or scream indicated that more often than not, their bolts were finding a target. The men knew their task and were confident that the other three divisions were on the move and would soon be able to offer support to them now that they were under fire.

Arimas and his syndicate were pulled into the conflict soon after as the rogues attempted the same flanking maneuvers on Dayle and Garron's position. Arimas could sense their approach and ordered his crossbow men to ready themselves while Arimas and the other four royal guards clung to the leftmost wall of the sewer and moved toward the junction that would lead farther east toward the main conflict.

The surprise attack only took advantage of the first five men to turn the corner. Even in the darkness and gloom of the sewers, Arimas and the others could see the whites of their eyes widen in shock as the rogues stared down at the crossbows leveled at their chests. The first volley was fired and the border detail stowed their crossbows and drew their blades to assist Arimas and the other four. *Retribution* swung free and wild as several of the lesser trained rogues cried out that Arimas was upon them in an attempt to warn the others. Arimas couldn't have planned it better. The young fools created a panic among the other denizens as the 'legendary' priest-king with his savage battle maul hunted for blood beneath the sewers.

Some of the rogues scattered and broke rank. Cries of terror coming from above echoed in the hollow passages of the sewers as some attempted their escape through the main sewer entrances now guarded by Anton and the honor guard. However, those with more training and discipline stood to fight. These men were definitely better trained than Arimas had expected, for the fight persisted for quite a time. Two of the border detail actually saw their proficiency in training and tried to stow their blades in an attempt to reload their crossbows for a second shot. One of the rogues clad in dark black and crimson studded leathers feigned a retreat to gain some distance before he leapt up and to the right launching two small throwing blades directly at the men reloading their crossbows. Arimas spun around to look at his men but they were already dead—one had a blade buried in his left eye and the other had caught a blade in his throat.

Arimas almost began to wonder if these men possessed better training than his own royal guards. They gave no ground yet they could not take any ground either. Aside from two losses in Arimas' division, no other blood was spilt on either side as the clang of steel on steel rang throughout the sewer lines. Finally the tide of battle shifted. Hadrin and Rorrick had completed their western sweep and were converging upon Arimas and his position. Flanking the rogues, another quick volley of bolts was launched into their ranks catching several off guard before the skilled rogue in the dark leathers ordered a tactical retreat. Several small, round devices were dropped on the ground which exploded into a thick smoke that completely filled the tunnel where the rogues made their stand. Divisions one and two rushed toward the smoke as Arimas and his men withdrew seeking cover, not sure what threat would surface from the smoke when it cleared.

The smoke shield lasted not even a minute before it dissipated and revealed an empty sewer. Arimas cast forth his senses and thought he felt a small group heading farther southwest toward the main exit line where hopefully Commander Barros' mounted border detail were still actively patrolling and would catch the few who were slipping through the noose.

Arimas nodded at Hadrin and Rorrick as they all regrouped, reloaded their crossbows and made their way east toward Dayle and Garron who had been fighting without assistance for some time now. Unfortunately, the rogues had consolidated their position within a small service line that provided the only way into their main defensive position. There were no other lines that intersected with it to provide a flanking opportunity and those down the service line were not prepared to charge Arimas and his men blindly, knowing that the soldiers of Lorenth also brought ranged weapons. It appeared to be a standstill.

When all five divisions had regrouped together in the far southeast of the sewers, Arimas looked over his men and was relieved to note that no one else had fallen. Arimas told the royal guards to sheathe blades and free their large gilded shields from the backs of their cloaks and breastplates to create a shield wall to advance down the service line. This was a less than ideal formation in such tight quarters for the service line could only fit four men across. Four walked low holding their shields to protect the legs of the wall while the four behind them held their shields high and on a slant, covering the lip of the other shields while diverting any stray bolts up and over the formation. Hadrin was ordered to stay back and guard the rear with his thirty men while Arimas and his twenty-three royal guards began their slow advance down the service line.

Arimas could feel the darkness of the men ahead of him as they began to deteriorate into disarray. Once they saw the gilded shields of the royal guard, all knew for sure that Arimas was among them and the earlier cries of their comrades within the chaos could now be trusted. Waves of bolts continued to streak toward the shield wall, some lodging themselves into the shields while others were deflected into the top of the sewer line or redirected over the small group of twenty-four men.

Watching the steady advance of Arimas, and *Retribution*, the rogues launched several more of the small canisters down the sewer line, causing more smoke to fill the sewers. This smoke was not as benign as before. Arimas could *feel* that something was wrong about the nature of the sudden fog. Suddenly his men began to cough and choke as the noxious gas began spreading throughout the formation of his elite soldiers. Arimas could feel the effects upon him as well and it enraged him with righteous fury.

In the briefest moment of clarity, he realized that his fury was combating the effects of the gas. He concentrated within himself allowing the zealous devotion to consume him. Within the sickly green gases that surrounded his men, trying to break their formation and render them exposed to the barrage of bolts that were now being withheld, Arimas stared at his hands as they began to illuminate with a soft amber-colored light. Arimas felt a strong presence within him as he dropped to his knees and began to pray aloud in a tongue not his own.

"Deim anoth hesid adon. Tovendi noctu elsarii et enchasad etum fiallis!"

The amber light within his hands burst free and radiated out in all directions, instantly neutralizing all the gas around him and his men. Those that had begun to wane under the gas were returned to their full strength. For the briefest of moments, the entire sewer was filled with the light that radiated from Arimas, illuminating the faces of their enemies before submitting them all to the darkness once again. None of the rogues waited around for Arimas and his men to gather themselves again. Arimas and his royal guards shook off the effects of the gas and continued to advance quickly upon the position formerly guarded by the rogues. Arimas stood down the shield wall and extended his senses down the service line sensing nothing in the immediate area but noticing that there was an excavation dug out into the sewer wall.

Arimas nodded his orders sharply and the small party advanced slowly upon the excavation. Their advance was cut short as the tunnel suddenly exploded, sending dirt and rock through the hole in the side of the sewer. The impact of the blast sent all the men to the ground but thankfully no one was close enough to be seriously injured. Arimas knew this was not an attack maneuver but a deception maneuver designed to conceal their path of escape from the sewers. The noose was broken. Despite all of his planning and orchestration, many of the rogues had found a way to exit Arimas' grasp, allowed to live and plot another day.

"My lord... is anyone hurt?"

"We are merely shaken Hadrin. Aside from several small cuts we were not injured in their escape. We are done down here, men. I did not take into account a potential escape route from within the sewers other than the main lines that were created. We will need to appoint new engineers shortly. I want reports on what lines have been compromised and I want the routes re-excavated to discover how these rogues escaped so that we can protect the security beneath our city and prevent situations such as this from happening again. Let's move out men—back to sewer entrance twenty-four."

The organized retreat was conducted without any further event. All in all, the total number of enemies killed numbered at fifteen while the soldiers of Lorenth sustained two deaths of their own. The magister would be tasked with the retrieval and identification of all the bodies in the sewers once the engineers were ready to begin their reconstruction efforts.

There were mixed emotions among the men once they exited the sewers. While the hope now was that the sewers were finally purged and the city completely cleansed, the nearly wasted morning took a toll on the men. The horns were blown and the soldiers in the lower city and on patrol were recalled into the fortress to give their reports. Anton had little to report. Only a few of the rogues had attempted an exit through the sewer entrances that were being guarded, and no one on the patrols noticed anyone exiting the river or fleeing the city. Added to that frustration, two of Hadrin's finest were now dead, only a handful of the more poorly trained rogues were killed, and the majority of the skilled degenerates had found a way out of the city unscathed.

None of the royal guards made mention of the remarkable display of power that Arimas had shown that morning. Each man had served with Arimas in battle, in grief, in victory and in pain. They also knew that reports about unknown powers from their priest-king would not be of any value to the men right now and would only add to confusion. Everyone knew something had changed with Arimas—he was more focused, he saw things more clearly, and even his reflexes in battle seemed somehow sharper. He was as agile now in his middle to late age than he was in the prime of his youth. No, the royal guards had nothing to say to the others. They stood in pride beneath the shadow that their priest-king cast. They were even more honored to serve him now than ever before.

The men were dismissed to partake of their noon meal. Commander Barros was to debrief his border detail afterward while Arimas himself debriefed the royal guard. Lead Counselor Bethanin would also convene with the priest-king in the afternoon once the debriefings were complete in order to begin the planning stages for the securing of Lorenth. Arimas left his royal guards to their meal while he returned to his chambers for his own, and hopefully, some conversation with his queen.

Elorn and Cael, Arimas' day servants, bowed at the arrival of the priest-king as he approached his chambers. Cael indicated that his meal was inside awaiting him and Arimas nodded and thanked them both before entering. He was slightly surprised to learn that Verona was not in the chambers and it did not appear that she had yet eaten her midday meal either. Arimas quickly devoured the flavorful soup prepared with thin slices of beef and vegetables and made quick work of the fresh bread, the sharp cheese and the wine. He wiped his mouth and then went to the bedchamber to pray and meditate on the events of the morning.

When he was in the bowels of death, noxious gas swirling around him and his men, he did not feel fear like he expected himself to feel. It was a righteous anger that he felt. Zeal had coursed through his veins and sharpened his mind. It was then that he felt the power of the deadly gases begin to lose their hold on him. How did he know that? He wasn't sure, but he distinctly remembered drawing on that power within and feeling himself pulse with divine rage. The more he drew in, the more he seemed to become sensitive to the threat not only around him, but also all of his men. He saw the gas as if it were nothing more than the same darkness that resided in Dean and his followers. Once he could see all the gas, including what was poisoning his men deep within their chests, the power flowed out from him and cleansed the entire area of all the darkness. The sensation was exhilarating.

He had felt the need to surrender—to surrender his mind and will to this divine presence. When he did, the prayer that was uttered was nothing that he possibly could have understood, yet it was the key to the release of the power within. He felt somehow contained inside until he unleashed the light of life through the power of the spoken word. He began to ponder the words that he spoke, clear as day within his mind. *Deim anoth hesid adon. Tovendi noctu elsarii et enchasad etum fiallis.* It was like poetry that flowed like silk off his tongue yet the meaning of the words escaped him. He had to finish the whisperings of those words in his mind because even in his light whispers he could feel the power building again. It was unlike any language he had heard before. He quickly penned down the words on a parchment as best as he could sound them out and carefully stowed the words within his desk.

After spending a short while longer in meditation and prayer he got up and set out to report back to the fortress to prepare for his debriefings. As he made his way out of his chambers he stopped and turned to face Cael.

"Cael, have you seen the queen at all this morning or near midday?"

"Not since she left for the libraries shortly after you headed out this morning, my lord. Did you wish to leave a message for her?"

"No. Thank you, Cael. Perhaps I will search for her myself after I conduct my business in the fortress. Good day to you both."

"And to you sire."

"Good day, my lord."

XIX

$\mathcal{I}$n the few short days since they were forced to abandon Lorenth, the exiles' new settlement was already showing tremendous signs of progress. The heavy rains two nights past had done more to motivate the men and women than any whips or threats could have. The exiles wanted shelter and some semblance of order in the midst of all the recent chaos and Dean channeled their frustrations and bitterness into effective and efficient work output. Those crafters who had the presence of mind to bring much of their supplies were already setup and established as they began to fashion tools and wares for the use of all the exiles. The supplies that were scavenged from the riverbank, as well as those that the exiles had the foresight to bring with them, made the process that much quicker.

Economically, Dean and the others were in ruin. There was no currency among the exiles and no way to determine equitable treatment for others. Dean imposed only one rule upon those he considered as 'his' people in order to direct their work and curb their greed—that only the individuals who gave of their time and labor for the benefit of the whole would eat. Basic essentials became the concern for all. There were no squabbles about cost or trade and bartering was nearly done away with initially. After the first thief among them had tried to steal foodstuffs in order to provide for himself without the burden of serving the others, there was not an issue again with theft in the camp.

Dean did not kill the thief, which was what many expected the former seneschal to do. Instead, the ill-doer was stripped naked and tied to a beam that had been secured between two trees. He was hung just high enough for his toes to touch the ground, and his three meals that day were replaced with a savage session of beatings at breakfast, midday meal, and then at the evening meal. Camp discipline improved tremendously and the former thief never again raised any concern about working for the benefit of others.

Throughout the initial few days, several more of Dean's devoted arrived from Lorenth. Among them were two of his favorite bedmates, Kasee and Lianne. Apparently Tiana was too thoroughly bruised by Dean during his last romp with her, and had chosen exile from the man instead of his protection. The two females did not enter the camp together, but in each set of eyes was the same excited light. Dean found that instead of being pleased to see either of the former servants, he was filled with a raging temptation to tear into them for their obvious power mongering, yet he paused and thought about their motives more carefully.

Why would they choose exile, away from all the public attention that he thought they were after, and away from the level of safety and security that a city as well built as Lorenth could provide, if not for something more tangible than position? Could these licentious chambermaids actually be choosing exile out of some sort of real affection for Dean?

The thought baffled him but aroused him all the same. Perhaps it was time to openly inform Kasee and Lianne about each other and force them both to share him—at the same time. He returned their gazes with a wickedly seductive glance of his own as he wiped the smirk from his face and focused his attention back on the work around the settlement.

It wasn't until several days later, just past mid morning, that the last remaining exiles arrived into the camp—all of them from the assassin's guild. There were far fewer numbers than Dean had been expecting, and he hoped, for their own sakes, that those missing were dead.

Dean turned over the supervision of the workers to Commander Zorn after spotting Dhax and Otto, accompanied with several other Drucharii and assassins, approach the encampment. With the slightest of nods he led them out of the settlement and into a small copse of trees nearby where he quickly counted up what remained of his assassin's guild. Forty-seven men and women, including the few thieves and assassins who had arrived earlier, that were trained to kill and gather intelligence, all reduced to outcasts for the second time in their lives. Perhaps the southern townships of Dunnham and Larriot, and maybe even Rallorn, could provide some sport for his thieves as they began to rebuild this settlement into a city worthy to challenge Lorenth.

"Have we no more eyes within Lorenth, Dhax?"

The Druuarc slowly shook his head, not sure whether his life would be forfeit with such a staggering failure. "Arimas was... exceedingly thorough in his 'cleansing' of the city. He started nearly six days ago now with the purge of the council and the upper city, then continued on to sweep through the lower city. It was like he could sense anyone who was not loyal to him. He targeted cooper and innkeeper alike; even the magister was examined, and his own royal guard! Those who did not leave the city when the offer of exile was extended were executed where they stood, whether it was in their shops, their homes, or in the streets themselves.

"Then once he secured the city, he completely surrounded its borders and every sewer entrance with guards, including patrols along the river and the roads leading out of the city, before leading an assault on our position within the underground.

"Arimas actually pursued you in the sewers?"

"As unbelievable as that seems, it gets worse, Seneschal." Even Dean took pause at the tone of soberness of Dhax's tone. Dhax was by far the most skilled Drucharii assassin. Dean even doubted his own abilities in combat when compared to the agility and skill that Dhax had shown on multiple occasions. This report was already making him sick to his stomach yet there was news even more disturbing that this? Dean nodded for Dhax to continue.

"For a brief moment, we actually thought we had Arimas and his royal guards defeated. Otto led an assault force out through one of the false sewer panels in an attempt to flank half of their party who were hiding to avoid our crossbow fire. At that point we did not know that Arimas and his royal guards were in the sewers as well. Otto and his assault force met Arimas and his small detachment of nine men—"

"Eleven men... I killed two of them first before we withdr—"

"Whatever... eleven men then. They were engaged in combat for a time, neither gaining any ground besides the initial barrage of bolt fire that took out Wade and several other junior thieves and two assassins. Otto feigned back and killed two of Arimas' men but then was flanked by a third party of soldiers. They fired another volley of bolts at which point Otto screened them all and those few who remained pushed for their fast withdrawal and leapt into the sewer waters heading out the exit line.

"Then, all three of Arimas' parties converged on the main service line leading into the guild. It was a standstill for the longest time until Arimas ordered his royal guards to form a shield wall which, even though it was only four men wide, rendered our bolt fire useless. They began to advance on our position until we tossed several noxious canisters into their formation. We almost had them! The front line was buckling and even Arimas was down for a time until the unbelievable happened. It must have been Arimas for all of a sudden we heard this deep booming voice praying down in the sewers. The prayer was followed by a blinding flash of amber light that completely eradicated all of the gas and fully healed all his men."

Dean looked like he was about to protest this sudden revelation until Dhax raised both his hands, indicating that Dean was to let him finish. Dean scowled but said nothing, leaving Dhax to continue.

"We didn't wait around to let them advance on us any further so we abandoned our hold and set the fire casks alight to collapse the guild and seal off our escape route. Fortunately, Arimas had no idea we had an entrance leading to the sparse forest, so our route remained unpatrolled. We only had to wait for about an hour before Arimas called off his dogs.

"There was no warning that Arimas was going to attack us beneath the city so there was no opportunity to claim our mounts from the lower city. We headed out on foot and followed the river to the Ardun Ford where we met up with Otto and the others. Our little walk from Lorenth took us nearly three days, but now we are here and Arimas holds Lorenth in the palm of his hand."

Curious, Dean asked, "How did you slip past the patrols that were watching the road and the water, Otto?"

"There were only two small patrols following the river itself. The rest were on the roads covering all the ancillary and primary entrances into the city. Bullio actually suggested we follow one of the patrols for quite some time before we went under the water as they turned around and began their back patrol to the city. The second patrol was even easier to slip past. As they began to approach us from the road initially, they could not even see into the water until they got tremendously close to our position. It was right then that the retreat horns were blown and the patrol abandoned what they thought was a 'useless' search to return to the city. We left the water and made for the trees across the shore as we too headed for the ford."

Dean was ready to explode with the hate he felt toward Arimas, yet he forced himself to hold his temper in check, knowing that he could not afford to lose any more men as a result of ill-guided anger. Ever since he was awakened that night when the dream was dramatically different, things were changing around him. This was now the fourth independent report testifying to Arimas' sudden transformation and endowment with unnatural gifts. Then again, Dean was also experiencing much of the same changes. His own senses were sharpening and he could nearly touch the swelling pool of power deep within him. While he had not yet learned the secret to unlocking this power, he knew he would soon. It was his primary ambition right now. Once he could unlock this restless energy within, Dean had no doubts that Arimas—and with Arimas, all of Lorenth—would finally fall at his feet.

Looking back to his men, Dean let the anger dissipate as he began to rework his assassin's guild into the city planning matrix nestled safely within his mind. It was a prime time to begin pillaging some of the southern townships, now before Arimas had an opportunity to reinforce defenses all around Lorenth. There were much-needed supplies within these townships that would certainly enhance their own efforts to become self-sufficient.

The northwest tip of Innin Lake would be the focal point of their new city. Innin Lake was the last source of life in the southern lands and luckily for them, its immense size would help sustain the city for years if they were careful to protect its cleanliness and supply. Easily four or five times the size of the entire city of Lorenth, it was impossible to view the opposite shore of the lake when standing on the northeast tip. Initially, Dean's plan was to begin fishing the lake to augment the dry foodstuffs that were already gathered or brought from the exiles' former homes. How long the fishing would last was not certain, but Innin Lake could potentially offer several years of it if they controlled their efforts.

The one thing Dean learned about city planning from Arimas was how *not* to build a great city. Nearly every tree and stone surrounding Lorenth was chopped down and excavated in the efforts to make Lorenth the city of splendor that it was. Dean already knew that careful thinning of a finite resource was the key to sustaining that resource for as long as possible.

Dean looked over the census information gathered several days ago. Two of the replacement engineers that had worked in the Lorenth sewers were among them and they would be a valuable asset when he needed to begin constructing the foundations of the city. He knew already that he needed to assemble a city planning council consisting of a chief engineer, a blacksmith, a quarry loadmaster, a forester, a provisions quartermaster, a military advisor, and a member from his intelligence network. Using the term 'assassin' among the city planners would not properly obtain the needed acceptance of his twice-exiled men and women of the underground. Shortly after assembling this council, training divisions would need to be established to increase the productivity of everyone that now considered Innin Hold their home.

The climate this far south was considerably warmer than Lorenth so the grain operations might not be as successful, but it was something they would have to try. Even the subject of livestock management was a point of concern. There were far too many matters before Dean, all which needed to be addressed relatively soon before the tenuous order within the developing settlement began to degrade into absolute chaos.

"As you can see, we are well on our way to recreating order and society for the considerable amount of exiles among us. As Drucharii, assassins, and thieves, my only caution now is to consider everyone here an exile, even as you have all become exiles. Train your blades and pillage the homes of those loyal to Arimas and not those here among us. There is much that the townships of Dunnham, Larriot and maybe even Rallorn can offer us if we strike fast and with subtlety.

"If we can operate with silence and only steal modest amounts of goods from various people at random times, we may be able to procure more supplies in the end than if we simply raided the townships and raised the general alarm within Lorenth. The last thing we need now is to breach Arimas' 'noble' offer of peace by violating his command and perhaps bringing all three border details and his royal guards down upon us in force. Let the fool think we have left his lands for good while we pilfer goods and supplies slowly over time. While their suspicions build, our covert recovery missions will continue until we are better able to mount a defensive stand against them if they eventually pursue us."

The assassin's guild members felt a renewed sense of purpose in light of their largest defeat and Dhax once again was gleaming with vile intent. There was no longer any need to trouble themselves with information gathering—at least until their new city was well under way. In time, Dean would begin spying on Lorenth once more to gather any precious intelligence that may give him a foothold again in Lorenth. Right now, the priority was growth and survival, and the Drucharii would be the leaders in the procurement of the much prized 'extras' that they would be missing as a result of their hasty withdrawal from Lorenthian society.

Dean told his assassins to get settled and refreshed. He asked Dhax to meet with him much later on, after the evening meal, to discuss some of his plans for Innin Hold. The assassins all dispersed among the other exiles as they began to reintegrate themselves among the citizenry, grabbing a decent meal from one of the several cooking areas spread out among the camps and resting a bit more before the action was driven higher on the days to follow. Dean then called Commander Zorn to his side once more after circling several names on the census sheet.

"Yes, Seneschal?"

"Erran, I want you to speak to these individuals for me this afternoon. I want each of them to gather all the crafters within their field and elect or appoint one industry leader to represent them in the city planning council. Tell them that the industry leaders are to meet with me here after the evening meal. I want you to attend as well."

"Yes, Seneschal. Is there anything else?"

"While you are speaking with these people, try to obtain an industry report from someone there as soon as you can manage it. I have been walking the area northeast of here on the edge of the lake. I believe that will make an ideal location to begin construction of the main keep and the city itself. The housing and trade centers that we have already begun building here will continue to be developed with some more properly detailed planning, but I want to shift the base of our military and the industry leaders toward the northeast, directly on the tip of Lake Innin."

"An excellent idea, Seneschal. That will provide a great vantage point to observe all the surrounding area, the water, and the industry here. Being that close to the water will enable some other more modern comforts perhaps that many in the old settlements have done without."

Dean nodded. Commander Zorn clearly understood that Arimas held onto much of the luxuries of the modern society within Lorenth, while those in the townships had much more meager lifestyles. Erran was a commander, yet even the commanders of the border details did not enjoy extravagant standards of living. They were paid considerably better than the regular soldier, but the battlemaster and commander ranks were nearly similar in pay with the only considerable differences being in the privileges that each level of authority was granted. It wasn't until one reached the rank of covenal that the soldier could expect a much better quality of life, with all the pleasures that modern city living could afford them.

Dean knew that his planning would make him abundantly more popular than Arimas as he began to promote the message that all should be equals in society and that need, not greed, would determine the flow of resources.

Dean dismissed the commander to complete the two errands he assigned to him while he began to look over the census list once again. He could not believe how many unskilled people were on the list. Those from Lorenth were definitely the worst. Nobles were the most useless people in society, in Dean's eyes. They talked and indulged themselves all day then gossiped and caroused all night, comfortable while sitting on purses fattened through business earnings long passed down from their fathers.

This was something else that would need to be discussed at the meeting tonight. Each industry would be appointing a skilled leader this afternoon who would be detailing to the council of city planners how many apprentices could be trained. All unskilled laborers would need to decide on a trade or else become part of the military branch to begin training with Commander Zorn.

Dean was starting to get a headache with all the planning involved in building this city properly. He would need to appoint capable people in various positions to ensure that he was not the sole enforcer of the vision, for this would be impossible for one man to accomplish. Dean wanted to take a short walk to clear his mind but decided against it, mainly because he did not know when Erran would return with his industry report and he was eager to know the progress on the quarries to the southwest.

Dean was already actively supplying eight stoneworkers, three of which were easily master-level qualified, with whatever they needed to restart their trades. They had brought several apprentices with them but more were needed, and many laborers as well would be required to assist with the hard manual task of quarrying. The amount of stone slabs produced on a daily basis was dismally low at present, but this would change. His goal was to increase stone production by at least four-hundred percent. This was the one resource that appeared limitless in the area and as such the focus needed to shift from forestry to stone working.

Kasee and Lianne had tried to see Dean over the last several days, and though his carnal appetites were starving for them, he could not yet indulge in the lascivious amusements his bedmates offered until the camp was slightly more permanent and could afford some privacy—especially for him and Kasee, as she loved to make excessive amounts of noise when Dean played upon her body. He knew that he would also need to get those two wenches into some sort of industry. Servants within the Lorenth fortress appeared to have only one skill set and he did not want those two offering their talents to the others in the camp when they could be doing something more valuable. Each person was an asset to the strengthening of this vision and even his bedmates could be employed at something useful for a change.

Within the hour, Erran had returned to the command tent with his industry report, just as Dean had requested. With an authoritative nod, Dean dismissed him once again to his regular duties of overseeing camp disciplines and the general flow of work throughout camp. Erran and his men were the backbone of Dean's enforcement. Whoever was discovered not working would not be eating with everyone else during the next meal so the men in arms became quite respected rather quickly.

Dean began to see figures that showed promise. The quarries were expanding much faster than he had initially hoped once he ordered several extra grinding wheels to be fashioned as a priority, while the blacksmiths were using what little reserve ore they had brought with them to forge picks and sledges to work the stone around them. Apparently the limestone was far easier to excavate and work with compared to the basalt and granite found north of the river near the Icecrown Peaks. Dean only hoped that the bricks of limestone would be sufficient for construction purposes but the stoneworkers seemed pleasantly surprised with the quality of the rock. The yields were actually starting to catch up with the demand of the other laborers as several more foundations to these smaller stone houses were being laid according to the rough zoning diagram that Dean had provided.

He didn't put much thought into the arrangement of housing but left those matters up to the people building them. His only stipulation was that they conserve building materials by joining several houses together, arranging the houses in blocks of units each sharing up to three walls with various neighbors around them. While the housing began to resemble some odd looking military formation, the logic behind the construction was apparent and exiles from various townships began to pull together as they collectively began creating these joined housing complexes made of stone.

There were minimal supplies of lumber which was to be expected, but at least the few small patches of forest in the area would provide enough lumber to create a suitable stockpile until plans could be created to take advantage of the much larger forest near the eastern shore of the lake. Some questioned why Innin Hold was being built so far from the forest, but they lacked the vision that Dean had. The north-western tip of Innin Lake had some trees, an abundant source of stone, access to the lake, and most importantly, it was fairly close to the western sea and Dean had hopes of expanding in that direction in time, so that fishing and perhaps other aquatic resources could be tapped into.

Agriculture and livestock management was barely adequate. Dean had already provided the fields southeast of the proposed city area for grazing, beyond the areas designated for the grain fields. Fencing was also an issue. The sheep and the cattle were grazing together and it was becoming increasingly more difficult to manage the herds of animals that were being gathered from across the townships. Slaughtering was currently forbidden due to the relatively short supply of animals and Dean wanted to promote breeding as quick as possible to ensure the success of the operation. There was so much yet to accomplish.

Dean paused when he encountered one unique idea that was submitted by the appointed agricultural leader. While it was a known fact these dry lowlands in the south were not nearly as fertile as the lands north of the river, Barrett Otenbright suggested creating shallow concrete cisterns with small stonework intake lines that connected with the river to feed the cisterns. What was even more brilliant was the idea of perforating the cisterns with several small holes to allow the siphoned water to infiltrate the dry soil beneath the seeded fields. The cisterns themselves could also be linked to each other with a similarly perforated stone transit line to moisten the ground between the cisterns as well as around them. Dean was lost in some of the thought and planning that went into Barrett's suggestions but he could follow his logic and the idea had tremendous merit. This was certainly going to be discussed at length tonight during the city planning meeting.

The salvaging and scavenging reports were becoming more and more non-existent now that they had successfully retrieved all the abandoned supplies from the river's edge and had begun amassing their stores near the command tents. Dean would call off these efforts entirely tomorrow and reassign those workers to the fields or the quarries.

The textile and leatherworking industries were non-existent at the moment, due to the lack of control over the livestock and the lack of pens or designated areas to begin any sort of operation. While the valuable wool and leather from the sheep and cattle would be needed eventually, it was not a priority yet. Breeding was the priority, which required pens and yards with ample access to grazing fields for the livestock to maintain a decent state of health.

Dean set the industry report down on his poorly salvaged desk. He could not handle any more reading about these matters, even as important as they were. It was nearly midday and already he felt restless. Dean left the command tent and decided to take a walk around camp. Being holed up in the command tent was not at all good for anyone's mental health when all that filled it was shoddy furniture, and a view of the thin ugly walls.

Impatience was beginning to nag at him. Dean wanted everything completed now. The city, the planning, all the industry established, supplied, and producing—yet all this would require a great deal of time, even considering the tremendously fast progress they had made already. Dean counted up all the names that were on the census already. Four-hundred ninety-four men and women, not including children under working age, left their homes to choose exile with Dean—this wasn't including himself or the majority of the forty-seven members of the assassin's guild which had arrived today. Over five hundred strong and all engaged in some form of industry to make the city prosper as quickly as it was prospering; over five-hundred hands that would all want some form of revenge on Arimas and those who had vaulted them all into exile.

XX

*D*ean's mind was continuously swarming with incessant thoughts of all that needed to be accomplished in Innin Hold. The burden of time, specifically the lack thereof, was also beginning to hang around his shoulders like a weight. True, they were accomplishing more than anyone expected, but the uncertain future was a variable playing with Dean's mind as the possibilities put pressure on his rational thoughts. Thankfully, his labor force was anything but typical.

A typical settlement team consisted of fifty skilled tradesmen who would elect to leave Lorenth or be nominated to leave from the surrounding townships, if need be. Usually there were incentives to encourage men to leave their homes and undertake the tasks of establishing a new settlement. And it was those fifty who would set up all of the industry infrastructure and housing for their families, seed the fields, create stables for the barracks, pens and yards for livestock if needed. Then, once the town was reasonably established, they would return to Lorenth to notify Arimas, usually through the magister or through Dean, that the township was ready.

Then, their wives and children would pack up their belongings and set out to the township to begin a new life. Tributes to Lorenth were considerably less for those living in the townships. The town watch would also be supplied from Lorenth, leaving the tradesmen able to pursue their interests or barter and trade with the surrounding townships. Many of these tradesmen led fairly profitable lives if they were among the original founding tradesmen of the town.

Dean's settlement team was at least ten times the typical size now that he had the actual census figures, although the quality of the workmanship left some things to be desired. Nevertheless, having such a number of people doing something beneficial was still considerably faster and more effective than being limited to a team of fifty skilled men.

Military matters would be another concern. Each of the border details was supposed to consist of two hundred and fifty men, though the eastern border detail was much smaller and Erikk Masaad's northern detail was actually quite a bit larger. Having Arimas devastate the southern detail the way he had certainly would not help matters. His military support was now slightly below one hundred men, all of whom were currently charged with the task of ensuring camp discipline, conducting scouting patrols, and even assisting in labor around camp when things were quiet, which was often. Once the foundations of the city were laid, and those unskilled laborers pushed into either industry or military training, things would begin to flow a bit smoother. It was this starting transitional period that was the most frustrating.

Dean continued to walk throughout the camp noticing little things here and there that could be improved. As of yet, there was no plan for the human waste and the camp was beginning to smell as many emptied their chamber pots wherever it was convenient, supposedly out of the way of higher traffic areas. This would not do for much longer. Prior to the foundation of Lorenth over twenty-five years ago now, there were several sicknesses that arose simply from not managing human waste properly, which had led to the construction of the sewer lines below Lorenth. It wasn't a perfect system, but it was adequate. Dean would attempt to improve even upon that aspect in the planning of Innin Hold. This was yet another thing that Dean had overlooked already. If he did not intervene soon, sickness could possibly break out in the camps and the cost on productivity would be great if that should happen.

Many of the citizens and soldiers alike stopped to address Dean by title, or simply nodded their heads respectively as he passed, intent on continuing with their work. Dean moved on throughout the quickly forming residential areas, noticing that the limestone bricks were a rather attractive color stone and when he tested the strength of the few walls that were nearly complete, he was pleasantly surprised at the strength that the wall and the mortar provided. Lorenth would not be the jewel of the west for long.

Dean left the residential area and continued farther northeast toward the area designated for the keep and the center of industry. The area would not be quite as large as Lorenth when completed but it was a good start, and expansion could always continue around the lake if needed. Once the Keep was completed he would need to begin stockpiling much stone for the city walls, which he already envisioned encircling the Keep and enclosing the housing to the southwest. The industry farther southwest within the stone hills would not be protected but should the need arise, Dean would think of something. He walked toward the lake and sat on the grass on the shore—the only real green grass in the area due to the abundant water supply.

With all the planning efforts, Dean had become distracted from his daily practice of drawing upon that awareness that for some time now had rested deep within him but always just slightly out of reach. He turned his thoughts inward and concentrated on the power that was boiling just beneath the surface of his mind. He began to smile as his senses sharpened. Dean's awareness began to increase, and he was soon seeing once again with his senses instead of just his eyes.

A small moth rested on his knee and without opening his eyes, Dean could sense the minute life energy within the moth. He could almost touch the energy. He trained his thoughts upon that tiny spark of life and concentrated. Sweat began to bead on his brow as he channeled more of his mind into understanding the depth of these sensations and what the meaning of it all was. He could almost feel the moth gently twitching its wings, probing its environment with its antennas, and even shifting its weight among its various legs. Suddenly the connection changed and became more distant as the moth began to fly away from Dean.

It happened so fast. A surge of anger welled up inside Dean when his efforts were thwarted by something as insignificant as a moth, yet what happened next defied explanation. The seneschal opened his eyes and saw the moth, dead, on the ground before him. It appeared blackened as if it burned from within. He pictured that same boiling cauldron of power deep within him and in those briefest of seconds, he imagined the blood, or whatever it was inside the moth that sustained its life, beginning to boil. Dean smiled a grim smile. Arimas was not the only one to be gifted with unnatural abilities it seemed.

Dean focused on the now dead moth and extended his senses again. Even though it was dead, he could sense something else even more easily than the effort it took to sense the creature's life. Within this lifeless husk Dean could sense potential of some sort. He extended his right hand over the dead moth and began to feel that awareness inside of him prompt him and guide him. The harder he tried to do *something* the more distant the awareness inside of him became until he finally stopped trying to make something happen and submitted himself to this strange presence within. The instant he submitted totally, he recoiled his hand as if he was bitten from a viper. A small tendril of black light shot from his hand into the dead moth.

Dean's eyes widened in horror and in amazement as he watched the dead moth flip over and attempt to fly once more. The black energy surrounded the moth and like an acid it began to consume its outer coverings revealing an insubstantial skeletal structure that could not sustain itself in flight. The moth that was returned to life quickly dissolved into nothingness. What Dean had just accomplished seemed impossible. He had terminated life, and then resurrected it, first with his mind and then through using the awareness inside. Dean's thoughts spun furiously. How far could this power be used? Could he cure death? Could he channel his mind into an enemy causing their blood to boil like that of the moth? Would a larger creature survive the resurrection better than something as small as a moth? Question after question coursed through his mind as the endless possibilities threatened to completely overtake him.

It was then that he felt a presence gazing upon him. His heart beat faster, his mind quickened, and he immediately turned to face the southwest, beyond the stone hills. His eyes closed yet his mind saw the isle so clearly. There beneath a dark mist waited a vast army... mindless minions surrounded by several robed wielders of the dark energies. Their faces were blurred as if the image was still yet a dream, or an uncertain destiny, yet one of the robed servants looked straight into his very soul and uttered one single word.

"Master..."

The vision of the isle ended. The presence left him as well, leaving Dean to ponder the significance of what had just taken place. Again he felt that odd loss of control in his life. He wasn't sure whether he liked this particular part of the changes that were happening yet he knew deep inside that he would not impede the changes in any way. He would have to embrace the destiny before him and grow in strength and power to overcome whatever the hands of fate threw his way.

Dean stood up from the water and extended his senses beneath the surface of the lake. He saw hundreds of tiny focal points of life swimming about and in a brief moment, he became aware that if he wanted to, he could quench that life among them all with a thought. He refrained from testing this idea out because all those fish would be a key resource in the feeding of the masses that he was now responsible for. He smiled again, knowing the time was near for Kaaldean to be unleashed—then all life would suffer at his hands.

Dean returned to his command tent to find search out food. Thankfully, Erran had placed a bowl of soup, now cold after sitting out for so long, with a piece of slightly stale bread on his desk. It was filling and not particularly bad tasting. He needed more leaders like Commander Zorn around him. Men that could lead without prompting, make adjustments when needed, and anticipate events before they happened.

Dean had already told Erran to begin selecting his chain of command and telling them to hold off on building their housing within the general housing area. Dean wanted to reserve some nicer housing for his leadership staff on the northeast section of the city opposite the common housing. Dean, the commander, his deputy commanders, and then if needed, division leaders, along with all of his full Drucharii and the appointed industry leaders would be given preferential housing according to their status within Innin Hold.

Ranking structures would need to change slightly to reflect their own culture instead of adopting Lorenth titles for everything. That too would be discussed tonight, but for the mean time, at least Erran could choose his leaders and be ready to give report tonight. Dean picked up the industry report and resumed his reading of the progress made throughout the past day. Some things were incredibly boring to read again but at least he could see progress and improvements in efficiency along the way. The exiles of Lorenth, soon be identified as citizens and founders of Innin Hold, were embracing the changes upon them and were working diligently at creating their new home, their workplaces, and eventually their new city.

The afternoon thankfully passed without incident or interruption and Dean even managed to take a quick nap in the latter hours of the afternoon before the evening meal began cooking. Likely another soup once again with more of the stale bread, but this was to be expected for now. All were eating adequately and once the fishing was started and hopefully once the assassin's guild began augmenting their stores with some variety of food items from the townships farther north, morale would improve even more around the camp and the daily requirements would be continued.

Looking over his list of goods already gathered or salvaged, Dean noticed several large bags of flour that still sat unopened, as well as the presence of plenty of seeds for vegetables, and more grain seed yet to be sown. A bakery would be another eventual endeavor, along with every other building and industry that needed to be completed. Once livestock breeding became more successful, a butcher shop would also be established, but that was several months away at the earliest.

Dean left his command tent to find some food and possibly sit with some of his men to see if he could learn anything from the idle chatter around the cook fires. Full soldiers would often talk and reveal things unintentionally that they may forget when giving reports to their commander or to their seneschal. Unfortunately there was nothing new to learn as the men ate their fill and returned to their posts for the evening rounds which lasted until the end of the first watch of the night.

The men would rotate their sleep with each other throughout the second, third and fourth watches to minimize disruption to each other as much as possible. This modified schedule for the night watch was typically only quarter strength and the shifts were broken up into four separate two and a half hour shifts. The current watch methods had some flaws but there had not yet been any issues with the citizens after dark so the system was working.

Dean nodded to Erran that the planning meeting was to begin shortly and the two men rose from their seats, placed their bowls near the cleaning station, and made their way into the command tent to rearrange the inside to accommodate the industry leaders. All those the seneschal had requested to be present were there, and Dean looked over the gathering of Innin Hold's leadership team. For the most part, he was impressed with what he saw. He vaguely remembered meeting some of these men and women in Lorenth years ago but all their names escaped him, except for Barrett Otenbright, who was obviously selected to lead the agriculture industry.

"Welcome to the first official city planning council meeting. I hereby recognize each of you as the elected or appointed industry leader for your field and with that title will come proportionate benefits to your station, beginning with accommodations of higher quality that will be established in the city proper as we develop and move toward our goals."

Smiles broke out all around the circle of leaders, including Erran. Dean knew that loyalty could be bought and secured through appealing to everyone's sense of greed or by affirming inside each of them what they thought they deserved already.

"I now invite each of you to address the council and state your name, trade or specialty and the industry that you represent."

Dean then took his seat as one by one each of the industry leaders stood and spoke.

"Huron Alliston, master stonecutter and leader for the guild of masons."

"Philip Fairchild, master carpenter and representative for the foresters."

"Barrett Otenbright, farmer and agricultural advisor."

"Erran Zorn, commander of the armies of Innin Hold under Seneschal Dean."

"Stefan Collings, chief engineer."

"Deanna Fairchild, master tailor and industry leader of textiles."

"Karl Feldegan, master blacksmith and foreman of the mines."

"Ainslie Verigan, stores quartermaster and chief clerk."

"Renwold Jessop, tanner and head leatherworker."

"Jared Pyne, breeder and lead for the livestock operations."

"Kaylee Aston, herbalist and chief apothecary."

"Vincent Sutherland, alchemist and chief scientist."

As the last counselor reclaimed their seat, Dean stood once again and looked over his shoulder, nodding toward the shadows cast by the ill-displaced candlelight within the command tent. Dhax took one step into the light much to the shock of all who were gathered, and Dean faced his attentive audience once more.

"Dhax is my chief intelligence agent. You may see him from time to time, but you likely will not. He is in charge of all scouting reports directly, even those conducted by the soldiers, and will as well be being responsible for the monitoring of all enemy movements as well as all tactical planning. Together with my commander these two are my military advisors and strategists. Dhax and his men report to me directly and will not normally attend these council meetings, but for the interests of fair disclosure, I have introduced you all to him today. Thank you Dhax, you are dismissed."

Dhax nodded once and slipped around Dean, deftly weaving between the chairs of those seated in the tent before ducking through the tent flap and vanishing into the night once more. Dean facilitated the communication within the meeting, calling on various industry leaders to highlight what was working well, what could use improvements, and what was not working at all. Problems were brought to light and possible resolutions were discussed at length until a consensus was reached by all. The most challenging part of the evening involved the layout of the city and how constructions needed to begin.

Preliminary ideas concerning waste management were improved upon by one industry leader, a man named Barrett. Others in the tent could not even grasp the concepts of using the waste from humans and animals to improve soil conditions but Barrett insisted that his pasture fields back in Bonnin grew thicker and greener every year as the waste from both the cows and sheep were left in the field where it eventually became part of the soil.

This led to Dean asking Barrett to expound upon his ideas to infuse water from the lake into the grain fields. The stoneworker head, Huron, nodded at the logic, stating that the stone work required would be possible to make in sections and joined with mortar later. Stefan also thought these ideas could improve sewage management and perhaps a collection area for the human waste could be created to test this theory out in time, while providing a way to ensure immediate waste removal now. Kaylee and Vincent also expressed some interest in these ideas as fertile ground was in short supply. The ability to grow herbs and reagents faster, larger, and potentially more potent was a very promising idea.

No matter what the outcome, everyone agreed that tomorrow the priority would be on creating sanitation points to proactively manage the health of everyone in the camps. Regulations needed to be created to ensure compliance with issues as simple as waste management before things became even harder to control.

Huron also reported that the granite and basalt grinding stones from his old quarries were much harder and that working with the softer limestone would extend the life of the grinding stones tremendously; however, the replacement stones would be fashioned in limestone and the life spans on those stones were not encouraging. Deanna, Karl, and Renwold also expressed a desire to begin setting up their industries but Dean advised them that this wouldn't be possible for a time. Karl would be the first one of the three to be re-established as the services of a blacksmith were already being missed around camp, but leathers and textiles would have to wait until Barrett and Jared were well established with their agriculture and livestock breeding operations.

Such was the way of starting over. Priorities needed to be set and all did agree that the priorities as set out and voted on by the members of the planning council were fair and logical. It would also provide a clear path for those to follow as together they built Innin Hold. Dean then informed the industry leaders about the need to maximize stone production through the establishment of multiple quarries, masons, and master crafters willing to apprentice two or more apprentices initially to bolster the exploitation of this nearly limitless resource around them. Once bricks were flowing like water, they could begin to stockpile the brick for use in bigger projects like the city while meeting the daily requirements to continue with housing, sanitation and now agricultural demands that were being placed on the precious yet abundant stone.

Huron knew all of the other master crafters and assured Dean that while the process of having multiple apprentices was unheard of, all would be willing to serve Innin Hold in this matter to speed up construction efforts around the entire camp.

Dean also told Philip to continue thinning the forests near the hills to the southwest and then to move his operation to the small forest northeast along the lake. The medium sized forest near the coast of the western sea would be last. Dean made it clear to Philip that he and his foresters could reduce the smaller forests to nothingness as all this land could conceivably be used to expand to in the future and would need to be cleared regardless.

Philip then suggested gathering seeds from the trees and potentially trying to replant the forests after they were cleared in hopes that in time they would have another resource to tap into. Dean commended Philip for the foresight and told him to gather the seeds as they cut but to wait on replanting them until he had a chance to determine where the best location of a forest would be in relation to the city and the industries. These sporadic forests would at least provide an adequate supply of timber until they could concentrate on a larger forestation project on the southeast shore. Before that could even be considered a possibility, the city would need to be well underway and all the industries had to be up and running.

Philip also volunteered to train some laborers and teach them enough basic skills to be able to assist Jared with building some pens and fencing to control the animals a little better. Nothing fancy would be done yet, but at the very least something useful could be constructed to help in the interim. Stables would also be needed soon as several of the men and women that had fled their homes had brought wagons with at least one or two horses leading them. The soldiers that were cast out by Arimas had not been allowed to bring their trained war mounts, but some of the soldier's wives thought to bring their husband's mount without adornments, as they had more time to plan for their departure then the men had. Still, there was a deficit of trained mounts. Fortunately, among the citizens there were many fine bred horses that, with some training, would suffice.

The meeting ended late and with much heaviness laid on everyone as they all began filtering out the command tent toward their own accommodations for the evening. All knew their responsibilities and tomorrow morning Dean would address every man, woman, and child capable of learning a trade to choose a profession by midday and register that choice with Erran on the census sheet, or else a profession would be chosen for them as the needs of Innin Hold dictated. Many of the unskilled folk were simply cooking or cleaning up around camp which, though necessary, was not a trade. All would work a trade and then be expected to share the load in all matters of camp life and cleanliness.

Tomorrow would begin with sanitation education and construction, assigning of trades to everyone in the camp, and then maximizing stone output. Next would be the completion of the housing units, infusing the grain fields with water according to the new proposals from Barrett, and then considering the creation of the stables after the pens and fences were erected.

With those achievable goals set before them, the next stages would involve the stockpiling of resources and the creation of a large sewer network beneath the foundations of the city. With only two engineers in the camp, their expertise would need to be optimized. Training an apprentice engineer was one of the more difficult things to do because it required months of intensive work with someone keen, someone who possessed a sharp mind, and someone who was able to think methodically and not haphazardly. Those candidates were in rather short supply, Dean feared, but perhaps tomorrow would reveal some people wanting to apply themselves to this profession. Dean could hope at least, but he would not hold his breath.

Now was the time for Innin Hold to rise from the ashes of exile. Dean would maintain his hopes over the following months that all would advance at more than a steady pace. Winter was fast approaching. Even though it was considerably warmer in this new location, there was no intelligence gathered about the climate this far south to know what could be expected in terms of weather. Addressing these most basic of plans would be at least one variable well within Dean's control and he fully intended on maximizing what could be achieved during this uncertain period of silence between Lorenth and the exiles.

XXI

The dwarves had now been drawn into the troubles of dragons and elves. While the prospect of forging alliances with these other races was all well and good, the dwarves still found time to grumble about matters that had very little bearing on the current situation but helped satisfy some innate need to grumble nonetheless. After the rather interesting meeting in the Ellorian highlands, all the ten clans reunited in Thunderhammer Hall to properly end their meeting with another fine feast, much merrymaking and of course, the chilled spiced mead made famous by the Ellorian clans.

The Hammul and the Nuragg clans had dismissed their water elemental escorts, completely forgetting about how it was that they were able to travel there in the first place. Their watercrafts were currently in Elloria and a rather imposing waterfall now stood in their way, effectively blocking their path back home. Grumbling ensued once again as the Nuragg and Hammul clans slumped down at the entrance of the Stormgarde clan. The two clans of the south vented their frustrations to any and all who would listen.

"And how are we to be gettin' a-back home then?"

"Calm down Fodrin, 'tis our own blasted fault we are in this predicament now ain't it? Maybe we can find more of dem water people to fetch the boats later."

"Aye, and by the time we get back maybe we will find our sons married off to them dryad folk with little bearded tree-children runnin' around now too!"

"Fodrin! Elof! That's enough chatter. Elof is right. It's our own fault we're here and we best be a-thinkin' of ways to remedy this problem and not just sniveling about it. Any suggestions, then?" Clan Chief Gimmel Thaineson was as burly and tough as the Nuragg clan came and once he got involved in any squabble, things usually sorted themselves out pretty fast. No one ventured any suggestions for a short time until Clan Chief Forin Hammul III offered his suggestion.

"Has Orin left yet?" The Silverfists had left at dawn with their ingenious engineered devices of metal and steam. Those from the massive hold of Barak'Dûm as well as the grays from Ur'Akam had left late last night due to the extremely long return trip they all had. They wanted to reach the Silverfist battlekeep, the first milestone in their long journey, by the next day. They turned down the air elementals offer for assistance in favor of consuming inordinate amounts of mead and walking off their sore heads and bloated bellies on the trip cross country.

But no one had seen the ten Bloodstone Clan leave on their massive stone allies and it became immediately clear what Forin was suggesting. The clan chief left his band of dwarves and his Nuragg kinsmen behind for a moment as he turned back toward Thunderhammer Hall to find his Bloodstone kinsmen. Within the half hour Orin and his nine elite, led by Forin, approached the remainder of the Hammul and the Nuragg. Orin stopped at the top of the stone walkway, tucked his hands in his girdle and proffered a proud smile to Gimmel.

"You lads be needin' a bit of a carry then?"

"Aye Orin," answered Gimmel. "We'd be much obliged if your stone friends could carry us and our crafts down and around to the river below the falls."

Orin let out a boisterous guffaw much to the displeasure of the Nuragg and Hammul dwarves seated beside him. "You must see the humor in all of this Gimmel. I have a mind to help yer crafts reach the shore while you all walk down and around the falls. You won't soon be acceptin' help like that again and then so easily dismissin' it. But I can't do that to you don't worry. Let's go get yer crafts and see you right on your way then."

The representatives of the three dwarven clans made their way out of the large stone-cut entrance that was shaped like an inverted battle hammer, wide at the bottom where many could enter and becoming narrower toward the top of the grand entrance for larger items, or races presumably, to also enter. As with everything the dwarves did, this entrance was also done in excess. It was covered with masterfully etched faces within the sides of the hammer's opening itself and was decorated with several arcs of forked lightning chiseled into the stone beside it to depict the Stormgarde Clan.

Orin reached into his long red beard and pulled forth an ornately carved horn fashioned from some sort of bone that hung from a leather strap around his neck. He sounded the horn once—a long and clear blast that resonated deeply in the lungs of all those within earshot.

The ground began to shake. Gimmel and Forin exchanged glances and then looked to Orin who stood beaming, his right arm raised and pointed to the low hills directly beside the mountain range. The watching dwarves suddenly realized that the hills were actually the stone elementals. One was even hidden among the rock face of the mountains. From rest to rumbling life the five massive elementals of stone stood tall and advanced toward Orin, the bearer of the bone horn.

After a brief exchange of words between Orin and the elementals, one of the five extended its pace and quickly traversed the open highlands toward the river where the two dwarven watercrafts were resting along the shore. One in each hand, the elemental lifted both of the barges into the air and returned to the others before handing the second barge to a different elemental.

"Let's get on with it then," shouted one of the Bloodstone elites as the five elementals knelt down to allow the ten Bloodstone dwarves to mount the living stone and secure themselves to the back within their leather harnesses. The two elementals carrying the watercrafts rested them down long enough for the Nuragg and the Hammul clansmen to board their respective crafts and then they were off toward the path down from the highlands to the southeast.

Luckily, the only ones to witness this odd sight were the Bloodstone dwarves, but those from the other two clans knew better than to hope that this story would not become public knowledge. That being said, the Nuragg and the Hammul did agree many weeks later that the stone elementals were surprisingly fast for their massive size. Their slow and measured pace, once you factored in the distance covered between each stride, was easily as fast as a horse, if not faster—and the elementals were only walking. The thought of a running miniature mountain was simply terrifying and all the fae were glad that these massive creatures were allies and not enemies.

They made incredible time down the south-eastern path as they turned west toward the entrance to the Silverfist Clan. The edges of the *Illu'Dar* were now clearly seen as they began to walk along its northern border toward the lower Ellorian waterfall and the river that would bear the other two clans home. No one even considered that the elementals covering the ground as fast as they did would make the journey to the river's edge *that* fast. Forin and Gimmel were tempted to start grumbling along with the other dwarves when they started to overtake the other clans that left a day earlier on foot. As the ground trembled with each step of the elementals the other dwarves near the entrance to the Silverfist battlekeep stopped and looked on with amusement at their kinsmen.

King Torgrim Varr and Korigan Goern of the Gray Clan both were reduced to their knees in laughter but it was Clan Chief Hrimir Ingar of the Silverfist Clan who was first to manage words.

"You lost your river Gimmel? You should've been more careful." This only made the laughter more infectious as even some of the dwarves within the floating watercraft began to chuckle. Gimmel and Forin endured the fun-hearted mocking with patience, choosing to hold their tongues to maintain what little dignity they had left.

The barges were lowered into the river gently while the Nuragg and the Hammul waved their second set of goodbyes to their kinsmen and began their own return home, trying to distance themselves as fast as possible from the laughter behind them.

Orin shared more of the details of the late morning with the others while still comfortably harnessed to the back of his stone friend. When all the laughter had finally died out, Orin waved his second goodbyes as well before he and his nine elites atop the five elementals turned back to the east to resume their own journey to the Red Rock Cliffs, far to the southeast of *Illu'Dar*.

Hrimir and his clansmen had overtaken those from Barak'Dûm and Ur'Akam nearly an hour ago but they chose to wait at the entrance to admit the others into the deep passes of Kel'Zarûl. Ever since the silence pact was issued generations ago, the dwarves had never considered traveling through the human lands in order to reach the west. When the first of the Silverfist Clan arrived north of the elven forests and began to delve beneath the lower Ellorian waterfall, they unlocked a world of subterranean beauty that would later prove to be a key discovery for the unification between the eastern and western clans.

The Silverfist created their greathall, built their forges, and established their centers for rune working as all dwarves did, until they found a natural tunnel in the north-western mines. After breaching the wall that hid its existence from them, the early founders of the Silverfist Clan stumbled into a cavernous world that glittered with silver and truesilver veins all through the rock walls that spanned for league upon league. With very minimal excavation, the Silverfist were able to dig through some of the more occlusive barriers in the cavern without compromising the natural supports that maintained the integrity of the chamber, and thus, the deep passes of Kel'Zarûl were born and with it, the Silverfist Clan got their name.

The deep passes of Kel'Zarûl stretched far to the northwest into the frozen wastes, twisting and contorting beneath the more shallow bodies of water that had completely frozen over near the *Dsa'carii* islands. Among the numerous open areas that glittered from the truesilver and silver, as well as sapphire and diamond deposits throughout, massive natural stone columns and the lesser stalagmites and stalactites gave the immense chamber a feeling of timelessness. Where the chamber came close to the surface, ice twice as thick as a man covered the underground chambers and allowed a diffuse blue light to penetrate the darkness beneath, refracting off the gem deposits and illuminating the chamber throughout the day and allowing for work to be conducted.

With the setting of the sun came the end of all work in the deep passes. Though there was talk with the grays about obtaining some colspar crystals to provide an alternate light source in the passes, so far this remained as just talk, simply because of the sheer length of the passes. It was an eight day journey beneath the ice and snow before the passes opened up. Once daylight ceased and the sight of most dwarves began to wane, they would often stop for the night to rest and eat before resuming their journey at first light.

Having the grays with them this time would allow them to travel longer each day. There was one journey during Runeveld many generations ago when those from Barak'Dûm traveled with the grays through the deep passes. It cut a day or more from their travels, and since that time, the two clans had often tried to plan their long journeys together. Sometimes the other clans actually envied their gray brothers for reasons such as this. Living in the depths for so long actually made their eyes hurt in the light of day, yet when darkness would blind many others, it was the Gray clan who could lead in almost no-light conditions.

Once they successfully exited the long and narrow passes of Kel`Zarûl, the crisp air of the lesser Icecrowns coupled with the snow falling among the mountain passes made all the dwarves loathe both ice and cold. Those of Barak'Dûm would rest and warm themselves in the dry and dark depths of the Gray Clan battlekeep before completing the final stretch of their own journey along the Great Stoneway.

Hrimir knew the long travels that still awaited his kinsmen so the offer was made as usual for all of them to rest and enjoy some of the Silverfist comforts before starting the long journey through the deep passes. Those of Barak'Dûm and Ur`Akam welcomed the hospitality of Hrimir and elected to remain among the Silverfist Clan for the evening and would set out for Kel`Zarûl at first light. There was something uniquely pleasant about staying among the Silverfist Clan. Though they were not as large as the grays or even as large as the Stormgarde, their halls were magnificent, their ability to not only kill, but to cook the large Ssaraki was a testament to their creativity and skill, and the sheer beauty of everything beneath that glittered in silver always inspired a deep sense of admiration and appreciation within the visitors for the talents of their kinsmen.

The Silverfist armory, another sight to behold, was filled with truesilver weaponry, polished silver plate armor and chainmail woven out of an iron and truesilver alloy, among many other creations. It was the Silverfist who provided the initial truesilver ore to the Gray Clan to create the tempered propellers for their famous bronze furnaces, before they delved deeper and discovered truesilver veins of their own. Even their mining tools were rumored to be among the best quality. Silver mining picks and hammers fused with diamond tips or edges made quick work of nearly all other rock deep within the mines and the deep caverns. Perhaps not as battle-ready as the grays or the Stormgarde, the Silverfist did pride themselves on their vast armory collections of weapons, armor, and numerous other strange devices and parts used in their engineering passions.

Ask anyone about what defined the Silverfist Clan and all would tell you it was their engineers. Stone molds in more shapes than anyone could believe littered the forge halls and storage areas as iron or silver was carefully poured and cooled to create a warehouse of hundreds of things that no one, not even some of the Silverfist engineers, could determine the use of. Experimentation was the rule among the engineers. What worked was refined and improved upon; what didn't work was discarded as soon as repairs were made to the areas that often were quite damaged after a failed experiment went awry. But their crowning achievement was a turbine system powered by nothing more than harnessed steam.

Iron and steel piping linked to massive boilers fuelled by burning wood in great amounts allowed the dwarves to create land wagons that could move at great speeds without horse or any other means. Loud and awe-inspiring, these fusions of dwarven engineering were the crowning achievement of the Silverfist Clan, though these devices were not without their limits. They had tried to replicate the same boiler system on watercraft but the weight displaced too much water and the barges simply would not float. Air travel with this amount of weight was ludicrous, not to mention unthinkable, for everyone knew that dwarves were creatures of the earth and flight was just... unnatural. Even the consumption rate of wood as fuel for these massive boilers was astronomical. Each land wagon required a hopper built behind the boiler that held at minimum forty stone worth of cut lumber to burn. Impractical yet effective, these beasts of iron and steam were but the beginning to even more research and experimentation in the Silverfist's never ending quest to adapt these concepts into much smaller and much more efficient designs.

The kinsmen of Barak'Dûm and Ur'Akam rested well that evening and as planned, the two clan representatives with their handful of comrades thanked Hrimir for his hospitality and set out for the deep passes where along their left and right sides of the cavern, well off the main path, worked many Silverfist miners already—making use of every ounce of daylight that the low-light caverns provided. While the air was temperate now, all knew the drastic drop in temperatures that would await them throughout the many days of travel ahead. Korigan and his grays then took up the lead, secured their packs, and took their initial steps down along the tortuous path before them as those from of Barak'Dûm followed, each checking their own packs for the additional provisions that Hrimir provided them for their journey. Into the darkness they would journey; into the daylight they would eventually emerge.

XXII

The reactions in Newhaven were much the same as they were in Falstad. Everyone stopped what they were doing when Covenal Guilian, reported to have fallen during diplomatic negotiations by the orchestration of Dean, raced through town accompanied by one of the forest inhabitants, a woman who rode atop her pale steed without saddle or harness. Her hair was the color of honey, her skin as fair as starlight, her eyes a piercing blue, and her face comprised of features so pure that the onlookers felt as if they were suddenly trapped within a dream—yet this was no dream. Under the light of several torches, the two dismounted near the inn, not even bothering to hitch their horses but simply speaking plainly to the animals and telling them that they would be going inside for the night.

It was late in the evening when the covenal and his guest entered through the sturdy oak door of the inn. The innkeeper dropped one of the mugs that he was drying behind the bar when Farin walked through his door—a sight that the innkeeper never thought he would see again as the rumors of the covenal's death had circulated fast throughout the townships.

"Covenal Guilian! These old eyes rejoice that you still live. Please come in... come in! You must have a bite and I will fix you and your lady-friend a modest room if you be stayin' tonight."

Farin offered a wide smile as the burly innkeeper stepped over the broken remains of the mug, embracing the covenal in a large hug and then clapping him on the back before shutting the door behind them as the two stepped inside.

"That would be most generous, Earl. It's been a long day and the horses need a rest and a good grooming might not be a bad idea. But I seem to be light on coin since my flirtations with death and I would have to pay you back anoth—"

"I'll not even pretend to have heard you talk to me about pay, Covenal. Your coin ain't no good here and besides, it's the least I can do for you."

"Thank you again, Earl. We need to get back to the city tomorrow and Arimas must be informed about a plot even now that may threaten his rule."

The innkeeper gave Farin an odd look. "You haven't heard about Arimas' new decree then?" Farin shook his head. "Or about the ex-seneschal and the exiles?" Again Farin shook his head in shock at the news spilling forth from the innkeeper.

The stable boy quickly left the front entrance to tend to Atarax and Laenos for the evening while Harriett, the innkeepers wife, brought two decent-sized helpings of what looked to be a meat and vegetable stew with thick, richly seasoned pepper gravy, along with several slices of bread that had been baked earlier that day. Tavendia declined the stew graciously, leaving Farin to explain that it was not customary for the elves to eat meat. Harriett nodded and quickly offered the elf some thin vegetable broth she had finished that night in preparation for the next day's meal, along with some cheese from the pantry, which Tavendia accepted gratefully.

The stew was delicious, though Farin wasn't sure whether he was offending his beautiful guest by eating what she had refused. This was his first hot meal in over a week and when Earl brought out two flagons of ale for his guests, and one for himself, his night was even more complete. Earl certainly had a way with the hops and the grains, for Newhaven was renowned for having one of the best ales in all of Lorenth. What shocked Farin though was that Tavendia actually sipped the ale and found it to be rather flavorful and said much the same, to the great pleasure of the innkeeper.

Earl went on to explain to Farin and Tavendia the events that had occurred in the last week—as best as he could gather from the rumors that made their way into the tavern nightly. When the thick-set older man finally sputtered to a stop at the end of his tale, he leaned back and took in the amazement on Farin's face, and the curiosity on his companion's.

When Farin continued to sit, speechless, as he processed the new information, the innkeeper took it upon himself to encourage conversation and asked them where they were traveling from. When he learned that the two had left the forests of *Illu'Dar* early that morning, the innkeeper was amazed. He asked how they had covered that much ground so fast, and Tavendia simply explained that the elves had ways of strengthening all life, and that the horses ran as fast as they were willing and able... nothing more.

Conversation dwindled again as Farin continued to say very little, and after a time the innkeeper led his guests both upstairs to a single room—arguably one of the nicer rooms the innkeeper had available. Farin blushed and then requested a separate room for himself in order to ensure some privacy for the lady. Tavendia flashed an amused smile to the innkeeper as she nodded in acceptance and then looked to Farin wishing him a pleasant sleep. The quarters provided for Farin were barely adequate but then again, a soldier did not require more than a bed this late in the evening. As he removed his outerwear, laying the clothing gently on the chair in the corner of the room, he climbed into his bed, noticing with chagrin how stiff the mattress was and how flat the pillows were in comparison to the comforts he had enjoyed in Avalide. Even though Farin was not tired, sleep eventually came to him once he was able to get his mind off of Tavendia and onto the unclear destiny that would await him and the elven druid once they reached the capital city.

Farin awoke to the gleaming rays of sun that burst through the open window of his second-floor room. The slight stiffness in his back told Farin that even his body preferred the elven beds. He splashed some water on his face and dressed once again before leaving the room to head downstairs where the inviting smell of bread was calling to his hungry stomach. Tavendia was already downstairs finishing off what appeared to be a fruit platter set before her while Farin enjoyed some baked beans with molasses and fresh bread, along with a cold glass of milk.

After the meal was done, Earl escorted them to the stables where Laenos and Atarax were waiting patiently. The stable boy was grooming Atarax this morning once again but stopped as the three approached. Earl clapped Farin on the back once again and wished them both safe travels before heading back inside the inn to begin circulating his own rumors about the return of Farin from the dead.

Farin stroked the side of Atarax's neck gently then mounted him as Tavendia expertly climbed onto Laenos' back. No further words were exchanged as the two set off for west, the rapidly rising sun clear behind their shoulders. As had happened last night, the first few laborers, shopkeepers and farmers that saw Farin responded with the same shock as Earl the innkeeper, pausing to wave at the covenal as he swiftly passed by.

Autumn was fast approaching. The mornings were colder than before, yet the sunshine and the dew that glistened upon the leaves of some of the low lying shrubs around the township made this morning a pleasant one. All around Newhaven, Farin could see the recently harvested grain fields in various stages of preparation for the winter freezing that would soon be upon them. The large windmill to the southwest of town was already grinding wheat into flour and the unpleasant smells coming from the local tannery indicated that the leatherworkers were also getting an early start on their curing jobs.

After leaving behind the unfinished road between Falstad and Newhaven, the well built cobblestone road between Newhaven and Lorenth made travel much more pleasurable. They chose not to venture into Rallorn as it was still morning and at the pace their horses were setting they would likely make Lorenth again by early evening. How they were able to shave nearly an entire day off of a three day trip amazed Farin, especially since it was the horses setting the pace, not Farin and Tavendia. It was as if they were showing off their true capabilities and testing the limits of their own potentials after their encounter with the elven warden.

The dual tolling of the evening bells were just sounding the start of the first watch of the night when Farin and Tavendia reached the massive gates of Lorenth. He had only been away for little under two weeks but the familiarity evoked a sensation of contentment within the covenal. While Farin did miss the elven wards and the architecture grown from the very heart of the trees, Lorenth felt solid like the rocks from which it was made. There was an aura of permanence about the city that made Farin feel proud to be human.

Emotion welled up in the heart of the normally stoic covenal when the night watchmen ordered the immediate opening of the night gate to admit Farin home. For years, Farin had locked away emotion, suppressing both fear and sorrow, yet after his immersive time spent with the *Illu`Dar* creatures of the balance, simple things that he never would have responded to were now evoking long-suppressed feelings of appreciation. How this man, who made himself into an emotional wall for so many years, was to function as a covenal again, Farin was unsure. As Farin and Tavendia began to dismount, he noticed that one of the guards was a member of his detail. Amid Farin's attempt to show strength in front of the men, the sight of one of his own sent his thoughts racing about the rest of his men who by implication were likely within the city and not currently tasked outside.

Those at the gates were shifting between genuine happiness that the covenal was alive and fascination at the elven beauty that stood patiently beside Farin. Tavendia did not speak. She showed no signs of impatience or displeasure. She merely observed the exchange between Farin and the other humans with an obvious interest, studying their interactions silently. It was less than ten minutes after their arrival that Commander Barros stood before his friend.

"You're late, Covenal," Hadrin stated flatly, no sign of emotion on his face.

"I lost an argument with a crossbow, Commander. My apologies for burdening you with command duties for the last week."

"You're excused. Just don't let it happen again." Now Hadrin's smile broke free. He walked toward Farin and they clasped arms. "The priest-king will likely have heard about your arrival by now and will be eager to have a report from you directly." Hadrin looked toward Tavendia. He took in her beauty, her pointed ears, and the odd clothing of her station before inclining his head. "And welcome, lady of the woods. Lorenth is honored to have you among us."

Tavendia inclined her head in return as she spoke, "It is I who am honored to be the first elf among your race. I hold my breath in eager anticipation for what is yet to happen as our races begin to entwine." The other guards did not know what to make of her slightly cryptic talk but it mattered not. An elf was in Lorenth. History was being made in front of soldier and citizen alike as Commander Barros extended his arm back toward the gate. Farin and Tavendia guided their mounts by resting their hands on the sides of their faces as the continuously growing procession followed the small party up the streets of the lower city approaching the upper city gates.

More soldiers from the eastern border detail came to pay their respects to Farin and he waved to them in greeting, the smile never having an opportunity to leave his face. The second gates to the upper city were already swung wide to admit the commander and his honored companions. As they passed into the upper city and walked along the stone channels that siphoned some of the water from the mighty Ardun waterfall that fell freely behind the citadel and the fortress, Farin paused as he saw his old friend Erikk standing near the entrance to the fortress with Arimas, several of the royal guard, and Lead Counselor Bethanin close at hand.

"The council welcomes back Covenal Farin Guilian of the eastern border detail and requests his report of the diplomatic mission of nearly two weeks past. The council also recognizes the elven diplomat among us, and accords her the honor and respect due to one of her position. We invite you to speak plainly with us for we are most interested to hear what you have to say." The Lead Counselor spoke with grace as the official formalities were exchanged. Tavendia nodded once more and informed those present that she had much to share and that time was not a pressing matter for now.

Arimas stepped out from beside the northern border covenal to address Farin. Farin almost looked away from Arimas but stopped as he noticed a new strength that now resided behind those piercing eyes. Farin tried to extend his senses over Arimas, attempting to see in the same way as he had when he tried observing the Illuallarii and then when he tried looking into the soul of Atarax. For the briefest of moments all he saw was light—a brilliant amber colored light that blotted out the priest-king's facial features and his robes. Then the image was gone. But, though Farin believed his seeking to be undetectable, when Arimas paused in mid-stride as Farin extended his senses, the covenal wondered if somehow Arimas had felt the subtle probing. Arimas resumed his step, and, stopping before Tavendia and Farin, he offered a quick smile to Farin in answer to the unspoken question coursing through his mind.

"Many were broken in spirit when we heard of your fall. How it is that you now stand before us whole, in body and in spirit, is something I will be very interested in learning about. You have changed, Farin. I have changed, as well. There are forces moving about us that we have long been ignorant of but are now making themselves known. You have ridden hard today and I offer this evening to you both. Show your friend what you will of Lorenth, Farin; enjoy the evening, get some rest, and tomorrow we will convene for a special session of the council."

Farin thanked Arimas for his generous offer and looked to Tavendia, who appeared pleased at the prospect of being shown around the city. Arimas certainly had changed. Farin's last visit to Lorenth, bearing the dreaded news of the Dark Wood, was received with skepticism; now he was being treated with honor and given time to rest and sleep off the travel weariness in favor of presenting his report on the morrow.

Far be it from Farin to ignore the king's suggestion. He waved to Erikk and said they would catch up on news later on while Commander Barros accompanied the two of them away from the citadel.

"I will take my leave of you, Farin. I will begin debriefing the men for there will be many questions tonight. It's good to have you back, Covenal."

"I know the men were in good hands. Thank you for—"

"There is no need to thank me for doing my—"

"No... thank you, Hadrin. You have no idea what it means to me to have you as part of my leadership core. You bring honor to the armor and to the colors of Lorenth." The commander wasn't sure how to respond to the accolades of his covenal. He nodded and said nothing more, much to his credit, before taking his leave and returning to the barracks.

"What would you like to see first, Tavendia?" Farin asked gallantly as they stepped beyond the gate of the fortress.

"Perhaps we should visit another inn. I know you are hungry and we have not taken many breaks today. Even though I may not need to eat as often as you do, there is no reason for you to deny yourself what you need just for me."

Farin could not argue with the logic of her words and led his companion toward the only inn and tavern located anywhere near the officer quarters. The Gilded Swan was definitely an upgrade in aesthetics from Earl's tavern and inn back in Newhaven; however, the company was not nearly as friendly. Farin rarely had the chance to frequent this establishment because much of his career was spent in the field with his men on various taskings that kept him out of the city and out of Seneschal Dean's attention and sight. The innkeeper nodded in greeting when the two entered, and asked Farin and Tavendia if they needed a room or a meal, promoting his special for the evening which was a succulent lamb roast covered with thin, aromatic gravy along with carrots on the side. Farin reached into his pockets for some coppers and quickly remembered that he had carried no money with him since his rehabilitation in elven lands. The innkeeper was tempted to deny him service but when Farin promised to fetch some coin from his quarters in the officer district, the innkeeper suddenly recognized the eastern border covenal that had been reported dead and agreed to serve him and the lady upon his honor.

Tavendia inquired about a lighter fare, perhaps of cheese and breads, or fruit and vegetables, and the innkeeper offered her something called 'salad' with an oil-based dressing and some fresh bread. Farin explained that the salad was just a collection of vegetables with some spices infused in the oil dressing. It sounded appetizing and so she requested that.

"Why do you trade coins for food here? What does he use these coins for?"

"It is a way to trade between humans. We give these coins value and then we trade that value with others for goods or services.

297

The more coins you have, the more goods and services you can trade for. Some get coins for service rendered, like myself and the other soldiers, while others trade their wares for coins in the marketplaces or among other townships. It works fairly well but greed often motivates people to be dishonest in dealings in an attempt to increase the coins they receive per dealing—some will steal coins from others when they are not looking, and some will unfortunately kill for them."

Farin watched the natural light in Tavendia's eyes dim at the foreign notion of crime, and guessed that she cultivated a disdain and sorrow that she tried not to show. He practiced extending his senses again and his presumptions were confirmed. Deep within her heart was a sorrow for humanity. She could not understand how humans could exist so independently from each other when all she had ever seen in her generations upon these lands was unity.

Elves did not trade or barter for anything. They lived as the trees lived—patiently and interdependently. The celebration hall was always filled with food and those who gathered shared with all. Those who crafted and those who taught; those that learned and those who lead—elves lived in harmony with one another. Needs were met and greed simply was not an emotion that motivated an elf.

Dwarves were more like the humans in this regard, yet like the elves, they too held to strong beliefs in equity. Dwarves were independent as clans, yet within the clan structure there was a similar equality and harmony. All needs were accounted for and no one was ever in want. For those who delved, smelted, forged or crafted, all the excess was stored in large warehouses and then traded between their other kinsmen from the other clans.

But the individualism noted among the humans was disconcerting for Tavendia and she had to hold her tongue in light of what she was learning about this culture. Farin saw all of this in her as she looked at him and touched his face gently.

"Now I wish you were not learning as fast as you are learning, Farin. I am sorry for the way I feel, but this is just something that I cannot fathom—though I am trying."

"We are indeed different, but I hope in time you will find some good among humans. There is beauty among the darkness, which you have not yet seen. Even I see things differently now since spending time with you and your kin."

The couple finished their meals, feeling more subdued than they had during their travels, and left the inn, choosing to make the most of what remained of the evening. Tavendia wanted to see the university in the lower city, and the libraries of the citadel, but both were closed this late in the evening; however, Farin did promise to find time to show her those places before her return to Avalide.

Farin led Tavendia around the upper city, the officer grounds, the stables, and the magister's office before they finally ended up at the king's beloved temple. To the back of the holy building, within its courtyards, remained the last few trees left in the city. They were short and stunted, and Tavendia immediately quickened her pace when she saw them. The sorrow that was in her eyes began to dissipate once she approached the trees and let her fingers graze their trunks as she walked among them.

"They are hurting. The soil is not deep enough for their roots and the rains here are not sufficient to feed them. I must speak with them, Farin."

The covenal looked into Tavendia's stricken face and saw the purpose that filled her eyes, and only nodded, allowing the druid to speak and act as she felt compelled. He nearly forgot that this druid had spent all her years among the trees. It had to be difficult for her, so far away from all she knew.

Tavendia knelt to the ground, her head ducked and her long hair hanging like a curtain around her face, and began to whisper intently. Farin could feel slight vibrations beneath him as the druid focused all of her thought and all of her energy into the earth beneath the trees, not on the trees themselves. She worked slowly and methodically, not just fixing the damage that she saw, but attempting to change the cause of the damage. The ground vibrations became small tremors as Farin watched the ground before him swell. Farin closed his eyes, trying to extend his senses to see what was really happening, and what he saw amazed him. Somehow, Tavendia was rearranging the terrain beneath the trees, displacing the bedrock and opening the looser, more fertile soil to allow the trees to extend their roots deeper. She also began to raise the terrain all along the tree line, shifting more earth and soil from areas where it was not needed as much.

Then, the elven druid closed her eyes and began to sing in that uncharacteristically deep, multi-vocal voice that resonated musically throughout the temple grounds. Farin struggled to keep his eyes closed, to rely only on his inner sight, as Tavendia slipped fully into her treesong. He had to use all his concentration to hold onto the images that he saw as the elf's words projected like thin cords of light which began to encircle and bind to the trunks of the trees. He could sense warmth and love permeating the air around the druid as she spoke life into the hearts of the trees, their only thought echoing the one word command that the druid uttered in the treesong. One word over and over... *grow*. Farin released the sight and dropped to one knee in exhaustion from his efforts as his natural eyes revealed to him what his senses had already begun to see.

There before him in the temple grounds, the few remaining trees had thickened in the trunk as their roots began to dig deeper into the earth, shifting around the concrete piping that made up the tunnels within the sewer network and extending farther down to the water table that was supplied by the River Ardun. The branches were straightened and elongated just like the sapling that Narissa had bolstered back in Avalide—yet this was so much more than the infusion of strength. This was the infusion of life and the will to grow. In mere moments Tavendia had corrected years of deficiency and restored the trees to the size they should have been at their age, while also strengthening them and giving them the optimal conditions in which to grow even further.

"That is much better. They are at peace now. Tomorrow I will ask that Arimas protect the sanctity of this small glade in honor of *Illu'Dar*. It will be well received in Avalide if the humans can show some restraint in their uncontrolled slaughter of the trees." Tavendia then looked at Farin who was wiping the sweat from his brow as he stood once more. She canted her head to the right slightly and looked so deeply into his eyes that Farin felt his very soul smile in response.

For a brief second he thought of Jesslyn, of all the pain that loving her had caused him over the years. Then, as he looked into the eyes of the elven druid before him, Jesslyn's visage began to fade from the forefront of his mind. Aside from the normal attraction he felt when he looked at the beautiful elf, there was something else... he actually began to allow his mind to wander toward much more intimate things. It was the first time he saw an elf blush. Then guilt set in as she turned away breaking off eye contact with him.

"I'm sorry, Farin. I forget sometimes how short-lived your race is. While I may find you pleasing to look upon, I could never bind myself to you, emotionally, or physically. You must understand... your race passes into nothingness like a candle that is lit and then quickly snuffed out. Allowing myself a few short years of pleasure with you would only result in an eternity of pain after your eventual death.

"I also know that these were merely thoughts of yours and not actions and sometimes I curse myself for being able to see truth, as you too can see truth. Humans and elves cannot join together in this manner and it pains me to speak so harshly to you now. You have a beautiful spirit Farin, but I cannot let you deceive yourself with those types of thoughts."

Farin, though reeling inwardly from her words, maintained his composure by digging back down into that hardened resolve that once protected him from all the pain that he felt when Jesslyn was taken from him. Like the donning of his plate armor, he strapped that same determination and emotionless fortitude over his heart and mind in an attempt to numb his heart which so foolishly had begun to feel again. Farin knew it was not love that caused his pulse to beat erratically—he had only met Tavendia a couple days ago. It was life. Ever since being among the elves everything seemed somehow richer and more beautiful. The thought of war and bloodshed was nagging at him. Nature and all its beauty was starting to indwell him. And for only the briefest of moments he envisioned being joined to this druid like the trees were rooted in the earth—strengthened from their symbiotic relationship.

Tavendia couldn't even look Farin in the eyes as she continued speaking. "I know you do not fully understand the changes that are happening inside you, Farin. I think it is time you begin to comprehend even a tiny fragment of what resides deep within you. You are learning faster than I would have expected a human to learn—especially since you are among the first humans to become altered through a shift in the balance in such a long time. You are a truth-seeker, Farin."

"How is that unique, Tavendia? Arimas is the priest-king and has long been known for his pursuit of truth. The magister and those who represent the legal council of Lorenth pursue truth. Am I to cease being a soldier to become as they are?" Farin spoke like the covenal of the eastern border detail would speak, not as a man in love. He spoke eloquently and professionally, with an even tone, as his emotional wall was now fully reconstructed.

Tavendia witnessed the sudden shift in his demeanor and was moved nearly to the point of tears at how fast her wound to his heart had calloused. It would not heal. He would not allow himself to heal. But he would serve and pursue truth as his destiny unfolded—this she was sure of. Instead of focusing on this new wound, she let it be, knowing that perhaps this was a part of Farin's journey.

"You see what is, Farin—and not what others would want you to see. In time, lies will become as plain as day to you and you will have insight into whatever you wish to understand. As you learn to control your emotions and your mind you will begin to see with greater ease and efficiency. You began in the Illuallarii with my mother, though you did not fully understand what you were attempting to do. You did it again when you sought to understand Atarax. And now you have done it three times today—before Arimas, before me within the inn, and now here among the trees."

For a time Farin just listened with his ears. He already had some insight into himself and knew that he could not become the old Farin again, no matter how hard he wanted to try. He could not contain this new passion for life behind a heart of steel. There had to be a compromise that could allow Farin to flow with the changes already taking place inside without submitting his heart to more pain and disappointment. Everything that Tavendia said resounded with truth and at last he felt as if a missing part of his soul was put back in its place, making him complete. He had a purpose and a destiny, as uncertain as it was. He was marked and linked somehow to the Lightbringer that was yet to come. He was the guardian and the redeemed. And while he knew nothing at all about what that meant, other than the obvious significance of the prophesized Lightbringer, he trusted the elves and their wisdom. Everything they had shown him and told him felt right. Perhaps this was his 'gift' working on a subconscious level, or perhaps he was being blindly naïve toward the elves and their magic—believing them to be masters of life and agents of the balance. Those were matters to debate another time.

"Thank you for telling me Tavendia. And please forgive me for letting my thoughts wander. You are the guest of Lorenth and I will do my best to act in such a manner as to bring honor to my name and my king."

"There is nothing to forgive Farin... nothing to forgive at all." There was a moment of awkward silence until Tavendia started to walk away from the temple grounds. "Come show me the lower city before it gets too late and we become too tired to enjoy ourselves." She flashed her incredible smile at Farin as he shrugged of his malaise and tried to enjoy the rest of the evening with the elven diplomat—or was she his friend?

Together, enjoying the cool evening air, they walked along the main streets of the lower city, passing by the barracks before heading into the marketplace. All the shops were secured and few people were seen walking the streets as lights all over town were lit in various homes as the tradesmen spent the last evening hours inside with their families or some other relaxing activity. Tavendia imagined how this place would look in the morning when life and trade were alive and well in the open air markets.

Then at last they came upon the university, which was nearly as large as the elven Illuallarii. While there definitely were some less appealing parts to the lower city, the university and the immediate surroundings were such a sight. Farin told Tavendia that it was within the walls of the university where all of Lorenth's research and study took place. The libraries were still housed in the upper city within the citadel but it was here in the university where theoretical knowledge and assumption became applied knowledge and fact.

There were departments for alchemy and general sciences, herbalism and apothecary training, departments dedicated to thought and logic, and of course, the military academy. Officers in particular were required to learn about the art of battle, in addition to the practical learning they received regarding the use of both the sword and bow, before being deemed a trained candidate for a border detail assignment. Until they had completed this training, they studied. This was not enough though for some of the trainees and thus many chose to serve with the honor guard while completing their training.

Farin let out a slight yawn. Tavendia nudged his shoulder as she leaned closer to him, "It's late and I have enjoyed seeing your city very much. You can show me more another time—preferably when the sun is shining." She chuckled softly as Farin nodded. They made their way back to the upper city slowly. The guards of the second watch of the night were already well into their shift as they opened the gates to the upper city for the covenal, each of them expressing their joy at seeing Farin alive and well among them again. They walked past The Gilded Swan once more, noticing that the crowd had gotten much larger now that the ale was freely flowing within the tavern.

Tavendia lingered at the window for a moment to watch the men in various states of inebriation. She thought the entire notion of drinking fermented grains was somewhat odd but rather amusing. Though the dwarves were known to partake in behaviors like this, she did not remember hearing reports about them acting foolish after they consumed too much. An intoxicated dwarf was often a stumbling, bumbling idiot with a rather nasty temper, a sore head and quite an upset stomach that a long sleep or several dunks in cold water seemed to improve. These humans however appeared to become livelier and laughed more—very interesting indeed.

When Farin finally led Tavendia to his large, white-bricked estate which had housed one other covenal before him, he opened his door quietly and lit the candles within the main room, not wanting to rouse his staff. He yawned again and then led Tavendia toward the master bedroom where he invited her to sleep. Before she could object, he told her that there was also a spare room with a bed that he would be more than comfortable in. She lightly touched Farin's shoulder in thanks, and warmly wished him a pleasant sleep before closing the bedroom door. He whispered his own goodnights to the closed door before proceeding to the spare room where his long trusted bedroll was spread out on top of the spare bed.

Farin smiled sadly as he thought of the first time Jesslyn snuck into his bedroll during the establishment of Larriot so many years ago. They had been sleeping in tents, upon bedrolls, and she had left the apothecary tent late in the night to be with the man she loved. They had lain together for nearly an hour just holding each other, listening to the rhythmic beating of each other's hearts. Oh, how he missed her! Farin's smile faded once more as he returned to the main room to blow out the candles before returning to his bedroll and yet another dreamless sleep.

XXIII

"Farin is alive?" queried Verona when Arimas returned from the courtyard with the news. The priest-king, exhausted after the long day, wearily relayed to his wife what little information he had after the couple were reunited at the end of the day. What Arimas did not share was the discovery that he had made about the returned covenal's newly acquired abilities.

Farin really had changed over the last two weeks. Arimas had felt a subtle probing of his mind, and with his own strengthened senses, knew that it came from Farin. The gentle seeking was not malicious and Farin had none of the darkness emanating from him that Arimas normally detected in those who were harboring ill intent. Farin was loyal, and merely inquisitive, like a young boy testing out a new toy. Perhaps the elves would be able to enlighten him and Farin and all the humans about the mystical developments happening among them.

Arimas stirred from his deep thoughts as his queen and lover approached him and slid her hand beneath his shirt, laying her head down upon his chest. He encircled her with his arms and kissed her forehead before dismissing the pensive thoughts and removing his mantle of office and his regalia in favor of a much simpler and more comfortable robe. Verona had already prepared two cups of a mint tea for them to enjoy together as Arimas slumped down on their bed where his queen was now sitting. They sipped their tea and relaxed in one another's company for some time, speaking of Farin and the elf who was even now touring their city.

Verona was fascinated at the prospect of meeting an elf, and requested to be present at the next day's meeting, provided she experienced some relief from the terrible stomach sickness that had been afflicting her on a daily basis. Even Arimas had tried to dispel the sickness that was in her, but to no avail. This sickness made no sense to him or to the apothecary and Arimas would often spend the better part of an hour in prayer each morning, supplicating with the unknown power that he heeded to.

While the king and his queen were still deep in conversation, Arimas suddenly felt a strange sensation wash over him and he quickly rose to his feet. It was overwhelming. He walked to the window and looked down toward the temple area where he could barely make out two individuals among the short trees in the temple grounds. Verona joined him at the window and followed the direction of his gaze.

"Who are they Arimas? Is that..."

"Yes, that is the lady of the woods, with Farin. She is doing something incredibly powerful. All I see is light and life around her and I have no idea what to make of it."

"Look!" Verona cried out. "Can it really be happening?" Arimas watched in amazement as the ground began to rumble and the trees grew before their very eyes—even this far away it was evident what was happening. Branches were elongating and the foliage thickened. Verona and Arimas swore that they could hear the trunks creaking and groaning as they straightened out and grew in size. It was... miraculous. There was no other word for it. Even after the elf had finished and was led by Farin out of the temple grounds, Arimas stood at the window with his queen and simply watched the trees sway freely in the night breeze, the torchlight around the temple and the grounds casting eerie shadows all over. Dragons... now elves with mystical powers over living things... Arimas was almost afraid to learn what else was out there that the humans had not yet encountered.

Arimas pulled Verona close once more and delighted himself with the fragrance of her hair. He delicately kissed the back of her neck, and when she turned to look up at him he passionately kissed her full on the lips. They held each other for a time before blowing out their chamber candles for the evening, suddenly feeling quite small in a world that apparently was far bigger than either of them had ever imagined.

*   *   *

"I am truly sorry your Excellency, I have tried everything I can think of but this is a sickness that I cannot treat. I know it sounds false, but I cannot find anything wrong with her—in fact, her general health appears to be improving despite these morning occurrences. Sire, I have seen similar ailments like this before with some of the younger women when they are with ch—"

"Rebekah, thank you for your time and your professional opinions but you are now treading upon fragile ground by bringing up matters that bear a great deal of pain for both me and the queen. I will not have you building up false hope where for years there has been nothing but pain and regret. I am old Rebekah. I may not feel its full effects but I see the subtle changes within me and now with your queen."

"My apologies sire, I will take my leave." Rebekah Delling bowed deeply as she gathered her bag of tinctures and suspensions, elixirs, powders, and even some bitter herbs and roots that supposedly could help alleviate some of these pains with his wife. Since losing her mother before the founding of Lorenth so many years ago, the herbalist and now apothecary fuelled her passion for the healing arts with the pain she would always bear deep within. Even her marriage to the younger alchemist, Leon Delling, did little to deter her from applying her trade more and more. When Arimas had to appoint a new head apothecary shortly after appointing a new seneschal, Rebekah was already the best choice and to this day, he never regretted his decision in choosing her. Even still, her expert council on this matter was too hard for him to accept so easily. While these treatments did little to stop the sickness from recurring each morning, they did bring momentary comfort and apparently enabled Verona to carry on with her day without further episodes. For this at least, Arimas was glad that Rebekah was working so diligently with the queen.

One more morning of being awakened by the sound of his lover expelling the contents of her stomach. One more morning of no answers from the head apothecary in the university—well, none that he could reasonably entertain. One more morning of Arimas praying at length in intercession, pleading for the ability to heal his wife as he had healed himself and his men down in the sewers. He even tried to invoke the power of that prayer over his wife. He felt the strength build like before but he could not unleash it into her. Apparently the power needed a corresponding darkness in order to be released, and like the apothecary said earlier, she appeared to be in good health.

Arimas told Verona to rest and that he would check on her later to ensure she was feeling better, then headed down to the council chambers to begin the preparations for the special council later this morning. The sun was barely in the sky and there were at least four more hours before midday. The counselors would begin arriving within the hour likely and Farin and the elf would also be arriving around then as well so he had some time. Commander Barros and Erikk Masaad were to be present as well as the full council, less those members who chose exile. Surprisingly, five of the eleven counselors chose exile or death over repentance— Dean's reach had grown long indeed.

The morning passed quickly as the preparations were completed. All were seated in anticipation for the arrival of Farin and the elven diplomat. Arimas had also requested his twenty-four royal guardsmen to be present—not for show or security but to allow them the opportunity to share in the assembly and to ensure their words were heard should they have matters to share as well.

Arimas carefully studied the elf as she walked in with Farin. She was much fairer than he remembered from last night, likely due to the lack of light and the shadows created by the torches. Her eyes were of the palest blue—lighter than the deep blue that Arimas was known for—which stood out in stark contrast to her light-amber colored hair. She wore the most unusual garments that he had ever seen. She was clad in a simple robe that clung to her frame and was colored in deep earthen tones with a cloak that appeared to be made of leaves clasped around her neck. It would be folly to think of her as anything but simple, especially after what he witnessed her accomplish last night.

Typically the Lead Counselor would address those present before the council but Tavendia did not wait to be addressed or welcomed officially once again. She carried herself with dignity and grace as she extended a small, sealed parchment towards Arimas and then approached all who had gathered within the large council chambers of the citadel. The morning sun danced playfully upon the stone tiled flooring of the chamber while a gentle breeze passed through windows that gave free reign to the sun's light. Aside from those gathered around the council the only other visitor was a small sparrow perched on the ledge of the window chirping innocently to itself while Tavendia began to address the high command of Lorenth. Her confident tone and the long years of wisdom that shone behind her eyes immediately captivated her audience.

"Long have the elves been watching the steady and measured growth of the human nation and long have we anticipated and feared this day when communion between our two races would begin. I am Tavendia Amberdawn, member of the *Essen'dril* and ambassador of Avalide, the forest sanctuary of *Illu'Dar*. For as long as I dare remember, fate has sought to entwine our destinies and now that time is upon us. It is no coincidence that the events of destiny have begun to spill into your realm upsetting the delicate balance that you have struggled to maintain for generations. I know you all will have questions of me, as I have of you, and it is my intent to see those questions resolved as we decide this day what is to become of the relationship between our races.

"Before you all begin with your questions, I must say a few words. I have already lived a span that would encompass more than ten generations of men. Question not how this can be, for in time, even our histories may become open to you and it is not my intent to reveal the history of the elves during such a gathering. I command the forces of nature and am a practitioner of the corporeal plane, even as my kin may conjure and divine within the elemental and spiritual planes. Question not how this can be, for the *Trinactria* is a subject that I am neither qualified nor willing to discuss during such a gathering. A shadow looms in the southwest and even now has begun to corrupt those among you. This... you shall question, and this shall I answer.

"The Seed of Corruption grows strong and fast as he seeks to plunge our world in shadow and despair but fate has not yet been determined. The Lightbringer will come from the race of men and must face the Seed of Corruption at the appointed time when the balance shall once and for all be corrected. The fae races have met and pondered your fate and the plight that affects us all. If the lands of Caliyon, of which Lorenth is a part, are to stand under the oppression of the shadow, then we must work together, sharing in wisdom and knowledge as we seek to find and protect the child of prophecy that will decide the fate of us all."

The council sat stunned at the words that left the elf's lips. No one knew what to say in response to this. Something inside Arimas was building as if her words were stirring some presence deep within him. He clung to every word she said and somehow knew that this elf was an instrument of peace and not an agent of discord. Throughout every word she spoke her eyes remained fixed upon Arimas as if she were speaking only to him. Arimas remembered the words spoken from Sargeron the black to Covenal Masaad about Arimas being marked in the line of the Lightbringer. Now the elf made reference to this Lightbringer once again. Tavendia smiled as Arimas felt his soul being laid bare before her watchful eyes.

"You know the truth of which I speak, Arimas. You have heard about the dragons, I understand. Already you see things more clearly, though you know not why. I see the gifts residing in many of you here, yet they lay dormant. But you, Arimas, hold the key to unlocking the potential of the human nation and your time of discovery draws near."

Before Arimas could even ponder a response, a creature bigger than the entire chamber appeared before them. This had to be one of the dragons that Erikk had told him about for when he turned to look at the covenal of the northern border detail, the truth was written all over his face. He was the only human to appear only awed at the beauty of this magnificent creature and not shocked that such a creature could exist. Within seconds of the appearance of this dragon, the tiny sparrow that was perched on the window also flew into the assembly area as its form began to shimmer until the bird was no more and another elf—a male it appeared—was also standing before the council. The royal guard immediately drew arms and began to form a wall of security around the priest-king.

"Hold men!" cried Arimas but he was already too late. The male elf responded with amazing speed as he quickly uttered several words in an unknown tongue and ice immediately encased the lower legs of every armed guard in the council.

"Forgive the fear that our presence among you has evoked, noble one. We intend no harm to you or your men and they shall be released. Stay your arms and listen for we too bring tidings from the Icecrown Peaks, and my ally Larros brings word to you from the northern lands of the *Dsa'carii*. I show you but a glimpse of my true form but perhaps I shall take on a less assuming one to speak more openly with you all."

The massive dragon began to shrink and change before their eyes until it resembled another elf similar to the male in skin complexion but obviously female. The hair was the same color as the scales were but the eyes were not elven, they were the same reptilian eyes as before. The change was remarkable—even her voice softened when she spoke once more.

"I am Zharra, platinum dragon of the Icecrown Peaks, daughter to Valkyyrak and Dalaria the ancients, and representative sent on behalf of all dragonkind to entreat with the humans. Larros, please release your bindings and feel free to address them as well."

The elven male made a flourish with his hands and the ice prisons shattered as several of the guards fell to ground trying to regain their balance. The guards quickly stood and sheathed their weapons as they returned to their places and waited with expectation to hear what would be said next.

"Pardon my hastiness, Priest-King, but I know full well how efficient your royal guards are and I needed to act fast. As Zharra has already said, I am Larros Solan'dras of the Frostspire and *Dsa'carii* ambassador to the humans. I am a storm mage as are the rest of my kin and throughout the long years of the silence pact I have frequently watched your rise and development as a race. The silence pact prevented me from introducing myself earlier which is something I do regret as over the years I have come to find great pleasure in observing your race. Lady Tavendia, whom I have not yet had the pleasure of meeting, has touched on several points of great importance and it is the hopes of both the dragon nation and those of the Frostspire to also aid and guide the humans as the age of Lightbringer draws near."

Arimas stood and walked toward the three ambassadors with Farin still standing patiently at Tavendia's side. "Lorenth is greatly honored today. Only in my dreams did I picture such things coming to pass before my eyes. Indeed there are questions but as you already know we are a fairly ignorant race when it comes to your nations and the unseen forces that guide this Caliyon that you speak of. It is my intention that humankind will stand by and listen to what you would have us learn. Perhaps then many unspoken questions will be answered and the knowledge gained will further direct our future questions. While I cannot completely fathom how you have been watching us silently for all these years, Ambassador Larros, I trust your words and thus I am inclined to believe all the more strongly that you already know what information would be best suited for us to know. We submit to your wisdom in these things."

"Already you speak with a wisdom and humility befitting the best of your race, Arimas," began Tavendia. "I would begin first by applauding you for your purge of the city. I feel none of the taint of the Seed of Corruption among you and I believe that even though your decision was tough and wrought with sorrow, you made the right choice."

"And I have the dragons to thank for the guidance, Lady Tavendia. Lady Zharra, I am sure you already know that Erikk Masaad has had brief dealings with Lord Sargeron before, and his message was delivered to my very ears, and heeded. His warnings confirmed my suspicions about the former seneschal, though I regret that I trusted Dean too long as it was. I lost a good friend and counselor that day, and nearly lost one of my fine covenals."

"Farin has been a testament to the bravery and integrity that can be found in humans," added Tavendia. "Avalide was honored to have him among us for his time of healing. He learns exceptionally fast and will prove to be a valuable resource to Lorenth as he learns to harness his gift more carefully."

Farin saw the intrigued expression on Arimas' face and ventured to answer the king's unspoken question. "Tavendia has identified me as a truth-seeker, my liege. It is a role that is difficult to explain, but to fill this role I have been given an inner second sight that reveals to me what my natural vision cannot see. Emotions, inner workings, and even the effects of magic are laid out before me."

"You and I will definitely need to talk at some length about this new ability of yours, Farin. You were always a valuable resource to Lorenth, even before you had this gift. My only regret is that I did not see the truth quicker. I have said it before but it bears repeating—I too have changed and Lorenth will be led in its original direction once more. No longer will corruption be allowed to fester within the heart of this city or in this land. Dean will have much to answer for eventually, and I intend to see to this answering personally."

"My only caution to you, Arimas, is that you not underestimate the Seed of Corruption. In time he will be Dean no longer," Zharra warned. "I am told that Farin knows the truth of this matter as well. For years the prophecies have been shrouded for us in relation to this very matter and alas we have no insight to give about how or when this transformation is to occur."

While Zharra was speaking, Verona slid unseen into the back of the council chambers. No one saw her enter for she maintained discretion and did not wish to draw attention upon herself. Try as she might, nothing could slip by Arimas it seemed, for within moments of her entrance, something stirred within him and he immediately locked his gaze on to hers. Farin noticed the change in Arimas' attention and followed his eyes to Verona. Now that he understood a part of what his gifting was, he extended his senses over Arimas in an attempt to understand his feelings toward the queen's sudden and apparently unplanned arrival.

He tried to slow the release of energy that he expended, probing with more of a whisper than a loud shout. Within seconds of extending his senses he caught a sensation of concern about Verona and her sickness and whether or not she should have come.

Farin immediately shifted his focus to Verona and nearly fell to the floor as he was blinded by an abundance of light coming from her stomach and lower abdomen area. It was almost like staring into the sun. His vision shifted and he saw the light separate until he felt, not saw, something he was not prepared for—life was growing within her.

"She bears a child of light!" Farin exclaimed, before collapsing to the floor in fatigue. Arimas looked toward Farin's prostrate figure with incredulity, hardly able to believe that the covenal's words could be true. The council, the royal guards and the three ambassadors all looked toward Verona, who was blushing furiously beneath the weight of their gazes. She stepped from out of the back of the chamber and into the daylight in order to stand beside Arimas.

Tavendia knelt beside the fallen Farin and whispered in his ear, "Stand my friend. Today you have seen truth that will change destiny." She helped him regain his footing.

"The age of the Lightbringer has begun and the period of sorrow is soon to come," began Larros. "Hold to what we teach you and prepare your hearts against the shadow for as surly as you draw breath Verona, Queen of Lorenth, there will be those who will plot for your death to prevent your child from entering the world—this the elves of Frostspire vow to ward against."

"It is thought that the ancient dragons were created as an answer to the imbalance that began with the corruption of the deity Sarik. While I cannot see in the same way as Farin, I too can sense that life stirs within you and I too felt the presence of destiny as you entered the room. The dragons of the Icecrowns will be there when you need us most. We will shelter, guide, teach, and possibly even learn from you and those of Lorenth as we ensure safe journeys for you and the child. I, Zharra, do decree this on behalf of the dragons and this charge will be taken up by all in service to the light."

Tavendia did not speak for a time as she walked up to Verona and stood before her and Arimas. Verona stood in awe at the beauty of the elf standing before her. Feeling self conscious, the queen offered a small curtsy toward the elf as Tavendia smiled and stretched out her hand in order to touch the flat belly of the queen. Tavendia's eyes immediately lit up.

"What is it Lady? What do you see?" Arimas demanded. Tavendia began to cry softly but still refrained from speaking as she grabbed the right hand of Arimas and spun him around a bit so that his palm now rested on Verona's belly with Tavendia's hand overtop his. Tavendia channeled the imagery into both of their minds—slowly at first, but steadily increasing in speed as more time elapsed. Arimas saw life deep within his queen, yet that light of life would be wrought with danger and much uncertainty. Images of shadow and war, pain and death, and finally the sadistic smile of Seneschal Dean looming over a vast abyss brought great sorrow to Verona and began to incite the wrath of Arimas once again. The imagery shifted once more and focused on two young souls even now learning and listening to ebb and flow of magic that was coursing around them from within the womb. They had no form but they were the potential of a seed—a seed that would grow into a thing of beauty to rival the vileness around them.

"There are two children..." whispered Arimas in realization.

"Yes, there are, and one of them will be the Lightbringer. We all are learning together now for the shroud has blocked our minds from understanding and the future is no longer clear. The dream has ended and with that dream the prophecies are now stilled." Tavendia reclaimed her hand, smiling sadly. "I know that both joy and sorrow will be yours as a result of these two children, yet beyond that I am blind."

Anton looked to Rorrick and to the other royal guards watching from his side. Each of them answered Anton's inquisitive glance with a nod. Anton stepped forward and dropped to his knee as around the room the twenty-three other royal guardsmen approached Arimas and Verona and also dropped to one knee. With them, Covenal Masaad and Commander Barros also rallied to the side of the priest-king and knelt in service, prepared to issue whatever oath of life and service that Anton would make on behalf of those of Lorenth.

"Arimas and Verona, Priest-King and Queen, lead us into this new age. We pledge our lives and our obedience to you, and vow to serve you as your hand in battle and your arm of discipline.

We commit all that we are and all that we do to counting your lives above our own. Hail to the Lightbringer that is to be born among us! May those of us on bended knee be committed to the preservation of your lineage and to the safeguarding of the heir of the throne of Lorenth until that fated day spoken of among us. As we have long served you as king, may we also serve you as priest and learn of the paths to the unknown god. We have witnessed divine power and healing pass through you and we submit ourselves to you once more."

Arimas smiled at the dedication of his men, which humbled his spirit even as his devoted soldiers and friends were humbled. Tavendia receded back into her memories and began to smile while Farin looked on with wonder. The image of Zharra looked to Larros as both began exchanging knowing nods. Lead Counselor Bethanin and Verona simply stood where they were, caught unprepared for the sudden change that came over the priest-king.

XXIV

Arimas could feel that awakened presence within consume him, but this time it was not with zeal or righteous anger. Like he felt deep within the bowels of the sewer, the sole thought flowing through his mind was to submit to this presence and not to attempt to control or manipulate it. It was in the weakness and submission of Arimas that this power would make him strong and use him. Farin nearly rallied beside Hadrin yet something unknown cautioned him against the initial urge to rededicate his life to the service of the priest-king and the deity that had its hand upon Arimas.

The priest-king knelt where he stood and cupped his raised hands together as if forming a bowl and presenting an offering. All along the room while the sun still shone on the stone tiling in the council chamber, the candles that were only lit during the evening and during ceremonial times of prayer spontaneously burst into flame. The smoke from each candle began to waft toward Arimas who remained kneeling with his hands still in position until all the smoke began to form a swirling orb within his cupped hands.

The elves looked on in wonder. Zharra made every attempt to see with her truesight what was truly happening, as Farin did the same. The orb of smoke pulsed once and a sound similar to that crystalline song that shattered the silence those many days ago resounded within the council chamber. The orb of smoke split into two thin tendrils and entered though the nostrils of the prostrate priest-king, filling his lungs with the fullness of this unknown presence.

Arimas stood and opened his eyes. Zharra gasped as she saw the very same manifestation there that she had witnessed when Sycaris had revealed the lost prophecy of her youth. Where there once were deep blue eyes rested twin swirling orbs of cloud and a gentle spirit that commanded respect and attention. The voice that left the lips of Arimas sounded nothing at all like him and everyone, including Verona, stared in wonder.

"Anton and those who kneel before me, who have so pledged in their heart of hearts and soul of souls to be the protector of the Lightbringer, shall be held to their vow and blessed with my very presence. It has been the faith of Arimas my servant that has permitted my power to once again spark life in my creation. Though I am empty and imprisoned within the heart of the earth, so long as your faith in me remains true, I will harness your faith and bestow my presence and power upon you.

"I am Deimar, the God that breathed life into this world and it will be through Arimas and those in reverence before me now that will lead my creation back toward the balance that was severed so long ago. Children of Ethoni that stand among us now know this— your long suffering and preservation of life will not go unrewarded and even now my brother smiles in remembrance of you.

"Woe to those who follow blindly after my brother Sarik. As with all matters concerning the balance, with great perfection and power comes its equal in imperfection and weakness for the shadow of my brother grows strong. He has chosen his vessel and even now is moving him toward the place of final corruption where the gates to the shadowlands will be opened.

"Your faith will enable my bonds to weaken; your faith will set your own thoughts and minds free of the shadow. Now stand all of you. Draw your blades and receive my blessing as paladins of the eternal flame!"

Farin's heart missed a beat as Arimas, indwelled by the spirit of Deimar, stared directly at him when he mentioned the phrase about faith setting free his mind from the shadow. Arimas turned to face those who had now stood in obedience to the last command of Deimar.

"Incanus dominum et chalori requi fasado etum savadi de Deim!"

He stretched out his hands. The smoke that was behind his eyes was unleashed through his palms as the same amber light that had filled the sewers days before. Thin tendrils of smoke and light coursed into the twenty-six men that once knelt before Arimas. Their bodies and necks arched back as divine power infused them causing their eyes to burn with righteous fire and coating their dual blades in a thin sheath of the same amber flame.

Then it was done. Arimas dropped back to his knees and reflexively turned his hands upward again as the candle flames all around the room immediately went out while a flaming orb of amber light spontaneously appeared and floated above Arimas' upturned hands. His twenty-six paladins corrected their posture, all looking toward Arimas with a literal amber fire burning where their eyes used to be. Their blades, savage enough on their own, now stood like a beacon of righteous wrath.

The two elves and the dragon reached up to wipe away another solitary tear from their left cheek as they stood in shock at the communion with the presence of a deity in their midst. Joy filled them in a way they would never be able to explain as the sentiment from Ethoni was relayed to the three fae creatures in the room. While the elves had held dream records and prophecies regarding the *Sar'Eth'Deim* for countless generations, none had ever felt the presence of a creator spirit among them. For once the elves could fully appreciate what the humans must have felt in their presence, likening them to far superior beings. Words from either of the three would be inappropriate at this time so they simply stood and watched the silent exchange between the priest-king and his new paladins. Tavendia subconsciously slid her arm around Farin's, who tried not to give the gesture any further thought and returned his attention back toward his king.

Zharra understood what had just happened. Farin was on the verge of that same discovery and likely would have the full meaning before the day was over. The humans had not just become a fae race like some were starting to postulate. Zharra doubted if any human would ever be able to even touch the elemental plane, but the spiritual plane was another matter. Something in the words of

Deimar made it all clear. It was the faith of the humans that was weakening the bonds of Deimar.

Zharra never gave any thought to Arimas' title before: Priest-King. King was evident. Arimas was the undisputed ruler of Lorenth but what was he priest over? There was a temple built with the creation of Lorenth all those years ago. Yet what beliefs did they adhere to? Arimas, along with many other humans, believed that life apart from the influence of some divine entity was nearly impossible. From the majesty of all creation around them, the humans drew comfort from the theory about an unnamed deity and built a house of prayer to reflect upon this core belief in human society.

The call of the Tear of Deimar was therefore no accident. As the humans prospered, and as Arimas himself conducted his rule above reproach always attempting to honor the values of Lorenth and show respect to this unnamed deity, the bonds of the imprisoned Deimar were weakening. Their faith brought about the call of the Tear. Their faith was weakening age-long chains around their god. Their faith was advancing destiny to the point of the great conflict. And it was their faith that would unlock the gifts of Deimar's spirit and would prove to be a power perfected in weakness. Those who would submit to the urgings of the spirit would become like vessels in service to the god of life who first breathed the humans into existence. Against such a power, even the elves and the dragons with all their personal mastery over the spiritual and elemental planes feared they would not be able to compete against the influence of a god through the servants of men. The rise of the humans was now complete.

Anton and the other paladins finally sheathed their swords of fire. As the metal was hidden from sight, the flame of the blade and behind their eyes went out and they appeared as they had only moments before. Verona and the counselors still in the chamber were speechless and not even Lead Counselor Bethanin knew what to say in response to the unbelievable events that had occurred. Cirra, attempting to seek guidance of the priest-king, approached Arimas and began to kneel in his presence until Arimas stopped her.

"No Cirra, I am not Deimar. I am but a man and a servant and I will not allow others to think more highly of me then they ought to think. That will go for everyone here and this message should be loud and clear to all those loyal to Lorenth and to me as their priest and king. I will endeavor not to abuse their faith in me as a leader as I in turn become a greater servant to our god and to each other. Let the temple now be known forever as the Temple of Deimar and let that place be a sanctuary of peace, revelation, and prayer as I carry this eternal flame within my hand and entrust it upon the altar where our faith and reverence will continue to free the bonds that imprison our creator. If it is to be our faith that will define us, then let it begin here among those who lead Lorenth. Cast aside doubt and embrace the faith of Deimar as together we move forward—a chosen people with a common goal set before us. Royal guards, covenals, and Commander you are no longer. Farin, with your gift you are to be the Inquisitor of Lorenth. Where lies abound and mystery clouds proper judgment, I will look to you to be my council and aid my conscience. Will you accept this charge?"

Farin stood tall and proud with Tavendia still holding his arm, drawing strength and comfort from her while listening with great interest to the words of the priest-king. "I accept this charge Priest-King. My gifts, such as they are, will be used to aid you such as I am able."

Arimas smiled to his former covenal. "I hold you to that charge. Besides, one encounter with death is enough for any of my field covenals. You must be allowed to live to continue telling the tale of your existence, and your giftings will be better used here in the capital as my new seneschal—from this point on known as my inquisitor. I wouldn't want to waste your giftings on leading a division when I will need your help with leading a nation.

"Paladins of the eternal flame, you are to be my holy knights and disciples of Deimar. Your mission will be akin to mine and thus you each will be tasked with the protection of Lorenth and her people, the leading of our soldiers in arms, and the ministry of faith and healing that I hope Deimar will grant upon each of you. You will be messengers of peace and executors of judgment; with one hand you will minister to the ailments of the sick and dying while the other hand will remain dipped in blood as you guard yourselves against the advancing tide of evil. Will each of you accept this charge? Let me hear it from each of your lips."

One by one, the twenty-four former royal guards, the covenal of the northern border detail and the commander of the eastern border detail all accepted the charge as it was given. Arimas ordered the immediate forging of two additional sets of royal guard plate armor for Hadrin and Erikk but their blades would not be replaced as they had been blessed by Deimar himself. Arimas also detailed his request for a mantle and robes of toughened leather for Farin to wear beneath the covenal's armor. The inquisitor would be recognized by all from afar by his armor alone and the golden mantle detailing the amber flames of the Temple of Deimar would hang around his shoulders and drape down both sides of his chest. The scarlet cloak of command would remain and the leather robe beneath his armor would be dyed crimson to match.

"This brings me to another point that must be discussed now. Dean is a threat to the safety and loyalty of all who would call themselves Lorenthians. With this new threat, measures must be taken. Now is the time to prepare for war, before war is waged upon us. Why I stayed my hand that day when Dean stood at the gates of Lorenth, I will never fully understand. Perhaps fate had a role to play in my decision, but I will not be caught unaware to his devices again."

"How do you want to handle this threat, Arimas?" questioned Dayle. "Shall we recall the promise of safety to those who chose exile?"

"No, integrity and honor is first among all—but ignorance and unpreparedness will not do either. Now that the purge is complete within the city it will be up to you, my paladins, to ensure the purge continues throughout the remainder of the townships.

"Crafters are to begin gathering stone from the quarries and moving it to the river banks in preparation for a wall of such scale that it will dwarf those of the city. All the stone stockpiles within Lorenth will be emptied to assist in this process for I will not sanction any further additions to the city while our borders remain undefended and unwatched. I also want to rally the soldiers of the three border details and all of the town-watch guardsmen, who will gather outside of the city to witness the dismantling of the border details and the creation of the Lorenthian Guard. The new Guard will be halved, with one division to be led by the capable Hadrin Barros and the other by the equally as capable Erikk Masaad. As new paladins and seasoned troop commanders you two will be instrumental in maintaining discipline and cohesion while being responsible for the physical and spiritual needs of the men under your command."

Hadrin remained fixed in his professional stance but Farin saw right through his façade of stoicism to the doubts and surprise at the new appointment. "Hadrin, don't be so surprised. I told you and Arimas that you were ready for a command of your own before and I still maintain that position. It was long overdue, my friend."

The neutral face of Hadrin broke into a smile and an odd raising of his left eyebrow at how easy Farin saw through his resolve. Meanwhile, those of the council that were still gathered were becoming increasingly restless and feeling rather left out of the recent discussions. Zharra, Tavendia, and Larros stood patiently to the side, watching with rapt attention at how the humans were assimilating all these new changes so quickly. Truly these humans were an adaptable race and without any hesitation, Arimas was already creating plans for the deployment of his new skills and personnel while keeping the larger matter of the Seed of Corruption in the forefront of his mind.

Larros was taking the opportunity to speak with Tavendia now that Farin was engaged in conversation with the other humans, while at the same time Zharra was extending her senses over the audience, picking up the discontent that was building with the six counselors seated nearby. What was puzzling for Zharra was Verona. Since the revelation that she was with child, her hand never strayed from her flat belly, as if she was afraid to doubt and afraid to hope at the same time.

No one paid any attention to Zharra as she worked her way toward the queen. Arimas and Farin, along with Hadrin, Erikk, Anton and the rest of the new paladins were busy discussing matters of defense, training, recruitment, and rank structure as Zharra silently came to stand at Verona's side. Were it not for her appearance in projection form, she would have lightly touched the queen's shoulder in an offer of comfort. Tavendia suddenly noticed what Zharra was doing and shifted her eyes from Larros for a moment and nodded her head in pleasure that someone had noticed the troubled queen.

"Why do you fear believing this to be true, Verona? With all that you have seen today how can you still doubt?" Zharra's gentle soothing voice brought tears into Verona's eyes as she tried to step into Zharra's arms but instead passed through the illusion and then lowered herself to her knees and sobbed quietly. Arimas began to turn around until Farin rested his hand on the priest-king's arm and shook his head, knowing that this was something that Verona needed to process without Arimas' aid.

"I am overwhelmed, Zharra. Those images that Tavendia flashed through my mind defy all that I know to be possible. That you are really a dragon and somehow here but not really here is much to accept; that you are not an elf with strange eyes I cannot fathom either, yet in those images that flashed through my mind I saw you in both forms and learned of your name without being properly introduced to you here in the council chamber. And the babies! You have no idea how long I have dreamed of this day. My inability to bear Arimas a son and an heir has tormented my heart for more years than I care to remember and has been my cardinal failing as a queen. I have always felt that I was half a queen and half a woman because of this and now my entire world has been altered.

"She also showed me pain and uncertainty... and death. I do not know who dies and that sole thought is consuming me. I have lived for years without a child and now I must walk through life knowing that someone close to me will die as a result of this union? Is Arimas destined to die? Is there to be a successful plot against my life that will destroy me and my children? Will one of them be targeted as they age and draw closer to the day of their destiny? How can I survive with all this fear and pain mingled so closely with joy and anticipation? How Zharra? Could you fathom living with the knowledge that one of your family could die at the hands of evil?"

Verona spoke with anger and fear lacing through every hushed word that was whispered. While the men around continued to discuss matters of state, studiously avoiding the conversation behind them, Zharra looked into the eyes of the hurting woman sympathetically. Without shifting her gaze from Verona, Zharra nodded toward Tavendia, who immediately broke from her conversation with Larros and joined the other two females. Tavendia connected with the mind of Zharra for but a moment to understand the conversation that was just shared between the human and the dragon before Tavendia lightly touched Verona's face.

"What you have seen of the future is but a mystery, Verona. That you will bear two children is certain. That death will take someone close to you remains shrouded in the realm of possibility but not in certainty. You cannot spend your days in fear and worry while neglecting these children who are destined to change the fate of Caliyon. As much as the elves and the dragons will try to stand in the gap that will threaten to swallow whole the line of the Lightbringer, it is you and Arimas that will be the most pivotal forces in the protection of these children of fate.

"You have tremendous strength, Verona. I see it in your eyes and I understand the sharpness of your mind. While those around you may have thought you to be the silent, isolated queen, inside I know that you have never let a day go by wasted. This will be no different. Dare to believe and ready yourself for the most important battle you must face. Two children will soon depend on you for love, nurturing and above all, protection from harm—and protection from Dean. I want to know, will you accept this charge? Will you stand on their behalf?"

At the mention of Dean, Verona curled her lip in disgust and wiped the tears from her eyes. Conviction began to form deep within her soul, and from that conviction developed passion. That passion then burned into a flame of commitment and dedication toward the most important task that would ever be assigned to her.

"I will stand. I will believe. I will train myself and my children to guard themselves against Dean and against the corruption. Thank you both for your words. For a time today I felt lost and without direction—now you have clearly set before me a path that I will follow."

The now restless counselors began looking to Cirra for guidance and intervention in the council that was running out of control—at least from their perspective. There was no order; there was no flow of events, just random and haphazard conversations and plans that were tossed around between the priest-king, his new inquisitor and several of the holy knights of Lorenth. Plans to construct a permanent wall encasing their borders? Consolidating the border details and the various town watches into one fighting force? Cirra had not yet put an end to this mockery of the council so Renlar Fin decided to call order back to it.

"Your Excellency, what of the council? While your plans are grandiose and inspiring, and the appointment of this inquisitor may well provide insight that you have not yet been privileged to receive from us, I wonder where we fit in to these new plans?"

The conversation came to an abrupt halt as many of the paladins turned to face the outspoken counselor. Arimas, the orb of eternal flame still suspended in his left hand, turned to address the counselors.

"You have neither been forgotten nor excluded from the vision I have for Lorenth, but there are to be changes nonetheless. Firstly, while I may hold the office of both priest and king, I too am a man, and today I have been humbled. As I gaze into this eternal flame I am constantly reminded of my own failures and I now understand that there is nothing different between you and I save for the responsibilities and level of accountability that we maintain in our duties. If you feel compelled to address me by titles then by all means continue to do so, but as leaders one and all in this room I would prefer to be treated as an equal and for you to use my proper name instead.

Secondly, the council has been corrupted and debilitated over the years that I have stood faithfully by your side, heeding the wisdom of the council even when my own ideals were sometimes decided against. While you six remain loyal and have proven your allegiance to Lorenth, the time for sitting in the council chambers to banter ideology has passed. We have six major industries within Lorenth and coincidently we have six counselors to also act as representatives and advisors. Lorenth cannot simply exist in the minds of those living in the townships and sending tributes to the capital. I will ensure that all have access to the city and we will strive to enhance our industry, protect our borders, and augment our fighting force.

Lastly, I urge you all to embrace these changes. Lorenth is not the same as it was and it will not be the same years from now as it is today. We are entering a time of uncertainty and thus we must prepare. What may have worked in the past is being revisited, and you as my trusted counselors will now serve as my accountability, second to my conscience, which will be tested by this eternal flame that I now wield. You will serve as my advisors in industry and trade as each of you will be required to choose an industry to represent and liaise with between them and the city. We shall convene council as needed and not as scheduled, and it will become a functional council, not an ideological one."

Around the room the counselors sat in various stages of acceptance or disbelief. Some, like Cirra and Jarl Phelps, were nodding in approval of the new vision and the functional council ideas presented. Eventually all did agree that these changes made sense and would in fact be more beneficial to the city, and even more so for the townships in the surrounding area. Issues regarding sanitation in the lower city, fair access to trade among the townships and the city, and improved conservation and care of the limited resources around the city were also brought forth during the open council session where Farin, Arimas, and even Tavendia and Anton submitted several ideas to enhance the workings of the city and the land around it.

Verona rather unexpectedly began to submit well thought out plans to bolster the military of Lorenth through the relocating of the research, natural and theoretical faculties of the university to the several empty floors of unused quarters in the upper citadel to allow more efficient access to the libraries and allow for the conversion of the present university into a war academy with additional barracks for the junior soldiers.

The counselors pondered the idea, knowing the frustration of the university with the present location of the libraries. Arimas concurred with the idea as it did present a more efficient use of space and would incorporate lodging for the influx of soldiers that would be augmented into the Lorenthian Guard. The queen also suggested the dismantling of the honor guard, who would then be accorded immediate access to the war academy with salary to reward their current service and training while expediting the training of several hundred men with various levels of experience in the field. Surprisingly, the tremendous amount of changes that were thought impossible to occur in one day did in fact occur and the unity of Lorenth began in a well lit council chamber in the early hours of the afternoon, where human, dragon, and elf all exchanged ideas and plans to draw the land of Lorenth into communication with the rest of the allied races of Caliyon.

* * *

With the setting of the sun came the consecration ceremony of the Temple of Deimar, where heralds had announced to the citizens of Lorenth the open invitation from the priest-king to bear witness to the act. Never before had Arimas witnessed such support from his people as the entire temple grounds, the upper city, and the streets leading back into the lower city were packed with thousands of people. Where others were not able to hear, Tavendia amplified the words of the priest-king along the currents of air that danced around the newly strengthened trees in the temple grounds.

All spectators saw the burning globe of flame that Arimas led out from the fortress entrance and down along the streets toward the temple. Many were amazed that it did not consume his hand and others later told stories of what they felt as they gazed into the burning orb as it passed by them. Many reported feelings of conviction and yet an abounding sense of grace, while others reported experiencing sensations of joy and peace.

When Arimas finally dedicated the altar to Deimar and called for his paladins to raise their blades in a salute to the Divine One of Lorenth, the citizens of Lorenth dropped to their knees in reverence as they saw the paladin blades burst into an amber flame. From across the upper city, as the darkness became more complete, the now-burning eyes of the paladins were also seen and many knew that these men had been touched by Deimar himself. The name of Deimar resonated within each man, woman and child in attendance at the consecration ceremony as they at last knew the name of their Creator.

With the sheathing of the paladin blades, an overwhelming sense of contentment washed over all in Lorenth. In the heart of hearts of all who felt this presence wash over them, the only thoughts coursing through each of their minds was the phrase *"I am well pleased."*

With the end of the first watch of the night now upon them, the Frostspire ambassador directed his farewells to the newly established order of paladins and to the rest of the leadership of Lorenth, pausing to incline his head to Arimas before shifting into the shape of the small sparrow and disappearing into the night sky above. Zharra then told Arimas that relations between the humans and the dragons would only begin to improve once she related her reports to the ancients and the others within the summit. Wishing that she could offer some sense of reassurance to Verona once more, she instead opted to thank her for the pleasure of meeting her and promised that she would return soon. Verona offered a thin smile behind eyes now solid with resolve as Zharra released her projection, leaving Farin and Tavendia in the temple grounds once more with the newly strengthened trees, the paladins, and the priest-king and queen accompanied by the six counselors and advisors.

Thus the night ended. Farin and Tavendia returned again to his covenal estate for the time being, knowing that even issues such as lodgings would be discussed at length in the next few days. Farin and Tavendia spent another hour in conversation before they at last said goodnight, Farin heading to the separate room and his bedroll once again.

Arimas and Verona, now alone in the temple grounds with the citizens all returned to their homes, sat beneath the heavy curtain of one of the trees. Verona allowed the joy of the awakened lives within her to fill her heart, while Arimas permitted himself to cry his own tears of joy as he held his beloved close to his chest, not even giving a thought to any lingering Lorenthians who might be observing their intimate exchange. The royal couple sat together for a long while, until the stiff muscles in Arimas' legs began to tell him that perhaps a warm bath would be something more enjoyable to share with Verona now. Her seductive smile was all the answer he needed as the priest-king and queen, with Anton, Rorrick, Dayle, and Garron silently ensuring the safety of their monarchs from within the shadows of the upper city, returned to the citadel to enjoy that much needed bath… among other things.

XXV

So it was that the fae races and the nation of humans strengthened their alliance with each other as the winter chill descended upon Caliyon once again. Amid the arcane celebratory displays above the massive stone tower of the Frostspire, the *Dsa`carii* hosts with their *Illu`darii* guests made their best attempts at merriment. With all the issues that were being set before them, the elven celebration of Frostfire was much more subdued this year. The past three months had brought one of the bitterest winters down upon Lorenth and the lowlands below the Frostspire. Even the Ellorian highlands were considerably colder than usual and with Runeveld approaching, the dwarven hopes of the spring thaw occurring before their own celebration was becoming less and less certain.

The relationships between the dragons of the Icecrowns and the elves of Frostspire had continued to thrive over the preceding months. Following her extraordinary visit to the Icecrown summit, Nyssia did successfully enter into the *Aëolyys eth`Seloria* with Valeris Sy`yn and the other members of the council of three. That same excitement was contagious and within several weeks, small detachments of skilled storm weavers who shared her fascination with the dragons were sent with Nyssia on subsequent journeys. The blue drake flight form had gained in popularity as the dragons whole-heartedly welcomed the elves who were proudly declaring their respect of the dragons in matters as trivial as travel forms.

The dragons began to call these elves the *Azurakkis,* which in the common tongue meant 'the blue drakes.'

The name stuck as this handful of elves began to frequent the summit more and more, applying their knowledge in the mastery of the drake form and sharing their own knowledge of magical masteries to the dragons. Each of the elves tried to shape-shift into a variant of the drake that Nyssia was known for and in several weeks the results were rather appealing and quite diverse, ranging from the elegant, sleek drake of Nyssia, to a larger, scaled, and savage-horned blue drake that Adaonas had experimented with in honor of Sargeron. In total, there were twelve *Azurakkis* from the Frostspire, including Nyssia. Focusing their efforts, learning the dragon ways, and teaching the elven masteries to the dragons in return enabled very close and intimate kinships to be fostered between the twelve and the dragons of the summit.

It was as a direct result of the past three months that the dragons began to experiment with their own dragon flame, applying the elven techniques of elemental mastery with their own innate ability to summon the traditional elemental fire. Those of the blue found the mastery of ice magic to be far easier now and could alter their flame to absorb heat instead of produce it. This led to more experimentation, until the blue dragons could effectively drain all heat from anything, living or not... a trick which could prove fatal to warm blooded beings. Dalaria and Vaelis further refined their own breath weapons to be able to encase an object in solid ice.

Even now, during the Frostfire celebrations, several other dragons were applying the techniques learned from the blues to improve upon the form of dragonfire they were able to control. Zharra had begun changing her weak flame into a spray of chromatic dust that she sensed could cause blindness. Sargeron and the other blacks, who also were limited in their magical prowess, took their flame to a more combat-oriented role and discovered that they had a certain affinity for acids. Thus, they began changing their flame into a highly potent acidic gas. While the elves applauded the dragons for their new insights, it was hard not to fear these powerful beasts even more as they continued to find ways to rise above every other created race in terms of savagery and survivability. Introducing these new breath weapons into their already impressive arsenal of defensive and offensive tactics made a deadly foe even more unbeatable. Thankfully, the dragons would stand with the elves and humans and not against them.

With the Icecrowns still occupying much of their thoughts, Nyssia and the other eleven *Azurakkis* tried their best to enjoy the company of their elven kin to the south. They related some of the stories about the dragons and the new insights achieved from both races over the past several months, much to the amazement of the attendees from Avalide. One of the Avalide *Essen`dril* was speaking at length with Larros as he led her into the midst of the conversation.

Apparently Larros and this druid, who introduced herself as Tavendia Amberdawn, were making tremendous progress with the humans of Lorenth. Arimas, long known among the elven circles already, had taken a stand against the Seed of Corruption and purged the city of all who bore his taint. He had met disloyalty with compassion and exiled the traitors far to the south where even now they were rebuilding in stone and heat—and growing strong. Silence had spread across the lands of Lorenth as both factions of men began to regroup and reprioritize.

Tavendia also mentioned the new inquisitor, Farin Guilian, who had nearly passed into memory on the river's edge of the *Illu`Dar.* She told of his healing, his time spent among the elves with her mother, Narissa, and then of their journey to Lorenth and her stay in the capital city for nearly a week. Farin, Tavendia relayed, exhibited a gift very similar to that of Aerinyyr, and she told the others of how he was able to discern truth through his senses and not through the same truesight that Aerinyyr was known for. Arimas fully intended on allowing Farin's insight to guide the decisions of the priest-king as they prepared for the next encounter with the former seneschal. While the intentions of Dean were not clear, no one would honestly believe that he was rebuilding solely to aid those who chose to follow him. The plots of the former seneschal would likely continue and it would be only a matter of time before his eyes would be cast upon Lorenth once more.

What raised everyone's interest was the news about Deimar, the Creator of life. None of the elves had ever encountered threads of prophecy pertaining to the weakening of the bonds that now held the *Sar`Eth`Deim*, nor of the abilities of each deity to reach into their own creation. Now in hindsight, as they pondered the shrouded prophecies in the light of this new revelation, they could vaguely understand how this could be. Once again, it was a matter of the balance. The age-long struggle between the creation and the corruption has resulted in greater good and greater evil being thrust into the heart of this conflict that was consuming Caliyon.

This struggle had come full circle and now threatened the release of the very deities that were responsible for dividing the creation in the first place, and for bringing the corruption into existence. No member of the elven race had considered the possibility that something as simple and juvenile as faith in a Creator could be powerful enough to summon forth the blessing of Deimar himself, a blessing that provided the humans the opportunity to be the deity's own agents and delegates in the very world that had imprisoned him before the age of knowledge began.

Was this sudden shift something that would now generate more power to be focused within the Seed of Corruption? Or was this increase in power of the humans a response to the strength already growing far to the south? The reports from Zharra that passed through Nyssia to the council of three spoke of a growing mist far to the southwest, on an island off the shore. None of the dragons could see into the mist and now a living evil was encroaching over the southwestern tip of Caliyon. Apparently the dragons that had left the Icecrowns in favor of warmer climates were covered in this living evil, but Karros and Xarethia, the pioneers of this new gathering of dragons, claimed that they were immune from the taint.

The elves had long found the human emotion of worry to be something only a weaker mind would bend to, yet now thin wisps of doubt and uncertainty began to trouble several of the elves as the darkness made its steady advance. If its course were to continue as it was, the human capital of Lorenth would be the first place to fall into shadow, and shortly thereafter the dwarven clans, then the *Illu`darii* and finally the *Dsa`carii* and the dragons—if they were susceptible to this threat.

Yet amid all the fears and the worries there was hope. News of the Lorenthian queen being with children elicited great hope among the fae. Life was stirring all over Caliyon, and, in the minds of many, the best counter to death was life. The dryads were looking to the end of the spring where the population of the glades would increase. The treants groaned in anticipation knowing that more and more trees would be awakening soon to sing their own songs and stand against the shadow, while the dryads were bustling with childlike glee that a new cycle of dryad girls and Lifetrees would begin once more. The culmination of this life would then happen near the middle of the summer, when the Lightbringer at long last would be born into the house of Arimas, where he would then be protected, trained, and equipped for his eventual stand against the corruption in the human form known now as Dean.

Frostfire was supposed to be a celebration remembering the union of the two elven races, yet all around the Frostspire, elves from both north and south were gathered in conversations about matters of great weight and importance—matters that affected Caliyon and all the fae. Valeris, together with Tinovis and Yserth were deep in conversation with Cheyandra Silversong and her trusted truth-sage Aerinyyr. In a way, this almost felt right. Change was upon them all and even traditions that had been honored for an age would need to defer to the threat upon all life as planning and strategy occupied more and more of everyone's waking mind. It was no surprise at all when Valeris, with the rest of the high council of Avalide as well as Frostspire, approached the dais of the council chamber to address the large assembly of elves.

"Frostfire is nearing its end once again. While we all are blessed to have the honor of hosting our cousins of the south among us, it is evident what the main thing occupying our thoughts is. The Lightbringer is among us. An uneasy silence has been looming over Lorenth for the past three months now, and even Arimas begins to wonder what his nemesis is planning in the south. According to our last reports from Ambassador Solan`dras, which I understand from Cheyandra were also verified by Ambassador

Amberdawn, the weather along the southern borders of Lorenth has been amenable for the continued construction of the Lorenth border wall and at their current rate of building, they estimate its completion to be around the beginning of summer.

"Lorenth is training a military nearly four times as large as it once was and the few paladins that were commissioned by Deimar have been instrumental in their training, their protection, and their convictions. I dare say I have never seen the human race so organized before. They train with precision and they lack for nothing. Arimas has ceased all expansion efforts and cut all tributes to Lorenth to assist the townships around the city to become self-sufficient and prosperous. Trade flows from township to township and commerce has become a source of pride for the humans.

"The blessing of Deimar is evident in all that Arimas and his paladins do and it would be folly for us to think less of the humans any longer. While we command the forces of the *Trinactria* by our own will, they have submitted to the will of the Creator and it is divine favor that has positioned them to withstand the onslaught of the shadow. But the silence in the south and upon the Isle of mist across the great seas troubles both the humans and the fae alike. In this we are united and in this we must make decisions on how we are to respond."

Nyssia and the other *Azurakkis* grew troubled in heart when Valeris talked about the taint in the south. Though none of the elves had met any of the dragons that had chosen to start anew in the stone hills, Zharra and others of the Icecrown Peaks grew more and more worried for them. According to Zharra, her brother had promised some time ago to return to the Icecrowns to see Dalaria and Valkyyrak and to give a report on the situation in the south. Over the last three months there had been no visit and no attempt to contact them. Zharra had tried to reconnect with her brother's mind with her projection but the taint was aware of her presence now and cancelled the magic of her projections within minutes of her attempts. Her only means of communicating with her brother was through the *Skarlagnos*. She tried frequently but often heard nothing in reply. Occasionally Karros would reiterate his intent of returning to the Icecrowns but more often he would sever the tie with his sister as vague emotions of anger and bitterness permeated the link between them.

Valkyyrak was worried as well. Even now, while the elves were discussing matters in regards to the humans, Nyssia knew the dragons were engaged in long and drawn out discussions about sending a party south to meet with Karros and speak with him face to face. They were also discussing flying south to obtain reports on the progress of the human exiles to pass on to Arimas.

Apparently the priest-king had dispatched a solitary scout not long ago, but he had yet to return. Arimas was wary and wanted to conduct a different scouting mission that would present less of an opportunity for the scout to fall ill from the land itself, or worse, from the hand of Dean and his exiles. Zharra had offered to use her projection to observe them but Valkyyrak wanted to personally see this Seed of Corruption himself and also mentioned that both missions could be conducted at the same time. This plan would be beneficial to the humans and the dragons as each race sought to understand how serious of a threat Dean was becoming and how fast this taint was moving across the south-western region. Arimas also supported this idea and was eager to hear the news of the south.

Nyssia had mentioned the concerns of Arimas and of the dragons to the council of three several times, but they were unable to extend their farsight to the southwest. There was a growing blackness that somehow absorbed or cancelled every effort of using magic to aid sight in that area. The council of three informed Nyssia that Aerinyyr the truth-sage would be informed of these matters during the Frostfire celebrations and his expertise would be sought out to see if his truesight could penetrate the blackness that farsight could not.

As the discussions within the council chamber continued, the topics ranged from the dragons and the shared knowledge between them, the never-ending discussions about the reflection pools to be instituted in the ruling halls of their allies, and now the growing corruption. It was during this particular shift in the conversation that Aerinyyr stood up to address everyone while rebuking one of the *Dsa`carii* for an outburst of ignorance.

"We cannot know that for certain, Gilindahl. Why should fear—a human emotion—be allowed to run unchecked through our minds? Logic tells us that hope remains, and even now, that hope is flourishing within the heart of Lorenth. Our duties are clear. The responsibility to train and guide this race has fallen to us and woe to those who neglect this charge of such tremendous import!"

"That is all well and good Aerinyyr, but can you confirm what lies in the south? Our farsight cannot penetrate the blackness beyond the River Ardun. Silence has grown amid the plots of evil and so far our attempts to understand have been thwarted. You shame me for fear yet you neither confirm nor deny my rationale. Look for yourself! What can you see Aerinyyr?"

Aerinyyr grew pensive as all communication ceased around the council chambers. All eyes were on Aerinyyr as he gathered his thoughts and entered into his truesight. Of all the elves living in the north and the south, Aerinyyr was by far the most gifted sage among them all. His mastery over the spiritual realm and the arts of divination were reaching legendary status as he continuously applied his gift, honing his skill and sharpening his control of truth. Several minutes passed by as Aerinyyr stood in their presence, arms extended and hair gently dancing behind his head in an unfelt breeze. His eyes rolled back into his head, lost to the force of his trance, as he cast his thoughts southwest.

While in the truesight, Aerinyyr had no concept of time. His seeking was purposeful and his direction was true. As he crossed the Ardun River and ventured farther south he could feel the chill of death upon him. This was beyond evil. Even his truesight was limited. He made out the foundations of a large castle being built along the northwestern tip of the only lake in the area. He thought he could press his vision to see more but pain began to pierce his eyes the farther south he extended his truesight. The stench of decay began to fill his nostrils and the hollow sound of laughter coming from the castle below made Aerinyyr's stomach turn.

Aerinyyr pressed through the pain and directed his sight toward the laughter below. Nothing could have prepared the truth-sage for the sight that was abruptly before him. A human man dressed in riding gray hung, chained to one of the new walls of the large, unfinished castle. Somehow his eyes had been burnt out from within and amid his cries of pain and terror, Dean stood laughing. Suddenly, Aerinyyr did not see Dean as a man, but a creature of shadow and flesh who, with hands extended, had enveloped the chained rider in a wall of darkness.

The creature then paused for a moment as if sensing something before turning with lightning fast speed to face the presence of Aerinyyr. Tendrils of vile shadow began shooting toward the elf, until Aerinyyr released the sight and dropped to his knees. That same laugh followed Aerinyyr out of the truesight as deep within he could still feel the chill of death upon him. Perhaps it was time to fear. The Seed of Corruption was beginning to dominate the mind and the will of Dean and soon the transformation would be complete.

"It begins today… midwinter's night is upon us!"

Everyone gasped as Aerinyyr dropped to the ground, writhing in pain. Steam began to rise from his eyes, his face, and his hands as some unseen fire burned through his body. Tavendia and Narissa, along with several others from both the Æthanon and *Essen`dril*, immediately surrounded the elven truth-sage. The healing magic of the corporeal and the spiritual realms was invoked and began to coalesce around the hurting form of Aerinyyr. The ice mages witnessing this display of magic began to augment the efforts of their elven kin by channeling their own essence into the wounded elf without directly interfering with the healing efforts of the druids and the spiritualists.

Finally the ritual ended and the broken form of Aerinyyr rose to a sitting position to examine the extent of his damages. He could not see with his natural eyes but his awareness told him that this would heal with time and rest. Those who intervened in the healing process felt completely exhausted. There were no other conversations by this point, as every elf gathered around the small cluster of healers and the maimed Aerinyyr, who turned his attention to the kin he could not see.

"Perhaps some measure of fear is warranted after all, Gilindahl. I felt the chill of death surround me but did not realize the significance of this until I left the truesight. Midwinter's eve—tonight will bring upon Caliyon the longest night of the year and

Dean undoubtedly has experienced a great taste of the power that will soon consume him. The Seed of Corruption is nearly mature and soon the embodiment of shadow will be set free upon Caliyon. My truesight revealed a large stronghold being built far to the south along the lone lake in the area. Details were hidden from me but Dean was there and he is growing incredibly powerful. As Arimas has been able to harness the blessing of Deimar, so Dean is able to manipulate the force of corruption to do his bidding—for now. I pity Dean for in his lust for power he will lose the only thing that he ever really wanted—control. And it will begin soon with the lost control of his mind."

"Why were we not able to heal you, Aerinyyr?" Narissa asked with great concern in her voice. "Was it only because tonight is Midwinter's eve?"

"No, although perhaps that increased the efforts required to intervene. Your actions did save me, but only because you all acted so fast. Something about this corruption appears to negate our magic and that is the most troubling part of all. I am damaged on the surface only. My awareness tells me that I will see again with time and rest but if you all had not acted as fast as you did I would likely have fallen into memory myself. How we are to deal with this new threat I am not sure, but perhaps now is the time to use what magic we can to draw our allies together. While I was skeptical of the notion of the reflecting pools, perhaps there is wisdom in that idea. It may be that our common interests would be better served if we had a means of instant communication with our allies."

The conversations restarted around the Frostspire while Narissa and the other healers stayed near to Aerinyyr, taking upon themselves the task of restoring him to full health. Nyssia sought out Valeris as more discussions about the reflecting pools resumed as well as a novel idea to chronicle the wisdom of the allied races and preserve copies within the Illuallarii. While the Frostspire libraries were nearly as extensive as those in Avalide, even the frost elves conceded to the fact that the dual-planar structure would afford a greater protection to their words.

As Cheyandra was also a part of this discussion, it was her suggestion to send four elven cyphers to the various races to learn and scribe the wisdom and to be responsible for its safe return to the Illuallarii. When Valeris questioned how the Matriarch would select such people for this daunting task, Cheyandra offered up the names of the four keepers who, for years, had tended to the long-passed dreamers. Since the call of the Tear, those four had wandered aimlessly around the forest without a sense of meaning. Perhaps now this opportunity would grant each of them that much needed sense of purpose once more.

Aerinyyr, blinded yet still able to engage in conversation, along with the high council members of both realms, added the final touches on the matters discussed at length this evening while the second last night of Frostfire was concluded and the guests were shown down to their living quarters. Tomorrow would begin with more planning than merrymaking as the plans for the pools and the pressing need to communicate the seriousness of Dean's growth in the south to Arimas would be discussed at length once more.

Aerinyyr, led by Narissa, was taken to his guest quarters where Narissa tended to his eyes once more, already noticing improvements in the dangerously burnt skin on his face. Narissa thought about the matters of faith that the humans were so devoted to and cast a lone thought toward Ethoni, wondering if a time would come when their patron deity would also make a fantastical entrance upon the elven nation. Part of her felt that this would never happen and she suddenly felt somewhat odd at the sensations that went through her. If this was faith then perhaps it truly was a human emotion because the entire concept felt foreign and unnatural to her.

Narissa saw Aerinyyr to bed, then left his room in search of her own guest chambers. Even though she was tired, her active mind refused the needed sleep as she pondered the weight of all that had happened in such a short time. Time... again the elves were confronted with the one commodity that never interested those who were immortal. It was hasty and pressured all those who were constrained by it, and now time was beginning to irritate the even-tempered healer as she wished she suddenly had more of it to understand this changing world around her.

* * *

Darkness had descended upon the barren wastes and the bronze dragon of the stone hills was soaring through the night skies in his restless search for food. Xarethia was following close by, as were several others, yet their systematic thinning of the sparse wildlife was drawing to a close and it was time to seek out other food resources.

Melandra, the only living female red besides Sycaris, had still not been presented to the dragons of the Icecrowns. She did not have the advantage of being mentored by another red female and thus many were uncertain if she would develop in the same way that Fyysara and Sycaris had developed. Truth be told, those in the south were completely cut off from the recent events that were happening around them. While they had all felt the call of the Tear like the other fae races had, they had refused to respond to it. They did not know of Fyysara's death, and they did not know about the silence of prophecy. Thus, they clung to the hope that Melandra would develop into a red like the Guide and provide a link to the prophecies that might aid them in their isolated existence.

Melandra did recognize that there were some matters that were clearer to her than others, yet with the silence of prophecy, she had only experienced a small number of dreams. No one told her that she was to be linked to prophecy, so she shrugged those few dreams off as nothing important.

The pursuit of food was now becoming the driving force among the southern dragons, while the advance of the corruption had become little more than a curious interest. All the words that Karros had once told Zharra about the dragons in the south being the guardians of the stone hills seemed nearly an eternity ago. Somewhere deep down inside, these dragons knew that their gradual complacency regarding the living taint around them was dangerous, yet no one did anything about it.

Karros remained steadfast in his belief that this taint had not corrupted them, yet he also knew that his behavior over time was changing. That old bitterness regarding his father had returned even stronger than before, regardless of the concerned words from Valkyyrak that Zharra had relayed. His constant irritation toward the ever-clinging taint, that to this point had been benign, was now becoming a subtle rage. He saw the same thing happening among the others that had ventured south with him. They all were growing more and more apart, preferring isolation over communion with each other. It was only the pursuit of food that was unifying them now.

Perhaps Karros lacked the charisma that Valkyyrak was known for. Perhaps he was less of a leader and more of just a figurehead that represented a deviation from what was old and traditional in favor of something new and spontaneous. Either way, they all knew that there was no future for them back among the dragons of the Icecrowns. They had chosen their own path and Karros would not accept the possibility that he could have led his kin into the barren wastes only to succumb to this strange taint and die of starvation. Thus the search for food spread out over larger and larger areas as the dragons moved farther north into the lowlands and farther east along the coast.

These lands were called the wastes for a reason. It didn't matter where they searched; life appeared to avoid this place, other than the snakes, the small rodent-like creatures, and the numerous species of insects that dominated the region. Melandra had actually suggested fishing off the coast. The others immediately discounted the notion as they preferred the fresh taste of flesh and the thought of plunging into the cold waters like some common bird was not something that any of the others entertained seriously. Hunting as a pack was proving to be less than profitable so Karros suggested the dispersal of the seven across the north, the east and the northeast areas to scout out and retrieve what wildlife they encountered.

The hunt was successful. Two of the younger dragons had actually found some smaller beasts with hardened scales and odd fur patterns. Dracian retrieved three of these smaller beasts while Glauron retrieved two other beasts that were far less hairy but equally scaled. The feeding frenzy was savage as there was nowhere near enough meat to go around. Skoren actually growled menacingly at Dracian as the younger dragon attempted to share in the feeding before Skoren grabbed one of the five carcasses and flew away to his own lair to eat in solitude.

Even Karros noticed himself growing impatient with Xarethia and his sons. Kalset and Zuan still needed to eat as well, though thankfully not nearly as much, but Karros had chosen to eat last and once his family had ravaged much of the meat allotted to them there was hardly anything left. Karros had not tasted anything quite like this. There was far less sinew than other wild animals and at least with the three smaller beasts there was an abundance of meat once they peeled back the strange scales, which came off in odd sheets and with little effort.

No one gave any thought to these scales as the bloodlust had consumed everyone by now. Dracian and Glauron each reported in passing that there were large caves and one gathering in the lowlands filled with these beasts and they would proudly lead the others to this new and abundant food source.

It wasn't until the early morning that Karros and Xarethia realized what had been done in the darkness of night. Karros found the error almost humorous, but Xarethia and Melandra were visibly shaken from the knowledge that Dracian and Glauron had ravaged both a dwarven encampment far to the east along the coast and a fairly new human settlement in the lowlands.

Indeed, this was a plentiful and renewable food source aside from the fact that the dwarves were fae creatures like the dragons and the humans were the pathetic race mentioned in the prophecies. Karros knew now that any chance they had at returning to the Icecrowns was lost, yet a large part of him did not care. For years, Karros had acted on principles set forth by Valkyyrak, pursued crafts as suggested by Valkyyrak, and even remained distant and set apart from a world ripe for domination because of Valkyyrak. The dragons knew no equal! Why should they hide in lairs well into the frozen north where adversaries would not dare to look when the more temperate regions were teeming with life and fine treasures that could supply the fearsome dragons for generations to come? Should they deny who they were simply out of respect for the outdated ideals of an ancient dragon whose relevance in this age was now in question?

Karros was not alone in this line of thinking, for each dragon that left the old ways of the Icecrowns left for similar reasons. Dragons were predators, masters of their domain, and should be afforded the proper amount of fear and respect because of this. Melandra and Xarethia would come to follow whatever direction that would be set forth from the others so Karros gave little thought to their initial revulsion at the knowledge of their having feasted on dwarven and human flesh. In the midst of the frenzy last night all had commented at least once on the fine quality of flesh these races afforded and perhaps it was time to assert their proper position in the hierarchy of life in Caliyon. Dragons were everything that humans were not, and perhaps a scheduled thinning of this weak race would prove to be essential in the development of both races.

The time for holding meetings had suddenly ended. Already Skoren had made it clear that he wanted nothing further to do with the others. With his newly developed taste for human flesh, Skoren, Karros knew, would frequent these new hunting grounds regardless of prophecy or fate. Glauron and even his own two sons Dracian and Demodran also wanted to pursue this new form of hunting for they were too young to even understand the old truces and potential alliances that were supposed to have been made. Karros neglected to pass on any of the old wisdom and now the price of their ignorance was being paid.

Melandra was supposed to be their Guide, unbeknownst to her, yet the prophecies had not spoken to anyone living among the stone hills for some time, which further reinforced for Karros that these few dragons were on their own. Perhaps leaving each of the dragons to their own devices was the key in their pursuits of freedom.

While some would say that their gradual deviation from all the normal behaviors that the dragons were known for happened as a direct result of the living taint clinging to them for years, others surmised that choice was the final obstacle for these southern dragons. The very natures of dragons were incorruptible by any magic or act of the will, yet perhaps living under the constant oppression from this vile taint increased their irritability and lowered their tolerance for others, including those who also left the Icecrowns. The wizened ones of this age would later conclude that the taint was only the catalyst of change and the final debasement of the southern dragons came by individual acts of choice. Their pursuits of freedom and independence led them down a path that few would return from, and great was the displeasure and sorrow within the Icecrowns when these truths started to fall upon the ears of the ancients.

It did not take long for even Melandra and Xarethia to follow the lead of their mates as the attacks upon the humans and the dwarves began. Their taste for human and dwarven flesh clouded their eyes and their mates' obsession with gathering the armor and weapons and other trophies of their ill-fated meals was a new fascination for them. These beasts bore sharp teeth of their own and several of them began to resist and fight back, be it ever so futilely. Yet, for the dragons, the threat of danger lurking beneath polished armors and shiny blades was intoxicating. It presented a challenge for once, and as the attacks continued, the victims began to adjust to the tactics of the dragons in hopes of defending against them and eventually repelling them completely.

As the southern dragons grew more and more apart from each other, choosing new lairs away from Karros and Xarethia, their ability to conduct successful raids against either the dwarves or the humans began to wane. Certainly one adult dragon was a force to be reckoned with, but without the ability to overpower their quarry with the help of their kin, the victims learned quickly how to run to safe areas that were too small for the dragon to reach them while mobilizing their own defense. Skoren was the first to feel the sting of a human weapon as the adaptive lesser race created a machine that could launch a large spear-like weapon with enough force to tear through dragon wings or even exploit any weaknesses in their scale layout if it hit at an upward angle.

The human ballista, as it later came to be called, struck its mark when Skoren—in all his red-scaled arrogance—continued to launch his flames against the earthenworks that the humans had hid behind, neglecting to pay attention to the unfinished yet fortified foundations of the human city being built over on the lake. The ballista fired its elongated, heavy-tipped spear clean through his right wing and then embedded itself into his left hind leg as he recoiled from the shock and the pain. Skoren heard the distinct *click* of another round being positioned and immediately reacted, flying away from the human city and retreating to his isolated lair far beyond the stone hills. Thwarted from his meal and wounded in both flesh and pride, Skoren began to brood and curse these lesser beings who had surprised him with their ingenuity.

Removing the ballista projectile proved to be more painful than when he was struck with it and the roar he let forth echoed among the barren wastes for leagues. He had to channel his essence carefully to close the wound in his leg but his wing would be permanently scarred from the weapon that had torn into him. He was marked by the human beasts and in the darkness of his underground lair, where the vile taint was even more potent, his malice grew. His slowly growing collection of human and dwarven armors and weapons, and even some shiny rocks that the dwarves were fond of did provide him some measure of comfort knowing that they were still no match for the large red dragon.

The social structure of the southern dragons continued to crumble. Dracian and Demodran left the lair of Karros and Xarethia much sooner than anyone expected as they flew far away to the east to escape the taint and the corruption that was indirectly consuming their parents and the others. The two topaz brothers eventually settled near the dwarven holds of the Nuragg and the Hammul where they became known as the sand dragons, hiding in plain sight within shallow lairs dug into the dry, sandy edges of the riverbank or other locations. They moved often which gave the impression that there were far more than two dragons in the region.

The two sand dragons spent their days lying in wait for some small band of dwarves on their way to forage or mine, or simply patrol. No one knew when or where they would strike next until it was too late. One or two of these feared sand dragons would erupt from their shallow, concealed lairs, creating a large cloud of fine sand while bearing flame, tooth and claw upon their targets, often killing up to half a dozen dwarves before the remaining managed to escape. These attacks were constant yet somewhat predictable; the dragons would thin the dwarves' numbers almost on a monthly basis, sometimes more frequently, and then would remain hidden for several weeks. Beyond those facts, the rest was rumor and legend as the infamy of the two topaz dragons continued to spread among the dwarven clans and eventually to the rest of the fae races.

Even Xarethia began to distance herself from the enraged Karros, who had begun to kill the humans or the dwarves for sport and for trophies to add to his horde. When Xarethia eventually led Kalset and Zuan away from the stone hills in favor of the more temperate areas of the east, Karros grew wild with rage and unleashed destruction among the humans until he was finally consumed.

The lessons that Skoren learned were not passed on to Karros as the bronze dragon succumbed to the might of the human ballista. The humans found a weakness in the soft and vulnerable underbelly of the great beast, and it wasn't long until the dragon reign of terror was ended in the south as Glauron and Melandra, also wounded in lesser ways from the ranged weapon of Innin Hold, left their lair to occupy the abandoned lair of Xarethia and the now-fallen Karros.

Melandra finally pursued her initial plan of plunging deep beneath the waters of the great sea in search for larger animals that would sustain both her and her mate. While Glauron did prefer the sweetness of human or dwarven flesh, he found the aquatic change in diet to be more tolerable than he would care to admit. The occasional scout or harvester that ventured too far south would often be abducted by the red male and his cravings would be sated for a time until the next foolhardy human wandered into the stone hills.

The ever present oppression from the vile taint continued to erode the morale of the last remaining dragons in the stone hills, yet Melandra, the rapidly wizening red female, did her best to bolster her and her mate against the onslaught of the corruption, often bringing the larger Glauron with her as she plunged beneath the cold waters. For a red, this experience was not necessarily a pleasant one but in the high heat of the days when even sleep was disturbed, the cool depths were almost refreshing. Better still, their deep and rapid descents below the surface of the waters also brought the dragon mates a blessed relief from the ever-clinging oppression. The two reds were reunited in their bonds. They even took pleasure in each other's company before the eventual need for air forced them back to the surface and into the grip of the clinging, vile taint.

From all appearances it seemed that the corruption had indeed begun running its course in the south. It wasn't until the northern dragons of the Icecrowns finally decided to visit those who had long since left the cold peaks that Valkyyrak would finally learn of the fate that had befallen his son and the fractured relationships that were spreading throughout the wastes.

XXVI

The construction of Innin Hold was advancing at a tremendous rate. The past three months had been fairly quiet and Dean was in no hurry to break that silence while they still remained vulnerable to attack. Winter had fallen upon Lorenth by now but in the south near Innin Hold, the cooler air actually improved the working and living conditions in the area, bringing some relief from the suffocating heat that this new area was becoming known for.

The days were growing shorter and the industries had to make the best use of the daylight hours in order to meet the demands that Dean had placed on the laborers and crafters. Aside from the commanding presence of Dean, the recent attacks from these winged beasts instilled a sense of urgency and fear within the populace of Innin Hold which in turn fuelled their energies all the more as the construction of Innin Hold was the key to their defensive power. All of their achievements with industry and the steadily increasing warehouses of supplies for the laborers would be for naught if they could not resist these unexpected attacks.

Among the exiles in the camp was a man who had come from the township of Coren, and according to him, this was not the first encounter he had had with the winged beasts called dragons. A large red female dragon had supposedly been found dead in the river valley area and between Covenal Masaad, the town watch Captain, and Arimas, this news became public knowledge while

Dean was out losing his first major battle with the elves of the Dark Wood. How many of these dragons existed no one could say, but apparently they came in various sizes and colors. As three other dragons had come and removed the dead body within hours of its discovery, there had been no opportunity for anyone to study the creature thoroughly.

What was rather interesting, though, was the Coren exile's further retelling, of how the large black dragon, called Sargeron, had warned the peasants about Dean. This Sargeron, an ominous black creature, had stated that he and his ilk had no intention of harming the humans, yet the men and women of Innin Hold were being attacked by members of the dragon race without warning or provocation. Dean had to think fast and began speaking with the engineers about creating a weapon that could pierce the hardest armor with ease, if such a thing could be done. Dean also tasked Dhax to speak with the engineers as well, perhaps finding a way to implement some of the more deadly inventions that the assassin's guild had created with new engineering ideas to create an even better weapon.

These dragons were magnificent creatures, though. They could light up the darkness with fire from their mouths, and their savage, horned faces and razor sharp talons made them the most challenging beast humans had ever faced. Dean and Arimas had long been known for their prowess in battle against every kind of beast in these lands and in time Dean would discover the inherent weaknesses of the dragons and find a way to exploit them. A dragon head would make an impressive trophy in his new fortress. All he needed was some time to figure out this creature's limitations— and he was sure it had at least one, as every other beast or person he encountered had a weakness that a skilled tactician could use to his benefit.

Dean surveyed the additions around his command tent. Two months ago he had ordered a separate chamber to be built onto the tent to afford the seneschal an area for personal quarters where a large wooden framed bed was commissioned from Philip Fairchild, the industry leader of forestry and a master carpenter in his own right. Philip was honored to be considered for this work and the results showed in the final result. The large frame was expertly joined together and stained with a dark red finish, making this the finest piece of furniture the seneschal had ever owned, even in Lorenth. Dean also knew that once the city was complete and the industry leaders were relocated into the city, the bragging rights for Philip would only increase his business, as he would undoubtedly boast of his skills being commissioned by the seneschal himself. That in and of itself was reward enough for the master carpenter and with the exceptional quality that Dean observed, such bragging rights were indeed in order.

He smiled to himself as he looked to his sides where both Lianne and Kasee were sleeping. Lianne as usual slept nude while Kasee might have well been nude for the thin and transparent white silk shift she wore hid nothing from his eyes. Dean began to harden once more, but before he could consider what he was in the mood for from the two women Kasee awakened. Seeing the seneschal leaning over her body, Kasee smiled sensually and set her exploratory hands to the task of teasing Dean. Lianne, woken from her own slumber by the guttural sounds Dean was making, joined Kasee in pleasuring him until Dean's carnal appetites were eventually satiated... for now. While many were initially shocked when he admitted the two into his chambers and warned his men that he was not to be interrupted, the soldiers all became accustomed to the presence of the two women.

Dean was eager to rise this morning after he dismissed his bedmates back to their workplace. Not even they were above his new decrees as he made it abundantly clear that they were servants no longer but would contribute to the well being of Innin Hold in more ways than simple sexual pleasures.

Kasee worked with Ainslie Verigan in the stores area helping to manage the warehouses and assisting with the development of a system for inventory management. Lianne chose to work with the textiles industry, likely because it was a slow paced industry at the moment, though according to Jared Pyne that would soon change. The sheep pens and the segregation from the cattle were actually improving their health and mating was resuming like normal. They were able to shear their herd once so far, obtaining a rather fine collection of the longer fall wool and by spring they could obtain another decent coat to supply the tailors with.

Dean was rather pleased with the rapid growth of the city now. With the backbone of the industry sectors in high production, Dean was finally starting to see some progress in the city. The housing had been completed early last month and the quarries were now full. The limestone being carted to the main warehouse that was built beside the site where the keep would be erected was now overflowing. Dean did not care; stone was one resource they could not have too much of. Morale had markedly improved over the past three months even when factoring in the random attacks by the dragons. The improved housing conditions compared to the rugged townships the exiles had left behind, as well as the efficient sewage management system that had been constructed, made those living in these block housing units almost feel like they were living in Lorenth. Barrett Otenbright and Huron Alliston had managed to create the watering pipelines that the farmer had ingeniously devised and the fields were already showing tremendous improvement, especially after the initial and subsequent introductions of animal wastes into the soil, which somehow encouraged the production of much larger crops than even those in Lorenth.

Dean could already foresee great changes in industry being this far south. Frost was a thing of the past down here, which allowed the growing season to persist throughout the winter. The wheat fields were nearly ripe, and with the extra growth opportunities, Dean expected that they would be able to obtain at least three full harvests of grain per year. The fisheries were offering impressive yields, and the citizens were being adequately fed, especially when they were encouraged to create small personal gardens behind the housing areas. Innin Hold was finally established and growing toward prosperity.

Bartering, which Dean wanted to discourage initially, was decided by the council to be an essential motivator for the successful development of the tradesmen. Humans were selfish at the best of times—of this Dean knew rather intimately—and despite his tenants of equalization among everyone in Innin Hold, the lack of incentive to perform above what was mandated had been hindering the growth of the city over the last month.

So, now there was trade among the citizens. Currency had not been established as of yet but over the past six weeks a system of value became fairly clear and those working in textiles would trade for items from the stonecutters, or the carpenters, who also would make exchanges for labor in return for certain goods from the farmers and the fisheries. If items were not needed immediately by the seller from the tradesman looking to buy, then promissory notes were issued to serve as credit for future purchases. To prevent forgery, the seller would scribe the note details into official ledgers that would accompany them and scratch that entry in the presence of the buyer when they sought to redeem the note.

The system was rudimentary yet effective and once Karl Feldegan had smelted enough ore from his recently established and long overdue mine and forge, Dean would appoint a city treasurer to begin the minting of a new currency with the excess ore not needed for the city.

Dean had submitted his seneschal armor to Karl for some modifications—namely, to remove all signs of Lorenth insignias and crests in favor of the new crest and colors that would eventually fly atop the banners of Innin Hold. The silver, gold, and blue of the Lorenth lion and banner would be replaced with the black and crimson colors of his Drucharii. The banner of Innin Hold would be the black raven in flight bearing a pale rose in its clutches, captured upon a crimson flag.

Davic was one of his newest Drucharii. Mentored by Otto and an assassin of exceptional skill already, Davic thought of creating the banner with a black rose and forming a division of the assassin's guild known as the Order of the Black Rose. These elite assassins would only prey upon strategic targets, and would leave the hallmark sign of a single black rose upon the dead body as a message to all who would be foolish enough to gain the negative attention of Dean and his guild. Though overly poetic and slightly dramatic, Dean thought long about the idea but instead went with the pale rose and the raven instead—although the order of the black rose was an idea he filed away in his mind.

Davic was the illegitimate child of Baron Vingo de'Mordrey, one of the few chancellors of Lorenth living outside of Rallorn on his own estates. Vingo was an entrepreneur at heart and Arimas, in his benevolence, granted the baron land to cultivate in return for twenty percent of his harvest and wares. The de'Mordrey estate made the covenal estates look small and within its alabaster walls the baron and his numerous servants worked the lands and produced exceptionally fine grape plantations and wineries that supplied the upper city nobles, the fortress, and The Gilded Swan.

Davic was the progeny of one of the baron's few encounters with the much younger and naïve servant girls that lived on the plantations. While the baroness would often be procuring supplies to care for the servants and provide staples for the baron and his family, Vingo would occasionally accost some young servant girl and force himself upon her, threatening her with banishment or worse should she speak of the encounter to anyone. What made the ordeal worse was that after the baron established the 'rules' of the encounter, he deliberately went out of his way to pleasure the victim before he would satisfy himself within her. The stunned servant would be gently and passionately fondled and kissed and even given extra supplies to take with her before being released back into the fields. Often the girl didn't know whether to cry in pleasure or in terror at the events that just transpired and silence became the coping mechanism for them all.

Any servant girl unlucky enough to be impregnated by the baron and was not married or being actively courted by someone ended up contracting some fatal sickness or fell victim to a horrible accident on the plantation. This only happened twice, but the young Jenaya Falst, daughter of the widowed estate bread maker, Ilana Falst, soon puzzled out the fate that befell the two servant girls that had died mysteriously and made her choice to flee to Lorenth as a lower class peasant instead of allowing her pregnancy to become known to the baron.

Life had been hard for Jenaya and harder still when Davic was finally born. The young mother had tried to find legitimate ways of providing for herself and for her infant son but there was no one who wanted a servant girl with a child, and the only thing besides those skills that she had to offer was her body, which she surrendered over and over in silence so that she could feed and clothe her rapidly growing son… the only reason she continued to cling to her miserable life in the lower city of Lorenth.

Davic was lured into theft early, knowing of but not fully understanding the line of work that his mother was involved in. Initially it was food and small items of luxury that he stole to make the nights more bearable for him and his mother. But one night, when his mother came through the door of their small house, battered and bleeding from another night's work, Davic stormed out of the house to find out who was responsible. After nine fruitless days of hunting he finally learned who had beaten his mother so savagely and had tracked him straight to the man's own home. It was not long before his target made his way back to the hostel where he would likely attempt to aquire the services of some other young victim. He waited nearly a quarter of an hour before he entered for the first time.

"Third door on th' right young sir… though I wouldn't be thinkin' 'bout interr—"

"You can keep those thoughts to yourself if you value your life and this establishment." The defiance in the young man's eyes had silenced any retort from the owner of the hostel, the very place his mother frequented throughout his early years and even on occasion now—though her regular clients often paid enough for them both to get by on.

It had been surprisingly quiet that evening and aside from the owner, there was only one other patron fondling one of the house's attractions in the corner. Several other women, some twice the age of Davic, cooed and gently fingered the shoulder of the young man as he passed by in his search for the staircase that would lead him upstairs, but Davic ignored their advances.

As promised, the third door on the right was shut and the faint sounds of another woman crying under the abuse of this well-paying patron provided more than enough noise to allow Davic the chance to open the door slowly. The boy smiled to himself at the easy target the abuser's back made.

The look of surprise that flooded into the villain's face when his throat was sliced from ear to ear was enough to soothe the rage of the young Davic. The traumatized victim beneath the dead man did well to bury her face in the sheets of the bed to muffle her screams, paying little heed to the blood that spilled over her back and shoulder from her assailant. Before the death became public knowledge, he cut the man's purse, stowing it within a small, hidden pocket within his leather jacket, and then leapt out the window and into the shadows below. It was then that Otto presented himself to the young and passionate killer, and invited him to join the blood order and work for the man who really ran Lorenth—the noble and fearless Seneschal Dean.

Davic did not hesitate. He returned home to leave the purse and the small fortune it contained to his mother, who had since collapsed in her bed from fatigue and pain. He kissed her forehead and disappeared into the night to begin his long training with the assassin's guild. A part of him was stricken with the thought that his mother would awake day after day, and never know what happened to her only son, but Davic buried those emotions in order to concentrate on the task at hand. His mother was a survivor; she would learn to cope.

And so his training began. Quickly gaining the attention of both assassins and Drucharii alike, the young Falst was given more opportunities to prove his worth. What made Davic so incredibly cold-blooded was the final task—to kill a living family member. He immediately chose to kill the baron of Rallorn, but the guild refused to grant him his request because Dhax made it quite clear that the Baron de'Mordrey was a charlatan. He played both sides of the silent conflict between Dean and Lorenth and his allegiance was always changing with the wind. His bloodstained hands were always clean in public, and his business dealings were always kept by the book giving the impression to Arimas and the rest of Lorenth that he was a model chancellor and the investment made in him was a good one. Dhax also told Davic that the baron was one of the few allies that the guild maintained and could be counted on to help hide bodies or such when the guild was in need of outside help. Always for a price, yet usually a fair price, and that kind of alliance could not be squandered so easily.

Thus, like in the tale of turmoil that had helped create Llise into the weapon that she once was, Davic was reunited with his mother nearly two years later after his disappearance, to tell her how much he loved her and regretted having to do what he needed to do. The sadness in his mother's eyes never left her face as she whispered to him that she was dead already and her only regret was not being able to give Davic the proper kind of upbringing that he had deserved. Amid the unsettled turmoil in his heart, with Otto poised to kill the young would-be Drucharii should he fail this final task, Davic struck fast and true, slipping his poisoned blade straight through his mother's left eye and deep into her brain, killing her instantly.

He had clung to the knife even as his mother dropped to the ground, folding over her body as his tears began to mingle with her blood. Otto stowed the blades that were no longer needed as he flashed the new Drucharii his usual, sadistic smile, congratulating the young elite assassin as he put to death what remained of Davic Falst and forever took upon himself the name of Davic de'Mordrey, a subtle warning to his father the baron, should he one day dig too deeply into the past of the young assassin.

Dean had almost arrived at Stefan Collings' makeshift workshop where the engineer, with aid from Dhax, had apparently devised a weapon strong enough to take down a dragon. Since the initial attack on the hold, one large red dragon had tasked himself with the continual harassment of Dean's people. Not for much longer, though. Stefan was well under way with the foundations of the outer wall while concurrently working on the lower southern tower which now housed this new weapon launcher.

The final design of the fortress was rather unique. Instead of the typical symmetrically built keep with towers of equal heights, Dean and Stefan finalized the idea of the spiraling tower that would house the keep above and the engineering workshop in the basement. The towers would begin with the lowest tower facing the southern side and spiraling up and around the keep toward the right until the tallest tower would overlook the west but would allow observation of the north as well. Dean didn't even have to knock because Stefan opened the door first and excitedly bowed to the seneschal before pointing toward the southern tower and beckoning the seneschal to follow.

"I take it by your display of child-like enthusiasm that you have a working prototype of this weapon?"

"Yes Seneschal, but words are limited in explaining what only sight can explain. If you would follow me my liege—I know you will not be disappointed with the ballista."

"For your own sake you had better be right, Stefan."

The engineer swallowed hard and led the well-built seneschal up into the only real part of the city that was complete. The spiraling staircase was climbed with much effort and Dean noticed along the way several doorways already created that opened up into nothingness but apparently fit into the engineer's master plan for the keep. For being the smallest of the towers, this was certainly tall enough and Dean was actually relieved to reach the top of the tower where a small stone table held something like a crossbow mixed with a large spear.

"This... is it? You created a big spear? How is that supposed to accomplish anything against dragons that cannot be penetrated by even our best st—"

The engineer ignored the criticisms of the seneschal as he took aim upon a target dummy nearly one furlong away. The amount of power behind the machine was astounding as the mechanisms launched the heavy spear clear across the open field, and sending it through steel armor five times thicker than normal to end up embedded in the target dummy. Even from this distance, Dean could easily see how far the spearhead drove through the breast piece and marveled at the accuracy of such a weapon, even at this range.

"You have amazed me, Philip, and that is hard to do. I want one of these machines on every tower in the keep as they are constructed and I want you to begin thinking of different bolts to create for different situations... oh, and try making these iron-tipped ones with a barbed head instead of that crossbow style point. Think of a long arrow mounted in here... much harder to remove once embedded I would wager."

The engineer nodded, obviously pleased that Dean liked the ballista and had commissioned his work for several more of the platforms. The barbed arrow idea was a creative suggestion that the engineers had already thought up among themselves. Initially they had considered creating some sort of fletching to make the arrow-tipped spear fly true, but after proper balancing and weight-management the steel-tipped arrow-bolt for the ballista flew true anyways. Instead of troubling the seneschal with this matter he simply nodded and informed the seneschal that they would have a new design for him soon.

Stefan walked back down with the seneschal and left him to his wanderings while he ventured out to the dummy to retrieve his ballista bolt and take more measurements before modifying his design once more. Dean continued on his rounds around the foundations of the city. Several basement chambers were already completed, including a detainment area for lawbreakers with adequate tools to be used for corrective or interrogative procedures. The only structure fully completed so far was the south tower that he was just inside of and work was already well underway on the first two levels of the keep attached to the tower.

Dean had to admit that his two engineers were rather good at organizing the work efforts of the laborers. All the zoning was already complete. Several stakes were in the ground already where the foundations were to be set for the industry leader housing, the commerce district, and several other smaller industries that would occupy space within the keep. Plans were laid for an additional set of stables for the command division mounts, the butcher, the bakery, a quality inn and tavern with a local distillery and brewery nearby, and whatever else would eventually be thought of, as the engineer also factored in several zones for nothing which would allow for growth in the future.

Every day saw more and more laborers coming in from the industry sectors in order to begin assisting the engineers and several of the masons in the construction of the city itself. At this pace, within another six months or so, the city would be habitable and defendable, with all the final details added after. The sewage lines were already in place beneath the city foundations and would initially collect all the waste into four main containment areas that would be incinerated with high heat. The tar-like residue that was believed to be non-toxic would then be pumped into the lake afterward.

Dean was on his way back to the command tent when he heard the whistle of Warric in the distance. Dean stopped and spun around to look at his Drucharii who was riding fast toward him with two other mounts—one bearing the supple figure of Deidre and the other bearing an unknown rider bound head to hands with twine. Dean knew immediately what this meant. Arimas was growing curious at last and this was his initial attempt at obtaining some scouting information.

"You come to me bearing gifts, Warric?" Dean said archly, offering a cruel smile to his Drucharii which Deidre and Warric responded to with smiles of their own. Deidre spun her leg around from the back of her mount catching the scout behind his back. The force of her kick sent the bound rider reeling in pain off the mount, where he landed awkwardly on his back and promptly passed out from the pain.

"There was only the one, Seneschal. We stalked him from the Ardun Ford but he resisted our capture for the last two days. He is a master rider and skilled with the bow, as I found out a bit too late." Warric pointed down to his right leg which was heavily bandaged. "Deidre was the one to bring him down finally as we chased him farther southeast, preventing his escape back across the river. Every time he regains enough energy to resist, he fights like a crazed man and so we had to keep silencing him with pain while re-securing his bonds."

"This is rather fortunate. I want him secured in the foundations beside the south tower. You will find some iron chains and shackles there. I will want to question him once he awakens. Perhaps some sport is in order to boost the morale of the Drucharii. I am sure you all could use some practice in interrogation."

"Just don't let Deidre at him first. There won't be anything left of him when she's done." Warric winked slyly at Deidre as she chuckled softly and punched Warric's arm.

"No one is to kill him or else their life is forfeit to me. I am serious in this. I have my own 'tests' to run on this unfortunate soul and I need him alive to conduct them. He is to be alive when you are all done and I will hold both of you responsible if this message is not properly conveyed to any Drucharii who engages in sport with my prisoner."

"Understood, Seneschal. We will bring him to this holding area straightaway and will notify you if we glean anything of interest from him." Deidre spoke with no emotion in her voice even though the sudden change in Dean's demeanor had caught her off guard, sending a splinter of fear lancing through her. The two Drucharii picked up the bound and unconscious prisoner and dragged him across the grounds toward the foundations of the city and the detainment area that Dean had described, at least one of the assassins glad to be putting space between herself and the unpredictable seneschal.

Dean gave no further thought to the scout for now, knowing that his Drucharii could occupy several days of time in the exquisite and methodical torture of the prisoner. Until he eventually broke, the scout was their play toy. While they didn't get much practice at this art, the few instances where they did engage in it were beautiful to watch. This rider would succumb in time, and then Dean would begin his own inquiry.

The low rumbling roar in the sky meant that one of their dragon adversaries had decided to pay them another calling. By now, all the people were aware of the immediate threat as they all scattered to several bunkers dug into the earth or within thin clefts of the quarry walls. This time they actually thwarted him as, in rage and frustration, he began bathing the area in flames, scorching several of the industry structures and destroying with his fire some minor structures that would be easily replaced. Dean was thankful that stone was the major resource, and that it had been chosen for construction purposes, for the stone walls of everything did not combust the way they would have if they had been built with wood.

Dean watched the impressive beast flying around the bunkers of earth and stone as gouts of flame spewed from his mouth. The dragon wasn't even paying attention to the unfinished city behind him as Dean looked up to the south tower to see Stefan loading the ballista with a rather savage-looking spear, with the new arrow-tip concept already incorporated. Either the engineer created this prototype incredibly fast or they had already considered this idea before and were unveiling it now. They were very skilled indeed. Dean could not have asked for a better team.

Even from this distance, Dean could hear the distinct *click* of the spring mechanism engaging the bolt as Stefan turned the large mounted weapon around to take aim at the red terror in the skies. The engineer did not hesitate. The bolt flew fast and true and tore into one of the wings of the massive beast, throwing the red backward in pain before the bolt finally embedded itself into one of his hind legs. Stefan did not stop to rejoice in his success but immediately began loading another bolt into the ballista. Once the spring was engaged the second time, even the dragon could recognize the implication of the *click* sound and immediately vaulted himself into the air and retreated back toward the southwest, wounded and thwarted.

The cheers of the laborers and the industry workers filled the air as the red dragon withdrew from the sky above. Stefan disengaged the tension from the ballista and removed the remaining bolt, setting it down inside of a wooden crate which housed two other rounds. Stefan stood and made eye contact with Dean, and the seneschal gave him a respectful nod of appreciation before turning his attention on the cheering citizens. Dean was quick to bark out commands that the threat had passed and work was to resume, causing the crowd to fall silent and disperse as everyone deferred to the commanding presence of the seneschal.

Work continued around the newly forming city once again as Dean continued his walk through the foundations and then into the rest of the industry sectors, stopping near the agricultural fields and livestock pens to speak briefly with several of the workers. The mill was nearing completion and would be fully functional within the next few weeks, in time to begin processing the first harvest of grain into the much needed flour.

That dark awareness in Dean's mind had been growing restless, and all the activities involved with establishing Innin Hold did little to soothe it. For the last several weeks, Dean had felt stronger and more alive than ever. Seeing that captive scout almost made him tingle with energy knowing what kind of experiments he would soon be able to conduct on the corruptible soul. With the lack of cold weather this far south, it was hard for Dean to know what time of year it was but according to Vincent Sutherland, who was also in charge of developing a plan for a university within Innin Hold over the next year, his calendar indicated that they were nearing the middle of winter now, and soon the days would start getting longer once more, increasing daylight productivity once again.

The more he focused on Vincent's wording regarding the middle of winter, the more the awareness in his mind stirred. There was something significant about the middle of winter and his link to this awareness, yet he wasn't sure yet what the significance was. Since his experiment with the moth, he had tried applying his power in other ways. Several cattle and sheep were deathly ill during their close living arrangements before the pens were completed and when Dean looked at them with his senses, he could almost see the growing corruption of death within them. Like with the moth, he began to boil their blood but not to the point of death—his goal being to burn away the sickness like the apothecaries used to do with heated rooms and controlled blood-letting. Sometimes causing a fever would actually improve the health of the ailing, and when Dean applied that rationale to the animals, he could almost isolate the corruption even more. Once the blood was heated enough, he would place his hands over the animal and draw out the disease into himself where he felt it dissipate and neutralize within his own spirit. The awareness had cancelled the effect of the disease and thus he was able to heal the animals with his gift.

It didn't quite feel like healing in the traditional sense. For Dean it was more the absorbing of the corruption of death around him from other living things in order to amplify his own power, while indirectly setting the afflicted free from their burden of disease. The difference was subtle, and all that anyone else saw was the seneschal restoring life to those around him, a miracle that encouraged them to look past the change of his eye color to an alarming blood red hue. Aside from this one physical alteration, the townspeople could not see the evil awareness growing beyond the borders of the seneschal's mind, seeking a way to free itself so that it could endow Dean with a power greater than anyone could imagine.

The term 'blood healer' became used around the city as Dean's personal fame continued to spread. Arimas was not able to perform such miracles like Dean. They served the seneschal, and now the blood healer of Innin Hold, and Dean freely dispensed his abilities as he crossed the paths of his own people suffering in lesser ways. With each cleansing, Dean was growing more and more powerful and some days he felt like he was actually losing control of himself in his mastery of the blood magic.

Today was a good day for Dean and his control. He would likely give his Drucharii a few days to question the prisoner before he went to visit him. Until that time, he would continue to oversee the continual development of his city. He was becoming a master at harnessing the strengths of his people and giving them a vision to follow, a vision which motivated them toward more efficient and quality work. He spun the tale that Innin Hold was *their* city and challenged each of them to work as if it were their own building, for every citizen would have equal access to the walled city of Innin Hold.

The day passed quickly and the evening meal once again was fish chowder bolstered with some of the last remaining potatoes of the year. Some of the personal herbs from the nearby gardens were contributed to the kitchens in order to flavor the meals more and even Dean appreciated the subtle hints of spice laced in with the fish, potatoes, and cream. Many were looking forward to the spring when the harvesting cycles would become more abundant and more regular. The projected crops would nearly overflow the storerooms come the spring, so throughout the winter many spent considerable effort thinking of different ways to preserve or pickle some of the vegetables to guard against spoilage.

Dean couldn't be bothered worrying about such matters right now. He finished his meal and began to stroll near the southern tower again, this time hearing the usual silence shattered by the shrieks of terror and pain coming from the captive below. With screaming that intense, Arimas' scout obviously still had too much fight left in him. No doubt he would be much more malleable after the Drucharii spent the night softening him up. Dean smirked wickedly, knowing just how fast this pathetic whelp would beg for death once the blood healer walked into the chamber. Blood healer... Dean grinned to himself as he pondered the title that had moved swiftly throughout the city, passing from one ignorant fool to the next. Regardless of what those who blindly followed him thought the words meant, he rather liked the appellation... blood healer indeed. They had no idea what he was truly capable of. And once they learned? It would be far too late then to do anything about it.

XXVII

*I*t took four days to finally break the Lorenthian scout. Each morning Dean would venture over to the containment area to gauge his Drucharii's progress, and each morning he found the scout, still fighting with all his strength, and resisting the methods of torture that the Drucharii were skillfully applying. Dean couldn't help but be slightly impressed that the man continued to stand in pride and defiance against the will of the seneschal's servants. The fourth morning, though, there were no more screams. Through a process of slow and agonizing bleeding with cauterization by iron brands plunged into hot coals, the Drucharii finally forced the Lorenthian scout to relent. Dean's thoughts were proven right again—in time everyone broke. One simply needed to find the other's weakness. The scout's resistance was finally broken when one of the Drucharii crushed his smallest toe between two plates of hot metal. Granted, they had to break his other nine toes and four of his fingers in this fashion before the prisoner finally succumbed. Reduced to a crippled pool of crushed bones, blood, and tears, the scout finally began to talk in exchange for the promise of the quick death offered to him by Dhax.

The scout told them of the alliance between the dragons and the elves, and the new order of paladins that Arimas had commissioned while under the influence of the god Deimar. He also reported on the great progress made on the immense stone wall construction that would enclose the borders of Lorenth.

Dhax found most of these ramblings to be senseless, fragmented pieces of a greater story, but Garrin, who was aiding Dhax in the exercises that day, recorded every word that the broken scout uttered, senseless or not, for delivery to the seneschal.

When the questioning was finally complete, the scout begged for release from his suffering. Dhax only laughed, grabbing the man's head and licking at the stream of blood oozing from the victim's right eye before spitting it back into the scout's face.

"Your job is not quite finished. Death awaits, but not until after the seneschal has his turn with you."

What little blood was left in the victim's face drained at the ominous sight of the seneschal, who stirred from the shadows where he had been lurking, watching the last few exchanges between Dhax and the scout. Dhax took several paces backward as the seneschal reached for and took hold of the stirring of the essence within, even more intense than ever before.

"Look at me!" The Drucharii took an additional step back as Dean spoke, his voice deepened by a darker tone which laced around it. It sounded as if there were someone else echoing Dean's words, but there was no one else to be seen. The terrified scout looked up in terror to behold the swirling red orbs that made Dean's eyes appear full of blood. Once the eye contact was made, it could not be severed. All the scout could do was shake with fear and summon the weakest of screams as the seneschal stalked toward him, stopping when there was less than a span between himself and the prisoner.

Like he had done with the moth, Dean focused on the essence of the scout, noting several areas where corruption had already seeped in. Arimas' man was bleeding deep within his body from all the trauma his Drucharii had put him through; his groin had been reduced to little more than pulp, making his gender barely discernable; and the amount of broken and shattered bones were exceptionally high. Dean chose to concentrate on the flow of blood still pulsing inside his victim, raising its internal temperature while isolating all the corruption in the broken body. And, just as he had done with the ailing animals of Innin Hold, Dean summoned that darkness into himself.

The scout had no idea what to believe as he felt his splintered bones begin to knit back together, his wounds fuse shut, and his bruises begin to heal until he felt nearly whole again. Dean surged with dark energy as the air around him began to crackle as if a small lightning storm was forming inside him. Dhax and Garrin stood dumbfounded at the changes in their leader and for once, even they began to fear what the seneschal was transforming into. Yet it was this fear that also compelled them to remain safely in loyal service. Once all the corruption had been drawn out of the scout, Dean pressed on with the channeling of his essence until the scout began to scream once more with renewed vigor. The distinct smell of burning flesh wafted over Dean and his Drucharii, causing Garrin to lose his fortitude and wretch where he stood. The scout's eyes burst into flame as Dean set fire to the inside of the man like he had with the moth until the screaming ceased and the prisoner's body hung limp before him. Dean surrendered his will to the awareness within as he extended his left hand and launched those black tendrils of dark energy into the chest of the dead scout. The darkness enveloped the human as Dean could feel the awareness attempting to resurrect this soul once more. Yet, still there was an obstacle. The scout opened what was left of his eyelids, his charred out eyes staring blankly as the skin began to peel away from his skeleton, revealing the closest thing Dean had yet come to resurrecting the living dead. But, the final key to the resurrection process remained unknown to the seneschal. In his failure to supply the last of the missing ingredients, the darkness that had gathered around the reanimated scout satisfied itself on the remaining flesh until the chained body eventually disintegrated into a small pillar of black ash.

As the reanimation process was failing, Dean and the awareness within him became conscious of a foreign, otherworldly presence watching the activities from a distant place. Dean paused, leaving the cloak of darkness to cover the dead scout before swiftly bearing his vision into the empty space beyond him, where he beheld the visage of an elven male. No one else standing in the room was aware of the long-haired specter save for Dean, whose retaliation was swift. He extended his right hand toward the vision as he laughed maliciously, and sent the same dark energy that had destroyed the life of the Lorenthian scout streaking across the vast openness until it pierced into the vision only Dean could see. The elf attempted to draw back in time to avoid the seneschal's wicked lash, but Dean was sure that even though the elf's presence had abandoned the scene, it had not done so before feeling pain at his hand. Wholly satisfied with his growing powers, and his displays of them, he turned his attention back to the remains of the scout and then took in the state of his two Drucharii, who both stood in recognizable fear of what stood before them.

"You are wise to fear me, and you are wiser still to continue serving me. My power will only grow and those who have stood by me will also share in the gifts that my power will bring. Harness your fear and surrender your will to me and serve! I have trained you well my friends... and friends I still count you, so long as your service to me remains. Seek to oppose me and I will make death a pain from which you will never escape... and like the pitiful mess before us only moments ago, you will beg for a final release which shall not be granted."

Dhax swallowed his fear and dropped to one knee, "My body and soul are yours to command my lord, as always, and forever."

Garrin followed the example of his Druuarc. "I kneel before you in service as well my lord, as always, and forever."

"You both chose wisely. Now go. Tonight has been called Midwinter's Eve by the elves of the Dark Wood, and perhaps the truth I seek does lie beneath the trees. I must ponder on this matter and decide on my next course of action."

The Drucharii rose to their feet and regained their full composure as they made their way out of the containment area to return to their own guild hall north of the lake. Dhax and Garrin did not speak about what they saw—not even to each other. In many ways they were tied to the wave of Dean's terrifying power and they could not escape the devastation that would follow in its wake. Part of them reveled in the thought, while what little remained of their human morality and conscience was troubled beyond belief.

Dean was lost within his own mind. The awareness was surging with such tremendous power as it attempted to guide him... somewhere. Again he felt that there was something important lying in the midst of the forests but it was far more intense here in the south than when he had bordered the Dark Wood. He tried to listen to the whispers and shadows in his mind, trying to filter out the intent of the awareness without his own intellect and belief s interfering. Like the pull he had experienced during the brief vision of those who had called him master, Dean once again felt drawn, but this time it was to the middling forest found northwest, along the shore of the great sea.

Before he could think more about this sudden set of urgings, another prolonged roar tore apart the silence in the skies above as the other notorious dragon, the bronze colored one, flew into the area in a blind rage. Usually the dragons were methodical and showed remarkable planning and intellect in how they coordinated their attack. It seemed that desperation had altered the course of the dragons. While those of Innin Hold had repelled the red dragon with their new weaponry, it appeared as if the large bronze was preparing to finish the job.

The dragon's rage was completely unpredictable. He spewed his fire over anything and everything, crushing several homes as he landed hard on them before thrashing his mighty talons to unearth some of the bunkers that a few unfortunate citizens were hiding in. Several of those men and women exposed were torn to shreds by one single swipe of the dragon's razor sharp talons. Dean extended his senses to this devastating beast in hopes of setting a flame within the bloodstream of this creature, yet the second he extended his senses he saw and felt nothing—as if the creature could not be detected through his senses. Only his natural eye could confirm the reality of this monster. The seneschal found that he could not even summon a cloud of dark energy to envelop him. It was as if the creature was completely immune to his power. Luckily, the dragon would not prove immune to the ballista. In his blind rage, the bronze dragon paid no attention to the insignificant engineer who had loaded yet another of his large bolts into the massive weapon housed within the towers of the quarter-built hold, and took aim upon the furious dragon.

Once fired, the bolt penetrated deep into the chest of the dragon, entering through a small band of pale flesh that ran from the bottom of his jaw all the way down to the tip of his tail. This part of the dragon's body was not scaled like the rest of him, so the projectile was able to enter the flesh of the creature unhindered. The dragon lurched in pain and spun several times above the settlement before eventually collapsing, landing outside of the field in front of the southern tower. The dragons did have a weakness, and now the humans of Innin Hold knew how to beat this fearsome adversary.

It was just past noon now and the skies were completely quiet as hundreds of citizens began to gather around the dead dragon. With its wings furled along its body and with the incredible length of its neck and tail, this creature resembled a giant scaled snake or wyrm—a fitting term for the winged beasts that dug lairs deep within the earth.

"As fear has pierced our hearts because of these great wyrms, so let fear strike into their hearts now that we have found their weakness. This creature will be extensively studied and perhaps this dead wyrm will be of some benefit for all the grief he has caused us."

Many stood in awe at the size and savageness of the dead dragon, and some even reached out to touch the warm scales. For all the terror that these beasts had caused recently, some found the sudden death of such a magnificent predator to be humbling and emotional. Humans had finally conquered the most intelligent and savage of the beasts known to man, forever asserting their place as the top predator—a title that bore little honor but commanded much respect. In all their pride of their accomplishments many began to worry that they were being positioned for an even greater fall, yet no one could begin to comprehend where such a threat would come from.

Dean suppressed the awareness and its promptings about the northern forest for now. The greatest trophy of man would be proudly displayed within the keep for generations to come and perhaps the weapons and defenses of this great wyrm would be integrated into weapons and defenses for Dean and his best men. Vincent was excited beyond belief at the chance to study such a beast while Karl took one look at the scales and was already thinking of ways to incorporate them into an armor pattern. Renwold saw potential for the underbelly and perhaps other toughened hide that may exist beneath the hard scales while Jared suggested that the flesh beneath all the armaments of this beast might even be edible and would provide more meat for the city than all the cattle they had at present.

Dean nodded to himself. This dragon would repay the humans for the grief it had caused, for by his death the humans would propel themselves forward in new directions. If this beast proved to be so valuable in death perhaps Dean would even consider tasking Stefan to reduce the ballista if possible, to make it somewhat portable to hunt these mighty beasts. Or perhaps the skilled engineer could fashion a different bolt coupled with a net, or something to entangle the great beasts, making them easier to capture or kill. Dean smiled. The dragons picked the battle, and now Dean and the rest Innin Hold were positioning themselves to win the war.

* * *

"We have waited long enough, father!"

"Zharra, we have already discussed this at great length. Karros is avoiding us and if what you say about this living taint is true, then you are willing to risk the well-being of everyone who ventures down there. Karros has chosen his path."

"You helped him choose that path with your neutrality. He was the youngest, the son of the mighty Valkyyrak in whose shadow he felt inadequate. He needed something from all of us that we never gave him and now, while his beliefs are noticeably being distorted, you are prepared to ignore his fate once more because of your pride."

Dalaria immediately intervened before Valkyyrak's rage found release. "Zharra, let me speak with your father. Leave us for a short while. I will speak with you once we have come to any sort of decision."

"We have already decided our actions, Dala—"

"No we have not. Calm yourself, my love."

The large platinum dragon acquiesced to her mother's request. Valkyyrak turned his large bulk away from the entrance to his lair as Zharra departed, taking to the skies on her silent wings and bending the light around her, vanishing in plain view. First she mentions this request from Arimas to scout out the southern plains beyond the Ardun River, and now this, Valkyyrak said to himself. While the great dragon knew the course of actions set before him had merit, Zharra in her tremendous wisdom saw to the truth of the matter. Valkyyrak was proud. Deep down, while he regretted the lack of guidance he gave to his youngest, a large part of him could not, or would not, admit to such failure. Yet that failure was beginning to cost him far too much... his own daughter was now moved to dispense chastisement to the golden ancient.

"She is right, Dalaria."

"Of course she is right. I was wondering how long it would take you to figure that out. The question is... what are you going to do about this? We have discussed this matter too long as it is. Midwinter's Eve has come and gone, the elves are restless, and your son is still lost to us."

Valkyyrak let go of all the anger and frustration that had built up inside him as he turned to look into the affectionate eyes of his mate. This flight to reach both places, to speak with Karros and observe the taint for himself and then return back to the Icecrowns, would only take a week. He could afford a week. He needed to afford a week.

"I will go."

"No... we will go, as well as anyone else who feels compelled to visit their kin. Nostrimus and Vaelis especially want to see Xarethia again, and to meet the newest additions to our extended family. And are we to also assist Arimas in his request of us?"

"Yes, of course. It would be foolish not to aid them, especially if we are already flying past the area. Use this day as you will my love, tell whom you must, for we leave at first light tomorrow morning."

Dalaria rubbed up along Valkyyrak's side and nuzzled his neck before flying down to the summit where Zharra was speaking with Nyssia. Dalaria paused and gave the elf a questioning look for she was not due to be in the Icecrowns for at least another week or more.

"What brings you among us again little sister?"

"I come with warning, Dalaria. You all already understand what happened several nights ago during our Frostfire celebrations, but over the past couple days I have begun to worry even more about what lies in the south. Aerinyyr is one of the most powerful mages that I know and he was nearly reduced to shadow and memory that night. As an honored *Azurak* I cannot help but hold a special place in my heart for you all here and I fear what evil might befall you should you set forth to investigate these matters in the human exile lands and beyond. Have you as yet decided on your path or do the deliberations still continue?"

Zharra was about to speak but Dalaria interrupted her before she could begin. "We are setting out tomorrow to investigate the south, as well as to visit my son and his mate who have long been away from the Icecrowns."

Zharra was noticeably surprised that her father had actually conceded to this plan. "Well done mother. You certainly know how to reason with father."

"Naturally."

"Will you not reconsider, Dalaria? Zharra, please! You must be wise about this! This evil is beyond anything that we have ever encountered."

"Patience, Nyssia," began the ancient blue female, her peaceful tones soothing the agitation within the elven stormweaver. "We dragons are not known for making rash decisions. You can attest to this by the length this particular discussion took. We have always approached matters we do not understand with caution, and this shall be no different. We will stick to the skies and observe only, save for when we land to seek out my son where Zharra last saw him and his mate. Then we shall return."

"If I cannot sway your mind, then may I fly with you? I have no obligations to meet with Avalide for some time and the other *Azurakkis* will not be arriving here until later next week."

The blue ancient and the platinum elder exchanged glances and Zharra nodded so slightly that many would have missed it. Dalaria cracked a toothy grin and approved the request, stating that the dragons would be honored to have her with them while also mentioning that it would be a good time to study Nyssia's form and rate her flying mastery while testing her proficiency with her dragon fire.

Nyssia chuckled at the last remark, knowing that her dragon fire was still terribly weak after all her practicing. She could summon a flame but it had just not felt right, so she had followed the same paths as her dragon friends and tested her abilities using the color-specific strengths that each of the dragons had been working on. Unsurprisingly, like the blues, Nyssia easily mastered the art of frost breath, and also achieved further success with refining her frost breath into sprays of hard ice spikes that, while small in individual size, would fly like daggers and tear into anything made of flesh and bone. Vaelis was quite impressed when Nyssia first experimented with that idea, first in theory and then in practice.

The three talked for a while and Nyssia shared some new information with the dragons regarding the reflecting pools that were finally to be built for whoever wished to be a recipient of one. Dalaria thought the idea to be rather intriguing and knew that Sargeron and Valkyyrak would both see the merit of instant communication with their allies, and would approve its usage, at least while the magic of Caliyon could still be employed under their control. The largest fear of all the fae was the possibility that this advancing taint would negate all magic and effectively cripple many of their extraordinary abilities. In many ways, the fae felt defined by their connections to the other realms of magic and to be suddenly severed from that connection would be akin to losing a limb or a vital organ.

The reflecting pools would be constructed on a much larger scale than when Avalide and Frostspire were first connected. Instead of working in the original pairings from before, Larros, Nyssia, Thaelvin, and Draevor would all be working independently with other skilled mages from both the Frostspire and from Avalide to complete the fusions of the new reflecting pools. The forecasted locations were tentatively going to be established in the Icecrown summit, the Lorenth council chamber, King Varr's war room, Korigan Goern's clan hall, Edon Thunderhammer's battlekeep antechamber, Hrimir Ingar's planning council chamber, Orin Chorimson's Blood Hall, and the Kurganat chamber of Forin Hammul III.

Eight new reflecting pools to be established—such tasks were going to be quite a strain on the knowledge and resources of the *Dsa'carii*. Cheyandra had already offered the support of Avalide to learn and assist as needed should their *Dsa'carii* kin be overtaxed, and Valeris had already indicated that their assistance would be utilized. The dwarves knew that the majority of these pools were to be done for the benefit of the fragmented dwarven clans and thus made significant commitments to the elves of the precious truesilver that was theorized to be able to contain the elemental and crystalline energies that normally the elves would have considered the original unknown ore for.

Arcanite was the end result of their experimentation with the first ores of the frozen wastes. This magically infused metal, which the dwarves insisted did not exist, presented the elves some difficulty as they attempted to explain its creation to the dwarves, who undeniably, were the masters of metals and ores found beneath the earth. When the *Dsa'carii* had begun summoning and channeling the earth and stone needed to fuse together the Frostspire, they unearthed ores that were pale blue and pale green in color. The dwarves agreed that the pale blue ore could in fact be raw truesilver, but the pale green ore stumped them. It was not mithril, and the only other ore that sounded anything like this was the ultra-rare thorium that the grays had been fortunate enough to uncover in their deep delving. In any event, the ore was but a conduit, for arcanite was forged by magic and not by fire.

Yserth Tel'andris, one of the ruling council of three in the Frostspire, had tasked two storm weavers to accompany an arcanist of the Ætheron as well as a druid of the *Essen'dril* so that the four would be able to combine their knowledge of the elemental, the spiritual, and the corporeal facets of magic when working with the Silverfist engineers who would be providing the bulk of the truesilver. Nyssia told the dragons that this initiative was well underway. Baelanor Ol'yyran and Jamaela Iss'yss had already left the Frostspire to meet with Rurok Amgar, the chief prospector for the Silverfist, as well as Phaelen Sundancer and Rallegan Timberwood, the arcanist and the druid respectively who had been sent from Avalide. Their task over the next few weeks was to optimize the process of arcanite transmutation and potentially begin work on the castings and the binders that would be transported to the needed locations.

Nyssia was appointed to be the lead mage in charge of activating the reflecting pool within the Icecrowns and then within Ur'Akam, and she would be assigned a senior ice mage as well as an Avalide arcanist to both be mentored by her and assist as needed. The arcanite project would likely take several weeks at the earliest as formulations were refined, and then several more weeks to begin with the castings and binders, so Nyssia had no inner conflicts about her desire to fly with the dragons and scout out the south with them. Nyssia spent that first day with Zharra mostly, but also was asked to speak with Valkyyrak and Sargeron about the reflecting pools.

Early in the evening Zharra and Nyssia flew north to Sycaris' favorite place for solitude and thinking. Nyssia had only spoken with the red female once beyond the exchanging of simple platitudes but Nyssia already knew from that one meeting that this dragon was deeply troubled, yet in possession of a strong resolve. With Zharra's uncanny ability to locate nearly all those of dragon blood with only her mind, finding Sycaris was relatively easy. Sycaris had a temperament quite similar to her father Sargeron—methodical, patient, calculating, and even bordering on some introverted tendencies, but behind the crimson scales beat a heart that was linked to the prophecies and a mind critical enough to interpret and unveil the truths therein.

Even with the silence of prophecy, Sycaris was a valuable resource to tap into. Her mind held generation upon generation of dreams, visions, histories, and the like and should she consent to having one of these Avalide cyphers speak with her, the untapped wisdom of draconic lore and study would be available to all the fae. More importantly, that wisdom would be preserved for all generations to follow as it would stand the test of time within the incredible structure of their southern kin known as the Illuallarii. Sycaris smiled when she saw her closest friend descend upon the high snow-capped peak with a summit barely wide enough for the two dragons and the small blue drake to rest. Sycaris shifted her glance to Nyssia and inclined her head, while Nyssia did the same.

"What brings the Lightweaver and the *Azurak* elder to this peak to disrupt my solitude?" The red's attempts at mock-seriousness were foiled as she smiled again.

"We came to share the sunset with you Sycaris, and our little sister here has long been wanting to get to know you as I know you. I figured tonight was as good as any night to acquaint the two of you more."

Nyssia would have blushed if her blue scales permitted it but instead she just sent an inquisitive look toward Zharra. "I am sorry, Sycaris. While what Zharra has said is true, I did not think our friend here would have plucked those particular thoughts from me. I did not wish for you to be forced to speak with me."

"Oh Nyssia, you need to act more like a dragon," Zharra teased. "You elves mince words far too much. Say what you feel, be honest, and bridge gaps as you see fit. You will learn this in time, but many of the dragons still residing in the Icecrowns are family of one sort or another. It is part of who we are to get to know each other, and it is a failing to go through life as a dragon and be disconnected from your kin. Our unity is our greatest strength."

"Zharra speaks the truth Nyssia. Had I known this was your intent, I would have obliged you sooner. It is true that I frequent this peak more than I probably should. My dearest Maelyyk appears to understand my recurring need for space, and for many of our kin, if needed I am but a thought away... especially if Zharra is anywhere close by."

Nyssia made idle chatter with Sycaris and Zharra for a while, all three taking in the amber and red tones that lit up the sky as the sun began to hide beneath the mighty western peaks of the Icecrowns. Nyssia always found the dragon vision fascinating at night. While the elves had tremendous vision in both the light and the dark, the dragon sight was quite different, though equally as accurate. Sycaris caught Nyssia off guard after several moments of silence when she took their earlier conversation much deeper once the night was upon them.

"What do you see in the darkness, Nyssia? What do you fear behind that which blocks all natural light? I have been staring into the darkness since I was a hatchling. I have seen fear and worry eat away at the heart of a dragon among dragons. My mother was one of the four original ancients, as you well know, and she too spent her life staring into the darkness. But, unlike me, she feared it and ignored it, and I feel that she died because of it. I have tried to decipher the meanings and the intents of the corruption that is spreading. There are still prophecies in my mind that are only now becoming clear in light of the changes around us. The advent of the paladins of Lorenth was prophesized many generations ago, yet no one had the understanding of the phrases in the prophecies that spoke of *the six and twenty eyes of light.* Even some of the prophecies regarding the Lightbringer have become clearer. Listen to this... *and the chalice of Deimar that would deliver the twinning fate of the balance.*"

"How does that passage refer to the Lightbringer?" inquired Nyssia.

"I only recently divined the meaning of this when we received news that the bride of Arimas is carrying twins. Look again Nyssia... what is a chalice?"

"It is a cup. I believe Larros once mentioned that Arimas kept a sacred cup in the temple of his unknown deity for years."

"Think beyond a cup. I did not see the meaning in this phrase because I am not human, but even the elves and the dwarves share this in common. Also look at the word 'deliver.' I believe this entire passage has a double meaning which further clouded the interpretation from me. While the first meaning of the deliverance involves the bringing forth of fate—possibly two fates, or a twinned fate where one branch impacts the other—one fate refering to the balance should the corruption win, and the other being the fate of Caliyon if the Lightbringer is victorious. But it is the hidden meaning that is the most important for the word 'deliver' can also refer to the childbearing process unique to humans and all fae females who possess..."

"A womb... of course! The womb is shaped like a chalice, and it was the work of Deimar that blessed the union of Arimas and Verona. Now she bears twins in accordance to this prophecy."

"You now understand that which I only found out several days ago. These are the issues that worry me, Nyssia. This is the darkness that I fear. Like these fragments of prophecy that are only now being revealed, there are many more threads that I have no understanding of but as the corruption advances and truths become revealed, the hindsight will also reveal the meaning of these threads that have long been misunderstood or not understood at all. How do I wrestle with these many threads of fragmented meaning in which fear can grant an interpretation that reason would refute? How do I carry on each day with all this weighty confusion trapped in my head?"

Nyssia finally saw an opening to interject and the solution she offered was perfect. "Sycaris, write it down and let others share the burden of these prophecies. Avalide is sending four cyphers to catalogue the wisdom of the fae and of the humans so that it can be forever preserved in the Illuallarii—a building created mainly by the air elementals where time has no reign and the objects housed within are forever safeguarded between the elemental plane and the corporeal plane. Will you consider sharing your wisdom with those of Avalide? Like those of the Frostspire, many of the elves have devoted complete age cycles to the study and the interpretation of dreams and prophecy. Perhaps in collaboration you will find relief and understanding."

Zharra and Sycaris both were deep in thought with the flurry of ideas that just burst forth from Nyssia. Being among dragons for as often as she had been, she started to recognize when they were speaking privately with the *Skarlagnos*. Not wanting to interrupt, she continued to watch the silent exchange while the evening darkness brought back the evident chill that had been restrained by the sun.

"While part of me finds the notion of sharing my responsibilities as the Guide somewhat improper, I cannot argue with your logic. I will accept your cypher Nyssia, and like you merged with the mind of Zharra, so I will allow your cypher to merge with mine should he or she be so motivated. Perhaps rest will finally come to my weary soul."

"I will be sure to notify the Matriarch of your decision, Sycaris."

"I think I will actually look forward to this, Nyssia. Perhaps one day your kin might consider admitting me into the Illuallarii that you spoke of. Such a structure sounds quite wondrous and I would like to observe it with my own eyes."

"I will also pass that point along as well. I cannot foresee any issues with your request Sycaris, although perhaps you may want to study from the blues on how to reduce your form to be able to gain entry inside."

Zharra tried to stifle the smile that was crossing her face as Sycaris began to shift in her appearance until a red-scaled upright dragon the size of Nyssia stood before the two.

"I see someone has already taught you well."

"Zharra began teaching me shortly after your first visit, Nyssia. It is a remarkable gift that you have given to us."

"I too have been the recipient of gifts far greater than I would have imagined. The other *Azurakkis* are somewhat envious by what I have seen and experienced with you. I count it an honor to be considered as part of your world in this way and my life has been widely enriched because of our friendship."

Little more was said as the three collectively agreed to return to the summit to prepare for the evening. Nyssia was not sure how many dragons would be heading toward the human exile settlement before making their way to the stone hills, but Sycaris had already stated that she would not be joining the expedition, while Zharra expressed that she fully intended to see with her natural eyes what she had seen through her projections.

Nearing the summit, Sycaris wished the two safe flights and a hasty return as she changed her course slightly to head to her lair where Maelyyk was undoubtedly waiting. As per usual, Nyssia went back to the lair of Vaanadu and Zharra for the evening, much as she had done every time she visited the Icecrowns. The kinship between Zharra and Nyssia had only strengthened since the day that they had entered into the *Aëolyys eth'Seloria* together.

Vaanadu had finally completed his room of glass and was now working on a separate chamber even deeper within the heart of the mountain. Nyssia did enjoy sleeping beneath their vertical entrance chamber where the moonlight often illuminated a small patch of rock deep in the lair; however, she was pleased to try the new chamber once when Vaanadu was not using it. She did find that it certainly radiated heat much better than the other chambers. Somehow it effectively trapped ambient heat inside the walls themselves, which, melted through tremendous use of dragon fire, appeared to glow like nearly spent embers. Sure enough, Vaanadu was waiting for the two of them as they made their decent into the now familiar lair where more light conversation persisted between the three for much longer than any of the trio had planned.

Morning came suddenly and, for Nyssia at least, it was not welcomed. Vaanadu had announced rather matter-of-factly that he would be traveling with them. How much of that decision was based on his protective nature of his mate versus his actual concern for the wayward bronze dragon who had left behind all those in the Icecrowns so many years ago, Nyssia could only guess. The three ascended into the cold pre-dawn sky and made their way to the summit where a small gathering of dragons was already assembling. Valkyyrak, Dalaria, and Sargeron were present of course, as were Nostrimus and Vaelis. She also saw Ormaryn, Vasuni, Trakkenor, and Nagendra gathering and before she could voice the question to Zharra as they made their final approach toward the summit, the platinum dragon opened her mind to answer the elf's unspoken question.

"Ormaryn and Nagendra were very close with Xarethia even before those two became mates—Nagendra more so because Xarethia is her older sister. Vasuni always gave Maelyyk and Sycaris a hard time and frequently would be found flying with Karros as the age gap between them was not overly large. This leaves my son, Trakkenor, who silently was attracted to Xarethia for years and was little more than a younger brother to Xarethia and Karros. Karros was much more driven than Trakkenor was and won her heart long before Trakkenor even considered vying for her affections. Thankfully he put all those matters behind him which allowed fate to bring my son and Tanith together, and now Vespa is among us as a result of that union."

"I thought that Vespa had a twin sister? I distinctly remember hearing that."

"Another source of pain uncovered..." Even from the way she spoke, Nyssia knew that this topic was a troublesome one. *"There were two daughters hatched nearly the same time. Vespa whom you know, and Vuhla whom you do not know. As different as a topaz can be from an amethyst dragon, so were Vespa and Vuhla. The only other amethyst dragon to come before or after her is my daughter*

Athelinde, so beyond what I know from my own offspring, we know little of the amethyst temperament. Vuhla followed Xarethia out of the Icecrowns and she gave no real reason why she left. Did she leave out of curiosity or for adventure? Was it a final act of rebellion toward Trakkenor and Tanith or was it a way to be free of Vespa, the 'good sister?'

"It wasn't that Vuhla was appreciated any less, but there was a restless spirit within her and seldom did she heed the wisdom of others. Within that restless spirit was a dragon full of life and promise but she never let that dragon out of her heart and thus she became a recluse of sorts until she finally decided to follow Xarethia away from the Icecrowns."

Zharra paused for a moment and then Nyssia added, *"I find is so incredible that the dragon social network is built on such strong relationships between each other. While the elves of the Frostspire think of each other with a similar kinship mentality, we are a society that often spends much time alone in contemplation and study. We have gotten along like this for as long as I can remember and isolation and solitude are words very familiar with the elves, and of our choosing. I find the passion in the dragon bond so foreign and yet so inspiring."*

"This is what makes the choice for isolation of those who left the Icecrowns so offensive to many of us, Nyssia. In all true ways we are family. Almost all of the dragons are direct descendants of Valkyyrak, Dalaria, Sargeron, and Fyysara. Only myself, Maelyyk, Vaelis and Karros are purely descended from Valkyyrak and Dalaria, while only Sycaris, Nostrimus, and Vaanadu are pure descendants of Sargeron and Fyysara. I think you can understand the heartache that filled the ancients when Karros led Xarethia and several others away from our ancient birthplace."

Their conversation ended abruptly as the three landed. Valkyyrak nodded to his daughter, and spoke to her through the *Skarlagnos.* Nyssia only hoped it was something close to an apology for his harshness the day before. Sargeron approached those who had gathered and issued his own words prior to their departure.

"We have a long journey ahead of us, nearly as long as the journey to the east that we made to meet with the rest of the fae races. From what Zharra has told us, we fly south to the great sea and then southeast toward the new human establishment before we explore the stone hills in search of our kin. We are not to engage the humans, we are only to observe from afar and report their developments to Lorenth."

Valkyyrak nodded to his ancient friend as Sargeron took to the skies followed by Valkyyrak and the others in rapid succession. The eleven dragons plus the smaller blue drake spiraled out of the Icecrown summit and began their long flight to the south in search of answers that they would soon wish were never obtained.

XXVIII

The inquisitor, dressed in his new regalia, was stationed at the front gates awaiting the change in command between the town watch and the first watch of the night. News of a rider approaching the city from the east stirred him from his melancholy as he strained in the setting sunlight to see the silhouette of the solitary rider on top of a pale steed that he knew quite well. He ordered the opening of the gates well before the rider actually dismounted and made his way down from the ramparts to greet her.

"Tavendia, what brings you to Lorenth so soon? I thought our next meeting was in three more weeks—not that I mind seeing you again of course but I... ahem. Sorry." Farin stuttered to an awkward stop.

"It comforts me to see you again as well Farin," Tavendia responded smoothly. "Did I hear correctly that you will be returning with me this time to the *Illu'Dar?*"

"Yes, you heard right. Over the last few weeks I have been in council with Arimas at great lengths and my poor words cannot properly convey the majesty of the wood. If you are indeed prepared to have the priest-king within the Illuallarii, I believe that Arimas is most keen in learning of your ways in the same fashion that I was privileged enough to."

Farin motioned for her to come into the city as he also whispered his thanks to Laenos for the safe bearing of the beautiful rider across the eastern borders of Lorenth. Tavendia, clothed in her typical earthen robes, followed Farin while Laenos walked beside them at his own pace and of his own accord.

"We are indeed ready. How have your own studies, and further insights into your gifting, been progressing?"

"My learning has been rapid, yet I understand that each new truth has been built on foundational knowledge that I learned before. It is a process of learning and understanding and even trusting the guidance of my emotions. There is something that has been troubling me, though."

"Is it something you wish to speak of?" Tavendia probed gently.

"Oh, it's nothing that I would withhold from you. Arimas has been seeking the awareness of Deimar in the hearts and minds of those in Lorenth but aside from me, his new paladins, and of course himself, it appears that no others bear the mark of Deimar upon their soul. We are questioning the limited blessings and wondering if there is a plan or a purpose to this limitation."

"And what does your gift tell you, Farin? I am sure you have attempted to seek the truth in this matter for it is a question that is worth answering."

"The only answer I see tells me that the will of Deimar is to bless all who would bow their knee and surrender their own will to him—yet while he remains imprisoned, his abilities to extend his influence into the land is limited by us, his chosen servants at this appointed time."

"Then stop looking beyond what has been made clear, my friend. I can tell you this from my own studies and my many discussions with the Æthian. The humans are the first to be reunited with their Creator since the creation. Change is happening. The glades of *Illu'Dar* have roused from their slumber; the dryads are nearing the births of hundreds of new children who will awaken more of the guardians in the wood while bolstering the magic that sustains the *Illu'Dar*. The Lightbringer is alive in the womb of your queen, and now the blessing of Deimar himself, the Creator of life and the positive balance, rests among his chosen few—and all of this because of the humans. It is an exciting time we live in Farin.

Though there is much fear that threatens to shake the heart of the resolute, there is hope—again, because of man."

Farin and Tavendia continued their slow walk toward the citadel through the streets of the lower city. Over the preceding months, whatever lingering depravity and filth had left the city to join with Dean. With the new decree of Arimas canceling tributes, the conditions in the lower city had begun to improve. Farin remembered the rabble that had accosted him in the lower city only a few months before, and shook his head. Things were so much different now. It appeared that Arimas' theories were correct, and that the prosperity of the townships resulted in a corresponding prosperity for all the citizenry of Lorenth proper.

Farin was proud of what his priest-king was accomplishing. *Retribution* had finally replaced the scepter of complacency that had weighed down their patriarch and now the priest-king was a symbol of strength once more. As Farin reflected on his unique gift of uncovering truth, he began to appreciate some of the burdens that this new gift inherently brought with it. While Farin had become far more respected within the city and certainly throughout the townships, Farin already knew that mingled with this respect was a deeper fear and avoidance of the inquisitor.

The loyalty of the people that remained was no longer in question yet within each man, woman and child existed a certain need for privacy, and that need was violated whenever Farin was near. Fear of exposure of deeds done while no one was looking led to a general shunning of the inquisitor, which Farin was beginning to understand and accept. His was a position of nearly absolute authority for even Arimas would defer to the insights gained by the inquisitor.

"You are very pensive this evening, Farin. What troubles you?"

"I was reflecting on the burdens, as well as the benefits, of my gift. The more I learn and grow, the more I feel alienated from my own people as what I am becoming is something that many do not feel comfortable with."

"I do not think I ever considered that possibility before," Tavendia responded, a note of sympathy in her voice. "The elves, by nature, are a virtuous people and truth reading, while uncommon among us, does not bear any stigma. It is no different from our druids, arcanists or healers who all are gifted in various ways and use those gifts for the preservation of the balance."

"More often than not, I wish I was born an elf, Tavendia. Elven society rings with a certain purity and brilliance that I do not think humans are capable of, even considering the great changes already happening around us as a result of the awakening of the Tear."

Tavendia refrained from speaking as she looked over to her human friend in wonder. Farin had surpassed all expectations so rapidly and had become an intellectual worthy of speaking within elven circles. His insights were becoming more relevant and far deeper than she would have expected. Once again her thoughts drifted to this human male whom she found beautiful in form as well as in spirit and again she forced herself to suppress those thoughts. There lay no future in that direction, she chided herself silently. Tavendia turned her full attention back to Farin, taking in the pain slowly beginning to build behind his eyes, and sighed. He was learning to master his gift well for she could not even detect his subtle probing any longer.

"Why must it be like this, Tavendia?"

"You already know the answer to that, Farin. Please do not broach this subject again. It pains me to see you like this but we cannot change what is and what cannot be."

The two walked in silence for the last hundred paces before crossing the gates to the upper city. It certainly appeared to be livelier now that the university had been moved into the upper levels of the citadel near the libraries. She even saw life bustling around the Temple of Deimar. Farin noticed her interest in the gathering throng paying their respects to the deity.

"Many of us now come here to pray and worship beneath the ever-burning orb of eternal flame that Arimas set upon the altar. Those of us marked by Deimar himself have found that in our humility and servitude to others, and through genuine reflection and inner searching beneath the watchful gaze of the orb, we find our strength. Arimas and his paladins have met almost daily within the temple to pray and seek understanding of their gifts. The apothecaries have begun to admire the paladins who strike at the heart of sickness and disease faster and truer than even some of the concoctions created by the apothecaries. But the paladins maintain the efficacy of the apothecaries and have begun blessing the stores of herbs, flowers, and other reagents, as well as the apothecaries themselves to aid them in the creation of more potent medicines. The paladins understand that should they shoulder the burden of healing the sick, they would become ineffective in their other areas of responsibility; therefore, they use their gifts when needed and offer blessings when they are able in order to achieve the most benefit."

"So what was once the university has now been converted to your military academy?"

"Mostly yes, but there have been some minor issues with housing. The recruitment into the Lorenthian Guard has been far more successful than expected because of the exceptional command presence of the paladins, among others. My former commander, Hadrin Barros, is an outstanding leader in his own right, as is the former covenal, Erikk Masaad. The Guard is fortunate to have them leading the two principal divisions."

"You miss command very much." She said it as a statement, not as a question, and Farin nodded his head slowly.

"I stood by the side of my men in battle, shared in the joys of their marriages, even stood ready to settle them into the ground should fate wrest them from my hands. It is difficult to see my men smile with their eyes and not with their hearts when I approach them. I feel less like a man and more like a mystery and this is a loss that I have been privately grieving for as I venture into deeper areas of my responsibility to Lorenth."

"Mother was right. The times of suffering have begun. Try to hold fast, Farin, for you also know that our prophecies speak of a time when this suffering will end and your joy will be complete. How much of that fate remains undecided, I do not know. But I sustain my hope knowing that you are becoming strong and wise in your gift."

The two entered into the fortress, passing through the stone corridors on their way to the citadel. The presence of the elven druid still caused a stir of awe among the servants that were busy working, though the men and women who spotted her were quick to bow in respect.

Farin and Tavendia passed by the council chamber and noticed Cirra Bethanin conferring with her colleagues around some sort of map board, discussing the various needs and concerns of industry that they were to be tasked to represent. Cirra looked up as they passed, smiled, and offered a small wave. The elf and her companion waved back and continued on their way toward the citadel where they would likely find Arimas in his royal hall with several, if not all, of his paladins in close contact.

Nearing the citadel, they continued on through the former antechamber that Dean had once held during his command as seneschal. The broad hall had been slightly modified to reflect the new office of the inquisitor but still the cold stone with its banners of amber flame did little to brighten the area. Farin reflected that he had finally achieved the position he had envisioned himself occupying. He was the second in command of all Lorenth, yet he felt somehow empty and alone without the comforting presence of his men.

The two stewards opened the grand doors to the hall of kings to admit the inquisitor and the druid of Avalide into the court of the priest-king where his trusted four sat in conference with him. Dayle, Rorrick, Garron, and Anton—the four personal guards of Arimas now transformed into paragons of virtue and keepers of the eternal flame of Deimar, stood to their feet as the druid and the inquisitor approached the dais. Arimas nodded to Farin and offered a small bow to the druid as he stood.

"We heard of your early arrival, Lady Tavendia. How can Lorenth be of service to you? Do you bring news from the elven council?"

"Hail Arimas and peace to you, his knights of fire. I have come for two reasons. The first is to inform you that the *Dsa'carii* council has been motivated by recent events to approve the construction of several reflecting pools across the land in order to enable instant communication between the allied races. For generations, the *Illu'darii* and the *Dsa'carii* have remained in close contact through the original pair of pools created by the four Frostspire diplomats. Even as we speak, a joint work between elves and dwarves is taking place in the east, just beyond our northern borders. They are attempting to create the much needed arcanite in order to forge the required components that will be needed to bring everyone into contact with each other. Would this be something that Lorenth would desire?"

Arimas looked into the faces of his friends beside him before turning back to face the druid. "While I have no understanding of this arcanite or of the process by which you plan on creating this unique device, the notion of being able to coordinate communications instantly between man and elf, dragon and dwarf, is remarkable and would be a strategically sound benefit to all. We would be honored to have one of these pools created here in Lorenth. The main council chambers below would be the perfect location, I would wager."

Tavendia nodded in response before speaking again. "My second reason for coming is to inform you that the council of nine requests your presence, along with that of the Matriarch, to better learn of your ways as they are prepared to enlighten you on our ways. While I realize that only Farin was intending on accompanying me back into the *Illu'Dar* perhaps you may wish to consider joining us."

"This is an honor that I have no hesitation in accepting, Lady Tavendia. Once again I find myself at a loss for words at the many kindnesses that the elves have been willing to bestow upon us. My only regret is that it appears the humans are the only recipients in this exchange, and I long to be able to give something back in return to show the extent of our appreciation."

"You fail to consider what you have already offered not only the elven nation, but to all the fae races—you offer hope, which even now is growing within the womb of a queen. You offer the greatest gift ever to be offered—restoration to the balance."

Arimas, his trusted four, his inquisitor, and the elven druid continued to share ideas and conversation about the reflecting pools, among other things. Eventually the conversations turned toward the ever increasing threat of the shadow that was growing in the south, where Dean undoubtedly was planning his next move. Arimas had requested permission to bring his four closest paladins with him to Avalide to possibly learn from the elves as well, which Tavendia immediately agreed to.

Arimas would need to brief his remaining paladins on the upcoming travel plans and delegate command for the days that he would be absent from Lorenth. Tavendia had only just arrived as well, and a day or two of rest before traveling again would likely be appreciated so Farin suggested that tomorrow be used to rest and administrate the details in order to leave on the following morning to begin their three day journey to the *Illu'Dar.* All those present saw the practicality of this idea and the decision was finalized.

Arimas excused himself for the evening. Verona had still been experiencing her miserable mornings because of the pregnancy and now that she was a few months along, her body was showing signs of her blessed condition. It made Arimas treasure even more the time he spent with his wife. Not even matters of state could keep him from her. The four paladins then bid the inquisitor and the elven ambassador a pleasant evening as they left the hall of kings for home, leaving Farin and Tavendia alone again.

"My new chambers used to be the former seneschal chambers and you are more than welcome to stay with me there. I took the liberty of remodeling an adjacent room as an ambassador suite, knowing that as Inquisitor, the duty would fall to me to ensure all ambassadors to Lorenth rest in comfort."

"Well thought out indeed Farin. Are you tired already?"

"Not particularly. Was there something else that you wanted to do tonight?"

"Might we go to the temple? I am eager to look upon this orb of amber flame again. Since Arimas was overtaken by the spirit of Deimar I confess that I felt somewhat unworthy of being in the presence of a Creator spirit. Understanding more and more about the character of Deimar, I believe him to be a benevolent deity, full of patience and concern. I would like to see his orb once again, to sit within his presence and observe the flame in its constant flux."

"Then let us venture there together and sit in peace for a time."

Tavendia and Farin made their way out of the hall of kings, back down through the lower floor of the fortress and out to the courtyard once more. The sun had completely set as all around the upper and lower city torch lights were set alight by the citizens.

The night was clear and the cool winter air crisp as the two made their way toward the temple.

Farin had made sure to grab his heavier outer robes in preparation for the night chill but Tavendia, only in her thin silk robes, was unaffected by the cold in the air. A mistress of earth and nature... master of herself and of the corporeal realm... a vision of such incredible beauty... and an intellect as sharp as her personality was gentle. Farin sighed and then forced himself to think about other things as Tavendia's skin began to flush. Each of them were now able to sense the inner workings of each other's mind and such intimacy was uncomfortable when shared between two people who had resolved to be professional associates at the least, and close friends at best. While Farin found her ability to suppress her feelings with an almost impersonal-like ease admirable, he struggled to understand her reasons behind her decision.

The two arrived at the temple where several citizens were gathered to pray. Some were humming an oddly pleasant tune; others were kneeling in reverence before the orb of amber flame set upon the altar. Tavendia became oblivious to everything else around her as she set her eyes upon the burning orb once more. Farin remained near the back of the temple as Tavendia began walking slowly toward the dancing globe of fire. His eyes never left her—except when one of the citizens bowed on his way out, wishing the inquisitor a pleasant evening.

Tavendia approached the orb, her eyes transfixed on the depth of the power that was contained within. Her awareness began to extend around the room. Some people came to worship, some to seek guidance, and others still presented themselves in front of the holy fire in hopes that the sleeping deity whose spirit was partially contained here would heal them of a silent illness or deliver them from emotional pain.

Tavendia opened up her mind toward the orb as she found a seat a few paces away from its amber radiance. At first the orb's emanations felt like residual energy, almost like a signature essence of what had been. The arcanists within the Ætheron often experienced a similar residual effect when tampering with large amounts of elemental energy. The healers within the Æthanon experienced this phenomenon to a far lesser degree, but Tavendia remembered her mother and even Aaira speaking about something like a residual essence that would surround the benefactor of large quantities of healing. It was very likely that Farin would have had a residual essence after being brought back from the brink of the shadow. This was something she would look into when they returned to Avalide.

The more she quieted her spirit and cast her focus upon the orb the greater the sense of peace within her began to grow until she sensed several subtle alterations within the living flame. She subconsciously began to cant her head slightly to the right as she witnessed the soft amber flame flicker into shades of red and then into a bright white. The voice that echoed in her mind took her completely by surprise.

"Daughter of Ethoni, you seek answers to that which is hidden from thought and time. You already have the insight of my brother and with it you have done well to preserve the balance inasmuch as you have tried to understand it. Stand fast dear one for the creations of Sarik are no longer under his control and a new master has arisen to command the shadow as the shadow will eventually command him. My power is limited but the strength and fervency of my chosen will force destiny to collide with possibility. Go in peace daughter and stay your heart against the sorrow that shall soon consume you."

"Tavendia!" shouted Farin as her sudden collapse near the orb of amber flame prompted him to quick reaction. The few citizens who still were deep in prayer gasped when they heard the inquisitor shout and moved quickly out of the way as he leapt toward where the elven druid was now sprawled, across the crimson carpeted stairs that led up to the altar where the flame rested. Farin swept her up into his arms as his hand felt her forehead and neck for signs of life. Calm began to wash over him as he noticed that she was still breathing. Within a few short moments, she opened her eyes and found the concerned gaze of the Lorenth Inquisitor searching her features. She instinctively extended her hand to caress his cheek as two of her fingers crossed his lips.

"I am sorry that I frightened you Farin. Please, help me up." Farin, unsure of her strength, acquiesced and assisted Tavendia back to her feet. Several of the worshipers continued to look on—

some with simple curiosity and others with genuine concern. Tavendia leaned close to Farin and whispered that she would like to leave now to return to the inquisitor chambers where she could gather her thoughts better.

They refrained from speaking until Farin's chamber steward had escorted him and Tavendia to the ambassador suite within the inquisitor's manor. While his former covenal estate had several staff to tend to general matters, Farin was not used to having a personal servant, and despite his initial discomfort, he had come to greatly appreciate the luxury of entering a room and finding a fire already struck in the hearth. The steward offered to draw a warm bath for either the inquisitor or his guest, but Farin politely declined, dismissing the steward for the evening. He had been so busy recently with Arimas and his own day-to-day agenda that he still had not made the effort to even learn his servant's first name or to acquaint himself with the good man. He would definitely need to act on that quickly for service abused was not a practice he condoned.

Tavendia looked over the well decorated chamber with obvious approval.

"This is certainly more... human, than your old place Farin," she said with a teasing grin. Farin only laughed as he nonchalantly mentioned that Arimas was forced to hire him a decorator as he had little ability in that area. A sudden memory crossed his mind as he ventured over to his desk and reached beneath the hidden panel in his drawer to reveal his dream journal. He looked back to Tavendia as he produced the leather-bound book closed with a simple gray ribbon.

"What is that?"

"I will show you this after. If you still wanted to share what had happened in the temple then please go ahead and share. I will leave this with you tonight to peruse after we say goodnight."

"You tease me Farin, and I am not used to this feeling of impatience," Tavendia smiled again as she gathered her composure. "But I suppose I can wait. The elders of the council would be ashamed to hear that an elf was impatient—you are starting to affect me Farin..."

Farin slid away from Tavendia before his laughter consumed him and stepped into the kitchen area of the suite, where his servant had thoughtfully prepared a pot of hot water for his evening tea. He decided to prepare a second cup of tea for Tavendia and after he let it steep for several minutes, he added a touch of honey and presented the aromatic beverage to his elven guest. She inhaled the pleasing vapors.

"What is this Farin? Now you really are beginning to intrigue me."

"We call it tea. It is a simple collection of specific leaves and herbs that are set in hot water. The heat leeches the flavor into the liquid. Then we sweeten the concoction with a touch of honey, but you must drink it slowly because it is very hot."

"That much is evident Farin, but I thank you for stating the obvious," Tavendia retorted wryly. Farin seated himself near the elf and together they sipped from their mugs in silence. "This is quite pleasant indeed... thank you Farin," Tavendia eventually said.

"You are most welcome. Now, what about the events in the temple?"

Tavendia took another sip of her tea before shifting her position slightly to become more comfortable. "I spoke with Deimar from within the orb of fire."

"And..."

Tavendia was enjoying this game of impatience now that she was in a position to do the teasing. She grinned while taking another slow and prolonged sip of her tea, watching impatience spread over Farin's face. Finally, she drew breath to speak.

"What he had to say was difficult to understand. He said so much with so few words and once he went silent, I felt terribly alone and even slightly fearful. He mentioned that I would encounter terrible sorrow very soon and that I was to guard my heart against it. He also implied that all of the elven research concerning the balance and how it works may not be completely accurate—that in particular troubles me greatly."

"You are still hiding something about what was said, and what was not said."

Tavendia shook her head slowly. "I think I finally understand how the other humans feel when some of us can hear their thoughts as if they were spoken words. I cannot hide things from you now, Farin. That is both liberating and restricting."

"I could pretend that I do not know these things if you like..."

"Oh, stop. That would result in deceit. Deimar simply told me more about the workings of the Seed of Corruption. He mentioned that the creations of Sarik had found a new master. This is troublesome, for the only thing that Sarik created was death, followed by unlife after death, which was the abomination that Deimar and Ethoni sought to quench which shattered the balance in the beginning."

"That *is* unsettling. If there were creations of Sarik, where are they living now? Have you ever encountered these creatures before?"

"No, and from how they sound, I would not wish to."

"Well that satisfies what you did not say, but what else were you tempted to withhold from me?"

"Oh Farin... fine! Deimar mentioned that I would not only encounter great sorrow, but that I would be consumed by it. Whether or not the guarding of my heart will render myself immune from this consuming sorrow I do not yet understand... but I have never been led by my emotions in anything, and I find it hard to believe that such a phenomenon could actually occur now."

Farin finished the last of his tea just as Tavendia had. He removed the empty cups and returned them to the kitchen area before returning to Tavendia in front of the fire. Farin could sense the thick heaviness of emotion that Tavendia was trying hard to restrain. Farin knelt beside her, opened his arms and pulled the elf close to him in a comforting embrace. Tavendia, though initially reluctant to welcome Farin's touch, soon lost hold of her emotions, and, wrapping her arms around him, began to cry into his shoulder as all her pent up feelings burst forth. Farin simply held the distraught druid and let her weep her tears until, gradually, her sobs waned.

"Human expressions are so odd, Farin," Tavendia finally spoke. "Elves seldom touch each other like this and while I find it foreign, I also find your presence to be a great comfort." The elf eased her way out from his arms as she shyly wiped the last of her tears from her eyes.

"I think you need to stop analyzing everything, Tavendia. A hug is simply a way to show concern and comfort to someone we care about. I could discern the weariness of your spirit and it pains me to see you in such a state."

Tavendia marveled at this human before her as she smiled again and shakily recommended that they get some sleep before tomorrow. They had one more day to enjoy each other's presence and company before they set out for the elven forest with Arimas and his four paladins. Tavendia hoped Cheyandra would not be displeased with her initiative in this matter but like Farin was a man of noble heart and sound mind, she saw the same strengths in Arimas and his selected paladins.

Tavendia walked with Farin to the door of her suite. She lightly touched his forearm, conveying a hundred different things in that one small gesture, before retreating behind the door of her room. Farin stood a moment just where she left him before sighing to himself. He slowly and reluctantly returned to his own room and crawled into his large and lonely bed once more.

As Farin lay awake, pondering the events of the day and lingering over his thoughts of the beautiful elf that sent his spirit spiraling with confusion between love and friendship, possibilities and impossibilities, Tavendia wept more tears as once again her choices regarding this one human man frustrated her and led her to more unanswered questions.

XXIX

They all felt the cold in a deep and personal way that night as the eleven dragons and the lone blue drake made their way over the southern border of Lorenth to where the great sea awaited them. Many were surprised to see such progress being made on the sections of wall being built across the country side that would eventually be joined together to create the border of stone that Arimas envisioned. Once they had left the bustling life of the human lands, early in the evening just as the sun was setting, it was only a short while before the vast expanse of water confronted them. Though Zharra had seen this expanse of water before with her projected vision, it had been nothing like how it was now, seeing it for real. The opposing shore was beyond the horizon and with the setting sun casting long shadows upon the face of the water a surreal emptiness began to impress upon them.

For several hours the group continued their flight in silence while inside each of them the feeling of oppression began to grow the closer they got to their destination. It wasn't until the steady night breeze suddenly stopped passing over the waters that the first threads of anxiety began to form among the dragons. No one broke the unnatural silence until Dalaria began to speak to everyone in the *Skarlagnos.*

"What you all are feeling is not natural. We have crossed a threshold into the realm of the unknown. We must be vigilant and,

above all, we must stay together. Death surrounds this place. Even the waters here appear devoid of life as if the corruption has infected even that which lies beneath the waters. For now we fly to the shore where hopefully by morning the shadows of the night will not cling so heavily to us. Courage everyone!"

Dalaria's words sparked their fading hope as each of them, Valkyyrak and Sargeron included, checked themselves and forced the empty thoughts out from their minds while the dark and lonely night continued on. As they continued on their south-easterly course across the sea, Dalaria occasionally led the group up and over the dark cloud cover to partially escape the enclosed feeling that was continuously gnawing at each of them.

The wind never did return. The empty blackness pressed on throughout the night until finally the long awaited rays of the morning sun began to crest over the horizon revealing a shore line dotted with what appeared to be a moderately sized forest. The dragons gradually began to descend, altering their flight path as they approached the land, being careful to maintain a low profile while flying over the dense wood. According to the memories of Zharra, the new human settlement was not far now and within several minutes she thought they would begin to see signs of life in the area.

Ormaryn was known around the Icecrowns as the stone dragon, mostly for his dusky colored scales but also his uncanny ability to nearly vanish when he settled against the side of any mountain. Equally as savage in appearance as Sargeron, Ormaryn had four horns that protruded out from the back of his head before they eventually began to curl toward the front of his face in a symmetrical arrangement. His face had several smaller spines and barbs all over including a slight deviation in his muzzle which allowed two of his larger teeth to protrude over his lower jaw further adding to his menacing appearance. It was Ormaryn who first noticed the ring of death within the forest far to their right.

"I believe that may explain this overwhelming sense of death," he stated aloud.

The others followed the direction of his gaze, and corrected their course slightly while ascending to get a better view of this odd ring of dead trees nestled within a thriving and as yet untouched forest.

As they flew over the dead circle Trakkenor and Sargeron emitted a chorus of low growls when a sudden pain extended deep into their spiritual beings. Both being black dragons and exceptionally adept with the spiritual realm, they were more sensitive than the others to the nature of the evil that was below them. The rest of the dragons, sensitive to the discomfort of the blacks, increased their speed and passed over the area as quickly as they could. No member of the party was successful in getting a close look at the ground within the dead circle, but the mystery of it would have to wait. No one wanted to travel back over that place again.

Like Zharra predicted, within several minutes the dragons began to notice the typical signs of human life in the area. Industrialization and destruction of the natural balance of life permeated the area and the dragons quickly began to ascend even higher so as not to attract undue attention from the humans as they flew overhead. Sargeron marveled at the quick work these industrious exiles were making of both the terrain and their new settlement, which was already beginning to look impressive with its stone foundations measuring out its boundaries.

A fine dust was rising in the south, likely from all the workers excavating the large amount of stone needed for all their structures in the surrounding area. Dotting the land were several fields similar to those in the Lorenth area that Nyssia had explained were growing wheat, a plant of sorts that the humans could grind into a substance to make food out of. The collection of dragons passed by what appeared to be the beginnings of the main city structure, unfinished save for one lone tower that stood completed. Circling the tower a high distance from the ground was a platform that Nyssia, with her excellent vision, cautioned held an object that might be a weapon of sorts. No sooner had she expressed this concern, though, when Vaelis suddenly cried out in anguish as she looked to the ground below and saw the broken body of her younger brother being completely ravaged by the humans. Dalaria broke into tears as she then saw what her daughter saw, while Valkyyrak, moved beyond rage and well past grief, unleashed a roar of such strength and anger that the miniscule creatures below cowered in fear.

It was Nyssia and Zharra that held them together this morning, cautioning the distraught dragons about intervening. These humans had already proven capable of slaying one of their own and retaliation in blind rage was not the way to vindicate this atrocity. The hard stare from Valkyyrak made Nyssia swallow in a sudden flush of fear which plainly crossed her face. Realizing what his glance had done to the elven *Azurak*, Valkyyrak softened his gaze. He yielded to the counsel of Nyssia and his daughter, leading the eleven dragons and the blue drake on their path beyond the human area in search of Xarethia and the rest of their kin.

While the heat in this region was considered stifling by the standards of the Icecrown dragons and the *Dsa'carii* elf, the heat was not what really bothered them. Zharra had begun using her senses as soon as they began flying over the great sea, when the wind had vanished without cause. She had seen the taint then though it had not been nearly as strong as it was now, as she noted that the taint had spread over the last few months. The entire human area was bathed in it as it slowly began to creep farther north toward the small forests on its eventual path toward the lands of Lorenth. Nagendra and Nostrimus, the two green dragons in the group, tried extending their senses to find their sister and daughter yet neither of them could detect any sign of Xarethia.

The small band of dragons remained together the entire time in order to protect each other from potential harm. While this was well and good, it dramatically slowed their efforts to locate the dragons thought to be in the area for they chose not to separate to scout the terrain more efficiently. Zharra took the lead at this point as she began to hone in on the location that she remembered from her projections. As they neared the general area, their search was ended as they spotted two medium-sized red dragons resting atop what appeared to be an entrance to an underground lair burrowed into the smaller stone hills behind them. The red female took everyone by surprise for no one recognized her at all but the red male that stood by her side was none other than the youngest son of Manaseth and Sirrusa, Glauron.

Zharra had told the others about the living taint before but no one could fully appreciate the effects of it until they all noticed the vile blackness that covered the surface of the red dragons below. Their normal vision revealed nothing out of the ordinary as the eleven made their approach toward the two waiting dragons.

Zharra had warned them all to maintain their distance as proximity to the taint would inevitably draw its attention and could compromise all of the Icecrown dragons if they were not careful. They all landed many paces away from the two reds while Nyssia began to study the area with her own senses, noting something that perhaps the dragons had failed to notice. The taint was not uniform. It did not blanket the entire area but it swarmed around objects of life. It clung to the red dragons, the low-lying shrubs in the dry and scorched earth that characterized the barren wastes, and gathered around the smaller animals, serpents, and insects native to the region.

While elves were never characterized by the emotions of fear, even Nyssia could feel something akin to that human emotion rising in her throat and deep within the pit of her stomach as her mind began to spin with the possibilities of a sentient corruptive essence that was beginning to consume all life, regardless of shape or form.

Vaanadu, the father of Manaseth, Glauron's father, was first to speak to the red male. Vaanadu could see the oppression that haunted Glauron's eyes. An overwhelming sense of compassion began to build within him for his descendant who had submitted himself to an existence of never-ending battle with an evil more ancient that Valkyyrak and Sargeron.

"Glauron, blood of my blood, your presence has been missed among the Icecrowns and we cannot live in silence any longer. We have come to open communication once more and to ensure that everyone here knows that there is still a home among the Icecrowns for any who are exhausted of battling the vile taint that wreaks havoc in these lands."

"The hour of your coming is late, Vaanadu, for this taint, though not able to corrupt us directly, has torn apart the unity of us all and we are cursed as a result of our choices to follow Karros. We have feasted on human and dwarven flesh and found it appealing.

We have begun to assert ourselves as the superior hunter in these lands and we have amassed hordes of treasures taken from the broken bodies of the well-armed adversaries who have begun to regularly supplement our diets. While part of us wants to mourn for the debasement that we have indulged in, the greater part of us relishes in the surge of life that courses through us every time we hunt our prey. They are improving their defenses and devising ways to repel our attacks. It is only a matter of time before one of us will fall beneath their ingenuity."

"One has already fallen, Glauron, and you shame his memory by leaving his body to be ravaged by the humans." Valkyyrak spoke with a deep sense of regret and responsibility in his authoritative voice as Glauron and the other red female looked visibly shaken at the news.

"Who..." the gentle spoken female could not even finish the phrase before she hung her head in sorrow. For reasons yet unknown by the others, this red female seemed more segregated from the taint, as if she had a greater resolve and higher tolerance of the evil and its consuming oppression.

"Our son, Karros, is dead. He lies broken before the tower of the humans where they have been systematically harvesting his scales and flesh, talons and horns for uses we cannot fathom and we cannot stomach." Dalaria's normally soothing voice dripped with anger and inner turmoil as she fixed her piercing eyes upon the much younger red male who seemed to shift between genuine sorrow and subtle defiance.

Vaelis took a step forward as Glauron once again looked up. "Glauron, Nostrimus and I have lost two of our own to this place. Have you no idea where Xarethia is? And what of our youngest son Skoren, or even Vuhla?"

"Skoren has turned against us all, as did Vuhla much earlier. We have not heard or seen signs of the amethyst wailer for years now, but Skoren was lost to us only recently as his thirst for human and dwarven flesh has taken his mind. He flew farther southwest, toward the isle of mist that we believe to be the source of this evil."

The younger red female then began to speak. "Mother left father several days ago, shortly after he fell to hunting the humans for sport and trophies, rather than for food. Once mother fled east with the two youngest of my kin, father lost himself in a blind rage. It is likely that he summoned his rage against the human establishment and fell beneath their new weaponry."

Vasuni shifted his weight slightly before addressing the female who claimed to be the daughter of Karros and Xarethia. "There was a time when your father and I were nearly as close as brothers. In all the years that you have been down here, did he never speak of the Icecrowns or of us—the rest of your kin?"

"There was no need to burden the younger ones with old knowledge, Vasuni," Glauron stated with a noticeable amount of disdain in his voice. "We left to forge a new destiny and what myself, Skoren, Xarethia, Karros and Vuhla knew of the Icecrowns was left to pass on as memory only. Karros thought that such wisdom would confuse the younger ones and would only undermine his vision of creating a separate realm of dragons, free from the old ideals and free to develop as fate would have us develop and not as Valkyyrak would see us develop."

"Then it is my pride that has caused much of this turmoil." Regret dripped from every word that left the mouth of Valkyyrak as he looked hard and long into the eyes of Glauron and the younger red female. "I would ask that you consider accepting an apology from me—Karros never expressed his lack of satisfaction with any of the ideals that we collectively agreed upon generations ago. The Icecrowns function as it has for years because of the choices many of the elders and the ancients decided upon. That being said, I can understand how my son felt lost among the others. I failed to understand my son better and this knowledge has become a burden that I will carry forever."

The red female was wrestling with her thoughts as Dalaria began to extend her own toward her. The moment her thoughts penetrated the red female a painful backlash hit the blue ancient as the corruption severed the probing almost instantly, although not before revealing that the red female had fragments of confused thoughts about the past, present, and future—she was a guide but she did not understand it. When Dalaria lurched back in pain after the backlash, Zharra began to notice the taint creeping toward Dalaria. A short burst of flame reduced it to ash which startled many of the others who were not actively watching the taint advance upon their position.

"Your efforts only delay the inevitable advance of the taint, Zharra. Eventually you stop caring about the advance and then you tolerate its stifling presence until you stop caring altogether." Sargeron was growing impatient with the complete disregard that Glauron was showing toward the taint. The younger red female had been staring at Dalaria since she recoiled from the backlash until she finally spoke up.

"What did you attempt to do? For a moment I thought I felt you in my mind. How are such things possible?"

"Stay out of her mind, Dalaria! You are not welcome to push your ways upon us after we have chosen—"

"Silence Glauron!" Valkyyrak seemed to almost swell in size and ferocity as even the disrespectful red took pause, obviously remembering now just how powerful Valkyyrak was. "Were you not our kin, I would have tolerated even less of your insolence. It was never the Icecrowns that abandoned you, but you that abandoned us. We seek to repair the lost relationships and we *will* share those things that you have neglected to pass on to our descendants."

Dalaria could see a retort beginning to form on Glauron's lips but luckily for him, he chose to keep those words to himself. The ancient blue dragon turned her attentions back toward the red female.

"I know you see things that you do not understand. You have visions of what once was, of things that are, and of things that may yet happen though recently those visions have changed and they do not speak into your mind like they once did. You are a guide, young one. You are among the rarest of dragons. My sister, Fyysara, was the original guide until recent events took her spirit away from us and now her broken body lies atop the frozen lake nestled within the Icecrowns to commemorate her life and her wisdom. Her daughter Sycaris is now the guide and aside from her, there has not been another red female dragon... until you.

"There are many things that you do not understand, for you have been denied the opportunity to learn from your elders as is the practice within the Icecrowns. Dragons are a magical race of fae creatures each with differing abilities according to the color of our scales. I was simply extending my thoughts into your mind to discern the nature of the troubled look that was upon your face—it is a small talent that many of us have and it happens instinctively with several of us."

"I would like to learn more about this, but life with this taint is the only life that I know. Inside I see memories of things I do not understand and certainly have not seen before. I know your face, Dalaria, though I have never seen you before. In fact, everyone here is somehow familiar. But Father and Mother raised all of us to be fighters, self-sustainers, and independent. I would be free of this oppression more for my son Zyrre, but I could never leave my mate as easily as mother left father."

As the still unnamed red female shared her thoughts with Dalaria, Zharra leaned close to Vaanadu and began whispering softly into his ear. She realized the gesture was not necessary but part of her wanted to avoid using magic around the presence of this taint. Even the use of the *Skarlagnos* gave her pause for she did not fully understand how the taint advanced, although use of magic certainly was a sound theory. Vaanadu nodded and smiled when Zharra had finished as he slowly began to approach the two reds.

Glauron was preoccupied, busy struggling with his prideful desire to rage at the interlopers from his past, but the female noticed the advancing red elder and held a curious look in her eyes which changed into sheer terror as the elder red focused his sight on the taint that was covering the two reds and unleashed a sustained blast of dragon fire across them.

Sargeron nearly leapt toward his son but Dalaria stopped him as she began to understand what Zharra must have whispered to him. Vaanadu extinguished his flame as soon as he completed his pass over the pair but the nearby shrubs continued to burn within the small patches of charred ground. Zharra smiled as her senses revealed no hint of the taint upon the dragons and no sign of damage from the exposure to the dragon flame, confirming her long held, but barely tested theory about the dragon's immunity to some, if not all, forms of magic.

Zharra then stepped forward to offer an explanation to the stunned red dragons and the numerous Icecrown dragons looking on with a mixture of disbelief and curiosity.

"I do not apologize for how I asked Vaanadu to act. While we may all agree that this taint cannot corrupt us, which is something I found rather odd to conceive at first, we can all agree that this taint is relentless in its quest to break our will and oppress our thoughts. It was for that reason alone that I wanted Vaanadu to rid them of this taint for a time, at least until we have had a chance to speak with each other in honesty, without the influence of this taint clouding the minds of our red brother and sister before us. I do not think for a moment that this taint will not seek them out again, which it likely is doing this very moment now that the hold has been severed. As for use of dragon fire upon another dragon… it was a theory that I had wanted to test for some time since I first spoke with Karros about this natural immunity that he maintained we had from this taint."

"How could you even attempt such a thing simply to test a theory, Zharra? Even that seems a bit beyond you," Valkyrrak scolded.

"Father, you must know me better than that. I had conducted my own tests before. I studied the rapid decay of Fyysara and could not understand how the corruption of death could be so accelerated with the dragons upon their death. In life, Karros maintained that the corruption was rendered harmless to him. I tested my own dragon fire on myself and I found that I could not harm myself with my own flame—it never fully made contact with my scales. I asked Vaanadu once to bath my foreleg in his own mighty flame. He refused me for a time until I eventually convinced him of my theories, proving once again through his efforts that I was immune from dragon fire.

"My final test was little sister Nyssia. A skilled ice mage in her own right, I pleaded with her to attempt to encase me in ice or cast projectiles of frost at me. When she attempted to locate me with her elemental mastery to begin the channeling, she could not detect me, almost as if I was immune from the elemental powers that would enable her to use its force against me. She even blindly cast her ice shards in my general area, and like the dragon fire, every shard that nearly hit its mark simply dissipated before it struck. I cannot explain it in any other way other than saying that dragons are naturally immune to the effects of magic because we are in essence, birthed of magic. Once that link to the planes of magic is severed, our bodies fall into pure corruption quickly and completely."

Glauron's features appeared somehow softer and his expression more sincere since being released from the effects of the taint. He offered a gentle smile to his mate before turning toward Valkyyrak.

"Valkyyrak… and the rest of you… forgive me. First, I would offer up our condolences to you Sargeron. Never would I have thought to live in a time when Fyysara would not be around to lead and guide. Her death is a loss to us all. And second, while I may enjoy this respite from the effects of this cursed taint, I know that it will consume us again before the day is out. There is no escape. Its advance is sure and steady and soon all of the human lands will be covered in it. There is a great evil off the coast that we cannot see but that we can feel night after night as the shadow stirs."

"Then return with us back to the Icecrowns, Glauron," pleaded Nagendra. "The wisdom of the elves and the dwarves is being shared with the dragons as even the humans of Lorenth have begun to ally themselves with us. The Lightbringer is among us, and we have been charged with his protection so that he may face the corruption at the appointed time. There is a purpose for you among us, if you will only choose life over this death that surrounds this place."

Glauron looked into the eyes of his young mate which burned with desire to be free of this place. Glauron remembered the fates of Skoren, Vuhla, and even Karros—the visionary of their freedom who had died at the hands of a lesser race.

"I never thought forgiveness and acceptance could be extended to us once more. Karros made us believe that our choices had forever severed our ties with the summit. After years of no contact with the Icecrowns, believing his rationale became easier and easier. If we are to be free of this taint then let us leave this forsaken place with haste and fly before all of us become savages lost under its slow eroding spell."

Melandra smiled and quickly ducked into her lair to retrieve young Zyrre who was not quite as large as the young Criosys, one of the youngest dragons within the Icecrowns. The filth of the taint was all over the young dragon that followed his mother sleepily out from the lair, and already several traces of the taint were beginning to crawl back on Melandra. Glauron used the same technique that Vaanadu had demonstrated and quickly seared the taint from both his mate and his son before Sargeron and Trakkenor roared to the skies in recognition of the reuniting of part of their kin. While the issues of the others were yet to be discussed, the aggressive nature of this taint brought a quick conclusion to their scouting expedition as the Icecrown dragons, with Glauron, Melandra, Zyrre and Nyssia following in their wake, adjusted their course for the long flight back to the north, away from the taint and bearing news of great importance to Lorenth as well as to their own kind... the grave news of another dragon now passed into memory.

* * *

Dean was unreasonably angry as he stalked through the unexplored forest that had been beckoning to him since his arrival in the lands of the exiles. That same sensation of losing control over himself was happening more and more often and a small part of him was beginning to fear what would happen if he ever did lose complete control. Yet, the sense of exhilaration and life that he was experiencing alongside that loss of control was intoxicating— never had he ever wielded such potential, and the possibilities of more power enticed him to abandon his own cautions and follow his inner awareness blindly.

He walked on foot throughout the afternoon and now well into the evening before finally reaching the edge of the forest to the northwest of Innin Hold. He could hear the sounds of the sea licking the coastline off in the distance, yet there still was no breeze to be felt.

The trip would have been so much faster had Dean taken his mount, but the former seneschal had not been in the best frame of mind when he had stormed away from the surrounding exiles who had just watched their ferocious leader char one of his own in anger. All because of that blasted wyrm! Everyone wanted something from the carcass, whether it was the hardened scales for Karl, huge slabs of flesh for the newly appointed butcher, Brady Adamar, or the organs and other oddities for Kaylee and Vincent to experiment with for medicinal or scientific purposes. No one could have guessed that the wyrm would begin rapidly decomposing, yet Dean was outraged with the failure to harvest more of the rare beast and subsequently had set flame to the closest laborer he saw.

Even his command staff took pause when they saw what Dean did to the laborer whose blackened husk began to crumble into dust beside the swiftly deteriorating bronze wyrm. Only several days had passed yet Brady could not salvage any more meat from the beast and the once hardened bronze scales were now softening and becoming dull in color. What added to the confusion was the fact that whatever was removed from the dead beast did not decompose like the rest, but was somehow preserved once it was taken away from whatever magic was destroying the magnificent creature.

Dean did not even bother to check with his industry leaders as to their new inventory numbers after the initial harvest from the wyrm. After reducing his laborer to a husk he basked in the glorious infusion of power that followed every time he killed something with this ability of his. It was only after that sensation started to wane that he noticed the trepidation on the faces of his citizens and even some of his soldiers. He regained control of himself long enough to fully appreciate what he had done and then stormed out of the gathering, heading toward the northwest almost automatically in his quest to shake off this feeling that nearly resembled remorse.

What was happening to him? He was never sorry for his actions. He tried to justify his actions by telling himself that perhaps a small demonstration of his power would only increase his command presence. No one would dare question the authority of Dean now. He was rapidly becoming more than a man; he was a force of nature, something to be reckoned with—something that inspired fear and awe. Dean's feet continued carrying him toward the northwest as his steady stream of self-aggrandizement gradually began to bolster his uncharacteristically flagging ego.

Throughout his long walk through then night, the former seneschal one again mused on his recent failures in Lorenth: his plots that were thwarted; his assassins that were slain; and even those loyal followers implanted all over Lorenth, now either exiled or slain. And, he thought about Arimas, the hated priest-king, and the man's own rumored new abilities. Arimas was a fool. If he had half the mind and a quarter of the courage that Dean did himself did, he would have shot the traitorous seneschal where he stood that final meeting. For, in time, Lorenth would be laid open to its enemies, and it would be then that Dean would unleash his maelstrom of vengeance, a horror such that Arimas had never before seen. And then, Dean would look into the eyes of his former ruler and watch in delight as the broken ruler burned from within.

Like a team of horses being driven without a visible rider, Dean plodded along throughout the night until he finally came across the forest, its silhouette visible in the predawn sky. The awareness was jubilant within him as he set foot within the forest that immediately felt different from any wooded area he had ever been in. The trees felt old, as if nestled within their very bark were memories of a forgotten age and of deeds done before time began. Dean's pace quickened.

Part of him again felt that subtle caution. Perhaps he should not be in this place, at this time. But, ever since that night when he commanded the Lorenthian scout's blood to boil while also feeling the observing presence of the elf at the outer reach of his own awareness, something had been leading him here. The inner cauldron that smoldered like hot metal was growing beyond his control and he could almost taste his destiny, and somewhere within these trees Dean felt sure he would find his answer. He continued his search, stepping over fallen trees and paying no attention to whatever wildlife might be lurking in the shadows of the early morning until at last he came across a single tree, an earthen object that arrested his attention immediately and started his senses screaming in recognition.

Dean stared in open amazement. Shorter than everything else in the forest, the tree, as if defying all reason, was cloaked in ash-colored bark, and covered with twisted, curling branches. No leaves at all were seen upon what looked to be a hold-over from ancient times, long dead... yet, from deep within its cancerous surface Dean could almost hear the sounds of breathing. The dead tree was alive somehow, Dean realized, his heart racing. Whispers of shadows began to cloud his mind as his senses revealed a gateway hidden beyond the tree and far from the sight of men. Lost to himself, Dean continued to approach the dead tree until he stood in front of its gnarled surface at last. The bark of its trunk began to splinter and crack until it peeled back to reveal something that closely resembled an apple growing within the center of the tree. The more he studied this apple the more he realized that it was in true form, a seed—a seed that would unlock the potential within. All he needed to do now was to reach his hand out, to take this seed into his grasp, and to embrace the flood of knowledge and power that would alter his destiny.

The intensity of the shadows began to grow as Dean's eyes suddenly took in the putrid stream of a thousand lost souls drifting from the dead tree now completely split in two. The broken form began to calcify before his eyes as if the rising of the sun were somehow weakening it, and the cries of the dead clawed at him, screaming at him to do what he was meant to do. Without any further thought, Dean reached out his hand and folded it around the seed within the dead tree, clutching it in his palm. He held it for only a moment before the apple seed withered in his grasp, releasing thin tendrils of black and violet that began to entwine around Dean's hand, his arm, and then his torso until they forced their way down his open mouth and throat. He could not even let out a scream as the foreign energy began to somehow merge with the awareness within his mind.

The invasive process was certainly not something anyone could relax under yet Dean forced himself to resist the instinctual urge to constrict his muscles. Instead, he tried to allow the awareness to lead and guide him, much as it had when he first attempted to resurrect the dead moth. His spirit began to awaken to something more incredible than anything he could have imagined. It was a glimpse of walking among the spirits of the damned and harnessing their power to fuel his immortality. The tendrils of violet and black energy continued to course through him until the remains of the dead tree began to crumble into the ground revealing a circle of stone—almost like a ritual altar vaguely familiar in his dreams from the past. Once the final traces of the tree were gone Dean arched his back and a wave of shadow burst from his being and traveled into the nearby trees, immediately causing them to wither and die. The dark energies that coursed over Dean lowered him to the ground as his conscious mind felt several large roots burst from the ground and enclose him. The inner awareness, continuously echoing its subtle commands to relax, began to express its pleasure in Dean's servitude as the large roots drew him into the cold earth.

* * *

"What do you mean, they're dead?" Commander Zorn paced around the command tent in the early afternoon heat as Dhax, the chief intelligence agent, concluded the delivery of his seemingly far-fetched report to the second-in-command. This was a morning of troubled news. While Dhax and Alic were trailing the wandering seneschal the night before, a host of dragons had passed over the encampment where the largest beast anyone had ever seen let out such a roar that the very earth rattled in protest. Erran was not sure what prevented their superior force from immediately descending upon the vulnerable humans but he was thankful nonetheless that they chose to fly past the area and leave the humans to nurse their fear.

"We always stalk in pairs. We always have, and we always will, in case events go ill for us like they did today. I cannot fully explain what happened this morning but Alic is now dead and what he managed to tell me before he withered and turned to ash in front of my own eyes indicates that the seneschal also perished in the event. Had I been any closer to Alic, I would have likely been consumed as well for every tree in the immediate area burst into shadows and withered into nothing The forest is cursed! Feel free to verify my story if you wish, but you may want to appoint a successor before you explore your curiosity. I've never ran from anything before today, but after seeing what I saw, I will never venture into that dead wood again."

The commander carefully weighed the news from the intelligence agent before responding. Innin Hold was starting to become a death sentence, not a new beginning. The citizens were torn between uncertainty and fear. The soldiers were even losing faith in the long held beliefs that the seneschal would lead them into victory and prosperity against the selfish and unrealistic expectations of Arimas. Some even began to voice their concerns that perhaps choosing exile was wrong and others even began to regret their choices to leave their lands and homes behind.

And now this... Erran knew that something would need to be done, and quickly, lest the loss of their leader led the citizens to truly lose heart. A revolt would not help matters now, as Arimas had sworn to kill any man or woman who ever returned to Lorenth after choosing to throw their lot in with the exiled seneschal.

Erran would act in accordance with the seneschal's original plan and would continue to work on the completion of Innin Hold as before. All the plans had been discussed at length many times and the engineers maintained all the schematics for the city proper. Erran's task now was to enforce discipline and try to restore confidence and order within the camp.

News of Dean's death spread throughout the settlement like wildfire, yet in its wake followed the commander and many other smaller units that had been briefed on the situation and commanded to deliver the same news to everyone across the industry camps and those working on Innin Hold itself. Dean's death was to be presented as 'unconfirmed' and the routine orders as established by the seneschal would be followed in his absence while Commander Erran Zorn handled the administrative control of the city in his stead. Erran also tried to rally the citizens and bolster their spirits. He challenged them to think on their accomplishments in the recent months and take pride in *their* city. Nothing could steal that pride from them and Erran made it clear that the initial vision of Dean's prosperity for all those who continued to make Innin Hold a reality would be carried out whether or not Dean came back to assume his command once more.

His efforts were moderately successful. Erran did not possess the same charisma and command presence that Dean emulated usually, until recent days that is, but Erran's heart was true and his conviction was clearly seen by those he spoke with. The mood in the camp began to settle back into a gentle rhythm and the work eventually began to pick up by the late afternoon. Erran had tasked several soldiers to rig up a team of horses and find a way to drag the rotting wyrm carcass from out of the camp area where its very presence was a testament to the brutality that Dean had unleashed upon one of his own followers. By the evening meal, they had succeeding in moving the carcass several leagues away from the encampment, choosing to bury the rapidly decomposing mass into Innin Lake where the sight would trouble no one again. Life then resumed its previous pace but in the northwest, a new and unseen shadow was forming. Rumors of the deadwoods began to filter through the camp as the forestry leaders immediately began to think of new locations for their precious and rare timber.

But the work continued as the shared vision of a complete and self-sufficient Innin Hold became more and more attainable as the nights grew into new days, and then into weeks, and then into several months while the unconfirmed death of Seneschal Dean became more and more confirmed in the hearts and minds of the people of Innin Hold.

XXX

Arcanite was the most intriguing material the Silverfist Clan had ever encountered. Rurok Amgar, several engineers, and a small handful of smelters—along with the four elves from both Avalide and Frostspire—admired the finished work of the arcanite castings and binders that had been amassed and organized into even stacks for transport. What was anticipated to only take weeks in reality consumed several months of trial and failure until at last the elves and the Silverfist prospector discovered an ideal combination of one stone worth of raw truesilver, an eighth-stone worth of sapphire and surprisingly, a sixteenth-stone worth of diamond.

The volatility of the diamond was discovered to be the missing ingredient for the mixture after weeks of endless failures resulted in the inability to fuse the materials together. Rurok stood in fascination as the four elves, now rather efficient in their application of elemental energies into the raw materials, wove their strands of magic into the ore and gems. Some of the attempts ended in violent reactions that were thankfully contained in the same magic shell that the elves were using to accomplish the fusion, while other attempts resulted in a tainted form of arcanite that was useless for anything and could not even be smelted back down to recover the base materials.

It was actually the druid, Rallegan Timberwood, who suggested the inclusion of diamond after the dwarves had run out of ideas.

The initial attempts with the diamond were some of the most volatile trials of all and had immediately cautioned the dwarf from using diamond in any other trials, but as with all things involving life, there was a balance. Rallegan suggested that perhaps there needed to be that same balance in the arcanite and the inclusion of a tiny amount of diamond with the sapphire might lead to the perfect harmony they were striving for. When the Æther energies coursed into the raw materials, all natural light began to be absorbed into the blue ore that glittered with the diamond and sapphire crystalline matrix until the end result was a dull, gray mass of transmuted material that appeared to be yet another failure until the elves looked to each other in amazement.

The ore was very difficult to work with. Difficult is a relative term, however, because once the elves began to suspend the ore in front of them, they used the immense powers of their mind to shape and work the larger mass of ore into a form similar to a hollow ring of dark metal. They then began to heat the metal through an elemental fire that likely burned hotter than even a dwarven forge. The finished result was the successful creation of one arcanite casting. The determined group continued the process until at last, eight complete sets of arcanite binders and castings sat in front of the Silverfist dwarves.

The dwarves also discovered that the left over arcanite that was not used for the reflection pool could be fashioned into ingots to be used at a later date. Though not nearly as attractive to look upon, the dwarves had a few ideas about how to use the dull gray arcanite ingots, knowing that the magical properties of the ore would make it exceptionally useful.

Baelanor left the others to admire their work and successes while he made arrangements to travel to Avalide to inform Frostspire that the work was completed. Avalide was much closer to the Silverfist battlekeep than Frostspire was and Baelanor loved visiting the warm forest city to admire the many differences in architecture and application of magic, so his choice to travel there was a natural one. The ice mage was exceptionally adept at shape shifting and was known around the Frostspire as being the mage who never did settle on any given travel form. He constantly experimented and tried different forms—even going so far as to create species that no one had ever seen and that Baelanor alone could imagine. Today he chose a form similar to his arctic cat form that he used a fair amount. He adjusted the fur colorations so that he could blend in better in the abundantly green surroundings and strengthened his feline legs for increased power and speed before dashing from the entrance of the Silverfist battlekeep and heading straight toward the northern border of the *Illu'Dar.*

The sprites and the guardians paid no attention to the large, dark-striped cat that streaked past them and headed deep into the forest, for deep within the fae mind rested an awareness of life, with a special sensitivity to other fae creatures. Baelanor leapt past several mistrunners on their regular patrols. The journey took most of the day and many mistrunners waved in acknowledgement as he swiftly ran. He also passed by one of the wardens who was engaged in idle conversation with some of the wildlife that also called the *Illu'Dar* home. As Baelanor approached the center of Avalide, he could hear the various whistling calls that were likely informing the others about his presence.

Evianna Windrunner was first to greet Baelanor in his cat form as he released the image and returned to his natural shape to offer a slight inclination of his head to the elven ambassador.

"*Eth aloni tul'venarii,* Ambassador, I come with news from the Silverfist Clan."

"*Ashanda eth reiis,* Baelanor. Come. The Matriarch will likely want to hear of your news as well."

The Avalide ambassador led the ice mage up the stairs woven in and around the massive trunks of the great trees that held the city in its delicate embrace. Even during the evening hours Avalide was beautiful. Baelanor was always studying something, and the harmony within Avalide was something definitely worth his attentions. Baelanor saw the Frostspire as a magnificent feat of elven magic that was forced upon the frozen wastes, whereas he saw Avalide as having grown into its beauty with the awareness and full cooperation of the living trees that gave *Illu'Dar* its overwhelming sense of peace and tranquility.

Matriarch Cheyandra Silversong with her truth-sage, Aerinyyr Riftseeker, as well as three other elves—likely from the Ætheron— were gathered in the Matriarchal Commune to hear the latest report from the Silverfist endeavors. Baelanor bowed low to the Matriarch as the elven greetings were exchanged as was customary, and then the Matriarch began to address the gathering.

"Your presence here can only mean that your careful work has been completed, or else another unforeseen travesty has befallen us. I do hope you bring news of the former."

"I do indeed Matriarch. The arcanite transmutation was stable and quite successful once we found the right combination of ore and gems needed to hold the Æther energy within. I believe the finished product will work as well as the originals work, even though the arcanite was formed exclusively from truesilver and not the thorium that the dwarves suggest was also used in the original castings and binders. We are content with the final result and I would ask for access to the pool here to pass my report to the council of three in order to begin assembling the pre-discussed teams to begin work on the arcing of the power matrices and the final installations in their proposed locations."

"Permission granted. Well done Baelanor. Time moves against us, and the hour of darkness is near at hand. Our mistrunners as well as our healers report a growing shadow in the western skies that daylight does not pierce and that the wind cannot move. Over the past months, since Midwinter's eve, this shadow has been growing ever larger. Our seers, under the council of Aerinyyr, have been forbidden to attempt to use their sight to penetrate the shadow. For even if they would be successful, the costs could be severe as my truth-sage can attest to."

"It comforts me to see you well once more, Aerinyyr."

"The healing was slow and laborious but with the constant help of the Æthanon healers, I am able to see once again. Thank you for your concern, Baelanor."

"Matriarch, how is it that not everyone sees this shadow in the west? Are you suggesting that it rests entirely in the spiritual plane?"

"Yes Baelanor, that is what we have deduced. Those with little spiritual insight, like our Ætheron and like our *Dsa'carii* kin to the north, are blind to this shadow, while those with deep spiritual leadings, like our Æthanon healers and diviners, see the shadow as clear as day. It is a restless evil that is spreading, while the isle of mist rumored to harbor an army of death walkers also casts forth its vile taint into the southern regions of Caliyon. Contact the spire and ask them to dispatch their teams accordingly. I will also send these Ætheron here with you to aid in the transportation of the components to their destinations."

Baelanor used the reflecting pool in the Avalide council chamber to deliver his report to Yserth, Valeris, and Tinovis, who all immediately acknowledged the dispatch request, promising to send Nyssia, Larros, Thaelvin, and Draevor with two additional frost mages to join with Baelanor and Jamaela. The four elven teams were each composed of a *Dsa'carii* ambassador, who would teach and oversee the projects, and another *Dsa'carii*, as well as an *Illu'darii* assistant to both mentor the ambassador and assist in the final stages of the installation.

Baelanor, along with the three Ætheron selected to accompany him, began their journey back toward the northern border of the *Illu'Dar* where they would reunite with Phaelen and Jamaela at the Silverfist battlekeep. They chose to forgo their rest and accommodations within Avalide to travel during the evening in order to complete the journey by morning. Throughout the previous day, while Baelanor had been delivering his report, the dwarves had moved seven sets of castings and binders to the entrance of the battlekeep where Phaelen, Rallegan, and Jamaela were also waiting to receive further instructions.

Baelanor and the three Æthian arcanists released their travel forms and stood tall to greet the others who had gathered to meet them. Baelanor repeated all the information that was passed on to him regarding the next phase in the plans to build the reflecting pools, as well as the information regarding the spiritual darkness that had begun to grow in the west. This caught the rest of the elves off guard, except Rallegan, who finally had the answer to the troubles within his spirit.

Rallegan took his leave from the other elves and the dwarves, bidding them luck in their race to complete the pools at the prescribed destinations before the shadow fell completely upon the land. There were great matters for the druids to discuss in preparation for the advance of the darkness, especially if it made its way toward *Illu'Dar.* The protectors of the balance needed to find an answer to resist and hopefully repel the shadow and in order to effectively plan such a strategy, the druids wanted to summon the dryads and the treants together to feel the heartbeat of nature more clearly and divine an answer from the land.

With all the focus on the advance of the corruption, the joyous celebration of new life among the dryads had been dulled, even though several mistrunners and all of the druids and wardens had gathered to witness the births. Rallegan nearly missed the joyous moment when the myriad of dryads with child began to sing through the last stages of the birth. Oakenroot, the eldest of the treant guardians, raised his gnarled limbs into the winds of life that swept with sudden ferocity through the gathering as the dryad songs wove into one tune layered with what sounded like a thousand harmonics.

Within the heart of forest, the young Lifetrees that were linked to the new dryads began to shoot up from the ground as their juvenile root systems began to extend deep into the earth. While the thin trunks and short branches reached barely a span into the air, the winds of life that rushed throughout the glades began to awaken guardians from each corner of the forest.

Four of the ten dryad elders, Xe'Deiona, Xe'Talis, Xe'Nara, and Xe'Laenii, together with their mates, stood in their respective circles to call the four winds of Caliyon as they blessed the births and welcomed their new kin into the forest of *Illu'Dar*. The groaning of the trees awakening filled the circle of winds with laughter as the new dryad mothers embraced their daughters for the first time and began dancing in rhythm with the awakening trees around them. Even those back in Avalide could hear the laughter upon the whispers of the wind that coursed through the elven capital. The air elementals also felt the stirring of the winds and smiled to each other knowing what was happening in the heart of the forest at long last. The first spring of the new dryads had begun and great was the celebration of life throughout all of the *Illu'Dar*. For the briefest of moments, the elves in the planning councils and healing wards, even those studying their works of fire and magic, all forgot about the darkness that loomed over Caliyon as the spark of life filled everyone with hope that the balance would correct itself, and all life would have a chance to thrive.

The druids were lost in the songs of the dryads, and also in their own treesongs that sought out the new saplings and began to bolster them, giving them the added protection of the druids of the *Essen'dril.* Talonyyr and Allarielle were there, and of course, Bethalyyn, Rallegan, and the other druids as well. Tavendia had returned from Lorenth yet again, after spending more time in training with Arimas and his paladins. After his first four paladins had experienced the wonder of the Illuallarii, the elves were quick to consent to the bringing of the rest of his paladins to receive the same benefit of wisdom and practice as they all spent much time over the past months in Avalide and in the Illuallarii learning the elven histories and focusing their amazing abilities to summon light and life into the world at will, and as needed.

Farin once again had chosen to accompany Tavendia back into the *Illu'Dar* where he felt so much more at home than he did in his large estate within the citadel. Farin knew from Tavendia's excitement that the dryads would be celebrating life shortly and his request to witness this event touched Tavendia's spirit and filled her with joy and increased respect for the human.

Over the past several months, Farin had begun to develop a few strong friendships with the elves. Narissa always sought him out because of her intense time spent healing him, and because she could see the turmoil in her daughter's eyes every time she looked upon Farin. She held her words, for she did not yet understand the complexity of the prophecies that were tied to Farin and she did not want to inadvertently alter a thread of prophecy by her interference.

Talonyyr also drew Farin into a close friendship. Ever since his observation of Farin's bravery in the face of his own death many months ago, Talonyyr had felt a deep respect for the former covenal. He spent much time walking with Farin and Tavendia throughout the glades in the cool of the evening, watching the beauty of the *aethia'lyys* as they became visible in the setting rays of the sun, when dusk fell upon the forest. Talonyyr was like Farin in many ways. A martial combatant and a born leader, they both shared stories of their lives and their training, even though Farin had a much more colorful past to tell.

While the elves spent entire age cycles training in the use of arms and magic, there had not been any battles among the elven people. They trained in order to protect that which had never been threatened before. Now that the time of shadow was upon them, a sudden vigor filled the elves once again, knowing that of all the times in history to use their wisdom and skill at arms, it would be now.

Farin even started getting to know and understand a few of the dryads, including Xe'Anya and Xe'Kiree, two of the dryad elders. Tavendia had to teach Farin about the dryad ways quickly, for many of the dryads who had not been fortunate to mate with the first human captives, looked at Farin with incredible longing, even though Xe'Kiree made it abundantly clear that Farin was a friend of the *Illu'Dar* and was not to be mated with. Farin had a hard time not blushing around the dryads for they were an incredibly sensual race. Even though they were noticeably shorter than human women, they maintained very soft and curvaceous figures that they hated to hide from the eyes of men. Farin was often the target of many flirtatious jokes when the dryads were near, and Xe'Cali and Xe'Jarra, the two who flirted with Farin the most, had no issues with expressing just how they would pleasure him if they were given permission to. Farin made the habit of never being alone with any dryad, and specifically asked Tavendia to be near him whenever they walked into their parts of the forest. Whether it was fear of their blatant sexual advances or his uncertainty about being able to resist their charms he did not say.

Today Farin had no concerns about the dryads for every dryad, old and young, was enraptured by the celebrations of life that had blessed them. The ten dryad elders, together with their elven mates, rejoiced and sang new songs, the dryads in the whisperings of the trees and the elves in the words of their native tongue.

Spring had charged into the winter that did not want to let go of Caliyon and with its arrival, hope blossomed anew. Arimas had very much wanted to witness this event himself, for Farin's excitement about anything of import to *Illu'Dar* often held matters of great fascination to the human mind as well, yet Verona requested his presence more often now as her own time to share in the miracle of life was fast approaching. Another few short months would see the arrival of the fated Lightbringer, which also implied that the war of the shadow was nearer now than ever before.

Many of the dryad elders were intensely troubled with the growing darkness in the west. Amid the wondrous celebrations of new life, Xe'Deiona, Xe'Kiree, Xe'Laenii, and Xe'Brea frequently exchanged nervous glances between genuine smiles as the balance of nature disrupted their very spirits day after day. Oakenroot had mentioned a similar sensation regarding the shadow of the west, and while their eyes could not penetrate the din and the shade in the west, the very fibers of their being resonated with the truth that a great enemy of the forest was lurking and against such a beast, the treants and the dryads felt bare and defenseless.

Farin was not surprised when the dryad council, together with the elven druids and the few members of the high council present, all collectively decided to postpone their discussions until the follow day, to give the new mothers time to sing with their daughters and begin shaping their young minds in the dryadic ways of the forest. Farin walked beside Tavendia yet again, careful to hold his thoughts in check even as the simple fragrance of her hair enticed him.

They spoke of Arimas and of the paladins and their remarkable achievements over the past few months since Farin and Tavendia had first led them into the *Illu'Dar* to experience the magic of the elves firsthand. None were disappointed. Hadrin was actually speechless as he sought out the eyes of his friend and former covenal, finally understanding the passion that Farin held in his heart for this sanctuary among the darkness. The Dark Wood was a title never again mentioned among human lips for the priest-king and his paladins made it abundantly clear that these forests were the last bastion of hope and life in all of Caliyon and there was no place that was its equal. Erikk and Dayle, along with Varron, Treven, and Braenor, found genuine laughter spontaneously escaping their lips as they wandered through the mystical glades. Each of the paladins experienced emotions quite similar to the others, yet they also experienced thoughts and spiritual nudges that were unique to each of them.

Tavendia and Farin both agreed that the experiences shared between the humans and the elves had a profound impact on both races, and they were each becoming more appreciative of the other. The Æthanon healers developed a close fascination for the humans, especially Arimas and his paladins. Their gradually improving mastery of the spiritual realm in matters of life and healing sparked several conversations that led to stronger bonds forged between the two races.

While the paladins did not fully understand the explanations behind some of the miraculous powers that resided in their fingertips, the elves took steps to bridge their knowledge gaps. Much to the dismay of the elves, however, it was humans who creatively suggested that what could be done for good and healing, could be undone to cause harm and death during favorable conditions. Once again, the barbaric nature of humans, even the noble ones, was revealed, forcing the elven healers to struggle with accepting the humans with their inherent flaws.

As it often happened, Farin and Tavendia initially began talking about something relevant which ultimately led into several tangent discussions about matters of various importances, simply for the pleasure of conversation with each other. Farin finally began to accept that Tavendia had completely shut off her emotions where he was concerned, as he was unsuccessful in divining any further emotions or conflicts within her spirit. Somehow she could enjoy his company and engage him in deep conversations while keeping him at arms length, emotionally. If she could succeed in this, then he could too, but part of him wanted to feel the pain of longing again.

Since Jesslyn had been torn from his life, Farin had made a living of hiding his heart and soul within an iron vault deep within his being. Emotions often betrayed people and they were unreliable and grievous at best, yet he longed to feel like a full man once again. Even the pain of subtle rejection was enough to stir the ache within his heart. This ache was not debilitating like he envisioned it to be, but motivating. For the first time, he wanted to explore life in all its beauty, and the prophecies of the elves that he was exposed to all mentioned that his would be a life of sorrow that would lead into unexpected joy.

He finally felt he divined the truth behind his own mysteries as he began to apply this rationale to his own life. Perhaps Tavendia was intended to be the source of pain that would eventually lead him down a path of emotional healing and awakening. This notion was definitely the soundest idea about the druid that ever crossed his mind and within moments of thinking about it, he wondered if Tavendia had been listening in on his thoughts yet again.

Evening came once again upon the glades as the distinct musical songs of the *aethia'lyys* filled the night skies. Farin would often spend long moments of solitude listening to the life that bristled within the forest as he gently blew on his wooden flute. Such a tiny trinket had become a token of such importance to him now as he constantly found himself paying more attention to the little details in his life and in his world. He was learning to appreciate all life for what it was... potential... hope... opportunity. All of those things would be lost if this shadow was successful in consuming the land. Thankfully Arimas, his paladins, his inquisitor, and all of his new allies, had begun to walk a road of defiance to the shadow.

Farin noticed himself smiling once more as he settled into the incredible comfort within the elven chambers. Farin had little to smile about on most days until recently and now it seemed that the most inconsequential matters led him to experience a simple and unadulterated joy. With the shadow larks singing overhead in the dark boughs of the forest, Farin quickly drifted into a peaceful sleep.

Morning brought about the much anticipated discussions among the treants, elves and the dryads. Although they were more than organized, the collective insights and wisdom from the three fae races struggled to culminate into any sort of plan, even a rudimentary one. The dryads and the treants could feel the imbalance within their very spirit, far deeper than the elves could feel it, yet no one could suggest anything definitive that would be effective in this situation. After several unproductive hours of discussions, the only consensus reached was that someone needed to ascertain the true nature of what this dark energy was. Many began looking once again to Aerinyyr the truth-sage to guide them in this course of study yet even he would not leave the protection of the *Illu'Dar* after discovering that the fae were particularly vulnerable to this evil.

It was then that the eyes began to drift toward Farin—a human truth-seeker who had proven his worth to Avalide and to Lorenth.

Tavendia did her best to choke down her fear when she began to understand where this discussion was leading. Farin merely reached out and took her hand in his and whispered that the task was his and if part of his fate was to serve the elves and the humans in this way, then he would embrace the task, no matter how difficult it might prove to be in the end.

The dryads and the treants looked at the human with a mixture of curiosity and respect for his quiet acceptance of the burden that was laid before his feet. Tavendia insisted in accompanying him, as did Talonyyr and a handful of mistrunners who either directly supported Farin or were following their own innate desire to explore the western lands beyond the forest's edge. Farin informed the gathering that he would make haste first to Lorenth, to notify the priest-king of this development, before venturing south to discern the nature of this spiritual darkness. With any luck, he would be able to uncover a weakness to cripple its advance and quickly return with news that would benefit all who stood in opposition to the shadow.

Farin found it slightly frustrating that whenever a consensus was reached within *Illu'Dar*, action almost always immediately followed. Apparently the dwarves preferred to mull their decisions over a long draught of mead while enjoying some finer comforts of life—a practice the humans inadvertently mimicked through their use of banquets, committees, and various other time-wasting ceremonies. There would be no further discussion about this subject until Farin returned. Just as Farin and Tavendia began to make their way out from the gathering, the gnarled arm of Oakenroot lightly encircled the shoulder of Farin, gently forcing him to face the ancient guardian of the forest.

"Though we cannot see past earth and tree, we know that this evil seeks to deceive. Guard yourself most diligently, youngling, for you seek to understand the evil at the root of all evils and great will be the danger."

"I thank you for your words Oakenroot, yet what more can you tell me about this root of evil?" Farin's question barely escaped his lips before Tavendia was already speaking to Oakenroot in a calm and peaceful voice.

"*Tana aeis beth'allios nuve'en padar et fyiorii kasan Deimar etarra novendi. Pas'aiis echar vasarii et o'oveii nas anum fina dei.*"

"As you wish *Essen'dril*. May the forest's strength preserve you both."

"Come Farin, it is time for us to gather our things and meet Talonyyr near the western border."

The odd exchange between Tavendia and Oakenroot troubled Farin. His senses could only pick up fear and uncertainty from Tavendia as they began their walk back to the *Hannoth'areii*, which was one of the larger structures northeast of the Matriarchal Commune and was designed to accommodate anyone who had not yet grown a residence for themselves. Farin stayed there of course when he visited, as did Tavendia. She had left Narissa and Lŏnaen's dwelling years ago, but like many elves, she was in no rush to select and begin work on her own *Aen'areii*, as typically that did not become a concern until one had chosen a mate.

"What did you say to the guardian Tavendia?"

The druid looked back toward Farin and for a second she thought she saw a glimpse of his soul laid bare before her. The vision caught her by surprise. She focused back on the question that she desperately wanted to avoid and then hesitated a moment before answering, "I cautioned him about the prophecies."

Farin knew she was leaving something important out but what she did say was true to a certain extent so he could not actually accuse her of lying. He chose to leave the matter alone as they continued their walk through the forest world of *Illu'Dar* approaching the *Hannoth'areii* where they would grab their travel clothes and pack a few simple rations for the journey back to Lorenth and beyond.

The relatively short walk back to the western border of the forest took much longer than usual. The Matriarch, the magister, the truth-sage, several healers, and even a small group of arcanists that Farin was briefly introduced to over the past few months all sought him out along the way through the forest. They never arrived in groups of more than two or three but when Farin reflected on the number of visitors that came to wish him well, or to stay the course, or even to remain in the light, Farin's awareness began to surmise that something larger was amiss—something that Farin did not yet understand but apparently many others did.

Tavendia remained quiet during their walk out of the forest. She certainly had learned to discipline her thoughts for Farin could not sense anything from her other than that same uncertainty that had been present ever since he decided to investigate this shadow in the west. Atarax and Laenos were both waiting for them as they emerged from the forest and crossed the shallow section of the Ellorian River, Tavendia parting the river out of instinct as she always did so that they passed along the dry ground to the other side. Farin lightly grabbed Tavendia's elbow before she mounted yet she would not face him. A tear began to run down the side of her perfectly featured face.

"Tavendia please... what is it that no one will tell me? Is there something you know that I do not? Please do not keep me in the dark like this."

At the mention of keeping him in the dark, Tavendia turned to face Farin before leaning into him so that the hair atop her head brushed his bristly chin. "I'm sorry Farin, but we have crossed into the heart of the shadow and we all fear that which we do not understand. This is no different. There is something stirring that we cannot fathom and the uncertainty is playing with our thoughts and our emotions. You, my friend, are caught in the middle of a war that has been raging since the creation of Caliyon. You did not start the war, you had no reason to be part of the war, yet your race will ultimately decide the end of the war—for better or worse. Please do not ask me about this again Farin. The pain I experience every time I see your questioning eyes is becoming unbearable for me for there is nothing that I would want more than to provide you with all the answers that you seek."

Farin released her elbow as she stroked the side of Laenos' neck before mounting. Atarax began to nicker and then he nudged Farin to rouse him from his malaise. Farin shook off his disquiet, whispered his own greetings to his equine friend, and then mounted Atarax just as Talonyyr and several mistrunners leapt from the shadows within the forest. Talonyyr, plus five other mistrunners, crossed the river with far less grace than Tavendia and came to stand by the druid and the inquisitor. Farin recognized two of the mistrunners aside from Talonyyr but the other three he did not remember meeting before. Tavendia actually smiled again and chuckled to herself as she looked into the face of her brother Gildar, one of the three Farin had not yet met. He suddenly realized that he knew a fair amount about him already from Narrisa and Tavendia.

"Gildar... coming for the adventure or because you actually have some concern for me and this human?"

Gildar flashed his mischievous smile to his older sister and proffered a well rehearsed and lightly mocking bow. "I come for both sister-dear. Your friend has quite a reputation already for one so short-lived and our trusted *Ryl'idohan* cannot be allowed to have the exciting tasks all to himself."

Talonyyr chuckled before inclining his head to Farin and Tavendia, "Farin, this is Gildar, as you now know... to his right are Kassn and Elaryyn, and to his left are Soral and Daeryyk whom I believe you have already have met before."

"*Eth aloni tuvvarii* mistrunners, I am honored to meet you."

"Almost Farin, keep practicing and you will get it right... it's pronounced *tul'venarii* but even the attempt brings us honor, my friend." Daeryyk smiled to Farin as the rest of them acknowledged his elven greeting in the traditional manner.

"Are you ready to begin Farin?" Talonyyr queried.

"I am ready... but where are your mounts?"

"We are called mistrunners for more reasons than you know. Do not worry about us, for it is we who have to worry about you keeping the pace."

Tavendia nodded to Farin as the small party of mistrunners began their quickened run, almost flying across the hard plains as their shapes began to shimmer and their form began to change. The two on horseback actually had to whisper to their mounts to run free and wild, almost spurring them on with allusions of competition with the six in order to catch up. So began another journey to Lorenth, yet this time Farin sought an audience with Arimas prior to undertaking the second leg of their journey. The priest-king would need to know about the recent events in *Illu'Dar* as well as Farin's plan to investigate that which would bear them deep into the southern lowlands where the spreading darkness awaited and the human exiles led by Dean now resided.

XXXI

"Do what you must, Nyssia, but understand that there is nothing but death awaiting those in the south. Now is the time to watch and wait. Hasty actions are unpredictable and will produce results even more unpredictable and such things must be avoided at all costs."

"I understand Sargeron, but you and Trakkenor cannot become complacent, especially when there is a certain connection between the black dragons and this shadow. There is a chance that you possess certain strengths that can work against this threat."

"There is a similar chance that we possess a certain vulnerability to this threat as well. You will not move me in this Nyssia. We will watch and wait, and perhaps learn the nature of this vulnerability or strength as the events unfold. The humans have begun to exploit a weakness with the dragons, the taint has likely consumed the human settlement now, and a shadow within the forest grows ever larger. We will all wait together in this calm before the storm is unleashed upon us. Let us do what we can while we can, and respond to the threat as options become clearer to all."

Nyssia knew that the words of the ancient black dragon held great wisdom and she shamed herself with these sporadic feelings of impatience. The council of three had said much the same things recently as a general sense of unease fell upon all the fae races. Since Aerinyyr was dreadfully wounded, many of the fae began to question how effective they would be in the face of this shadow and as a result, patient anticipation became the mandate while eyes began turning to the humans to see how they would respond.

Valeris had passed on to Nyssia that the reflecting pools were now ready for installation as well as additional information given from Cheyandra Silversong regarding the expected births of the dryads within the heart of the forest. Valeris had also mentioned that a prophecy-bound human with well developed ties to Avalide had chosen to investigate the shadow in the west with the aid of a small elven party. They would likely be arriving in Lorenth shortly, where they were planning to speak with Arimas before continuing on toward the south.

Nyssia left the Icecrowns the day prior and made the flight with Arcyn Ly'yrs, a mage of well respected talents who would be assisting her with the arcing and fusing process. They flew throughout the day and night, arriving at the summit by dawn. Nyssia had already spoken with Zharra and Valkyyrak that morning and now she was in the middle of discussions with Sargeron as the two *Dsa'carii* awaited the arrival of Braena Jadelight of the Ætheron. According to Valeris, she was transporting two sets of castings and binders for use within the Icecrown summit and then within Ur'Akam. Braena arrived while Nyssia was still speaking with Sargeron and the evident sense of awe at observing the dragon summit for the first time was clearly seen on Braena's face as she placed the arcanite materials on the ground and abandoned her great eagle flight form.

"*Eth aloni tul'venarii seitas Dsa'carii.*"

"*Ashanda eth reiis seita Illu'darii et sorendii nin'aloth benin ay'amara.*" Nyssia turned her attention back to Sargeron and inclined her head. "I will defer to your wisdom in this matter Sargeron and trust that our inaction may yet prove to be the wisest course of action. I will take my leave now for my sister from Avalide has arrived and there is much work for us to accomplish."

"Sycaris has just contacted me. If you have no objections, she would like to join you in your work to observe."

"That will be fine, Sargeron." The immense black ancient nodded and then vaulted himself into the air, extending his massive wings as he took to the skies, leaving the three elves together to begin their time-consuming work.

*   *   *

Arimas led Larros and his two elven companions down to the council chamber where Cirra Bethanin, Melsa Vilarin, Renlar Fin and Jarl Phelps were already discussing matters of industry again. Arimas had previously briefed the counselors on the reflecting pool idea and the day was finally upon them. Shae Solarwind and Illios Var`eth had arrived from the Silverfist Clan battlekeep with two very strange looking rings that would apparently be used to create these communication devices—one of which was to be located here in Lorenth, and the other to be located in the large and hidden dwarven hold of Barak'Dûm.

Arimas and the other humans collectively stared in awe as the twin massive rings were suspended before the elves as they walked down the large corridors. Each of the elves had one hand extended toward the arcanite ring that they controlled, which appeared to float in midair as they walked. Their path was less than ideal because they had to adjust their course a number of times to find the larger doorways that could permit these rings to pass through. The three elves, along with Arimas and a now very pregnant Verona, all entered into the council chambers. The four counselors present also stared at the logic-defying situation unfolding before them as two metal rings entered the chamber without apparent assistance while the five followed after.

Illios placed his casting near the entrance of the council chamber off to side of the doorway, also setting down the binders he held with his other hand, while Shae began to orient her casting over the location that Arimas was guiding her toward. Larros then informed the priest-king that if at all possible, the humans would have to continue on with their day to day activities for there were several weeks of work still ahead of them.

Arimas walked among the counselors and began repeating much of what Larros had conveyed to him when a runner arrived in the council chamber seeking the priest-king. Arimas waved him over to hear his report.

"Tegan, isn't it?" The runner stood proud and smiled, shocked that the priest-king would remember, let alone even know, the name of a runner.

"Yes, your Excellency. I bring news from the main gate. Two riders with six large black beasts chasing them are approaching the city at great speeds."

Arimas could sense the fear in the young man's heart and he rested his hand upon his shoulder, infusing the runner with a sense of strength and calm while extending his senses toward the eastern road, not noticing any of the darkness that would typically be seen within the heart of an enemy.

"Open the gate, Tegan. Did you by chance see the inquisitor mantle on one of the riders? And was there both a black mount alongside a pale mount?"

"We could not make out the mantle from their distance, but yes, now that you mention it, there was a black and a pale mount."

"I will come with you Tegan. They will likely already be at the gates by the time we get down there for I do not ride nearly as fast as you anymore. The inquisitor and the Elven Ambassador have arrived again, and I can only assume that the six black beasts you mentioned are another mystery of the *Illu'Dar* that we do not yet understand."

Arimas leaned over to kiss his queen, and rested his hand upon her swollen abdomen for a moment. He smiled a warm smile before lightly kissing her again and headed out with the runner behind him. Once the pair stepped out of the fortress entrance, Anton, Rorrick, Garron, and Dayle took up their usual flanking positions behind their Monarch as the small party mounted up and made their way through the upper city. Arimas waved to the upper city gate guards that hailed him and continued down toward the main gate where another runner had been dispatched out of impatience. Arimas waved the second runner down and sent him back to the gate with orders not to fire at the beasts but to open the city to the riders and their guests.

The second rider was quick to comply and within several moments, Arimas could hear the iron portcullis being raised. Arimas and his party continued out through the main gate where they waited for the party that was nearly upon them as Arimas had predicted. Sure enough, his loyal inquisitor stood atop the war mount that he somehow controlled without bit or harness, while the beautiful druid of Avalide rode beside him. Arimas subconsciously cast his senses toward the six black cats that were following the horses, one of them with a very distinct silver colored mane and a savage appearance. His senses told him nothing though; he could not discern any ill intent from the beasts and thus he waited in calm with his four paladins beside him while his runner excused himself in order to return to his post.

Farin waved to the priest-king as the inquisitor came to a halt before him. Before Arimas could even ask the unspoken question, the silver-fringed cat along with the other five began to shimmer and shift until six other elves stood alongside Tavendia and Farin. The six were not at all like the elves that Arimas and the paladins had met within Avalide during their few weeks of training. They were far more rugged in appearance, though their faces were still pure, unblemished, and unmarred by the facial hair that was typical of human and dwarven males. What was even more distracting though was their rather peculiar clothing that shifted with the light and almost blurred their image to any who tried to focus on them too long. Arimas even had to turn his eyes after a short time.

"Welcome back Farin. I sense heaviness in your spirit which partly explains your quick return. Welcome to you as well, travelers of the forest."

Talonyyr stepped forward to greet the priest-king while Farin held his own words, "*Eth aloni tul'venarii* Arimas. Long have we waited for this momentous time where the hope of Caliyon is now near at hand. I am Talonyyr Silverleaf, *Illu'darii Ryl'idohan* and shadow hunter of the glades. These are my friends and brothers of the wood: Gildar, Daeryyk, Soral, Elaryyn and Kassn." Farin then addressed the priest-king once Talonyyr finished his greeting.

"Something is happening in the south Arimas. I know not what, but the elves cannot see past the shadow, and many believe it to be something spiritual in nature. I have chosen to study this shadow in hopes that a weakness can be found."

"Then it is worse than I thought." Arimas paused as he looked to his four ever-present paladins. Farin could sense a similar weight in the priest-king's spirit as he turned back to face him. "Though I did not expect you for some time, I am glad you both are here. I wanted to bring this to your attention sooner but with the dryad celebrations nearly upon you I knew that I kept you here too long as it was. Reports from Dunnham have been coming in about a strange sickness affecting several families. The local apothecary is overwhelmed and now she has become affected by this sickness, as well. Like you alluded to, it appears to be spiritual in nature because physically, nothing appears to be wrong. Yet, the strength of these afflicted people is waning, emotions and tensions are rising, and fear has begun to strike at the hearts of our people in a way that they have not experienced before."

Anton took off his helmet and ran his gauntleted hand through his sandy colored hair as he added to Arimas' words. "We have sent two paladins to Dunnham to try to divine the nature of this illness yet they have not sent any messages back to Lorenth as of yet. Perhaps you could pass through the township on your way south to help guide their search for the cause before moving on."

Farin nodded, "Of course Anton. If my insights can help focus their healing efforts then we will head there first, although I did plan on crossing the Ardun Ford farther upstream near..." Farin shook his head softly as Tavendia rested her hand upon his forearm. "It won't be a detour at all actually. We will pass through Montague and then continue south over the Midland Bridge following the road toward Dunnham."

Farin cast his glance toward the south, unable to see the same shadow that the elven spiritists and diviners could see, but aware of the evil, nonetheless. He felt it almost as sure as he felt the heavy inquisitor mantle that now decorated his shoulders. He did not know what would bring comfort to him right now. He subconsciously began stroking the wooden flute in his pocket while staring off into the unseen shadow.

"What do you see Farin?"

"I see nothing, but what I feel... Arimas, pray for me?"

Arimas laid his hands upon the inquisitor as he began to infuse the strength of Deimar into Farin's weary and uncertain spirit, praying in a tongue that Farin did not know. He took a deep cleansing breath and when Arimas released his shoulders he stood taller, and more confident. Farin clapped Arimas' shoulder gently in thanks.

"I would normally stay for the day but I do not think time is favoring us any longer, Arimas. If you have nothing more for me, I think we will simply head out from here. We won't make Dunnham until tomorrow as it is, and we had best be getting started for the elves and even the dryads and treants are expecting me back soon."

"Then go with the blessings of Deimar, each of you. Know that you all will rest in our prayers as we hold to the belief that the gifts imparted to you will bring about the will of Deimar. And Farin... hold to the faith. As you enter this darkness, let faith set your mind free from the shadow and persevere until you have the answers that you seek."

Farin caught himself staring blankly at the priest-king with the final words he mentioned. There was something oddly familiar about that particular choice of wording yet Farin could not place where he had heard it before. The four paladins saluted the inquisitor as he remounted Atarax, while Tavendia mounted Laenos once more and the mistrunners began to shift into their black cat forms. Farin looked deep into the zealous eyes of Arimas and then took in the majesty of Lorenth behind him before setting his focus on the long travels ahead and gently whispering to Atarax that it was time to go.

* * *

Tavendia grew more and more withdrawn as the small party rode south across the Midland Bridge in the dark of the night. This bridge marked the halfway point in their journey. As they passed through Montague hours earlier, Farin could already sense the fear lurking in the citizens there, much farther north than the reported events in Dunnham. News traveled fast, and bad news traveled even faster, it seemed, yet Farin could not sense anything worthy of more than the usual concern in Montague.

The spring weather was warmer than expected, even during the late night hours while they made their steady ride toward the southernmost township of Dunnham. The six mistrunners faded in and out of sight as they provided continual security for Farin, Tavendia, Atarax, and Laenos. Farin smiled as he noticed that he was now considering Atarax and Laenos part of the party and not simply mounts to bear them into the unknown perils ahead. Farin reached down and patted the strong neck of his black friend which elicited a gentle nicker in response.

There was something captivating about Talonyyr and his mistrunners. In many ways they represented the darker side of all that was fair and good. Their adherence to and protection of life and the balance was never in question, yet it was in the dark hours, when the light of day had failed, that the mistrunners were truly at peace and in their element. Farin saw among the six a deep camaraderie and bonds that would stand the test of time.

Farin had never seen a panther before, but Sorel had mentioned before that these tremendously powerful cats were found within the Illu'Dar along with many other forms of animal life that had fled the human destruction of the west or fled the corruption from the south. Farin still could not understand the nature of the balance and how the elves functioned within it. The panther was a known predator according to Sorel, and while the panther would hunt and kill within the forests, the elves agreed that this was all part of the balance of life. While humans and dwarves also killed beasts for food, the elves refrained from the consumption of anything that required the slaughter of another creation of life. Farin shrugged off those thoughts as he gently and carefully extended his awareness toward Tavendia.

Her mind might as well been reinforced in iron for all that he could discern from her. He had tried speaking with her once several hours ago but she only grew more and more stoic every time Farin attempted to pay any attention to her. So he let the one-sided conversation end and placed his focus on the road ahead. By noon, or shortly thereafter they would at last arrive in Dunnham. They had spent longer than he would have liked in Montague, which set them back a few hours, but even still, this next leg in their journey was nearly complete.

As they traveled along the dark, lonely road, trusting to the sight of Tavendia to lead their small party through the blackness, Farin became aware of something else in the darkness. Something... curious. Something that had been following them for a long time and something that did not wish to be seen. He leaned over toward Tavendia to mention this observation and she actually stirred when he brought the matter up. She closed her eyes and then faintly smiled as she nodded.

"Ith ala'hanos tavaris etanii."

Farin was actually surprised to see the elemental appear beside him. Her features were almost human in appearance and he often wondered if they chose their physical forms much like some of the more talented elves could choose their travel forms. The air elementals were magnificent creatures that could bend their image at will, choosing to be invisible like the wind, or partially substantial, enough to interact with the corporeal world and enough to allow their translucent features to be seen.

"Hail to you Redeemed Guardian. My apologies for keeping my presence hidden so long but I have followed for much the same reason the others have followed. We all seek truth and understanding, and through you we believe that this truth and understanding will make itself clear in time. I am Chamoiset and I have come to represent the final part of the balance."

Farin nodded to the elemental as he pondered her words. He sought the truth of the matter within and very quickly he understood the reference she was making. As Farin had once studied back in the Avalide Illuallarii, magic was apart of something called the *Trinactria* and within this force were three distinct planes. Tavendia, and to a lesser extent the mistrunners, represented the power of the corporeal plane, for that is the area where the druids, wardens, treants, dryads, and the mistrunners focused their abilities. Chamoiset obviously represented the elemental plane of magic, which left Farin as the representative for the spiritual plane, which did make some sense as he understood that it was the blessings of Deimar that had given rise to his 'talent' in the first place.

For some reason, Jerarin, Chamoiset, and every other air elemental he encountered all referred to him as the Redeemed Guardian. What initially unnerved him before when Narissa had first led him into the Illuallarii, now gave him little pause. He had reconciled that there were events that were unfolding that he did not yet understand; events that were prophesized about but not shared with Farin out of fear of altering the fragile threads of prophecy. Farin knew that he was treading the course of prophecy—a tenuous balance with a fate that he assumed was not yet defined but would soon be revealed if the sternly unemotional state of Tavendia was any indication.

The long night hours finally gave rise to the morning sun, yet even its gleaming rays seemed somehow dim the farther they pressed on toward the south. The mistrunners had shifted back into their elven forms, which apparently did not slow them down at all for their feet barely touched the ground as they crossed the lowland plains. When asked why they chose to switch between forms, Kassn only smiled and told him that fatigue did occasionally set in while they were in their panther forms for prolonged periods of time. Apparently running in their natural forms was one way for them to regain much of their essence.

Farin had consumed the last of the travel rations acquired in Newhaven when they stopped to see Earl and Harriett at the inn. Even the aging innkeeper knew there was something amiss happening in the south for he could barely afford giving Farin what little he could spare in light of the fallout that could affect the harvests from Dunnham that Newhaven partially depended on. Farin held to the belief that things were not as bad as Earl thought they were and items as basic as travel rations hopefully could be obtained with little effort once they reached Dunnham.

The morning passed without incident as the human, seven elves, one elemental and two horses continued their quick pace along the well kept road that would bear them to the township. As the sun reached its apex high in the noon sky, they finally made their approach into town. The mistrunners, once again in panther form, began to spread out as if they sensed something foul. The air was filled with a spirit of oppression and hopelessness as many town members walked throughout the town with nothing but blank expressions upon their faces. Immediately Farin extended his senses and reeled backward as the sensatory overload blinded him with pain, causing him to fall from his saddle.

"Farin!" shouted Tavendia as Laenos stopped to let her dismount. Farin picked himself up off the ground and turned to face Tavendia whose face was now stained with tears. The mistrunners also released their panther forms once more as they ran back toward Farin to see what had just happened.

"It's everywhere! There is a living taint upon everything that lives in this town and it is corrupting all that it is coming in contact with. This is far too great for me to handle. We need to find the paladins that are here and work together to repel this taint. Tavendia, can you see this taint with your senses?"

"No, I cannot, but I feel it everywhere. I believe that I can aid you by feeling alone for this is something that is affecting the balance of life here and I will work on restoring that balance."

Talonyyr lifted his nose into the air as if attempting to sniff the wind. Somewhere along the journey, Farin realized that the wind suddenly stopped. Talonyyr snapped his head to the left as he made two quick noises with his mouth signaling his mistrunners to follow toward his location. Farin and Tavendia also followed on foot as they walked into the center of the town. There, they found two of the king's paladins being overwhelmed by a large number of people pleading with them for help.

Wellan Spiers and Nate Duchamel looked up in relief when they noticed the inquisitor and the druid approaching.

"People of Dunnham, let the paladins move freely and we shall all work together to heal this town. Fail to listen and we will remove you by force and healing will find you last—not first."

The plagued citizens of Dunnham saw the conviction within Farin's eyes and immediately recognized the same conviction that filled the eyes of the priest-king when the spirit of Deimar was upon him. They moved back in accordance with Farin's directives, allowing the paladins to break free form the group.

"Thank you for coming, Inquisitor. For the past few days we have seen nothing but this consuming spiritual agony. We have done our best to banish it, but it is a sickness we cannot heal for more than a few hours at most. We feel the oppression in the air but we cannot locate the source of this evil."

"There are few who can, Wellan, and all I can tell you is that it clings to life like a parasite seeking to corrupt and utterly consume everything that it comes in contact with. Surprisingly, I sense none of this taint upon you, which makes matters easier. Wellan, Nate, this is Tavendia, *Essen'dril* of Avalide as you know, and with her are six of the mistrunners who protect the sanctity of *Illu'Dar's* borders. Talonyyr, Kassn, Sorel, Gildar, Daeryyk, and Elaryyn."

The paladins nodded toward the new members of their group before Nate looked toward the druid with a heavy spirit, "Lady Tavendia, Arimas has charged us with the cleansing of this town yet we cannot see that which plagues everyone. Can you bridge our minds briefly with Farin so that he can show us the truth of this corruption?"

Tavendia marveled at the suggestion from the paladin as Farin raised his eyebrows and nodded his agreement with the suggestion. Tavendia first merged with Farin and immediately saw the taint as he saw it. A living taint was indeed an accurate description. It clung to life yet avoided all things elemental if at all possible. Tavendia immediately understood that this was a spiritual evil, attacking the spirit of its victim before the body became compromised.

Tavendia released the merge with Farin and then stepped toward the two paladins, placing her hands on the side of each of their faces to enter into the *Aëolyys eth'Seloria* with them. She did her best to keep the exchange brief for not all humans were mentally fit enough to process the tremendous flow of information that sometimes occurred with this ritual. She communicated that this taint was spiritual in nature and not physical. Through the imagery that she shed into each of their opened minds she also provided words of her own insight about the possible vulnerability to elemental forces such as water, fire, earth, and air. Wellan looked into the face of Nate as understanding dawned. Tavendia released the merging ritual once more and a terrifying look began to cross the face of the elder paladin.

"We spent the past few days trying to heal people afflicted by this taint when we should have been pronouncing judgment upon the taint itself." Wellan's words resounded with authority as Nate nodded in understanding. "If your theory is in fact true, then perhaps it is time to introduce this taint to the amber flames of Deimar himself."

Both of the paladins dropped to one knee and removed their gilded helms. With one gauntleted fist held across his chest, Wellan, and then Nate began to pray to Deimar for the strength and ability to accomplish that which they could not accomplish on their own. Farin and Tavendia took several paces back, noticing that the scattered citizens were once again drawing closer to the praying paladins.

Talonyyr and the other five mistrunners assumed their panther forms once more as they leapt into defensive positions around the paladins. They began growling at the ever advancing line of people that again began to question their resolve in the face of this new threat in the form of these large black cats.

When Wellan and Nate had concluded their prayers, they both stood tall and proud, donning their helms once more and then drawing their blades from the scabbards at their sides. Their dual balanced blades immediately burst into the amber flame of Deimar while their eyes also began to burn with the same fire. Talonyyr and the other mistrunners looked back and silently watched in amazement as the humans became filled with the presence of a creator spirit.

Tavendia silently began to summon the winds from the far north, and Farin, who had extended his senses to follow her actions, smiled to himself as he realized what Tavendia was beginning to do. She did not simply blast the corruption with the untainted northern wind, which likely would have worked to a certain degree. Instead she channeled the north winds to encircle the entire township while keeping the calm of the storm over the gathering of the people around them.

Wellan and Nate, their eyes aflame with righteous wrath, could see the taint plainly now that their eyes were linked to the spiritual essence of Deimar. Farin stayed their arms initially as he whispered for them to wait for another few moments before unleashing their divine fire. Tavendia began to perspire as the effort she expended in controlling the distant winds over such a large area began to tax her strength, yet she pushed on and began to increase the speed of the encircling winds to create a vortex that siphoned every bit of the corruption and taint that was in the town and began to pull it together in front of her. All those who were inundated with the taint collapsed in relief as the druid ripped it off of everyone with the force of the north winds. When Farin could no longer detect the taint anywhere else in the town other than in front of them, he released the arms of Wellan and Nate and bid them to do what they were led to do.

Nate crossed his flaming swords in front of him. Wellan mirrored his actions as they both advanced on the large flowing mass of taint that floated before the druid, restrained by the elemental forces of wind. Wellan and Nate both thrust their burning blades deep into the mass of darkness while shouting in unison,

"Deim anoth sanctu etum fiallis en sorche!"

The amber flame that was plunged deep into the center of the darkness erupted into a pillar of fire, sending the paladins flying backward, while knocking down Tavendia, Farin, the mistrunners, and all of the townspeople.

Tavendia released the north winds and began to pant in exhaustion while the paladins stood once more and cast their burning vision over the town. It was done, but no one assumed it was over. This taint may have been annihilated in this small part of the land, but those from Avalide and from the court of the amber flame knew that this taint would shrug off this minor setback before advancing once again.

Nate approached the exhausted druid and sheathed his blades to quench the righteous wrath of the paladin so that he could impart some strength into her. Within seconds of his hands making contact with the soft skin of her forehead, Tavendia began breathing slower and her perspiration began to cease.

"Thank you Nate... you heal nearly as well as my mother."

"I should, for it was your sister, Aaira, who worked with me."

Tavendia actually chuckled as she regained her footing and surveyed the town. Many of the townspeople broke down into tears of joy at the sudden sense of freedom, while others, mainly those posted to the town to ensure the construction of the border wall, began to approach the deliverers in search of a way to bolster the defense of this land against another attack.

This time it was Tavendia who spoke. "The taint will take some time to advance upon your position here again, but unless we alter the land slightly we cannot prevent this from reoccurring. I can feel the scar of the land from where this taint crossed the western fork of the Ardun River. There is a wide yet shallow place where the waters nearly stop flowing that has made the lands of Lorenth vulnerable to attack by this taint."

Kyle Mathis, the lead engineer tasked to oversee the Dunnham section of the border wall suddenly questioned, "The Ardun Ford?"

Farin confirmed the engineer's questions as Tavendia continued. "We must push the remaining corruption back across the river. I will then pull the river borders closer together and eliminate this ford completely which will restore the force of the western river. But, even this is not a permanent solution. Evil will always find a way and thus the task will fall to us to ensure that we find other measures to ensure your lands and your people are protected."

While Nate began to minister to the townspeople in need of aid, Wellan followed with Tavendia and the others along the river's edge for nearly a league until they saw remnants of the taint still clinging to the eastern shore of the river. The large stone border wall appeared to be complete all the way down this section of the shore yet Tavendia began to summon the magic deep within the earth to aid her as she felt her way back along the scar in the land to the wide ford many leagues away in the northwest. Projecting her control of the waters from this distance was nearly as difficult as pulling the northern winds as far as she pulled them yet within several long minutes she felt the earth begin to respond to her nudging. Every rock and stone she displaced from the center of the ford was used to close the gap between the river borders until the face of the ford began to change. What once was a wide and lazy section of the river was transformed into a narrow, deep, and rapid section that also swept away the final remnants of the taint on the eastern shore. From what Farin could see, none of the border wall foundation stones had even shifted. She truly was a master of nature.

This time it was Wellan who sheathed his blade and began infusing the druid with strength as she conducted her efforts from afar. While she was still greatly fatigued from the effort, she was not nearly in as bad of a condition as before, being able to remain on her two feet while making the walk back toward Dunnham once more.

Satisfied with their efforts for the day, the restored town celebrated their deliverance with the elves and the inquisitor as the paladins began making their own journey back to Lorenth to report to Arimas all that had occurred. As tempted as Farin was to assume that they had obtained the answers they were sent for, something nagged at his spirit, a voice insisting that there was more to this corruption than what they had found in Dunnham. Farin could feel the darkness southwest of the town, and knew in his heart that he would be unable to return to his king's side without fully exploring it, first.

In any event, Farin's rations were gone, their party had not slept in over a day and the afternoon was nearly over, so there was nothing to be gained by immediately leaving Dunnham. Farin went to the local innkeeper and requested meals and a room for himself and another for Tavendia. Talonyyr declined the offer of an indoor shelter, more content to sleep alongside his mistrunners under the stars. A gentle breeze began to flow through the town again as Farin stopped and frowned. This taint truly was adverse to any elemental forces for even the wind was restrained in the wake of the clinging darkness.

The townspeople all returned to their homes for the evening, finally being able to rest peacefully for the first time in weeks, while Farin and Tavendia both shared a simple supper of bread and cheese and a small glass of the fine wine from the Baron of Rallorn—a shadier character Farin had never met, yet the man had a business as clean as they came. Fatigue set in quickly as Farin and Tavendia finally entered into real conversation for the first time in over a week. Tavendia actually initiated the conversation. Farin had no idea what prompted the sudden shift in her aversion from him over the last few days, but he did not complain as he indulged her questions and open conversation for several hours until the innkeeper hinted that their chambers were ready and that he was wanting to retire for the evening himself.

The inquisitor of Lorenth and the ambassador of Avalide thanked the innkeeper for the meal and the time to converse as they made their way up the stairs and down the hall to the rooms assigned to the pair. Farin wished the beautiful elf a pleasant sleep as she began to close her door and then he too entered his room and had nearly shut his door when Tavendia, having reemerged from her room and crossed the hallway, extended her hand and restrained the solid oak door. Farin, startled but ridiculously hopeful, stood still, his eyes not moving from her face. A moment passed, an eternity, and then with a sob, Tavendia threw her arms around Farin and pressed her mouth to his. Farin, unable to think, unable to speak, simply encircled her waist, holding on to her for balance. Keeping her lips against his, Tavendia gently led Farin fully into his room, and without looking or thinking, closed the door behind them. No words were shared that night and no candles were ever lit as Farin and Tavendia finally lost themselves in each other.

XXXII

The departure from Dunnham went smoothly. Many of the townsfolk had come to reiterate their thanks to the druid for her miraculous assistance. While she fended off her new admirers, Farin stocked up on rations to last at least another week, which he hoped would be all the time he needed to study the shadow in the southwest, uncover its weakness, and return to Lorenth and Avalide with news to share. Despite the grim tasks before him, though, Farin couldn't stifle the permanent smile that seemed etched onto his face.

Even Gildar nearly commented about Farin's pleased expression until Tavendia scowled a warning in his direction. Her brother was forced to stop himself in mid-sentence and instead burst into laughter while shifting into panther form. A laughing panther was by far the oddest sound Farin had ever heard and even he began to chuckle at the unspoken questions now actively circulating throughout the elven party as they left the town of Dunnham behind and approached the border wall at the river. Kyle Mathis was already on the scene, supervising the construction of the wall which had created an impenetrable barrier along the river's edge. When asked about any gates or incomplete sections, Kyle rubbed the stubble on his face and then pointed out that there was an unfinished section not even half a league to the southeast.

Farin thanked the engineer and wished him well on the completion of the wall as the party continued on their mounts across the open ground along the border wall. Eventually they came upon the large gap that had been described to them. The next section of the wall ran from this point down along the river for several more leagues at least until Farin assumed it began heading northeast to run behind Rallorn and Newhaven, where it would finally loop around the new settlement of Falstad before running across the plains back toward the large cliffs northeast of Lorenth.

Tavendia could feel the darkness of the corruption on the opposing shore as she calmed and parted the waters long enough for her and the rest of the party to cross on dry ground. What little of the taint that tried to seize the opportunity to cross over on the dry ground was instantly swept away when Tavendia released the waters once again. Farin immediately felt the temperature change as they crossed the river and headed southwest into the full force of the taint where again, the winds ceased completely. The party stopped as everyone could feel the weight of the vile taint hemming them in from every side. The pressing burden of responsibility laid upon Farin's shoulders increased even more as he took in all that was before him. As the mixed party from Avalide and Lorenth made their way into unknown lands, Farin cast his thoughts toward Deimar, trusting in the prayers offered up on his behalf. Setting his eyes ahead, he decided that there was only one way to complete this quest and the fate of his entire party depended on this one thing... he simply took a step forward.

* * *

He stood alone in the darkness, There was no sense of time. No sensation upon his skin to tell him whether the air was warm or cool, and no sight to guide his wanderings. To him, a day might have well been a year, or perhaps only the passing of a single minute. His memories were fragmented and greatly distorted. The awareness within was still there, nudging him onward, forcing him to take blind steps of faith within the great emptiness around him.

There was a moment when he thought himself dead. Visions of a seed in the shape of an apple residing in the heart of dead tree consumed him. Shadows... living shadows... a ring of death... and then he was drawn into this darkness, a place where light could not penetrate and where hope could not exist.

Being driven by an internal compulsion that he could not easily control, Dean submitted once more to the pressing powers within, his thoughts ever-plotting and calculating while the continued promise of tremendous power waited only a short distance away.

The veil of darkness began to peel away from his eyes as an ethereal green glow started to pulse in the distance, aiding him in his vision. What he thought to be nothing but darkness was nearly as large as a world unto itself. What stood before him was a world of stone, with pools of tears where lost souls had been banished. Dean walked farther into this impossible world. The echo of his footsteps was the first, and only sound, Dean could hear. As he continued on through the shady place, the aura of his surroundings began to impregnate within him a deep respect for the unknown. His head full of wonderment and confusion, he stopped to reflect, dropping to his knees to beseech his inner awareness for wisdom and guidance, inviting that presence to embody him once again.

He could almost feel the rush of power course through his veins as he finished his meditation. He opened his now blood-filled eyes and took in his new surroundings. What was lost to his human eyes was now revealed in his devotion to this awareness. The intricate stone work revealed a craftsmanship far greater than time would have thought possible and the intricate webs of magic that preserved its integrity were astounding. Truly, whoever created this place was someone far more familiar with magic than even the elves or the dragons. Again he paused and reflected... there were no spider webs, no rats, no bilge odors or evidence of decomposition. It was as if this place had been magically sealed away. Who would have ordered this action? What traces of these people would remain to reveal their knowledge and wisdom? For this he had no answer.

As he neared the first bifurcation, he sensed more than heard a distant hum. Instinctively he followed the sound through various other passages and forks without fear or apprehension. He stopped... why did he trust his instincts so much in this? There was a strong possibility for peril, yet Dean felt certain that the hum was actually a pulse of the awareness leading him to the center of magic within what he now believed were the ancient ruins of a lost race. He moved on. Step by step. Without hesitation he finally turned the last corner as the strength of the hum increased to its full intensity.

There in the center of the room stood a stone altar with various glyphs marked on the wall, and other ritualistic-looking diagrams across the stone floor. Without taking another step forward, Dean paused, and then like he had done several times before, he submitted his will to the awareness. Within seconds he felt his eyes glaze over and his will usurped by a stronger power. The awareness took over while Dean, trapped in the confines of his own mind, watched the next series of events unfold before him.

"Nos etachi khalum ve'er theet yaruch sor'bek tan dorijha!" The unknown words spoken in a harsh guttural tone flew from his lips and instantly the hum ceased as the pale green incandescent glow began to intensify and localize around the altar of stone. Whether he made the gestures or whether it was the awareness, Dean was not sure, but his shining red eyes focused ahead as he walked with purposeful strides toward the altar. He reached his left hand into the green flames that had begun to burn on the altar

"Soract Fa'os!" He spoke again without understanding, and then removed his hand from the altar. A green ball of flame floated above his upturned palm to shed light on all his surroundings. With a final act out of his control his left hand lashed out and released the netherflame from his hand which shattered the far wall of stone revealing a hidden room larger than the antechamber that he currently found himself in. With that, the sense of control returned to Dean.

Silently whispering his thanks to the awareness, he walked to the newly revealed chamber and paused in shock and disbelief. The librams and tomes that were revealed before him spanned the entirety of the chamber. More research than twenty lifetimes potentially existed in here and his only thought was that within this well of wisdom was a key that would unlock his destiny. As if his will was linked to an entity within the libram hall, a solitary scroll of parchment floated from the wall space to his right, perhaps fifteen spans down, and came to rest in the air in front of him. He instinctively reached out to grab the scroll while a sharp pain stabbed him behind the eyes followed by a booming voice within his mind and in his own tongue,

"The Faithful has entered and may seek the wisdom of ages. That which you seek dwells among much disarray and anger. As that which is precious is often surrounded by that which is common, so are the words that you seek. But woe unto you should you try to remove anything from this place. For should the light of day touch anything hidden in the crypts of night you and all the knowledge you bring shall return to the dust from whence you were created."

The pain subsided as he reverently retrieved the scroll. He pondered how to read this scroll in the failing light of the crypts, and again, as if his will bore the authority to command that which resided in these crypts, a small green flame sparked and grew above a thin pedestal stand in the exact center of the crypt of night with a small stone receptacle that appeared to hover just above it. The flame began to trigger several other similar receptacles around the room to magically light up with the same familiar green glow, bringing full light to the hall and enabling him to better study the scroll. He scanned the lettering on the scroll and realized that it was in a script he had never seen before. An altar of mist and shadow began to form from the ground until a surface for Dean to place the scroll upon rested before him. He rolled the scroll out and began to scan the first section of unrecognizable words.

Again he surrendered himself to the awareness that was raging inside his mind. Dean could feel his eyes filling with blood once again as the deeply rooted malice within his very soul began to burn and swell. As if commanding the foreign script to become clear, he began to see the lettering shimmer and shift while the cries of the dead began to amplify within the chamber. His own mind was forced backward within himself as if his intellect were somehow interfering with what the awareness was trying to accomplish. Dean looked upon the script once more, this time not trying to understand the words but simply observing the flow of the characters upon the page, as if the meaning was already there waiting for him to find it.

Clarity was on the brink of his mind as the awareness inside kept surging. There was definitely something integral to this scroll and the vast pressure building within his mind told him that the awareness also thought that this particular reference was important. Dean felt like a puppet again, being led by something that was without question far more powerful than he, yet the thought of losing his control to someone, or something, incited his anger again. He had been Arimas' puppet for years until he began to position himself differently... think differently... bribe differently. Now he was living in the shadow of a new master and the very notion of blind servitude caused that calculating mind of his to begin considering ways of bending this awareness to his will.

With a sudden resolve, he forced his mind back into control of the awareness that almost appeared to be ignoring him. That sudden effort reduced him to his knees as he fought for control of himself in the arena of his mind. The more he grew intolerant... the more venom and malice that began to fester in the depths of his soul... every action that he took to dominate that which was dominating him resulted in a deep sense of pleasure from the awareness, as if this inherent struggle for control was essential for something.

When at last he felt the power of the awareness fade, Dean did not let the anger inside cool. Like that same cauldron of molten metal within, his emotions and senses were peaked during the height of his anger. Everything was clearer. His own self-awareness was sharper. He found that even the spirits of the dead could be clearly seen now that he had entered into that blood-rage once more. Surrounded by a host of the damned, he looked long and hard into the partially decayed or grossly distorted faces before him and again he thought he heard several of them whisper almost inaudibly the single word he heard from his vision of the isle of mist.

"Master . . ."

He looked back down at the scroll which he could read as clear as day now that the blood-rage had consumed him. The parchment even bore a reddish hue as if it were responding to the darkness that was within Dean. He made a vow that day that he would never surrender the blood-rage, for it was the only thing holding his mind together and he would never allow this power to utterly consume his will. Little did Dean understand that this was the last vow he would ever make. Dean subconsciously clicked his metal greaves together to rid them of mud that was not there as he stared down at the parchment before him while also summoning a second scroll through the application of his will. The second scroll came of its own accord and set itself down beside the first as Dean began to pour over the wisdom before him...

With the rise of the shadow people will come a time of darkness throughout the new earth. The balance will shift and the abominations of the deep will once again plague the land. The nightmares of Sarik will cross the veil and the living will stand in judgment by the dead. In retribution will Ethoni's children stand against the darkness that will not yield while Deimar's Hand of Light summons disciples to measure his wrath upon the nightmares. But the nightmares will withstand the fires of Ethoni and the strength of men will wane for a great host will fall in abject humiliation and worship. The price of betrayal will be met by the soul stealer's left hand while blessings to his followers will flow freely from his right.
~The Awakening: Chronicles of Tzar'ech, Volume I

And it will be that in the time of the great abomination, the Hand of Ethoni will extend to measure his wrath upon the creations of Sarik. The Creator of death could only watch and mourn the corruption that now would threaten his brothers and all that was and could yet be. The lands of shadow would be opened and the Faithful will be imparted with the ability to rule both the realms of life and death in order to shift the balance of this war. Enter the revenants—reavers and wraiths of a long dead age with power over the blood and flesh. Infused with the charms of darkness and hanging both control of death and life in either hand, the Faithful will be a maelstrom unto himself. Within his hand will be the unleashing of blessings and cursings for the land will shed tears of blood.

There will also come a time when his Faithful will master the Ætherstorms. Immortals will fear the Faithful for even the past

will be brought to bear upon the present. The living will dream and forget while the sands of life and death swirl around the Faithful as the myriad of mortals begin to shiver in the fear of imminent death. Praise to the shadow for unleashing his Faithful into the war. All will hear his cry when they awake and it will trouble even the brave of heart for ne'er shall they forget those four words... Sedara Ut'kamon Num Lycharax! And the laugher of the dead will outlive the living and their wasted prayers for this nightmare to end swiftly.
~Book of Jyx'narag: Vizarian Prophecies Volume III

So many things he did not understand yet he absorbed it all, believing that in time the understanding would come. Unfamiliar names were littered throughout these scrolls, and while he could deduce that Sarik, Ethoni and Deimar were obviously men of considerable power, the references to their struggle with corruption confused the matter even more. What interested him greatly were the references to the 'Faithful' and the 'soul stealer.' The initial voice that rang in his head addressed him as the Faithful and if this were indeed true then he was well on the track to unlocking the secret of the powers revealed in these scrolls. Command of the living and the dead... master of the Ætherstorms... and then the revenants, the mere possibilities made him nearly drunk with a sense of unstoppable power.

Fueled by his thirst for knowledge, he began to scour the crypts for anything that could aid him in his search to unlock his destiny. As the voice had warned, he read what felt like hundreds of collections of nothing more than the rants of the dead, of injustices suffered and cries of lament or revenge. Some were even gathered like the words of a song in their unilateral message of death and destruction that they would bring upon the land once they were free.

Dean regained no concept of time here. While he was suspended in this crypt between what he surmised was life and death, he felt no bodily urges or needs. It was as if time ceased within this place and he would have as much time as he needed to learn that which was required for him to ascend to his rightful position of power. Of all the scrolls that he had read, only a small handful contained anything of real value and those he set beside him as he continuously extended his will and desire to retrieve various scrolls. There was no rhythm or order to his search.

Several scrolls were actually nothing more than a blank piece of parchment with a seal, yet once he broke the seal, he heard a piercing shriek and a very unnatural wind began to blow through the crypts as he was overcome with a sensation that someone, or something, had just been released from a prison of sorts. What remained of the blank parchment began to decay within his hand until it was nothing more than a pile of ash. Day and night, though he had no sensation of either, passed as he read and reread from the scrolls. There were two larger tomes as well that were most interesting. The ink used to create these works was not ink at all but appeared to be some form of a black resin that clung to the page as if alive. One of the tomes detailed a chronology of sorts that spoke of their creation by Sarik who was not a man like he originally assumed, but a deity of sorts, which led him to assume that the other two that were frequently mentioned were also deities. These creatures spoken of in the tome used to be human apparently while some were actually beasts that had died off a long time ago. Sarik had brought the dead back to life in a manner similar to what Dean had attempted several times yet could not properly achieve.

The entire process of their reanimation was incredible. While there was a definite link between reanimation and submission, Dean was unsure whether the submission was to be from him or from the target that would be reanimated. He assumed it to be the former simply because how could the dead submit to anything? Much of the process he had already been divining through his various experiments but the one thing he knew he was missing could only come from the awareness within. After reading scroll after scroll, and perusing through the few tomes, he knew that the key to unlocking the power within Dean was the awareness itself.

He found himself attracted to the tome about reanimation. The art was called necromancy, and while Sarik's curiosity spawned a chain of events that apparently was not intended, inwardly, the deity smiled as he watched his creations begin to flourish and spread. Deimar and Ethoni could not tolerate what Sarik had done and with a final counterstroke, the three deities were imprisoned within the depths of the earth while their divine essences dissipated into all the creation. The ripple from the immense discharge of Æther energies had a rather counter-productive effect on Sarik's creations. The very nature of their life, or unlife rather, had changed and from that moment until now they remained trapped in this realm of spirits where they could not influence the lands of the living any longer. But that was about to change.

Dean could feel himself and the awareness begin to merge slowly as he continued to read and learn. What once was a battle of wills began shifting into a partnership of sorts. While the blood-rage was not released as he had vowed, he found that he needed to restrain the awareness less and less as he learned more from the tomes before him. There were several scrolls that specifically dealt with the soul stealer who would unlock the shadowlands. Perhaps this was referring to Dean and his present location... yet it mattered little. Every time he stumbled across another blank scroll and inadvertently freed another trapped spirit he felt himself become stronger. This power eventually became too great for him to contain and after a time he began to feel himself pulse with that dark energy as an aura began to emanate from within him, continuously expanding around his body like a ring of death.

At long last he broke the seal to a very peculiar tome that seemed to absorb all light—both natural and unnatural. It was a book of complete darkness, fastened with seal of light and no matter how hard he tried to force the seal, the light held back the darkness that swirled across the covers and the spine of the tome as if it were little more than a book of shadow and smoke. He studied the tome for what could likely have been days but the seal finally broke when he began to filter the whispers of the many freed spirits that had begun to commune with him since their release. Dean could barely detect the awareness within himself any longer and at first he thought that it had left him but he immediately knew that to be untrue and thus he reasoned that he and the awareness were becoming one—an inseparable synthesis of the physical realm and spirit realm that the lost souls called a phylactery.

The whispers all mentioned the need to consume the light that held the seal in place. While the idea was simple, its process was incredibly difficult for no matter how much darkness was forced around the light, something inherently powerful about the light always made the darkness shatter in its presence. It was then that the idea filled him. It was impossible to overcome the light with darkness, but it was not impossible to corrupt the light and bring about the darkness from within. Where force had failed, subtlety would prevail as Dean grabbed the tome and pressed it against his chest. The light reacted to the darkness that Dean was harboring within, and the former seneschal felt the seal of the book burning against him. He held the tome in place for a time too long to measure. While he tried to ignore the hissing sounds and the smells of his chest being singed by the light-bound tome, he focused all his thoughts upon corrupting the very nature of the seal by continuously exposing it to the dread and the shadow. He was unsure how much time had elapsed when the seal of light shattered and book of shadows opened against him, healing the brandings caused by the light as his final merger with the awareness was now complete. He took the book away from his chest as his once blood-filled eyes began to pulse with the same sickly green light that glimmered throughout the crypts.

There were no words in the book of shadows, only images and rapidly changing glimpses of events that were yet to come. He felt as if part of his soul were now merged with this book and while it remained in the crypt of shadows, he would partially remain bound to this place, immune from the effects of time.

How all of this came to be, he still did not know, yet he sensed that even these questions would become clear as he explored the depths of his power. The book of shadows drew his attention back as he opened his mind to the messages that were contained within. It was hard to make sense of it all initially as the rapidly changing message flooded his mind with fragments of whispers and understanding.

The Faithful must... BEWARE the Lightbringer... invoke the dark light to bridge the planes... the shadowlands will only be opened when the... submission must be evident for the revenants... the dead will lie before his feet and will answer his call... Deimar himself will choose his hand of light to bring forth that which can repel the shadow... immortality shall be granted with the liberation of the shadow phylactery... immune from all sources of magic, these creatures of the balance fly toward... summon the past to bear against those of the present... even the Faithful will cast fear upon the children of Ethoni as the darkness swallows the light before their eyes... guard the phylactery above all for the protection of life cannot be guaranteed should the link to the spirit plane be severed... will summon unto himself an army of light to vanquish the Seed of Corruption... for therein the requirement of the balance will be fulfilled and Chronos will stand where the Sar'Eth'Deim once fell... fear the redeemed for his will shall not be utterly destroyed... and the world will be plunged into darkness as the soul stealer arises from the depths of the earth waging his war upon those who would enslave him as they that were liberated were once enslaved.

Dean shut the book of shadows as he closed his eyes and meditated on the fragmented passages. That there was meaning hidden within meaning he was sure of, yet there was much that was alluded to that escaped his understanding. What Dean did know was that he would search out this Lightbringer and put to death that which could rise against him, and he knew just how he would accomplish this task. His Drucharii would make the perfect reavers for his plan. Perhaps the young de'Mordrey with his plans for an elite order marked by the black rose of death would bring Lorenth into a new era of fear that no one would expect.

Dean extended his arms and tilted his neck backward as he drew a deep breath. He could feel all the ambient shadow of his surroundings being pulled within him as his unholy aura surged with renewed vigor. The Faithful's transformation was nearly complete. He placed the book of shadows back down upon the altar of mist as he commanded it to be stored back in its place once more, along with the other tomes and scrolls that were beginning to mount up upon the altar. Dean turned his back to the crypt and began to retrace the route that he had already traveled what felt like nearly a lifetime ago. Dean felt no older, but he knew he was far wiser after his intense time of study. He did not hear the hum that led him here in the first place but that did not matter, for somehow, the inner awareness had fused with his own awareness. He realized he possessed intimate knowledge about the layout of this place which was but a piece of what could be called the spiritual plane.

Dean grew more and more aware of the entourage that had begun following him from the crypts. The whispers of the dead quickened as their lust for vengeance began to peak in light of their eventual release from this plane. Instinctively, Dean knew that he could and would command these spirits to do his bidding and once he set foot upon the land that represented the corporeal plane, the bridge between realms would be created and Dean's transformation would be complete.

With every step he took, he could feel the aura around him pulse, serving as a beacon to the lost spirits seeking release. The shadow master was among them at last and woe to the living once Dean unleashed the full force of this darkness upon them. Stepping out from the narrow corridors that led to the crypts he once again stood in awe at the vast expanse of stone and the ocean of tears that rested at his feet. He raised his hands and began to alter the terrain with forceful nudges from his mind, creating a smooth path back to the gate that first drew him into this realm. Then in his full voice, he raised his arms and uttered his challenge to whatever remained hidden beneath his sight, summoning all those who were once trapped as he spoke of their freedom.

"Creatures of the night and spirits of the dead I summon you! No more shall the light imprison you here. I am the Faithful... the soul stealer... and the master of the book of shadows and I have come to bridge the gap between my world and yours. If you would be free, then follow me and vengeance will be yours."

The howls of the dead filled the chambers with its ominous music as Dean continued his march toward the gate that began to open the closer he drew near. Like a rift in space, a thin vertical line of green netherfire pierced the darkness and began to pull apart like a curtain revealing the now dead forest that he remembered wandering to in his rage so long ago.

Dean turned back to face his army of the damned that stood behind him and offered a twisted smile as the blood-rage began to consume him once more. He turned his attention back toward the piercing light of the day and crossed the threshold between the spiritual and the corporeal as a single clap of thunder rolled across the clear, sunlit sky.

* * *

The day lapsed into evening once more and though Farin thought about sleep, he knew that he would not be able to under the effects of the looming shadow. His only comfort was Tavendia, who sat in perfect harmony atop her pale steed. There still were no words shared between the pair this morning as the elven druid kissed him once again before leaving his side in search of her robes that she hastily abandoned the night before. She almost blushed as she watched Farin admiring her body while she dressed and began to laugh as he reminded her of how he first felt when she had walked in on him having a bath in Avalide.

Tavendia looked over at Farin and produced that smile... that one smile that caused the left side of her delicate lips to curl up more than the right. A smile he had not seen since she first met him in the healing chambers of Avalide. Farin would definitely need to speak with her about last night. While he thought he knew her stand on their relationship... or the lack of one... he tried not to over analyze their night of passion.

As the night wore on, Farin could feel the evil in this area begin to take a toll on his emotions. The smiles had finally faded and even the mistrunners stayed in panther form—ever alert and watching for the veiled threat hanging over their heads. Farin noticed a small forest to their left that showed signs of lumbering and caution began to fill everyone as they realized they were now in the lands of Dean and the exiles of Lorenth. Farin silently wished that Wellan or Nate were here with him. While his ability to discern truth was well and good, even Farin was envious of the holy knights of Deimar who could invoke the creator spirit's righteous wrath simply by drawing their blessed blades. Farin felt dreadfully alone all of a sudden as a cold chill ran down his spine. The darkness of night somehow felt more complete this far south, and Farin began quietly praying for the morning rays of sun to stifle the darkness again.

Finally, dawn broke over the horizon to their back and began casting long shadows across the warm, dry ground as yet another forest rested a few leagues ahead of them. Why Farin was heading for this forest he could not say but Tavendia also confirmed his suspicions about this unholy place. While the skies above him were clear, and the sun began to rise, all that Farin could feel was shadow and the ever-present chill of death all around him.

The mistrunners began to make low warning growls as they approached the border of the forest. Farin knew this had to be the place he was destined to find, for his heart began to pound with fear. He closed his eyes and swallowed hard before setting his resolve on the task at hand. Farin and Tavendia dismounted and stood before the forest with the others. Talonyyr had shifted back to his elven form and gripped Farin's forearm firmly. Fear was lurking behind the eyes of the shadow hunter.

"Farin, something is terribly wrong about this wood. It is dark. It is evil. Everything here is slowly dying. I listened to the trees, Farin, and heard nothing... they are all dead, though some do not know it yet. The ground thirsts for blood and within the center of this evil is a focal point of darkness that I cannot discern. If you can divine the weakness of this place from here, then well and good but do not venture into the center—the trees speak of a ring of death."

Farin extended his senses again but all he could see was the pull of the darkness within the center of the forest. There was... something about the center that was the key to this entire darkness and Farin knew that to know it, he would need to investigate it, for that was the sole reason for him to venture to these forsaken lands and he would not leave without the answers he sought.

Tavendia returned to her wary silence and then drew Farin into an uncharacteristic embrace, holding him close and stealing another passionate kiss but saying nothing. Then, she pulled away from him, and after exchanging a look with Farin that he wished he could lose himself in, the group began to march into the dead woods. Farin saw death everywhere. There were no bugs, no insects, no forest dwelling creatures, no birds singing, and again no wind whistling through the trees. Even the leaves were all in various stages of whither and decay. Chunks of bark were rotting from the inside of the trees outward and the only smell was that of decomposing plant matter.

The sun was nearly full into the sky when they came across the ring of death. There was at least two hours before noon and the blazing sun felt hotter than the sun in the mid-afternoon as Farin waved down the others and told them to wait while he approached its center and began to extend his senses. All he could see was the evil around him. The truth that he sought eluded him as fear began to choke his spirit. The hair on the back of his neck began to rise as old memories that he had forgotten about began to surface in the forefront of his mind.

As he stood halfway between the ring of dead trees and the center where the nexus of evil was pulsating he quickly looked down at the ground and fear washed over his face. There embedded among the decay of dead trees and plants was a ring of stonework that yelled out from his dreams and nightmares of the past. Before he could summon the strength to move, a deafening clap of thunder shattered the silence of the dead wood and suddenly, upon the very altar of stone that had haunted Farin for years, was Dean.

Standing upon the altar with the maelstrom of dark magic swirling around him, Dean raised his hands in submission. His coal-black eyes flashed with a green nebulous glow as shadowy vapor began to slowly seep from the corners of his eyes. The sky steadily darkened as an unnatural storm formation grew directly above and a thick cover of greasy clouds spread, smothering the sky. Tendrils of ebony and violet light reached down like boneless fingers and began to twine around Dean as he maintained his position. Slowly, Dean began to change in appearance. First his hands and his head, then his torso and legs, until what stood on the altar was physically nothing more than a remnant of the man, a grotesque caricature who maintained a mere shadow of Dean's features and the ever-condescending eyes whose gaze now pulsed with a sickly green color. Peals of thunder rolled across the sky, the implied lightning not witnessed until Dean dropped his arms and took a deep breath, drawing all the shadow and the darkness into him. A single column of lightning blasted into Dean at which point the sky cleared and the sun reappeared.

"What have you done Dean?"

"I am Dean no longer... I am Kaaldean. I am your doom!" Anger and fury boiled behind those green eyes as the newly birthed Kaaldean thrust out his arms and unleashed two entwining tendrils of violet and black shadow with lightning speed, enfolding Farin in a vice-like grip and sending him to his knees in agony.

"Submit Farin, and I will spare you more pain than you could ever imagine."

Farin could hardly breathe let alone speak, but the defiance in his eyes gave Kaaldean all the answers that he needed. Farin gasped with pain as Kaaldean altered the flows of magic that were coursing through his body while behind him, what appeared to be a gateway into another realm, began to shimmer as his senses discerned a large host of spirits spilling into their land.

Farin heard the stifled scream of Tavendia, and assumed that Talonyyr had restrained her. His only prayer now was that they could escape. Farin returned his defiant gaze back toward Kaaldean and determined in his heart that he would not give Kaaldean the pleasure of watching him die weak and broken. The green pulsating eyes shifted into the color of blood as Kaaldean spoke the last words that he remembered hearing before he died a man, and was born again as a twisted servant of Kaaldean's will.

"Death is not your destiny Farin. I feel your soul and it is mine to do what I will with it. You will be my harbinger of woe and I will undo Arimas and all that he sought to accomplish in life by subverting you and forcing him to destroy you lest he perish before the darkness that you will unleash upon Lorenth."

Farin's eyes closed for the last time. The final sound he heard was Dean's dark laughter as even darker magic corrupted his flesh and imprisoned his mind in shackles of servitude to the soul stealer.

*　　*　　*

The six stood amid the hordes of undead and shadow-spawn and glared into the mist that enshrouded the isle—all sensing the sudden breach between realms and knowing that their master had fulfilled his call. No words needed to be said among the six as Jyx`narag raised a skeletal hand and pointed toward the waiting waters that would lead them on their long march toward their master and toward their promise of vengeance.

*   *   *

"The veil is sundered... the rise of the Seed is complete."

"What of Tavendia and Farin? Aerinyyr, can you not determine the fate of them either?"

"I dare not lead my truesight into the shadow again after experiencing only a hint of the corruption's power. Something has been violated... this I feel, though it is more than the violation of nature. My hope remains in Farin and in the others who escort him into the very heart of evil, yet the truth of this sensation that we feel will not be apparent until I can sense their presence on our side of the river."

The Matriarch nodded solemnly as she paced within the Matriarchal Commune. The trusted advice of her truth-sage hardly brought the relief that she was hoping for yet she knew that there was little that could be done until word reached the glades. If hope were to remain, then Farin would indeed be bringing back word about a weakness to this spiritual evil that loomed in the west... yet hope was fading in the light of prophecy and the silence that hung over the *Illu'Dar* was unsettling many, as the search for answers continued to produce very little to build any sense of hope.

*   *   *

The relative silence of the Icecrowns was shattered once again as Sargeron, Trakkenor and the younger Ysiel collectively roared in frustration... sensing something unnatural deep within their very beings. As their eyes found each other, understanding between the three black dragons became clear. Fyysara once warned about the Seed and what his arrival might cause... a warning that Sycaris was all too familiar with. After the sensations experienced by Sargeron and Trakkenor as they passed over the ring of death, Nyssia's ideas about this link were becoming abundantly more plausible, but the decision to stand and watch would remain.

466

The discussions that would follow between Valkyyrak, Dalaria, and the three elves, busy at work on their communication device, would do little to mediate the threatening feeling that was hanging over the summit. Zharra and Sycaris—although the increased time they spent together was a comfort to both—would continue to wrestle with the link between the three blacks, the arrival of the soul stealer, the taint that was growing in the south and the fragmented threads of prophecy that continually were becoming clearer in the light of recent events.

Zharra cast a lone thought toward Xarethia, wondering if she had felt the same sensation that the other three black dragons had felt earlier. She reserved some hope for her and her young ones... hope that Zharra could find them eventually and lead them back to the embrace of the Icecrowns as they had done with Glauron, Melandra and the young Zyrre.

"I shall hope with you, Zharra." Zharra smiled as her closest friend had obviously been listening to her inner monologue as Zharra and Dalaria were notorious for doing to others.

"I know... hope is all we have left for now."

Appendix

The silence has come...
A force that would stand in opposition to the balance has arisen
and seeks to undermine all that the Sar`Eth`Deim had sought
to create. A dark, brooding energy begins to pulse in the heart
of creation, its tendrils seeking to corrupt and entwine around
all that is pure and noble. Its sole purpose is to destroy. Where
it could not destroy completely it would content itself to corrupt
and twist the essence of both life and magic and morph the entity
into a creature that would bend and serve the darkness. War
came for the first time upon Caliyon and war still remains even to
this day.
As one would imagine, the world was not always at war like this.
Once there was a balance between life and death, magic and
nature, creation and destruction. The Sar`Eth`Deim created unto
themselves creatures of bone and flesh, of magic, of elements, and
even those that were later created from unlife—which the learned
of these lands postulate was when the seed of darkness first came
to sunder the world and corrupt all life. The
Sar`Eth`Deim were not merely the source of all balance, they were
the perpetuators of all that had come after them. Every thought,
plan or dream was enabled by the vision set forth and imprinted
on the creation. All was thought to be in harmony, until the war
of ages began and the very heart of creation was broken and a
tear would fall in bitter acceptance of what had been lost.

~ The Lightbringer Prophecies: the arise of shadow volume I ~

*Of the Sar`Eth`Deim there were three: Sarik, the creator of
negative balance, Deimar, the creator of positive balance, and
Ethoni, the regulator and guide of the creation who stood ever
vigilant to protect the
sanctity of the balance.*
*For Sarik, death was the perfect conclusion to life; destruction—
the stabilizer and regulator to prevent order from quenching the
spirit of change. His was the idea to create life from unlife even
against the admonitions of Ethoni and Deimar. Those who have
come after believe that it was in this inner conflict of the three
that the spark of corruption was birthed and took corporeal form
in the midst of these creations.*
*Until this day, magic was used as a tool of governance, yet with
this corruption, even magic would be perverted and altered,
resulting in dark arts and twisted servants of undeath that would
arise. Woe to him who breaches the veil of the netherworld to
master the darkness in the wake of the silence which shall come.*

~ The Chronicles of Origins: the Sar`Eth`Deim volume II ~

*For it was Deimar, the creator of positive balance, who sought
to bring harmony where there was natural chaos, life to that
which was devoid of life and reparation to all things which fell
to disorder. While he understood the ambitions of Sarik to bring
life to that which had fallen to death, there was a certain sanctity
and finality about the negative balance that Deimar respected
and even admired. To tamper with this finality and sanctity
was not part of the balance.*
*Deimar populated the lands with the three primal forms of life—
plant, animal and human. His creations grew and flourished,
yet it was the humans who showed remarkable adaptability and
mastery over the rest of creation.*

~ Caliyon Histories: visions of Deimar volume II ~

470

Between the positive and negative creation, maintaining and enforcing the balance stood Ethoni. He was the enforcer. Where Sarik and Deimar created, Ethoni would watch, govern and guide the creation so that the balance would not be altered. It was through Ethoni that the "magic" of Caliyon was born. Ethoni would regulate, and direct the creation. Sometimes through subtlety, other times overtly, yet always in the wake of his passing, magic would be infused into the creation.

Some of this essence would simply dissipate, as it often did when Ethoni would intervene with humankind. Some magic would be retained in the creation and would strengthen or bolster it in some way. It was in this way from the passing of Ethoni and his interaction with creation that the elementals of earth, fire, water and air came to be.

Guardians of nature and of the balance, these elementals were sentient and incorruptible. On rare occasion, the magic of Ethoni would transform the very nature of the creation, sparking a new form of life better suited to maintain balance. It was through these means that the fae creatures were born.

~ *The Chronicles of Origins: the Sar`Eth`Deim volume IV* ~

Yet the most notable of all the fae were the two races of men that were forever changed and altered to such an extent that none would ever think of them as human. Within the realm of earth, there existed stone elemental guardians and the forest guardians later named as the treants, or the silent watchers. The humans in these two regions of forest and stone were fused with the magic of the lands and of the guardians and thus were the dwarves and elves brought into existence. The dwarves were akin to men of stone. Stout in stature yet filled with the strength of earth, these creatures came to prefer the earth and the rock as suitable terrain to build in and beneath.

The magic that transformed them left little residual effect upon these creatures and thus the dwarves were forced to become a self-sustaining race, living off the land and beneath it in solitude, distancing themselves from the humans who sought to master everything above the ground. The dwarves were long thought of as nothing but a myth for humankind had no aspirations of delving beneath the earth
to find other things to dominate and conquer.
The elves were an anomaly of creation. Though humanlike in appearance, these particular creatures took in the very essence of the forest. Their features were pure and unmarred; their bodies grew slender and even slightly taller—elegant as the forests they preferred to inhabit. Unlike the dwarves, where beards were a symbol of age and respect, the elves were incapable of growing facial hair and were often thought of as the immortal youth—creatures of beauty and grace. Unlike the dwarves, the magic that transformed them lingered and the residual effect was unexpected. These fae creatures would not die of natural causes and the aging process was incredibly long making the elves a creature to envy.

~ The Physsalia Dream Records: of dwarves and elves ~

The darkness spread throughout the creation. Even among the Sar`Eth`Deim unrest began to fester. The creation was continually getting more out of balance. Magic was no longer contained but became a synergistic power that embodied and surrounded life and now the creation was learning how to harness and use this essence. Once the effects of the corruption were seen by the Sar`Eth`Deim, Ethoni sought to suppress this imbalance as he would any other, yet the nature of this corruption was not something natural, but spiritual. With every effort to guide and enforce the balance, Ethoni only saw more changes that were unexpected. Sarik took note of all these changes and marveled at how things were getting more out of balance. His creations and the inadvertent creation of dark magic were in part needed now to balance the spontaneous creation of the dragons and the rest of the fae, especially the elves, yet his brothers would not concede

*to this line of thought. Sarik, though partly troubled by his resolve
to create life from unlife against the advice of his brothers, still
retained a fascination at this new marvel of his creation and
through this fascination he himself began to become further
corrupted in spirit.*

*It was on midwinter's night, the day that ushered in the longest
night of the year, that the corruption born in the ignorance and
pride of Sarik became a sentient being and indwelled Sarik. The
corruption changed him as he had changed the creation, twisting
both his mind and body, perverting his countenance and isolating
him from his brothers. The Sar`Eth`Deim was broken. United
against their brother, Ethoni and Deimar sought to imprison
Sarik in the depths of his perversion of nature. Yet before the
magic of Ethoni could complete the bindings around Sarik a
backlash erupted in the heart of creation. Never before had one
of the three sought to manipulate any part of their brothers until
this day and the ripple that echoed throughout creation would
be the spark of alteration that forever would send Caliyon into
a spiral of change that the Sar`Eth`Deim would not be able to
intervene in. For in the moment that the magic of Ethoni came
into contact with the divine corruption of Sarik, the foundations
of the balance were shattered and the three became shells of
their former selves—their essences depleted and released into
the creation with the corruption fully grown. The corruption was
now complete and the Sar`Eth`Deim were united once more, this
time imprisoned together and silenced for all time, only able
to watch from beneath their creation while magic, life, death
and corruption grew on its own accord—the balance forever
destroyed.*

~ The Lightbringer Prophecies: the silencing of the three ~

*While compiling the records of the dreamers I have come to
understand a similar theme that now brings some light to
the prophecies of old. There is more than just a mystery that
surrounds the events of midwinter's night. The popular belief
as perpetuated by several of the spiritual leaders and arcane
practitioners of the races, a large portion of them being female,*

whether they were dwarf, elven or other, had recalled dreams
containing a similar element even though several of these people
were living in completely different geographical locations. It was
thought that Deimar, prior to the backlash that reduced and
imprisoned the three together in the depths of creation, shed a
tear for his corrupted brother. This solitary tear, shed in pure
sorrow, was a literal part of Deimar's essence. As it fell to the
ground, it became an orb of magic—pulsating with the light of
creation and entombed with the three following the backlash.
Where hope was now lost, the Tear of Deimar responded to that
lack of hope and down in the darkness, while the three stood
motionless, the tear began to wait for someone... something pure
and with purpose that could channel all the hope and power
contained within and use it
to restore the balance.

~ *The Illu`darii Dream Records: the prophecy of the tear* ~

Glossary

Aëolyys eth`Seloria: elven ritual whereby one or more of the participants can share memories and wisdom through touch.

Aerinyyr Riftseeker: truth-sage of Avalide and master diviner able to see tremendous distances through the use of his truesight.

Aethia`lyys*: Native to the forests of *Illu`Dar, this surprisingly large bird, also called the shadow lark, can only be seen in low-light conditions present during dawn and dusk.

Æthian: elven enclave of spell casters. Separated into two divisions based on either an elemental focus (Ætheron) or a spiritual focus (Æthanon).

Apothecary: traditional herbalist and healer dedicated to the prevention and elimination of disease and/or illness through their application of various poultices, tinctures, and elixirs.

Arimas: Human priest-king of Lorenth, husband to Verona, and wielder of the intimidating battle maul *Retribution*.

Avalide: The forested capital city of the *Illu`darii* elves.

Barak: dwarven word for a hold; Barak`Dûm was established as a hold between three individual clans: Dûm`Ald, Dûm`Keld and Dûm`Eth. Represented by King Torgrim Varr.

Battlemaster: Subordinate officer position within the Lorenthian command structure typically responsible for camp discipline. Assigned a smaller division of soldiers and accountable to the Commander and the Covenal of the border detail. Identified by the crossed swords insignia.

Blood Order: secret rogue guild hidden within and below Lorenth in service to Seneschal Dean. Later disbanded and reorganized as the Order of the Black Rose.

Chase Harman: Covenal of the southern border detail of Lorenth.

Cheyandra Silversong: elven Matriarch and sister to Valeck Silversong.

Cirra Bethanin: Lead Counselor of Lorenth.

Colspar: a crystalline formation that exudes a pale blue glow when set within stone, typically used by the Gray dwarves of Ur`Akam as a subterranean light source.

Commander: Junior officer position within the Lorenthian command structure typically second in command of a border detail and adjutant to the Covenal. Identified by the crossed swords and crown insignia.

Council of Three: *Dsa`carii* leadership council that co-jointly govern the Frostspire: Valeris Sy`yn, Tinovis Fyr`eth, and Yserth Tel`andris.

Council of the Nine: *Illu`darii* council composed of elves in high standing within their disciplines that assemble to support and advise the Matriarch in matters of great importance: Edarath Lightweaver, Sereven Windsong, Valeck Silversong, Bethalyyn Leafwhisperer, Lŏnaen

Amberdawn, Taelon Grayylan, Symphia Gladerunner, Onaeria Willowleaf, Essalla Soulfire.

Covenal: Senior officer position within the Lorenthian command structure typically assigned a border expansion detail of no fewer than one hundred guardsmen.

Cypher: *Illu`darii* historian charged with the task of recording the events of the past, present and future as they are revealed. Formerly known as Keepers, this responsibility has been given to: Sylande, to preserve the knowledge of the fae races; Llaine, sent to the ten dwarven clans; Ashandi, sent to both the humans and dragons; and Illisa, responsible for the wisdom of the elemental races.

Dalaria: ancient blue female dragon, adept of the Icecrowns, and mate to Valkyyrak the golden ancient.

Deimar: God of the positive balance and one of the three Sar`Eth`Deim imprisoned within the heart of Caliyon. Creator of all human, animal and plant life.

Draevor Tel`yys: Frostspire ice mage and ambassador to the dragons.

Druarc: Master Drucharii and operational leader of the Blood Order assassins: Dhax Brenigan.

Drucharii: elite member of the Blood Order of assassins.

Dryad Elder Council: Xe`Deiona, Xe`Talis, Xe`Nara, Xe`Laenii, Xe`Anya, Xe`Kiree, Xe`Brea, Xe`Cami, Xe`Asara, Xe`Eraena.

Dwarven clans: Gray, Dûm`Ald, Dûm`Keld, Dûm`Eth, Hammul, Stormgarde, Silverfist, Nuragg, Ironheart, and Bloodstone.

Edon Thunderhammer: Clan Chief of Stormgarde clan.

Erikk Masaad: Covenal of the northern border detail of Lorenth.

Essen`dril: One of the few Avalide elves gifted in the mastery of the treesong and member of the guild of druids.

Ethoni: Enforcer and regulator of the balance and one of the three Sar`Eth`Deim deities imprisoned within the heart of Caliyon. Attributed with the residual magic left in his wake that caused the alterations of creation, namely the fae races and the elemental creatures.

Farin Guilian: Covenal of the eastern border detail of Lorenth.

Farsight: the ability to cast one's vision great distances through the mastery of the spiritual plane, not nearly as powerful or revealing as truesight.

Forin Hammul III: Clan Chief of the Hammul clan and protector of the eastern section of the Glar`orok Pass.

Frostspire: A massive feat of elven magic, ice, and stonework built in the frozen wastes that house the *Dsa`carii* elves, enables research, and serves as a battlekeep.

Furlong: Originally defined as the length a plow team was to be driven without resting. Later standardized to be forty rods or two-hundred twenty yards.

Fyysara: ancient red female dragon, historian and guide of the Icecrowns, and mate to Sargeron the black.

Gimmel Thaineson: Clan Chief of the Nuragg clan and protector of the western section of the Glar`orok Pass.

Great Stoneway: a feat of dwarven genius and engineering that tunnels beneath the Icecrown peaks connecting the fortress of Ur`Akam with the hold of Barak'Dûm.

Hrimir Ingar: Clan Chief of the Silverfist clan and keeper of the passes of Kel`Zarûl.

Icecrown Summit: the large plateau high in the Icecrown Peaks where the dragons of Caliyon first emerged and dominated.

Illuallarii: Elven library of Avalide created in both the elemental and corporeal planes.

Illu'Dar: The sentient glade and home of many fae races bordered by the Ellorian River and the Red Rock Cliffs.

Korigan Goern: Clan Chief of the Gray clan of Ur'Akam.

Larros Solan'dras: Frostspire ice mage and ambassador to the humans.

League: a measure of distance. Considered to be the distance a man can walk in one hour, which is approximately three miles.

Lifetree: a tree with a life bond with a dryad: as one thrives, so shall the other; as one perishes, so shall the other as well. While the majority of Lifetrees rest within the heartwood and remain in an unawakened state, the elder dryads were bound in life to several of the ancient forest elemental guardians.

Lorenth: The crowning achievement and capital city of the human empire built around the majestic waterfall of the Ardun River.

Matriarch: a master arcanist in her own right, Cheyandra Silversong is also the elven monarch of Avalide.

Red Rock Cliffs: large mountainous region along the eastern coast of Caliyon and home of both the Bloodstone clan and the stone elementals.

Lightbringer: the child of light and balance mentioned in countless threads of prophecy as being the one to come that would stand to face the corruption and determine the fate of Caliyon.

Nyssia Dv'arek Frostspire ice mage, ambassador to Avalide, and elder *Azzurak*.

Rod: Originally being a straight branch or poll. The rod is currently standardized as five and a half yards.

Orin Chorimson: Clan Chief of the Bloodstone clan.

Ryl`idohan: Elven leader of the mistrunners.

Sargeron: ancient black dragon of the Icecrowns and guardian of the night skies, mate to Fyysara, father to Vaanadu, Nostrimus and Sycaris.

Sarik: God of the negative balance and one of the Sar`Eth`Deim imprisoned within the heart of Caliyon. Creator of death and decay who ventured into the realm of necromancy against the will of his brothers.

Seneschal: Second in command over all Lorenth and accountable only to the priest-king himself.

Shandari: Avalide Lorekeeper, Air elemental visionary behind the development of the Illuallarii and pioneer of the alliance between Avalide and the air elementals.

Ssaraki: A large burrowing predator often exceeding ten feet in length, easily recognizable by its twin tusks protruding from its mouth and the various shaped holes arranged asymmetrically over the surface of its flat head, presumably used for hearing. These asexual hunters are very defensive of their territory and often do not associate with other members of its species.

Stone: unit of measurement equal to fourteen pounds.

Tavendia Amberdawn: Avalide ambassador to the humans and member of the *Essen`dril*.

Thaelvin Ar`ys: Frostspire ice mage and ambassador to the dwarves.

Torgrim Varr: Dwarven King of Barak'Dûm.

Trinactria: elven concept of the three planes of magic representing the corporeal plane, the spiritual plane, and the elemental plane.

Valeck Silversong: Ætheron arch magus and brother to Cheyandra Silversong.

Valkyyrak: ancient gold dragon of the Icecrowns, mate to Dalaria, and father to Zharra, Maelyyk, Vaelis, and Karros.

Xe`: dryad prefix ascribed to a newly mature dryad capable of mating.

Troy C. Reeves has been an avid fantasy reader for much of his life. He serves in the Canadian Armed Forces as a nursing officer and works in a home business while pursuing his writing career. He and his wife, Melissa, have three sons and live in Edmonton, Canada.

LaVergne, TN USA
25 March 2010
177200LV00009B/1/P

9 781440 191848